0.5

SILVER TONGUED DEVIL

LORELEI JAMES

Silver Tongued Devil

by Lorelei James
A Rough Riders Prequel Novel
Copyright © 2020 LJLA, LLC, All Rights Reserved.

Ridgeview Publishing

ISBN: 978-1-941869-04-8

Visit www.loreleijames.com

Cover Design by Meredith Blair
Cover Image © Mliss/Depositphotos.com/34836693
Edited by Lindsey Faber
Interior Design by BB eBooks Co., Ltd. – www.bbebooksthailand.com

Rough Riders Series

(in reading order)

ONE

Outside Sackett's Saloon
Labelle Unincorporated Township
Crook County, Wyoming
May 1897

EVEN IN THE dark, Silas McKay sensed the attack coming. Although he couldn't get his knife out in front of him in time, somehow he managed to turn his head, so the first blow landed on his cheekbone instead of busting his nose.

Still hurt like a son-of-a-bitch.

Then the bastard who'd taken that cheap shot aimed punches number two and three at Silas's gut, doubling him over.

Sharp pain sliced through him and he sucked in a quick breath.

An elbow connected with the back of his head and Silas's hat hit the ground.

But before Silas could straighten up, Zeke West kicked him in the butt with enough force that Silas landed face-first in the dirt. Dust filled his mouth and he started coughing.

"Gimme back my money," Zeke yelled.

More dust eddied around him, making it impossible to see in the pitch black. Making it hard to breathe—even before Zeke changed tactics and kicked Silas in the ribs.

He felt the wetness coating his side.

"Dirty rotten cheater like you belongs in the dirt," Zeke sneered.

Silas wheezed out, "I won fair and square."

"Liar!" A flurry of kicks connected. "You've never played fair. I'm gonna beat you until you pass out and then I'm takin' back what's mine."

Like hell.

But Silas only managed to grunt in response.

Zeke shuffled until the toe of his boot connected with Silas's spine, punctuating each kick with insults—"dirty, rotten, no-good, lyin', lily-livered, cheatin', son of a whore"—while Silas attempted to protect his head.

"Ready to give me my money back?" Zeke taunted. "Or should I bring this up with your brother?"

A commotion sounded, bootsteps hitting the wooden planks outside the saloon, then boots thudding across the ground as people shouted and raced toward where the beating was happening.

About damn time.

Silas took a chance, uncurling his arms from around his head to glare over his shoulder at Zeke. Then he gritted out, "Typical, West, that you were hidin' in the shadows to jump me. Ain't man enough to face me head-on—"

The last thing Silas saw was Zeke's boot heel above his face before everything went dark.

TWO

JONAS MCKAY REACHED the scuffle just as Zeke West tried to stomp on his brother's face again.

Yelling "Hey!" he shoved Zeke hard, knocking him off balance, away from Silas, who was out cold. Heart racing, he crouched down to see if Zeke had actually done the unthinkable and killed Silas this time.

Blood covered Silas's face. Jonas couldn't tell if the blood on Silas's mouth was from his lip being busted open or just run-off blood pouring from someplace else.

Before he could roll Silas over, Zeke stumbled forward, as if to take another shot.

Jonas held up his hand. "Touch him again, West, and I'm haulin' you in."

"I thought you were off duty, *Deputy* McKay," he spat.

"I'm never off duty. And I'd arrest any man beatin' on another man who can't fight back. Now step aside."

"Make me. You think that big tin star makes you a big man?"

"No, but this big gun does. Step aside."

"Do as he says, Zeke."

Jonas looked up at Zeke's brother, Zachariah, who'd shoved his way through the circle of onlookers.

Zeke sputtered, "B-but he cheated—"

"Now is not the time." To ensure his smaller brother complied, Zachariah tugged Zeke back away from the scene. He said, "We're goin'," to Jonas but added, "But we ain't done with this. Not by a long shot," to Zeke.

Fucking West brothers. They were notorious for tossing out threats, but the hell of it was, they nearly always followed through. Or at least Zeke did.

Silas groaned, garnering Jonas's attention. Then he started to cough blood.

"Easy. Let's get you off your back."

When Silas didn't move of his own accord, Jonas shoved his brother's shoulder hard, forcing him onto his side so he didn't choke on his own blood.

Silas promptly passed out again.

Jonas glanced up and saw Jimmy, the twelve-year-old orphan who worked odd jobs around Labelle, holding Silas's hat. "Is he gonna be okay, Deputy?"

"I don't know, Jimmy. Can you run over to Doc's place and let him know I'm bringin' Silas in for a look-see?"

"Sure will." Jimmy raced off.

A snort sounded, then Robbie O'Neil crouched down across from Jonas. "Stubborn lad, yer brother. I be warnin' him against playin' poker with Zeke West again, knowin' that bastard was spoilin' for a fight since the *last* time Silas beat him at cards."

"Appears my brother didn't listen."

"Never does."

"I reckon Silas won?"

"Aye."

Jonas sighed, studying Silas's bloodied face. "And to think I've always considered him the luckier twin."

"Bein's West had just gotten paid from the railroad and Silas cleaned him out, that's still likely true."

"Well, at least he has money to pay Doc this time."

Robbie snorted. "Silver lining, I s'ppose. I'll help ya carry him to Doc's place since he ain't gonna make it on his own."

"I'd appreciate it."

They each grabbed one of Silas's arms and legs. While Silas wasn't overly heavy, they stopped twice to catch their breath on the trek to Doc's cabin, which was tucked back in the trees at the crossroads outside of town.

After the third time they stopped, Jonas huffed, "We shoulda thrown him in the back of a wagon."

"Aye," Robbie replied, puffing beside him.

Jimmy met them at the tree line, holding a lantern and wearing Silas's hat. "Doc says to bring him around back."

Doc Moorcroft and his wife had lived in the area since before Wyoming had become a state. At one time Doc did all his doctoring in the log cabin. These days patients were seen in the addition on the back of the house near the stables, which also had a three-bed recovery room.

For years Doc's place had been neutral territory. He offered settlers, ranchers, cowboys, Indians, whores, outlaws and law enforcement all equal medical treatment as long as they could pay.

Doc stood in the doorway, a robe thrown on over long johns, his white hair sticking up and his eyes narrowed behind his round spectacles. He harrumphed. "Silas again?"

"Yes, sir."

"Bring him in." Doc's gaze moved to the gun belt hanging on Jonas's hips, then he locked his eyes on Jonas's. "Then I'll expect you to step out and remove that, Deputy."

Jonas knew the drill—no weapons of any kind were allowed, no exceptions. He gave Doc a chin lift in acknowledgement and Doc stepped aside to allow them to enter.

After hefting Silas up on the table, Jonas retreated and was surprised when Robbie followed him outside. Jonas raised an eyebrow. "You got a knife in your boot or something?"

"Nay. I be thinkin' you'd rather have me lookin' after that gun than young Jimmy."

"True enough." Jonas slid the leather strap free of the clasp and passed the gun belt to Robbie. "You don't mind waitin'?"

Robbie fastened the belt around his own waist before he answered. "No sir. Nice night. I'll just sit over there in the shadow of the rain barrel and keep me eyes open."

"Fair enough."

"What about me, Deputy McKay?" Jimmy asked.

The last thing Jonas needed was Jimmy back at Ruby Red's

Boardinghouse or Sackett's Saloon, running his mouth that the deputy was unarmed. Trouble rarely came to Doc's place, but Zeke West was a whole different kind of trouble. "You stay here on lookout with Robbie and hold onto Silas's hat. If Doc needs anything, I might send you back into town."

"Sure thing."

When Jonas returned inside, he noticed that Doc wasn't alone. Miss Dinah Thompson was setting out supplies as Doc instructed her. Rumor was Doc's wife had taken ill, and Miss Thompson—their boarder and the local schoolteacher—helped Doc out when she wasn't teaching.

From what he could see in the dim light, she was a pretty little thing, with honey-colored hair pinned up to reveal a slender neck and a strong jawline. Jonas had heard that Miss Thompson suffered from shyness, but bein's he wasn't a church-going man, and Miss Thompson wasn't the type to set foot in Sackett's Saloon or act in a manner to get herself arrested, their paths hadn't crossed this closely in the past year that she'd lived in Labelle.

Her voice held a soft twang when she inquired, "Deputy?"

"Yes, Miss?"

"Would you kindly help adjust your brother's clothing so Doc can examine him?"

Naturally she wouldn't be stripping Silas down to his skin. Even in the lamplight Jonas noticed the red tinge to her cheeks and she wouldn't meet his gaze. "Of course."

Then she moved to the end of the table to set a bowl of water and a stack of cloths next to Silas's bloodied head.

Doc removed Silas's vest and tossed it aside.

That's when Jonas noticed the blood stain spreading across the bottom of Silas's white shirt.

"What the hell is that from?"

"Language, Deputy, there's a lady present," Doc said. "Dinah, dear, could you hand me the scissors? It'll be easier to cut this shirt away than peel it off."

"Yes, Doc."

He sliced the shirt straight down the middle of Silas's torso. The blood hadn't clotted yet, since there wasn't an open wound for the fabric to stick to because a small knife was still lodged in the flesh above Silas's hip, clean through his shirt.

Christ. Had West stabbed him? Then Jonas's eyes narrowed on the hilt of the knife—a familiar-looking knife.

Doc sighed. "Well, this is unexpected."

"Yeah, especially since that knife belongs to my brother."

"You're certain?"

"Yes, sir, I have one exactly like it. I'm guessin' he pulled it out, intending to defend himself, and ended up stabbin' himself instead." Jonas had begun to think maybe he *was* the luckier twin.

Doc leaned down to examine the area closer. "It's mostly a superficial wound. Not too deep. I suspect the jiggling when you carried him caused the blood to leak out around the edges of the blade. He's not suffering from excessive blood loss. I recommend cauterizing the puncture rather than stitching it. Less likelihood of infection. What say you?" Doc glanced up at Jonas for confirmation.

"Do whatever you think is best, Doc."

Jonas watched as Doc directed his assistant. At the bench laden with supplies, she lifted the globe off the lantern and increased the size of the flame as Doc chose a flat, wide knife.

Turning the knife over the flame, Doc said, "I'll need you to hold his legs, Deputy, while Miss Thompson immobilizes his upper body."

Jonas frowned. "She's a little bit of a thing, Doc. Shouldn't she—"

"I'm stronger than I look," the schoolteacher interjected, "and no stranger to this procedure. How about you worry about *your* half, Deputy, and let me worry about mine?"

Without waiting for his response, she wedged Silas's limp left arm against his body and pinned it in place with her hips as she leaned across his chest to clutch the other side of the table, pressing her elbows into his right arm, holding him down.

Well, that worked pretty slick. Guess she did know what she was doing.

Jonas took the same position with his brother's legs.

Doc quickly removed the knife lodged in Silas's side with one hand and pressed the red-hot cauterizing knife over the wound with the other hand.

As expected, that woke Silas up.

"Son-of-a-bitching, cocksucking, mother of a whore—"

"Pipe down, Mr. McKay," Miss Thompson said through gritted teeth as Silas tried to arch his back. "And for all that's holy, please hold still!"

Silas went so motionless that Jonas assumed he'd passed out again.

But as soon as Doc said, "Done. Let him go," and Jonas released Silas's legs, he glanced up to see Silas had one hand holding Miss Thompson's throat and his other hand circling her wrist.

Silas demanded, "I'm dead, ain't I?"

"Please—"

"I'm dead and in heaven because I've got a beautiful angel like you fussin' over me."

Oh for the love of god, Silas…really? Flirting the second you open your damn eyes?

"I assure you that you're very much alive," she said softly, "but if you don't release me right now, I might kill you myself."

Silas's smile turned into a wince. "I take it back. I'm dead and I'm in hell, bein' tempted by a fallen angel with flashing eyes and a feisty tongue."

"You are the very devil, Mr. McKay. Or you're very drunk."

"I'm neither. But I am feelin' light-headed when I look at you."

"Cut it out," Jonas said sharply. "And let her go."

"But she smells like spring and sugar and all good things."

"Silas!" Jonas snapped.

Silas released his grip on her and squeezed his eyes shut. "I ain't gonna apologize for puttin' my hands on you, darlin'. I was afraid you were tryin' to get away from me."

Doc chuckled. "If he didn't already have a head injury, Dinah dear, I'd allow you to cuff his ears. He'd be easier to deal with."

"I remember exactly how to deal with him, Doc."

"Good. Then I'll let you coax him into drinking this tincture."

Jonas watched as Miss Thompson murmured to Silas, urging him to finish the entire glass, which he did in one long gulp as she held on to the back of his neck.

His brother didn't put up a fuss—which wasn't like his stubborn twin at all.

What in the devil was going on?

Doc continued his exam, asking Silas questions about where he had the most pain. Testing Silas's ribs for breaks, half-rolling him onto his left side to check his back. After he finished, he gently patted Silas on the shoulder. "Got bruises up and down your spine, no protrusions that I can see, but you'll be sore for several days. Same with your ribs, maybe a fracture or two. We'll wrap you up tomorrow before you leave. It'd be best if you remained overnight. Just in case I missed something." He pointed to Silas's head. "Once Dinah gets you cleaned up, I'll take a closer look at that hard noggin of yours."

"Thanks, Doc."

"One of these days, Silas, you ain't gonna be so lucky."

"I don't feel lucky today."

"Well you *are* lucky," Miss Thompson declared. "Especially since Doc isn't lecturing you on the dangers of fighting."

"Hey. *I* didn't start it."

"This time," she sniped at him. "And don't bother pretending there won't be a next time."

Jonas addressed the feisty schoolteacher, who seemed way more familiar with his brother than he'd imagined. "You've seen to Silas before?"

"Twice. But never for an injury this serious."

His jaw dropped. "But…you weren't here the last time I brought him in."

Miss Thompson finally met his gaze.

Good lord. Her eyes were the pale blue of a winter Wyoming sky.

She lifted her chin. "Then logic would dictate, Deputy, that you're unaware of your brother's most recent escapades."

Dressed down by a schoolmarm? Huh-uh. Not happening on his watch. He was the damn law around here.

"Or logic would dictate that my brother is sweet on you, Miss Thompson, and his previous injuries were so minimal that he didn't mention them to me, lest I see right through his ruse to charm you with that silver tongue of his while you're doctoring on him," Jonas countered.

She blushed and turned away.

"Leave her alone, Jonas," Silas said groggily.

"Deputy, if I could have a word with you outside while my assistant cleans up the patient?" Doc said.

Neither Silas nor Miss Thompson glanced his way—or at each other—but Jonas got the distinct sense they wouldn't keep their distance when both their chaperones were gone.

THREE

A S SOON AS Doc and Deputy McKay left the room, Dinah expelled a deep breath.

She unclenched her hands and looked over at Silas, sprawled on the table, blood still covering his face.

The laudanum hadn't taken effect yet, as he was staring at her with an intensity that caused her to blush ten shades of red.

Silas held out his hand to her. "Come here."

"You're injured. It's not wise—"

"It ain't wise to deny an injured man comfort. Unless you want me to hop down and come to you?"

"You're impossible," Dinah harrumphed as she erased the distance between them. "But I'm not holding your hand."

"That's fine, darlin'; I'll hold yours."

"Mr. McKay—"

"Silas," he gently corrected as he caught her fingers in his. "If I'm gonna be courtin' you, there'll be no more formality between us."

"When did I agree to let you court me?" she retorted.

He flashed that charming grin at her for a brief second before he winced in pain. "When I was here two weeks last? Doc gave me his blessing."

Dinah bit her cheek to keep from reminding Silas that she was old enough to make her own choices. But since she lived with Doc Moorcroft and his wife, she did owe Doc the courtesy of letting Silas make his intentions toward her clear. "I thought you'd forgotten."

"Have you changed your mind?" he asked softly.

She shook her head. "Did you purposely pick a fight so you'd have an excuse to be in Doc's office and see me again to make sure I *hadn't* changed my mind?"

"No. That bastard Zeke West jumped me after I beat him at cards." He attempted another smile. "But it was worth it since I get to see your pretty face."

"Stop trying to charm me, Silas McKay. You wince every time you smile." She released his hand and reached for a cloth. She dipped it in the water, wrung it out, and began to clean his face.

"That tickles."

"Better than it hurting."

"Oh, it hurts too."

She stopped mid-swipe.

He reached for her other hand. "But *you're* not hurtin' me, darlin'. Keep goin'. And talk to me, please. I'm getting sleepy."

"I imagine so. You should sleep. Your body needs to heal."

"Will you be here when I wake up?"

"Not here in the room with you"—*like last time* went unsaid—"but I'll be close by."

"Good."

Dinah continued to clear the blood from his face. His *handsome* face.

Lord, Silas McKay defined a good-looking man. His facial features were rugged—square jaw, wide cheeks, surprisingly straight nose for being a brawler. The stubble on his cheeks and neck was the same midnight hue as his wavy black hair. Thick slashes of his dark eyebrows highlighted his piercing blue eyes, eyes that seemed to bore right into her soul every time they regarded her. His height topped hers by a solid foot. And speaking of solid…her gaze traveled down his exposed chest. Beneath the dark hair that grew in the center, she saw the sloped definition of his muscles. Lots of muscles.

What would it be like to touch him? To sift her fingers through his chest hair, to trace the cords in his neck, to smooth her hands over the bulges in his arms?

Her body went hot just thinking about it.

"Dinah?" Silas mumbled.

She threw him a panicked gaze; had he caught her admiring his near nakedness? Luckily, his eyes were still closed. "You are supposed to be sleeping."

"Almost was, but I gotta say this first."

"What?"

"Don't let Jonas scare you off."

She froze. "Will he try?"

"I s'ppose so. Me courtin' you is gonna be a shock for him. I, ah…hadn't told him yet."

Dinah didn't know how to respond, so she didn't.

"I wanted to wait until I had you on my arm for sure to make the proper introduction since he's the only family I got."

That confession allowed a small smile as she dabbed away the crusted blood on his cheek. "Worried he wouldn't believe you?"

"Maybe. Truth is…since our folks died, it's always been just me'n him. Bein' twins made us look out for each other even more. Jonas is happy bein' married to his badge. Says his job'll likely kill him, so he don't need to make some unlucky woman a widow."

"I knew you were twins; I hadn't understood you are *identical* twins until I saw the two of you side by side tonight. That mirror image surprised me. Granted, I've only seen the deputy from a distance, but he's always seemed so much…meaner looking than you."

Silas chuckled. "He is. Prolly why I'm considered the better-lookin' twin."

Dinah shook her head, even when she was charmed by his audacity.

"Although, you'd likely argue that point tonight."

"Perhaps." The skin under his eye had already discolored blackish-purple. In the short time he'd been here, the left side of his face had puffed up. He had scratches on his forehead beneath the dirt and blood. His lower lip had quit bleeding. It probably didn't need stitched—that was one positive.

"You mad at me for fightin'?" Silas asked softly.

"If I say yes because seeing you beat up scares the life out of me…will you stop?"

She couldn't blame his refusal to answer on the medicine.

Her gaze met his sleepy-eyed one before she glanced at the bowl of dirty water. "I worry about you. You claim you didn't start it, but I'm more concerned that Zeke West wants to finish it—and by 'it,' I mean you. This isn't the first time you've tangled with him, Silas."

"And it likely won't be the last."

"Why?"

"Because we seem to end up in the same places."

"Silas. There's an easy way to end that. Stay away from Sackett's. Stay away from him."

"Easier said than done, darlin', since West has had it out for me for a while…" He yawned. "He's always flashing that railroad money around, reminding me…"

A sigh. Then silence.

The laudanum had knocked him out mid-sentence.

When his breathing turned slow and even, she switched out the dirty water and rags for clean.

Before she started on the second round of cleanup, Doc and the deputy returned. She stepped aside so Doc could examine Silas's head and neck. Upon seeing no new undue swelling, he once again pronounced Silas lucky and in need of rest.

While Doc and the deputy handled the payment for services, Dinah continued cleaning Silas's face.

Doc cleared his throat. "Dinah, dear, the deputy would like to have a word with you."

Her heart galloped but she managed to nod.

"I'll need a nip or two before I can fall asleep, so I'll be sitting right outside with Robbie and Jimmy until you're done."

"Thank you, Doc," the deputy said.

Her nerves kicked up after Doc left her alone with Jonas McKay. She couldn't quite hide her shaking hands as she dunked the cloth and gently cleaned the scrapes on Silas's forehead.

"Doc tells me that you and my brother are courtin'."

"Silas *intends* to court me."

She felt him studying her before he spoke.

"Even after seein' my fool brother beat to hell…you haven't changed your mind about him?"

"No." That's when Dinah met the deputy's eyes. Eyes so like Silas's yet...not. "I'm looking forward to getting to know your fool brother, Deputy."

He smiled at that. "Since Silas has managed to keep it from me that he's needed doctoring, and Doc won't share the details, I'm askin' you to tell me when and why Silas was here before."

"Forgive me, sir, but if your brother would've wanted you to know, he would've told you."

"Oh, I've considered that. Trust me. But I believe the real reason he didn't share is because he wanted to keep you all to himself."

She barely withheld a snort. "Because Silas might've feared you'd get it in your head to court me too?"

"Perhaps."

"Well, that's straight-up wrong. Silas told me you're already happily married to your badge."

Deputy McKay laughed at that. "I can see why my brother likes you. Because that silver-tongued cowboy charm of his rolls off you like water off a duck's back, don't it?"

"Sometimes."

"So I'm askin' you, please, to tell me what injuries brought Silas here. I can't protect him if I don't know what he's done or who might be gunnin' for him."

Dinah dropped the cloth in the water and leaned back against the bench behind her, folding her arms across her chest. "What he's done, was tangle with Zeke West."

His eyes narrowed. "Which time was this?"

They'd clashed so often that even the deputy knew about it? Why didn't he stop his brother from fighting? "Months ago. I remember Silas telling Doc that you were at some lawman's meeting in Cheyenne."

"That'd explain why I hadn't heard of this incident. I ended up stuck in Cheyenne for two weeks because of that blizzard. So what happened between him and West?"

"Something that had to do with a girl at Ruby Red's." She forced her eyes to remain on his even when her entire body went hot with embarrassment. Good girls—church-going, virginal schoolteachers—like her weren't supposed to admit knowledge of a local whorehouse, let alone say the name out loud in mixed company, and especially not admit that she'd come face to face with the beautiful Ruby Redmond that night.

"Silas just *told* you that, Miss Thompson?" the deputy said skeptically.

Please Lord, forgive me for the lie I'm about to tell. "I overheard that part of the conversation."

He removed his hat, ran his hands through his hair and resettled the black hat on his head. "I beg your pardon for askin' this, bein's that it ain't proper to discuss my brother's questionable behavior with such an upstanding woman as yourself, but I'd be much obliged if you could share as many details as you remember about Silas's conversation with Doc."

Dinah's focus moved to Silas sacked out on the table, snoring with his mouth open. "I didn't hear why Silas was at Ruby Red's—if he'd been there a while or if one of the girls retrieved him from Sackett's thinking he was you when the trouble started—and quite frankly, I don't wanna know. But Silas stepped in when Zeke threatened one of the women after she refused to go upstairs with him. Zeke warned Silas to walk away, Silas didn't, and Zeke nearly broke his arm." She paused. "I say 'nearly' because that's what brought Silas here that night through a snowstorm. He was in so much pain Doc thought it had to be a break. We dosed him with tonic and he stayed here overnight. We got that same blizzard that stranded you in Cheyenne, so the next morning Silas was stuck here."

"Better here under expert care than anywhere else," the deputy said.

"Unfortunately, Doc's wife, Mrs. Agnes, had taken ill, so Doc looked after her and I handled the household, which included caring for Silas. He stayed in the recovery room. I kept the fire going, took him food, which meant we spent time together unchaperoned. A lot of time." She glanced over at him. "That's probably why Silas didn't mention it; he was protecting my reputation. It turned out he didn't have a broken arm, just a severe strain."

"His left arm?"

She nodded.

"Now I know why he'd been favoring that side. I imagine he'd've healed up faster if it *had* been a break."

"That's what Doc said. Before Silas left after the blizzard, he claimed he'd be back to square things about courting me, but I hadn't seen him until two weeks ago."

"What was the story with that injury?"

She shrugged. "Pain in his chest. When Doc pressed him for details,

Silas admitted the ache was from the fear he was too late, and I'd given my heart to another. Doc practically hauled him out of here by his ear."

The deputy snorted. "Bet Doc gave him grief after that."

"Yes, sir." A pause lingered. "Still…Silas had to get in the last word. He swore the next time he saw me it'd be with his hat in one hand and flowers in the other." She couldn't help but smile. "That man has a way with words, even if some of them are just hopeful thinking."

"That he does." Jonas patted Silas on the shoulder. Then he looked up at her. "Thanks for talkin' to me. My brother has been known to make rash decisions—"

"And you assumed I was just another one?" she injected sharply.

"Yep. But I was wrong. Silas is all I've got. While we don't always understand each other's thoughts and actions, I want him to have the life he's been workin' toward. If that's with you…I'm good with it as long as you know it ain't gonna be an easy road."

Dinah lifted a brow. "I wouldn't think I'd have to explain the difference between marrying and courting to you, Deputy."

"*I* understand them perfectly well, Miss Thompson. But Silas…in his mind, he's already put his ring on your finger and slid his boots under your bed."

Jonas McKay was a plain talker; she'd give him that much.

The deputy stepped back. "Jimmy is bunkin' in here tonight. You or Doc can send him to fetch me if Silas takes a turn. If not, I'll be back tomorrow afternoon to haul him home."

She held up Silas's sliced and bloodied shirt. "Will you remember to bring him something to wear?"

"Ah…I ain't goin' home. But it won't bother Silas none to walk around bare-chested."

It'll bother me.

There was no chance she wouldn't shamelessly stare at his chest. Especially that intriguing trail of dark hair that continued down his belly and disappeared into his pants. She picked up his tattered shirt. "I could try and patch it up."

"Best turn that into a rag. Ain't no fixin' it." He offered her a hat tip and he was gone.

No fixing it? She'd see about that.

With Silas asleep and Jimmy settled, there wasn't a reason to remain out here.

She and Doc returned to the house in silence, only bothering to say goodnight.

Dinah's small room in the log cabin was tucked in the far back corner. The space had originally been Doc's exam room, so it had built-in shelves along one wall and hooks in the ceiling to hang lanterns from for better lighting.

Her room stayed either cool or downright cold year-round, but she loved the cozy space, from her bed piled high with her handmade quilts, to the tiny nook opposite the door where her small writing desk, chair and sewing machine were lodged. A round-topped steamer trunk held her undergarments and the few treasured family items she'd kept.

Exhausted, she turned the kerosene lamp on high and sat heavily on the chair to untie her boots, freeing her poor swollen feet.

Ah. Heaven.

She wiggled her toes as she crossed over to place her boots on the shelf next to her dress shoes. She'd been in her nightclothes in bed—but not asleep—when Doc had knocked, requesting her assistance. She hadn't bothered with undergarments or socks, opting to shove her bare feet into her boots and don her day clothes.

After removing the dark brown apron that protected the front of her dress, she tossed it on the floor. She then shimmied out of the blue calico, hanging it between her other two everyday dresses, noticing she had four aprons left to get her through to wash day.

She swept her fingers down the black wool skirt and the high-necked white blouse that comprised her teaching uniform. With school out for the summer, the only occasion she'd have to wear her dressier outfits would be church.

Or when Silas McKay came courting.

That thought sent flutters through her belly.

She'd never been courted, but she'd listened to girls gossiping about how out here in the "Wild West" courting couples didn't require a chaperone. So she and Silas could go anywhere they wanted. He seemed the type of man who'd consider her opinion when choosing a destination, and the first place she'd ask to see would be Devil's Tower.

Thinking back to those "courting" conversations she'd overheard, she wasn't sure if officially courting meant she'd see Silas every day. Or would his visits be limited to Sunday since his ranch work kept him busy the other days of the week? Was it improper for her to ride out to his place if he couldn't come to her? Not that she knew where he lived beyond his vague explanation of "closer to Sundance."

Dinah retrieved her cotton nightgown and dragged it over her head, not bothering to fasten the buttons once she had it on.

She looked longingly at the book—*Nana* by Emile Zola—she'd been reading a few short hours ago. Instead of crawling back in bed, she took out her flat board and sewing supplies.

Silas's shirt was frontiersman style—a pullover loose cotton blend V-neck with laces and wide tipped collars. There was no fixing the jagged slice down the center. The best option would be to turn the fabric under on each side and create a placket. She could add two buttons and buttonholes so at least his belly would be covered. Plus, a button-up shirt would be easier for him to put on with his ribs being wrapped. If her quick fix turned out to be hideous looking, he could always wear it as a work shirt. She hated to see anything go to waste and wondered if Jonas's hesitation about bringing Silas extra clothes had been from his brother's lack of extra clothing options.

After trimming the center until both edges were straight, she folded and pinned the material. She moved the lamp to the shelf above her sewing machine and that provided enough light to run two long, straight stiches down each side. Then she repinned the shirt down center for button and buttonhole placement. A few stitches and wrapped thread finished the button attachment. She made the cuts for the buttonholes and did a quick whip stitch around the inside to keep them from fraying.

Once she'd had the shirt buttoned, she found the hole where the knife had been lodged and sewed it up.

It'd do. But she couldn't hand him back a bloody shirt.

In the kitchen, she poured cold water from the pitcher into a bowl, added some salt and dunked the shirt in. The blood hadn't had much time to set so it washed out more easily than she'd believed it would. She rinsed it once more, wrung it out and returned to her room, hanging it on a peg to dry.

Dinah moved the lamp back beside her bed. The cock's first crow would come in a few short hours, so she extinguished the flame, climbed beneath the covers and tried to sleep.

FOUR

JONAS AND ROBBIE walked back to town in silence.

They parted ways at Robinette's General Store. Jonas cut left, heading to the deputy's office.

The main sheriff's office was located in Sundance, the Crook County seat. While this settlement hadn't been officially recognized as a town, with a central railway line and several businesses, including a saloon and a bawdy house, it had all the problems of a town that required a permanent law presence. Currently there were only two deputies, Jonas and "Big Jim"—aka Jim Biggerman. During the day, the on-duty deputy was expected to be available in the building or around town. If the single jail cell had an occupant, they stayed overnight in the cramped office.

Although the hour was late, the last place Jonas wanted to sleep tonight was a bunk roll on the floor of the empty cell.

He relocked the door and headed to Sackett's. If trouble happened, it usually started in the saloon anyway. At least he'd be easy to find.

Sackett's and Ruby Red's Boardinghouse were separate businesses with a common purpose: cashing in on men's vices. Since the businesses were side by side, Sackett and Ruby had connected the whorehouse to the saloon via a door on the second floor. That way men could claim they'd been in the saloon all night and they thought their womenfolk would be none the wiser.

If you happened to be riding through the area, looking for a place to stay, you'd likely tie up in front of the two-story white clapboard structure with the sign announcing *Miss Ruby Red's Boardinghouse.* After entering through the fancy etched glass and brass door, you'd find a small reception area, fussy floral paper covering the walls, two small tables and four spindly, upholstered velvet chairs situated in front of each of the lace-curtained windows. A stand that resembled a polished preacher's pulpit blocked access to the only door, presumably leading upstairs to the rooms for rent. Hanging on the wall behind that pulpit was a sign that read:

NO VACANCY

As far as Jonas knew, that sign was a permanent fixture.

If you were also the observant type, you'd notice another small hand-lettered sign on the stand that read:

Ask about our specials

Shrewd-eyed Mrs. Mavis, a retired former madam, could size up a walk-in as a potential customer or a clueless gadabout in five seconds and dealt with them appropriately. For Madam Ruby, it paid to have good help—and she, in turn, paid them well.

Jonas strode through the door to the saloon, which had been propped open with a rusted cream canister to air out the cigar smoke and the sour smell of spilled booze and nervous sweat.

Although it was well past one a.m., Sackett's still had a dozen men sitting at the bar. Off to the right side he saw both gambling tables were full too.

Dickie, the bartender, who was also Mrs. Mavis's husband, caught his attention and gave the sign for Jonas to exit out the back. Then he bent down to tug the pulley that rang the bell in the Madam's room that warned of trouble.

After a brief nod, Jonas strolled through the space, ignoring the patrons as they ignored him, cutting through the kitchen and storage areas at the rear of the saloon and out the delivery entrance.

Five steps later he stood outside the back edge of Ruby Red's building. To the casual observer, there wasn't a door. He knocked twice. After a few minutes, a section that appeared to be broken siding opened a crack.

"It's Jonas."

Ruby herself opened the hidden door and beckoned him in.

He walked past her down a short, dark hallway. He heard her slide the metal bar that blocked the outer door as he entered her personal living space.

The vibrant color scheme in her parlor furnishings suited her. From the chaise lounge covered in sage-green velvet and embellished with gold tassels, to the double bench settee in vibrant blue, trimmed with a thick silk cord the hue of a robin's egg, and a side table with legs whimsically carved to resemble peacock heads. On the opposite side was a high-backed chair comprised of pale pink tufted fabric, decorated with dark pink satin piping and beaded fringe. Beneath his feet was a spongy rug; the curlicues and flowers in it contained all the colors of the furniture, pillows and wallpaper.

Since the building had no windows, save for the ones in front, she'd created what appeared to be a window behind the settee: a long curtain rod with ivory damask drapes swooping across and floral-patterned silk panels hanging below it. She'd placed candles and kerosene lamps on the side tables, creating ambiance to counteract the absence of natural light.

The room was wholly feminine. He felt like the proverbial bull among her delicate things and opted to sit in the sturdy rocking chair next to the small cookstove when they spent time in here—which wasn't often.

When she said, "Is Silas all right?" Jonas turned around and faced her.

God, the woman was pretty. Long, black hair, which, unbound, reached her waist. Eyes as bright blue as the cushions on her settee. Wide cheeks that tapered to a sharply pointed chin. And those lips. Those full, soft, luscious red lips that never failed to stir his desire.

She'd thrown a lavender embroidered silk robe over her nightdress—a nightdress created with sheer black lace that dipped low on her abundant bosom. Tiny bows and silk roses dotted the neckline.

Jonas had the overwhelming desire to rip each flower off with his teeth to get to the soft, fragrant, creamy skin that lay beneath.

"Jonas?" she said in that husky rasp.

His eyes met hers. "How'd you hear about it?"

"Millie said everyone ran out of the saloon when Zeke started shouting, so she followed." Her gaze searched his face. "Sounded like you got there quickly after it started."

Reaching out, he ran the backs of his knuckles down the smooth curve of her jaw. "Only because I was on my way here to see you."

She leaned into his touch. "He must be okay if you came back."

"Doc fixed him up." He continued to stroke her cheek. "Silas ended up with a self-inflicted knife wound. I can't believe that he let Zeke West beat the holy hell out of him again. I don't know that I've ever seen Silas lose a fight to any man other than West."

"What is it with those two?"

Jonas dropped his hand. Hardened his eyes. "Why don't you tell me?"

"Pardon?"

"Tonight I found out that Silas and Zeke got into it months ago over one of your girls."

"Oh. That."

"Why didn't you tell me?"

"Because Silas specifically asked me not to. And no, he didn't ask me not to tell you because he found out that you and I are...close."

He lifted an eyebrow. "And yet, you kept it from me that you and my brother are palling around when I'm out of town? Just how...close are you two?"

Those mesmerizing eyes widened before narrowing with anger, and he braced himself. "Bugger off, McKay. I'd never be *close* like that with your brother. I only knew about his injury because someone needed to take him to Doc, to discover if that fool West had broken more than his pride."

"*You* took him out there in a damn blizzard, Ruby?" Why hadn't Doc or the feisty Miss Thompson relayed that fact to him?

"Yes. Millie and I loaded Silas on the sled and hitched it to Daisy. Then I rode her to Doc's," she retorted.

Seemed both she and Daisy the mule were mule-headed enough to attempt something so dangerous.

"Besides, I only stayed there long enough to get Silas unloaded. I was back here, with Daisy safely in the barn, within two hours."

"Thank you for seein' to him," he said gruffly.

"You're welcome. But I didn't do it for you. The *last* thing I needed was to be stuck with an injured, complaining, delirious man demanding food, medicine and attention from my girls for however long the blasted storm lasted." She raised that stubborn chin and challenged him. "So did you stop by solely to give me your belated thanks or did you need something else?"

Sassy woman.

Jonas slipped his arm around her waist and hauled her close. "Oh, I'm in definite need of something else." He lowered his head and pressed his lips to hers.

Kissing Ruby always started out sweet and slow, but rarely ended that way. The woman consumed him with fire and need equal to his. She snaked her arms around his neck and held on as his forearm slid beneath her ass. Lifting her up, he began walking forward, his body knowing the way to her bedroom without the need of his eyes to get him there.

She tasted of the mint tea she drank before bed and the sweet heat that was all Ruby. Her mouth opened to his hungrily, her nails digging into the back of his neck as she pushed her body closer to his.

He stopped when the backs of her legs connected with the footboard and he gradually broke the kiss to set her on the bed.

Ruby surveyed him with the intensity of a hunter who'd cornered prey as he unhooked his gun belt and draped it over the bottom post of her canopied bed. Then he removed his leather vest and hung it on the peg beside the door. His hat went next to it. When he reached down to pull off his boot, she hopped off the bed.

"Sit. Let me do that for you."

"Ain't no way I'm sittin' on that fancy silk bedding with my dirty britches and dusty boots."

"Then sit on the bench." She deftly unhooked his trousers and yanked them to his knees, effectively hobbling him, before she practically shoved his ass onto the bench.

"Ruby, dammit, I'm dirty and smelly—"

"Hush." Cupping the heel of his left boot in her palm, she lifted up, tugging until his foot slipped out. She repeated the process with his right foot. After she removed his shirt, she tugged the top half of his one-piece union suit to his hips and stood. "I'll give you a quick whore's bath if you think your scent is offensive."

A whore's bath. That sly tongue of hers…that's the reason he usually obeyed her without question.

Ruby returned with a damp cloth and the ceramic bowl from the washstand. Making herself comfortable on his lap, she murmured, "Close your eyes and relax."

She wiped his face and neck slowly. Thoroughly. Her way of showing him how much she enjoyed touching him. "I like that you're clean-shaven. I'm not a fan of beards."

A fact Jonas was aware of...hence why he scraped his whiskers away.

Every once in a while, he'd feel the press of her full breasts as she leaned over to rinse out the cloth. Then she'd start in again. Lifting his right arm out to his side as she ran that cool rag from the ball of his shoulder to the tips of his fingers—and everywhere in between, following suit with his left arm.

Her powdery roses and mint scent filled his head. The soft swell of her ass resting on his thighs tormented him. Yet, he managed to remain relaxed until...she reached into the front opening of his union suit to fondle his hardness.

Nuzzling into his neck, she murmured, "Feeling cleaner, Deputy?"

"Everything 'cept my mind," he drawled.

Ruby licked his collarbone. "'Fraid I don't have a fix for that. But I had some dirty thoughts of my own about what I wanted to do to you." She scooted back on his lap as she kissed a path through the patch of thick hair covering his chest, her lips connecting with his nipple. She nipped, laved and flicked the tip until it tightened to a hard point.

Rather than switching to the other nipple, she planted kisses straight down his chest and dropped to her knees.

Jonas cupped her chin in his palm, forcing her bright blue eyes to meet his gaze.

Never failed to surprise him, humble him, that this beautiful, sensual woman wanted to freely give him what other men paid her for. He stroked her bottom lip with his thumb. "I don't wanna finish in your mouth."

"Maybe I wanna finish you off with my mouth so you'll have to lick me until you're hard again." She sucked his thumb into her mouth and swirled her tongue around it.

"That'll work too," he said gruffly.

"Thought you might say that." She glided her hands up his thighs and tugged on his clothing. "Lift up."

His ass went skyborne so fast he damn near scooted off the bench.

Then his union suit hit his ankles and Ruby...

"Ah fuck," he groaned as she sucked him to the back of her throat with the first draw of his flesh into her hot, wet mouth.

Her soft laugh vibrated up his shaft.

She pushed his legs open wider, giving herself more room to work.

And work him she did.

He grabbed a fistful of her silky hair, not to guide her because God knew the woman didn't need instruction, but to keep her hair from blocking his view. Watching her suck on him was an added bonus he stored up for those nights when he only had his hand making him feel good.

Ruby pushed him closer to the edge with each wet, deep suck. With every teasing circle her tongue drew around the cockhead after she pulled the foreskin back.

His legs began to shake. His sac tightened beneath her stroking thumb. Before he lost his head completely, he said, "Ruby. Look at me."

Almost as soon as that dark, determined gaze met his, his cock went rigid and he started to come. He groaned long and loud with each pulse, loving how she kept her lips tight around his girth each time he rocked deeper into her mouth. Feeling her swallow until he had nothing left was the closest he'd ever gotten to a religious experience.

So it took a few moments for his head to leave the clouds.

"C'mon."

Jonas blinked at her when she stood and tried to tug him to his feet.

"Whoa. Gimme a moment to find my balance since you knocked me for a damn loop, woman." He brought his hands to her hips and urged her closer. "My turn to tease."

"But I want—"

"Me eatin' that pussy. I'm gettin' to it. But first…take off the robe, Ruby."

The lilac silk floated to the floor.

"Now c'mere, up on your knees."

With her knees pressed into his hips, her tits were right in his face.

Perfect.

He might've growled after he'd opened his mouth over a lace-covered nipple.

Ruby squeezed his shoulders and arched back. "I can take this off."

"Mmm. When I'm ready for that, I'll let you know." He twirled his tongue around the wide pink circle, getting it wet, then sucking hard on the tight tip right through the lace. He paused to blow a stream of air across it, smiling against the full curve of her breast when her whole body shuddered.

He teased her, switching back and forth between her nipples and nibbling on the long, tempting sweep of her neck. Letting his mouth do the talking without any words exchanged.

Her every sigh whispered to his male pride that although her heart wanted no part of him, her body couldn't lie about how strongly his touch affected her.

Jonas slipped his right hand beneath the hem of her nightgown and smoothed a path up the inside of her thigh until his knuckles connected with proof of her desire. His middle finger met no resistance as he pushed it inside where she was so wet and warm, encouraging him to add another finger.

Her response was to widen her stance and angle her head to give him access to whatever part of her he wanted.

That surrender spurred him into action.

Ignoring the hard bulge lengthening against his belly, he rotated his wrist, so the bony side of his thumb rested against her sweet spot. Working those two digits in tandem with the rapid motion he knew she preferred nudged her closer to the edge of bliss.

This is mine. Every quiver. Every moan. In this moment she belongs solely to me.

Ruby's legs were quaking. When he felt her ass muscles tighten, he knew all it would take was his mouth on her other sweet spot and she'd unspool for him.

Jonas sucked on her earlobe. Tugged on it with his teeth until Ruby moaned. Her pussy clenched around his fingers as her clit pulsed against his thumb. He rode out every throb until she slumped against him with a muttered, "Goddamn you, McKay."

Grinning, he nipped the swell of her right breast. "That 'goddamn you' wasn't because I did something wrong?"

"No. You did everything right, since *I* taught you how to do it right."

"So that wasn't a complaint?"

She snorted. "Not hardly. More like an accursed expression of joy."

Jonas clamped his hands on her ass and stood. "Well, sweetheart, let's see if I can't get you to curse at me a couple more times before we fall asleep."

FIVE

J ONAS MCKAY WAS an amazing lover.

Then again…he should be, since she'd made him that way.

Ruby had barely caught her breath after he'd used that wickedly talented mouth to give her two orgasms and he was back at her, greedy for more.

He was stringing kisses up her torso from side to side, gripping her legs with his big, rough-skinned hands, creating space for himself to do what he did best: fuck her into a whimpering, mindless, sweaty mess.

It was great to be her.

Except…he was using those hands to flip her over onto her belly.

Her body—boneless and sated—was his for the asking. Silent asking, since Jonas in this hard and horny state was a man of few words.

Then he hiked her ass into the air, spreading her wide open for the hard snap of his hips as he drove his cock into her.

Ruby arched up, only to feel Jonas's hand between her shoulder blades, holding her in place as he picked up the pace.

So this was how he wanted it. Hard and fast. She was good with that.

Turning her head to the side, she happily absorbed the intensity of this man's passion as he pounded into her, his fingers digging into her butt cheeks, holding that soft flesh apart so he could watch his cock tunneling into her pussy. His breathing was a series of harsh grunts, a secret language between lovers that only she had been privileged to hear.

Drops of his sweat plopped onto her ass crack and rolled down her spine, the heat of her own skin causing the moisture to evaporate before it reached her neck. The sheets—although fine silk—abraded her nipples, nipples he'd spent a long time teasing through her lace nightgown, turning them more sensitive than usual.

"Touch yourself," he gritted out.

"Jonas, I'm wrung out. I'll just—"

He stopped moving.

After pulling out, he gently rolled her back over, his big body looming over hers. "I'll not take my pleasure while you just lie there until I'm done. I'm not like other—"

Ruby placed her fingers over his lips. "I know that."

"Do you?" His dark blue eyes blazed with a mix of desire and vulnerability.

"Yes. But this is better." She parted her legs and latched onto his hips with her calves as she canted her pelvis. "Because you can watch my face and *see* how much I love the way you fuck me."

"That right?" he said in a conversational tone as his cock found its way back inside her.

He stilled. Balls deep, his shaft pulsing so hard she felt it against her inner walls.

"You gonna give it to me sweet, Deputy?"

Then he was nose to nose with her. "No. Brace your arms above your head."

Maybe she smirked a bit because he'd fallen right into her honeytrap. Gripping the spires of her headboard, she said, "I'm ready."

Jonas rolled his hips in a long, sinuous movement like a big lion stretching after a long nap. "I know what you're doin'." A slow glide out, a pause, then an equally slow glide in. "But you're not callin' the shots; I am. Get ready to come for the fourth time." He kissed her neck in the spot that drove her wild and lowered his full weight onto her.

She gasped and felt him smile against her throat.

"Like that, do you?" His groin pressed against her clit with every single stroke. "Mebbe I'll keep us close like this. Short, shallow pumps do it for me." His mouth migrated to her ear and he whispered, "I'm pretty sure they'll do it for you too."

"You're a menace."

"Mmm-hmm. You created a monster, Ruby girl."

For some reason she melted when he called her that. But she wasn't feeling soft and lovey-dovey. She turned her head to sink her teeth into the ball of his shoulder then said, "Show me the beast, Jonas."

That's when he unleashed himself on her.

It was a hot, wet, sticky romp that left her moaning from another climax as he emptied himself into her.

Jonas kissed her after he'd begun to breathe normally again. Touching her face with reverence, petting and soothing her, settled something inside him too. He cared for her in the aftermath, using an old handkerchief from her nightstand to clean between her legs. Fetching her a drink if she needed one. He always returned to the left side of her bed and gathered her into his arms, patiently waiting until she found the spot on his chest that perfectly fit her head.

She never had allowed herself the luxury of snuggling and falling asleep with a man...until Jonas.

Her hair spilled across the pillows and he reached for it. Toying with the strands, twirling sections around his fingers, smoothing pieces away from her face. He'd done this from their first time together, proving that he enjoyed touching all parts of her, not just the obvious ones.

The man had a sweet side as wide as the Yellowstone River.

Ruby knew by the preoccupied way he stared into space he had a matter on his mind.

After a bit he said, "So Silas intends to court Miss Thompson, the schoolteacher."

"This came about at Doc's tonight?"

"Nope. Guess he's been workin' toward it for a few months. Was the first I'd heard of it."

She ruffled her fingers through the hair on his chest. "Do I hear disapproval?"

"Not sure yet. I like that she laughs off his charm. She also ain't put off by his fightin' nature. That worries me some. But at least since she's been getting medical trainin' with Doc he'll have someone to patch him up after he finds trouble."

"Maybe she'll be a reason he stops fighting." What she meant was:

hopefully Silas would have someone besides his brother looking after him.

"This wasn't the first time she'd tended to him; they were all familiar like." He kissed the top of Ruby's head. "Neither did she let on that you were the one who brung Silas to Doc during the blizzard."

"Sounds like you admire the young schoolteacher." She paused. "Or maybe you're jealous? Wishing you'd thought to court her first."

Jonas went still beneath her. "There's only one woman I'm interested in courtin' and she's turned me down every damn time I've brought it up."

This was a sore point between them. Jonas wanted to thumb his nose at the locals and let everyone know they were together.

She disagreed. She wouldn't put his job in jeopardy, nor have people questioning his character because they thought so poorly of hers.

TJ Louis, the deputy previous to Jonas, had been forced to leave his post after he'd fallen for one of Ruby's girls. Jonas could argue all he wanted that it wasn't that TJ had taken up with a whore; it was that he'd knocked her up and was living with her without the respectability of marriage that had aided in him losing his job.

But Ruby knew better. Big Jim, the other part-time deputy, had questioned whether TJ would show "poor judgment" enforcing the law in other instances. Big Jim and his wife were god-fearing, morally superior, judgy do-gooders who'd ban every activity except for church and daily bible study groups if they had their way.

As far as Ruby knew, Big Jim and Jonas got along well enough. But that'd change the moment Big Jim realized that his fellow lawman had spent the past two years secretly fucking the madam of the local whorehouse. Jonas hadn't even told his brother he'd gotten close with Ruby, mostly because Ruby forbade it. She'd seen this scenario play out too many times, with family relationships broken beyond repair due to disapproval, and she couldn't live with that for him.

So her only option was to live without him.

But the more time they spent together, the harder it was to watch him leave in the morning.

"Please tell me your silence is because you're rethinkin' that *no courtin'* stance," Jonas said softly.

Ruby sighed. "My answer hasn't changed. But I'm wondering how things will change for *you* when Silas is paired off."

Jonas took his time before answering. "I'd likely need to find a new place to live. That cabin is small for bachelor brothers. Be mighty cramped with three of us."

"Surely your brother wouldn't kick you off the land you both own."

"That land has never felt like mine."

"Why not?"

"I come to work in an office; Silas works on the range."

It wasn't bitterness she detected but his resignation. "You've mentioned a few times that you don't love being a deputy in an unincorporated township, but I'm sure if you told Silas you'd like to be more involved running and expanding the ranch, he'd welcome your input."

"That's the thing—I don't want to do that either. Silas would love nothin' better than to become a Wyoming land baron with thousands of head of cattle. I had enough of that life the six years we worked the cattle drives. As soon as I had a chance to make my own way, I did."

She tipped her head back to look at him. "Do you miss that part of who you used to be?"

"Sometimes. I mean, it was heady stuff getting deputized at age nineteen due a shortage of lawmen. Some outlaws took advantage of the Indian raids goin' on all over territories. They robbed, then killed, raped and butchered entire families, makin' it appear that those poor homesteaders had been set on by savages."

"And you saw that brutality?"

He nodded. "Still get bad dreams from it. Once the white men doin' them acts were featured on wanted posters, we went after them. Caught 'em too. Then other outlaw gangs started causin' problems for the railroads and the bounties were a big payout, so five of us banded together and we spent the next two years huntin' 'em down."

He rarely spoke about that time in his life and she wanted to keep him talking. "What kind of men were you ridin' with?"

"Determined. One guy was a former Texas Ranger, another one was rumored to've been a Pinkerton agent."

"Rumored to be," she repeated. "They don't wear that distinction like a badge?"

Jonas snorted. "Pinkerton agents are super-secretive. I've adopted a few of their 'don't tell' tricks and it's the damnedest thing that even other bounty hunters don't question you. Another guy had been an army soldier. Last member was part Blackfeet. Best scout and tracker I ever met."

"And you."

"Yep. Still don't know why they asked me to mount up with them. Bein' the youngest member of the posse…I learned more in them two years than in the previous nineteen years combined. During that time, Silas had gone on his first cattle drive without me and afterward, they dumped off here. He loved the area and bought a piece of land that already had improvements. Then he staked a claim for the land abutting it for me. He had to join up with another cattle drive before he could live on his place full-time. The outfit he worked for taught him where to find stray, unclaimed cattle. If he came across any here, he added them to his herd. Every penny he earned, he bought up more abandoned claims. Small acreages. Tough to make a living between sellin' cattle in the fall and calving season in early spring, so he worked for the railroad for a spell."

"He did? Is that how he knows Zeke?"

"I suspect that's where their bad blood started. Plus, Silas….ah…*supplements* his income with gambling, and West can't walk past a card table without losin' his shirt. Or so Silas says, and he takes advantage of that fact whenever possible. My brother is the luckiest damn card player I've ever known. After quittin' at the railroad—I'm guessing because of a row between him and Zeke—he hired out as a ranch hand. He's never said so, but it feels like he resents me. When I showed up here after takin' a break from the chasin' outlaw life, he'd already done all the hard ranch work. Now he's courtin' Miss Thompson. If anyone deserves a helpmate, it's my brother."

"Jonas. I asked about *you*," she reminded him.

"I know. But I wouldn't be here if it wasn't for Silas." Jonas sighed. "Most days, I feel a whole lotta guilt. If I was a better brother, I'd give him more of my salary so he wouldn't hafta play cards to try and win the money. Or I'd resign as deputy and go after more bounties and invest the money in the ranch."

"Would that make you happy?"

"Probably not. You're about the only thing makin' me happy these days, Ruby. I know you don't wanna hear it, but it's true."

Ruby didn't comment on that.

Silence stretched between them.

He yawned. "Sorry, I'm whipped."

She pressed a kiss on his chest. "It's fine. I am too. Go to sleep."

"I like talkin' to you, Ruby girl."

"I like being with you like this too, Deputy."

"Don't forget to blow out that candle."

Always looking out for her. "I won't."

After he dozed off, Ruby watched him. The glow from the bedside candle highlighted the masculine beauty of his face, a rugged handsomeness he normally masked beneath the brim of his cowboy hat.

Her thoughts rolled back to the first time she'd met the new deputy. Working in an illegal vocation guaranteed she had no love for law enforcement, but maintaining a civil relationship was a necessity. So Madam Ruby had shown up in the deputy's office, presenting herself as a businesswoman, donning her smartest outfit—a pine green, brushed wool skirt, a tightly fitted short jacket the color of ripe plums that ended at her natural waist, and a crisp white shirtwaist. She'd pinned up her hair with silver combs, and worn no facial enhancements.

It had been an unexpected delight to see Deputy McKay's tongue nearly hit the office floor—usually that reaction happened when she was completely naked, not fully clothed. Her attraction to the dark-haired, deep-voiced, blue-eyed lawman had been equally unforeseen, but she'd hidden her interest much better. At least at first.

The man had been completely baffled when she'd inquired how much it'd cost for him to continue looking the other way, skipping regular raids on her "boardinghouse." Then he'd immediately become indignant, assuring her the morals—or lack thereof—of her clientele was no concern of his…unless her girls or the men they serviced were in danger or blatantly breaking the law.

She'd liked him so much more after that little speech.

A few weeks after their talk, the boardinghouse needed his official presence after a drunken customer had nearly strangled Julianna. The deputy ended up knocking the drunken fool out cold and dumping the man on his front porch, informing his wife that he'd been permanently banned from Ruby Red's—not Sackett's—so there wasn't any confusion about where he'd been. Ruby also suspected the personal visit from the deputy was for him to discover whether the guy had been violent toward his wife too.

When Deputy McKay returned to see if there'd been any more trouble, Ruby had invited him into her rooms. What Jonas hadn't known at the time was Ruby never entertained men in her private space.

The poor guy had been uncomfortable from the moment she'd lured him into her parlor. Ruby wasn't one to shy away; her job was to get men to relax. So it wasn't until her second invitation and half a bottle of whiskey shared between them that he'd finally loosened up enough to tell her the truth of why she made him so nervous: Big, strong, tough, steely-eyed, Jonas McKay...was a virgin.

A twenty-three-year-old virgin who hadn't taken advantage of the few opportunities he'd had to shed his virginity, since he'd spent his youth riding the range, and his adulthood chasing outlaws, solely in the company of other men.

So Ruby had seduced him. Deflowered him. Instructed him. Turned him into a confident, caring sexual beast. Helped form him into the type of exciting lover she craved.

The first few months were spent teaching him stamina and all the ways to bring a woman to climax. Then she'd focused on communication so he could tell her exactly what he wanted or what he wanted to do to her. In explicit detail.

His innate sexuality had blossomed. He knew when to be rough. When to be gentle. When to take control and when to surrender. When to start teasing and when to stop. He learned the difference between passion and desire. Between longing and lust.

In mixed company they were professional. Cordial. Friendly, even.

In private they were untamed, unapologetic sex fiends, gorging themselves on pleasure.

Maybe Ruby could've kept their relationship strictly about physical release if Jonas had ever sneered about her profession, called her a whore or acted as if he was doing her a favor by fucking her.

But that wasn't the kind of man he was.

It truly did not matter to him what she did outside the time they spent together.

Jonas never offered to pay her.

He also never asked if she serviced other men between the times they were together.

Looking at him now...she could hate herself for letting him get so entwined in her life and in her heart. At one time she'd dreamed of finding a man like Jonas McKay. But now after she'd found him, she couldn't keep him.

It would shatter her soul when the day came that she'd have to turn him away.

Until then, she'd enjoy each moment as if they'd never have another.

She blew out the candle and pulled the coverlet over both of them.

SIX

W HEN SILAS WOKE up, his head didn't hurt nearly as much as he'd thought it would.

His body, however, felt like he'd been drug by a horse for a mile or ten.

He groaned and rolled to his side. Then he jackknifed into a sitting position. Keeping his eyes closed, he counted to ten before he opened them.

Not bad. Not too dizzy.

He heard a snort and peered over to see young Jimmy sprawled, snuffling pig noises floating out of his open mouth. Kid probably hadn't slept that well in ages.

Needing to take a piss something fierce, Silas lowered his feet to the floor, grateful his boots were still on. His ribs hurt worse than the gouge in his gut. Seemed to take forever to reach the door. But finally he shuffled out into the sunny morning.

He crossed over to the stand of scrub oak behind the barn and relieved himself, staring at the sky to try and figure out the time. Had to be after ten, which meant he was hours late checking cattle.

By the time he returned to the open doorway, hot and cold rolled over him. His stomach had twisted into knots, forcing him to lean against the building.

Damn laudanum. Easier to just buck up and take the pain than deal with this flop-sweat feeling.

"Silas McKay! What are you doing up and about?" a stern but sweet voice demanded.

Silas opened his eyes and his belly tightened again, but not from sickness. Dinah stood not ten feet from him, all pink-cheeked and pretty. Concern darkening her crystal-blue eyes. He couldn't help but grin at her. "Dinah, darlin'. I'd gladly take a beatin' every night if it meant I could see your beautiful face first thing every mornin'."

"I see your dance with the devil last night didn't dull your silver tongue."

"It weren't a dance. The devil merely twirled me a bit to make sure I didn't waste any more time before courtin' my very own angel."

"Heavens, Mr. McKay. I think you might have a more serious head injury than Doc believed."

He chuckled. "Nah. I'm just fine. And it's Silas, sweetheart. Remember?"

She raised one dark blond brow. "I don't remember giving you permission to call me sweetheart."

Silas pushed off the building and started toward her. "You'd rather I called you something else?"

"You shouldn't be calling me anything. You should be lying down, resting."

Two steps closer. "I could call you honey, 'cause you sure are sweet."

"Silas."

Three steps closer. "Or I could call you sugar pie."

"Let me guess...because it's also sweet?"

He stopped when his boots nearly touched the hem of her skirt. Staring into those expressive eyes, he held back a smile. The woman couldn't bluff to save her life. She liked this kinda love-talk.

Dinah didn't move when Silas tucked a loose tendril of her hair behind her delicate ear. Nor did she shy away when he traced the line of her jaw down to her stubborn chin. "Sugar pie is sweet. But that's not why I'd like to call you that."

"Then why?" she said so softly he barely heard her.

"Because sugar pie is my favorite dessert and I can't wait to eat it all up. Every silky, sweet, tasty bite. I'm torn between takin' my time enjoyin' it or gorging myself on it."

Her face flushed a darker pink, but she didn't look away from him.

Oh, she had some fire all right.

"Is that all right by you?"

She bit her lip then blurted, "But I don't know how to make…sugar pie."

So many ways to take that response. So very many dirty delicious ways. He managed a cool, "I'll teach you."

"Everything?" she said breathlessly.

"Yeah, sweetheart. Everything and then some." He leaned a fraction closer. "If you don't want me callin' you sugar pie, I got another word that'll work."

"What's that?"

Silas caught a whiff of her rose perfume when he whispered in her ear, "Mine."

She shivered so completely he felt her skirt move.

Jimmy broke the moment by butting in between them. "Hey, Miss Thompson. Didja bring us food?"

For the first time Silas noticed Dinah had a covered basket dangling from the crook of her left arm.

"Yes, Jimmy, there's food. Just be patient and go wash up." She lifted a cloth off the basket and held it out to Silas. "Doc had to cut your shirt off last night. Jonas told me to put it in the rag pile, but I mended it. I changed the style and added buttons, I hope you don't mind."

He stared at her. "Why?"

"Why'd I fix it? Because I figured you'd rather have something to wear than nothing." She harrumphed and glanced at his chest, then away. "Although your brother hinted you'd be fine running around half-clothed, but I wasn't sure if he was joking." Another peep at his chest from beneath her lashes.

If she was failing miserably at acting unaffected by seeing his chest, belly and bare arms on display, how would she react if he started flexing those muscles?

Faint maybe, you cocky jerk.

He told his brother's voice in his head to *shut up.*

"I can't thank you enough, Dinah." Taking the clean, mended shirt, he turned it around so the front faced him. "This'll work just fine."

She seemed confused that he didn't immediately put it on.

"I'll wait until after Doc wraps my ribs."

"I'm sure Jimmy won't mind breaking his fast with a half-naked man."

"But you would?"

She didn't respond.

"Dinah?"

Her eyes met his. "It's distracting." She tossed a look over her shoulder. "Jimmy. Come on and eat." She sidestepped Silas. "I'll set it up inside."

"Jimmy needs to get my horse and tack from Blackbird's Livery first."

"But I'm hungry!" Jimmy complained.

Dinah whirled around. "The boy needs to eat."

"Yes, ma'am, I agree. The promise of a meal will get him back here faster." Silas dug in his pocket and flipped Jimmy a coin. "Give this to Micah at the stables and make sure you tell him I owe him a quart of milk."

"A quart of milk?" Jimmy repeated, confused. "Why?"

"Then Micah will know *I* sent you."

"Oh, like a code?"

"Yep."

His eyes lit up. "Miss Ruby has secret codes too."

I'll just bet she does. "Micah will ready my horse and tack for you, but you aren't to ride him back here, Jimmy. Are we clear?"

"Yes, sir."

"Soon as you make it back with everything"—Silas flipped another coin in the air and caught it at the last moment before Jimmy could—"this coin and Miss Thompson's tasty food will be yours."

"Yes, sir!" Jimmy raced off.

"Don't know why you're so fired up to get your horse back, Silas. It's not like you're going anywhere," she said with a sniff and headed into Doc's recovery room.

Silas followed, waiting until she'd finished setting up the food—thick slices of bread, a jar of preserves and a crock of butter—before he spoke. "While I appreciate the idea of wastin' more of my day, that ain't the reality. I've gotta get home."

"You had a stab wound *twelve hours* ago. Your body is covered in bruises and you were kicked in the head. You need to spend today recovering, not cowboying."

"And while I'm recovering, who's gonna deal with my cattle? I'm also Garold Henrikson's hand, so I'm tendin' to his livestock. I ain't gonna lie abed when those animals need me."

"Silas. You can barely walk."

"Barely is still walkin', though. If I can walk, I can ride."

Dinah put her hands on her hips. "There's no talking you out of this?"

"No."

"Fine. After you eat, and after Doc checks you out, I'll ride with you to check cattle."

His eyes narrowed. "Why?"

"Because I don't trust you not to do too much, McKay."

"Concerned for my well-bein', sugar pie?"

"Yes." She raised that haughty chin a notch. "I'd prefer that the first man I've agreed to let court me not be too exhausted or broken down to do so properly."

Proper wasn't the word that came to mind as how he intended to court her, but it made him grin anyway. "In that case, I'll be extra careful today when we're ridin' the range. Wouldn't want to break any of my body parts you're so fired up about seein' *properly*."

"Silas McKay! I said no such thing."

"But you were thinkin' it, darlin'." He reached for a slice of bread, but she tapped his hand.

"Wash first."

"Yes, ma'am."

Silas had a feeling he'd better get used to saying that.

DOC GRUMBLED ABOUT Silas's "fool-headed ways" and dismissed him after tightly wrapping his ribs.

Dinah and Doc spoke in private after she'd exited the house carrying a bundle. Then she headed to the barn to get her horse ready.

She emerged on an old paint horse that should've been put to pasture years ago. "Is that yours?" he asked.

"No. She's Mrs. Agnes's." She patted the neck. "I'm riding her today because she's slow and steady." Dinah smirked at him. "Emphasis on *slow*.

Me riding slow means you'll have to ride that way too, instead of tearing off like we're in a wild horse race at the county fair."

"Well, darlin', there's *your* slow and *my* slow. Try to keep up."

The thirty-minute ride seemed to take three times that long even though they were traveling fast enough to keep from conversing.

Dinah had a good seat on her horse—better than he'd imagined.

And Silas had been watching her a lot, not only because her pantalets were on display with her dress bunched up to the saddle horn. He'd become enthralled with the way her body moved in the saddle, bouncing ass and bouncing tits, her golden hair streaming behind her unbound. But he also appreciated that she'd worn practical boots, not the high-heeled style other town girls favored. Plus, she'd chosen a wide-brimmed cavalry hat with stampede strings that probably belonged to Doc, rather than a fancy silk and lace bonnet with birds and feathers. She'd dressed to work, not to impress him, and that impressed him most of all.

He wondered what she saw when she looked his way—which he'd caught her doing several times. A brawler? A poorly dressed ranch hand?

That's when Silas knew his courting her would include the reality of what it meant to be married to a rancher. He'd rather be alone than spend his life with a woman who hated everything about his life that he loved.

Dinah seemed…lighter today. Looking around the land as if it was the first time she'd seen it. Tipping her head back to catch the sun's rays on her face. With that glow upon her, she appeared every bit a beautiful angel.

She caught him staring and smiled shyly.

He smiled back and took the lead, kicking up the pace as they zipped along the last stretch that led to Henrikson's place.

Garold was waiting outside when they rode up.

"Mornin', Garold."

"It's afternoon, McKay. You're late."

"Ran into some trouble last night that couldn't be helped." He swore Dinah snorted at that half-truth. "You been out at all this mornin'?"

"No. That is why I pay you. Cows are"—he gestured behind him and muttered in German—"same as yesterday."

A little blessing. The cattle had water and enough room to graze through today. Moving them could wait until tomorrow. He smiled at the grumpy German. "I'll get to it then and stop back by when we're done."

"We?" Garold said gruffly, looking between him and Dinah.

"Yes. This is Miss Dinah Thompson, the woman I'm courtin'. Dinah, this is my neighbor Garold Henrikson. I also do a little cowboyin' for him."

"Pleasure to meet you, Mr. Henrikson. Your home is lovely."

Garold harrumphed and walked toward his house without a word.

Wasn't until they were around the back of the barn and out of earshot when Dinah said, "Is he always so rude?"

"These days? Yeah. Never used to be. I reckon he's just heartbroke, so I forgive his rudeness. His meanness some days is a hard pill to swallow." But Silas had no choice but to smile and choke down that bitter pill. He had little doubt Henrikson would be moving on—sooner, rather than later— and Silas intended to be the one Henrikson offered the sale of his land to first. So if he had to suck it up, he would. All spring Silas had been fretting and planning and refiguring his financial situation, looking for ways to earn the extra money needed to strike a promissory lease-for-sale agreement before some other fat-cat greenhorn swooped in with a carpetbag of cash because he wanted to play at being a rancher.

Dinah stopped her horse and Silas had to rein back around. "Something wrong?"

"Why is he heartbroken, Silas?"

"I ain't gonna gossip about a man's troubles, Dinah."

"It's not gossip if you tell me. It's gossip if you tell everyone at Sackett's Saloon or Robinette's General Store. Besides, I'm trustworthy. How long do you think I would've lasted working for Doc if I blathered on about who'd come to see him and why?"

"All right. But it's one of them sad stories that'll need a handkerchief in the after-telling, and sugar pie, I'm fresh out."

"I've brought my own handkerchief."

Of course she had. Silas scrubbed his hands over his face. "I've owned this land for four years, but only been livin' here for three. Two years ago Henrikson and his wife overpaid for the land they're on. Land I wanted but couldn't afford to buy from the original claimant. They had the house, barn and corrals built before they moved in. They came callin' 'bout a week or so after they arrived. Margaret, his wife, was younger than him by about half. She'd grown up on a ranch in Texas and livin' here was her idea." He smiled. "Garold doted on her. Margaret teased him about it, but he didn't mind because you could just tell he was over the moon for her. I quickly figured out she knew her way around the cattle business and Garold was just learnin'. Last fall, I helped them with their round-up and she shared that they were expectin' a baby. Then she asked if I'd be willin' to help them with brandin' in the spring too."

"Of course you said yes."

He nodded. "I saw 'em around Christmas. With winter and all, it's easy to stay isolated. After I got back from Doc's after the blizzard, and knowin' it'd stranded Jonas in Cheyenne, I decided to see if my neighbors were okay." His hands tightened on his saddle horn. "I had to hitch the mule up to the sled and ride across the snow on my knees because it was still deep. First thing I saw was Garold sittin' on the porch with the front door and all the windows in the house open. He didn't even hear me crunching through the snow or sayin' his name. When he finally looked up, I'd never seen haunted eyes like that. He had a bruise on his head the size of a biscuit. I asked what happened and he started talkin' in German. Then he started cryin' and lord...I knew it was bad."

"Oh no."

"Don't know how long I sat there with him until he spoke English, but I know it was full-on dark by the time he finished tellin' me what had happened. He'd gone out to the barn to check on the horses when there was just a few inches of snow on the ground. Somehow he slipped, whacked his head into a beam and it knocked him out cold. When he came to, it was night. By then, the blizzard was ragin' and he knew enough not to try to make it back to the house. So he decided to wait it out until mornin'." Silas swallowed hard. "Except mornin' came and it was still snowing and blowing, and he couldn't even see the house. He had water, and hay to keep himself warm, so he rode out four days in that barn until it cleared. Took him half a day to dig a path to the house. And when he got there..."

Dinah reached over and touched his shoulder. "I'm sorry. You don't have to tell me any more."

"No. You oughta know it all. Margaret..." He cleared his throat. "The baby had tried to come durin' that time. Neither Margaret nor their baby boy made it. Garold couldn't keep their bodies in the house but he couldn't just throw them in the snowbank either. He'd spent two days in the house with them, lost in grief, not knowin' what to do..." From the corner of his eye he saw Dinah pull a handkerchief out of her pocket. "I took him back to my place, dosed him with whiskey until he passed out and then went back to do what he couldn't." He paused. "I found a spot over there"—he pointed to a cluster of trees—"where there was a snow break and the ground had some give. Took me a day to dig it deep enough and another day to bury them."

"Silas. You had a sprained arm."

"I know, darlin'. It hurt like hell."

"But you did it anyway."

"I had to. So that's why, when Garold's grumpy, I reckon he's got a right to it." He reined around and bit back a wince of pain. "Come on. Let's get this done." Then he rode off.

AFTER DEALING WITH his herd and Henrikson's, they rode to Silas's place.

Silas purposely didn't watch her face when she caught her first look at his home. It wasn't much—and that was just the outside. The barn was a lot nicer than the house, which he supposed said a lot about him.

He dismounted slowly and turned to assist her only to find she hadn't needed his help. "If you wanna stay a bit, you can hang your tack here while your horse is corralled."

She fiddled with her horse's bridle. "Do you want me to stay?"

"Yeah, sugar pie, I do. Very much."

"Okay then."

After they dealt with the horses and turned them out, Dinah did a slow spin. "How much of your land did we see?"

"Only the front section. I've been workin' on adding on some fence lines as markers but it's slow goin' when it's just me doin' the building. I've spent a lot of time at Henrikson's place this winter and spring." He scratched his neck. "That's why it took months for me to make it back to Doc's."

"Poor Mr. Henrikson. I can't imagine."

"It's even more frustrating for him since he ain't much of a rancher. Margaret dealt with the animals. His herd is twice the size of mine. I'm happy to hire out to him, but I'm getting behind. And I've gotta turn the bulls out in the next two weeks."

She frowned. "What does that mean?"

He grinned. "Putting the bulls and cows together in one pasture means in nine months I'll have calves."

Dinah blushed. Then she said, "Are you ready for a late lunch?" She pointed to her saddlebag. "I brought sandwiches."

"Darlin', you didn't have to do that. But thank you. There's a table and chairs inside."

"While I'm sure it's lovely, I'd rather be outside. I brought a blanket so we could have a picnic. And also, I brought…" She lowered her eyes.

Silas caught her chin in his hand and forced her to look at him. "Tell me."

"I brought the book I started reading to you when we were snowed in. You seemed to like it and I wondered if you'd finished it?"

Such sweetness in her. He just wanted to lap it up. "No, haven't had much time for readin' beyond the 'land for sale' section of the newspaper." Although the glove on his hand kept him from feeling the smooth warmth of her skin, he couldn't help but stroke the cute dent in her chin anyway. "I'd like to hear the rest of the story about a time machine. Who thinks up that crazy kinda stuff?"

"H.G. Wells has a vivid imagination, that's for certain."

"Tell you what. While I get us some water, why don't you pick a spot to spread out?"

"Sounds wonderful."

Silas grabbed a glass jar and lid from the cabin and filled it with the cold, clean water from the hand pump. One of the first things he'd done after buying this place was dig a well, so he didn't have to haul water from the creek.

He quickly washed his hands, forearms and face and set off in search of her.

Dinah had chosen a spot in the open meadow that resembled a wild-flower garden. Pale green sagebrush abounded as did purple bluebell flowers, clumps of yellow meadow gold, and the occasional scarlet patch of Indian paintbrush. She sat in the middle of the white blanket, her legs stretched out in front of her, her arms braced behind her as she tipped her face to the sun. Her relaxed posture and soft smile defined serene.

And he felt it too. Dinah being here gave him a sense of peace. Of rightness.

She opened her eyes as he approached, and her smile broadened. "I see why you love this place so much. I'm afraid I wouldn't get much ranch work done. I'd be too tempted to lollygag out here in the sun among the wildflowers."

He grinned at her. "I ain't feelin' a bit guilty about not bein' out building fence when I have a chance to lollygag with you."

"Let's eat first." Dinah pulled out the food she'd packed. Sliced pork sandwiches with a layer of salty lard smeared on the bread, wedges of pale-yellow cheese and some kind of dessert.

He poked at it. "What's this?"

"Apple spice cake with brown sugar frosting." She sent him a teasing look. "It's no sugar pie, but I think you'll like it."

"If you made it, I'm sure I will."

They ate in silence. He liked that she didn't constantly chatter like a squirrel. They shared the water and when he offered to make coffee later, they decided to save the cake for then.

Silas set his hat aside and stretched out on the blanket with his arms behind his head. "I'm stuffed. That was a treat, Dinah. Thank you."

"You're welcome." She'd resumed her previous pose of basking in the sun. He wished he could ask her to lie down beside him, but she'd probably panic so he let it be.

For now.

"What's goin' through your mind?"

"Questions. Lots and lots of questions."

"About?"

Turning her head, Dinah peered at him curiously. "You. Your life before you came to Wyoming. How you ended up in Crook County. Your family—besides Jonas."

He chuckled. "You do have lots of questions. Guess it'd be best if I started at the beginning. Me n' Jonas were born in Boston about a year after our parents came to America from Ireland. We didn't have nothin'. Lived in the two-room 'factory' housing that was a benefit of the manufacturing plant where they both worked. I remember bein' hungry. We were left alone a lot, bein's our parents worked or were sleepin' from workin' so much. We ran with a bunch of other kids who were in the same situation."

"Did you go to school?"

"Yep. Factory-run school, so at least we had one meal a day." He shifted positions when a rock dug into his bruised spine. "When we were ten, there was a big fire at the plant and both of our parents died."

She reached for his hand and squeezed. "Oh Silas. That's awful."

He threaded their fingers together. She didn't pull away, so he resumed talking. "We were luckier than other kids because our folks were devout Catholics. Seriously devout. The Catholic orphanage took us in. We had school and church every day, even in the summer, plus we had chores to do. Might make me callous to say this, but we were better off in the orphanage than when our parents were alive. But space was limited so at age thirteen they kicked you out."

"Just out into the street?"

"Yeah. That's when it paid not to've been a problem kid. Father O'Flaherty and our folks were from the same part of Ireland, so when our time to leave came, he booked us passage on a train to Denver with other orphans." He let his thumb steal across the silky skin on the inside of her wrist. "Talk about an adventure. Two town kids finally seein' what lay outside the smoke and grime of the city. After we reached Denver and we didn't have no one to claim us, then they'd let other people lookin' for kids or workers come in and talk to you."

"You got to choose where you went?"

"Sorta. I mean we wouldn't be allowed *not* to choose. Father O'Flaherty had given us paperwork that required me'n Jonas to stay together. It was an incentive because whoever picked us to work for them got paid double. This rough-lookin' guy wearin' the oddest clothes and boots that jingled was the first to talk to us. His name was Jeb and he was a drover. We didn't know what that was, and he explained he was in charge of movin' cattle all across the West. Down south from Texas, up north to Montana and even east to Kansas. He made it sound like heaven; ridin' horses on the range, roundin' up strays, movin' them across ragin' rivers and over the plains, dodgin' Indian raids and outlaws. Sleepin' beneath the stars every night. Eatin' by a campfire." Silas laughed. "Lord, he gave us the hard sell and we fell for it."

"What did he have you and Jonas doing?"

"We were 'camp boys' to start, which meant all the crap jobs plus learnin' to run the remuda."

"Remuda?"

"The extra horses. Each cowhand—cowpunchers, they called them-selves both—needed three horses to rotate in to ride, since we were on the trail for between three and five months. So me'n Jonas had to keep the remuda in line while the cowpunchers dealt with the cattle."

"How many cowpunchers were on the drive?"

"Between ten to fifteen, dependin' on how many cattle we were runnin'."

"You and Jonas had to deal with up to thirty extra horses every day?"

"Yep. Eventually we worked our way up to cowhands. I'd never been so tired in my life. Took two solid years until I got used to it. But them cowpunchers also taught us everything we needed to survive. How to hunt and fish. How to rope and ride. How to shoot guns and use knives. How to track men and animals. How to doctor men and animals. How to play cards and drink whiskey. How to charm the ladies. How to tell a good story. How to navigate by the stars. Never spent a turn cookin' with the chuckwagon, but everything else was fair game." He paused. "I loved it and I'm grateful every damn day that we were chosen to learn that life, 'cause a lot of other orphans ended up like Jimmy. But by the time I was nineteen, I realized I wanted my own ranch, responsible only for myself, my land and my own livestock."

"You never wanted to do anything else?" she asked.

"Nope. But Jonas did. While he did his part workin' the cattle, Jonas took to ridin' like he'd been born on horseback. He also stayed calm in situations that had other men reachin' for their guns. Whenever we'd come across marshals or a posse, he'd spend hours talkin' to them and one group deputized him. While he was excited he'd found his path, that meant we'd be on separate paths for the first time in our lives."

Again, Dinah squeezed his hand. "Was that hard?"

"Yeah. Especially since we're twins. We'd always been together. So for the first couple of months after he was gone, I'd pose one of the ridiculous questions that kills the boredom on a drive and the rider to my left would goggle at me as if I was crazy as a loon. I'd gotten so used to Jonas ridin' next to me that it was weird and sad when he wasn't. Anyway, I kept on movin' cattle. Saved my money. I found this place one day searchin' for strays. Campbell, the guy who owned it, wanted out. None of his livestock had made it through the winter and he was lookin' for a buyer."

"How long ago was that?"

"Four years."

"How old are you?"

He smirked at her. "How old do you *think* I am?"

"At least thirty-seven," she teased.

"Funny. I'm twenty-five. How old are you?"

"I turned twenty last month."

"Practically an old maid, then, huh?"

"Hush, you. Keep going with the Silas saga."

He sighed. "Let's see...livin' out in the middle of nowhere Crook County...oh right. Jonas tracked me down about two years ago. Said he needed a break from chasin' outlaws and sleepin' on the ground. Labelle had a job opening for a deputy, but I know it's boring work. He claims he's fine here, but I sense his restlessness. He helps out if I ask, but ranchin' ain't his thing."

"And you? Do you ever feel restless?"

Silas lifted his head and studied her. It seemed more than a casual question. "I don't have the itch to move someplace else. This is my home. But I do get impatient with not havin' the funds to expand the McKay Ranch as fast as I'd like. So I just gotta bide my time and build my ranch acre by acre."

Recognition lit her eyes. "That's why you play cards. To earn money quicker so you can buy more land."

"Sounds like a good way to end up with less money, don't it?"

"Not if you're skillful at it. Which you must be if Zeke West keeps challenging you."

His chest puffed out a bit at hearing how fast she rose to his defense. "I'm not wastin' this precious time with you by talkin' about that idiot. Now it's your turn to detail Dinah's life and how you came to be in Crook County."

Dinah pushed to her knees and reached in the saddlebag to pull out *The Time Machine*. "Let's save that story for another time. I'd rather find out what the Eloi and the Morlocks are up to in their story. Now where were we...?"

It was sweet that she'd bookmarked the page with the piece of paper he'd doodled on while he'd been listening to her read last time.

"*In a moment I knew what had happened. I had slept, and my fire had gone out, and the cold bitterness of death had come over my soul.*"

Silas concentrated on the sound and inflections in her voice. He could listen to her speak for hours.

After several pages of Dinah fidgeting, Silas promised he'd behave if she stretched out beside him and got comfortable.

That's how Jonas found them: Dinah lying on her front with her ankles crossed behind her and reading from the book as she rested on her elbows, while Silas laid on his side, head propped on his hand, enthralled with her and the story.

Dinah hadn't jumped up as if they'd been caught doing something wrong when Jonas's horse thundered up, young Jimmy on another horse behind him. She just pressed her finger to the sentence she'd stopped on so she wouldn't lose her place when she glanced up.

"What in the devil is goin' on?" Jonas demanded.

"He's resting, as per Doc's recommendation," she answered coolly.

"Silas was supposed to be *resting* at Doc's place until I fetched him. I went there and found out he'd left hours ago."

"You know that cattle don't wait until afternoon, Jonas." Silas sat up and grimaced from the sharp pain. "Dinah helped me with chores and we've been out here enjoyin' each other's company."

When Jonas appeared skeptical, Silas held up his hand. "Ain't it better we're out here where anyone can see what we're doin', rather than us bein' alone in the cabin, givin' people a chance to tell tales about what we *might've* been up to? Besides, ain't no one ever stops by to sit and visit a spell with me."

"That's because you're a damn hermit." Jonas sighed. "I wasn't gonna say nothin' about what you two were doin'. I intended to ask Dinah if she wanted me or Jimmy to ready her horse for the ride back to Doc's."

"Who said she's leavin'?"

"I figured she'd prefer to head out with Jimmy before it gets dark. Since you're 'resting' on Doc's orders and can't escort her back home."

"Your brother is right." Dinah rolled to her feet. "I have my own chores to finish before supper." She looked at Jimmy and pointed. "My tack is hanging over the fence."

"I'll get it right now, Miss," he said and spurred away.

However, Jonas, that nosy bastard, hadn't moved.

As Dinah started to tuck everything back into the saddlebag, Silas realized they hadn't eaten the tasty-looking dessert. "Can't you at least stay and have cake with me?"

"I'll leave both pieces here for you and Jonas."

"I ain't sure he's deserving of your special cake," he said sourly.

"Silas McKay. He *carried* you to Doc's after your fight last night, remember? You can share one piece of cake with him." She tapped his cheek and made a less-than-sympathetic clicking noise with her tongue. "You know I'll make more anytime you ask."

That perked him up some. Silas carried her saddlebag as they slowly made their way back to the corral. "When can I see you next?" he asked.

"When would you like to see me?"

"Tomorrow."

"Excellent. Church is at nine. Then there's a community social in Sundance after the various services finish." She crowded close enough to him their boot tips met. "And I'll remind you that is an all or nothing option *only*. You come to church and you can escort me to the social. But you cannot skip church and slide in next to me at the social for a slice of pie, Silas."

Shrewd woman had figured him out pretty quick. He pasted on a smile. "Guess I'll see you in church, darlin'."

She smiled. "I'd like that."

They didn't linger with further goodbyes. Still he felt guilty watching Dinah ride off with Jimmy when it should be him seeing after her.

Jonas had turned out his horse before he sauntered up to where Silas was watching the dust clouds swirling in the sun's dying rays. "Everything all right?"

"Yep."

"How you feelin'?"

"Like someone kicked the shit outta me."

"I figured as much. But I brought something that'll dull those aches." He waggled a bottle of whiskey. "You interested?"

"Heck yeah. Dinah left a couple of pieces of cake for us."

"Looks like we've got supper covered."

They walked side by side back to the house.

"You up for a game of cards?" Jonas asked.

Silas gave him the side-eye. "Why wouldn't I be?"

"Oh, you know that old sayin'...lucky at cards, unlucky in love. I think the reverse might be true now that you're *courtin'* Miss Thompson and you're lookin' all moon-eyed in love. I'd hate to take advantage."

"Shut up."

Jonas laughed.

Silas reached over and shoved him.

SEVEN

DINAH HADN'T EVER spent so much time getting ready for church.

Standing in her pantalets, she sorted through her clothing choices, wishing she'd had time to finish sewing the new summer lawn dress in cheery green gingham she'd started after school had ended. But so far, she'd been too busy running the house and helping Doc while Mrs. Agnes recuperated.

Her fingers stopped at the fawn-colored velvet skirt. It wasn't too heavy for such a lovely spring day. She could wear the buttercream-hued shirtwaist with it. Thankfully she'd fancied up the simple placket by embroidering colorful flowers down the center. Her only fitted jacket was winter-weight, so she opted for the soft-pink cashmere shawl her mother had knitted when times were flush for the Thompson family.

After dressing and buttoning up her white dress boots, she debated on hat choices. She loathed the current fashion of garish, gargantuan headpieces, feathered with entire birds' nests tucked into the fabric. She'd assured herself that even if she had the money to purchase the latest style, she wouldn't choose anything so gaudy.

Snagging a long pink ribbon from her sewing stash, she carefully tied it around her straw hat, twisting the ends into a bow at the back and letting the extra lengths hang down.

She turned sideways, checking her reflection in the mirror. Last evening before bed, she'd dampened her hair and twisted sections of it in rags to create the lovely loose curls that reached the middle of her back. She'd pulled the front pieces straight back and created a pouf with two silver combs. At least her hair would look stylish regardless of whether she wore the hat.

Two knocks sounded on her door. "Dinah, dear? Are you ready?"

"Yes. Be right out."

Doc had already loaded the basket of food for the social and hitched the horse to the buggy.

Dinah clambered up and took her place beside Doc on the wooden bench seat. Part of her felt guilty for leaving Mrs. Agnes at home alone; another part felt she deserved some social interaction.

And she was really looking forward to seeing Silas again.

Doc's place was on the outskirts of LaBelle, and a thirty-minute buggy ride into Sundance. Although several businesses from Sundance, such as Sackett's Saloon and Harker's Hardware, had opened storefronts in the township, complementing the existing mercantile, the area was still considered a "cow town."

Sundance, however, considered itself to be a "real town." Since Sundance was the Crook County seat, it had a lovely three-story brick courthouse as the town's centerpiece. There were also three churches, seven saloons, three general stores, a livery and blacksmith's, a hatmaker's and a dressmaker's, a shoe store, a barbershop, a hotel with a restaurant, two other dining establishments and a community center. The town also was proud of its municipal band and baseball team, which hosted tournaments that drew spectators from Wyoming and South Dakota.

Not that Dinah had personally partaken of any of Sundance's entertainments.

While Sundance had a daily stage line that ran from Spearfish, the mail only made it to LaBelle twice a week. But the "cow township" did have one advantage that Sundance did not: a main railroad extension to the thriving town of Gillette, via direct route from Cheyenne.

Although she'd spent the majority of her days the previous five years nursing her mother, in her free time she and her friends had an active social life in Cheyenne. She'd attended the fair, shopped at the variety of stores along Main Street, enjoyed community events such as plays and dances—even when she'd been too shy to actually dance.

After her mother had passed on, leaving her practically penniless, Dinah had no choice but to find a teaching job as soon as possible. "Frontier" schools paid a higher salary. When she saw the advertisement in the *Wyoming Eagle Tribune*, for a teacher for grades one through three, in a township outside of Sundance, that included room and board, she immediately sent off a letter.

Within two weeks she'd received a response from Doctor Alexander Moorcroft. If she accepted the teacher's position for two years, she would board with him and his wife. Any help she provided as his medical assistant—after her teaching hours—would be paid separately. Transportation of herself and her belongings from Cheyenne to Labelle would also be provided. Not only would she have her own room in his house, she'd also have use of a horse and buggy.

It'd seemed too good to be true—and in some respects, it was. Still, she accepted the position, sold off the last of her parents' household furnishings, keeping only the steamer trunks, a credenza, desk and chair, a mirror, and the sewing machine. She'd also saved all of the books her family had collected, fabric, quilts and bedding, and a few decorative knickknacks she hoped to display in her own home one day.

She'd arrived at the train station with all her earthly possessions a year ago.

Nothing had turned out as she'd hoped.

Yet, Doc had always treated her kindly and paid her promptly. Mrs. Agnes could be a real pill, but she treated Dinah like the help for the most part, and she'd gotten used to that with her own mother.

That's where her struggle was. Dinah was lonely. She looked forward to attending church, not to absorb the preacher's words, but to have social contact with people other than the infirmed.

Doc harrumphed next to her, tearing her out of her thoughts.

"Is that Silas McKay waiting at the bottom of the steps with his hat in his hand?"

Dinah squinted at the figure dressed in the black coat, politely inclining his head at the people passing by him. Her belly swooped and she placed her hand there to quell her sudden bout of nerves. He'd really come.

"Dinah?" Doc prompted.

"Yes, Doc. Silas asked if he could escort me to the picnic and I agreed—but only if he accompanied me to church beforehand."

He smirked. "Good to know."

Then Silas was there, helping her down from the buggy. "Dinah. You are a vision of loveliness on this fine mornin'."

"Thank you." Lord have mercy, this man looked every bit as if the devil himself had decided to come to church. A satin brocade vest with red piping peeped out from beneath his black suit coat. His shirt was also black but the jaunty tie at his throat was red. That far-too-handsome face had been cleanly shaven. His dark hair beneath his hat wasn't severely tamed with a heavy pomade, allowing the ends to curl in a charmingly roguish manner.

"Do I pass your inspection, Miss Thompson?" he murmured in her ear.

"Yes, Mr. McKay, you do. The bruises and scrapes on your face not-withstanding."

He chuckled. "Nothin' I can do about that now."

"Except keep it from happening again by avoiding fighting in the future."

"No promises on that, sugar pie."

That's what she was most worried about.

The three of them entered church together and Dinah couldn't help but notice the curious looks other girls—and even their mothers—sent his way. But he paid no attention to anything except making sure she was comfortably situated between him and Doc in Doc's preferred pew.

Silas glanced down at the floor, then turned to squint behind him and leaned over to study the pews across the aisle.

She whispered, "Is something wrong?"

"Where are the kneelers?"

"Excuse me?"

"The slide out benches with pads where you kneel?"

"Umm. This church doesn't have them."

"Bein's it's a poor country church? 'Cause it's the first one I've been in that ain't had 'em."

"This is a Methodist church. We don't use kneelers."

He blinked as if that didn't explain anything.

Doc shushed them and they stayed silent throughout the service.

Afterward, as they waited in line to shake the pastor's hand, Silas bent down to whisper, "So I'm guessin' no bowls of holy water on the way out neither."

"No."

The pastor seemed eager to talk to Silas. He clasped Silas's outstretched hand in both of his. "Deputy. It is a privilege to have you in our midst today."

"'Cept I'm not Deputy McKay. That's my brother Jonas. I'm Silas. I'm just a rancher."

Dinah frowned at his *just a rancher* comment on his occupation.

"I apologize, Silas," the pastor gushed. "It is still a delight to meet you."

"Likewise."

"Are you considering joining my flock?"

"Father O'Flaherty would have my hide. He didn't send me all the way out here from Boston so I could turn against everything him and the nuns taught me."

The pastor blinked. "Pardon?"

"Nothin'. This place will hafta do until there's a Catholic church built."

Silas ushered Dinah out before she could apologize for him—as if she'd do that.

But she stopped him in the vestibule. "How often does that happen?"

"What? Folks bein' surprised that I'm Catholic?"

"No. People mistaking you for Jonas."

His jaw tightened. "All the time. But Deputy McKay don't ever look like this." He pointed to his bruised face. "So truly, I don't get the confusion 'cause it seems I always look a little rougher around the edges than him and I'm certainly no gentleman."

Dinah stood on the tips of her boots to whisper, "You are a gentleman for escorting me to church, Silas. And I have no problem telling you and your brother apart."

"That right?" He angled his head until his lips were almost touching her ear. "You a bettin' woman, sugar pie?"

And...there was the appearance of his rascally side.

Clasping his hand in hers, she hotfooted it out of the church and didn't stop moving until Silas dug his boot heels in and pulled her up short.

"What are you so all-fired up about?" he demanded.

She whirled around. "You! Talking about betting! In a church!"

He shrugged. "So?"

"So...remember the Bible lessons about moneylenders? And Jesus warning against games of chance taking place in God's temple because they were a sin?"

"I musta missed those scriptures." He came boot to boot with her, so close his hat cast her face in shadow. "Did you hustle me outta there in case God opted to send a lightnin' bolt to strike me dead for breakin' some kinda Methodist no gamblin' rule?"

"Silas. That is *not* funny."

"Then you ain't gonna find this funny either. But I like seein' a little sass in you so I'll suggest it anyway." His cheek brushed hers. "What I'd been about to say, is you'n me ought to have us a wager."

"Absolutely not."

"Scared to lose?" he taunted.

She slapped her hand on his chest. "I can see why people wanna punch you in the face, McKay."

The man had the audacity to flash her that dimpled smile. "Now darlin', that ain't fair that you're tryin' to distract me with such sweet-talk."

Her mouth dropped open.

He laughed. "Anyway, here's the wager: let's each take a guess on how many times I get called Deputy McKay today."

"What's the winner get?"

Silas's gaze fell to her mouth. "That many kisses."

"But...then the loser gets kisses too."

"Mmm-hmm. That's why it's called a *sure* bet, sugar pie, try and keep up."

Oh, Dinah could continue to act prim, as if she expected Silas to work harder for a kiss. But she was desperate to know the softness of his lips as his strong, hard body held her close. So she boldly said, "Deal. My guess is three."

"Mine is nine."

"Nine? That's a lot."

"I expect a lot of confusion. A lot of your kisses will more than make up for it. I'm countin' down until we can leave the picnic and square up on our bet." He pressed his lips to the shell of her ear...just one time.

That small kiss vibrated throughout her entire body.

Silas stepped back and gallantly offered her his arm. "Shall we?"

THE TOWN COUNCIL held the picnic and pig roast feed at the racetrack north of town.

Right after they arrived, Doc found his cronies, leaving Silas to carry the basket of food to the community tables.

Someone had already spread newspapers down on three long tables. Women were setting out their food stuffs on pieces of cloth that drew attention to their picnic contribution.

Dinah should've thought to add a curl of ribbon around the mason jar of pickled eggs or the sour cherry preserves. However, she had pre-sliced the loaf of molasses bread and arranged the mound of whipped honey butter on a floral painted saucer. She lifted out the spice cake with the brown butter frosting and set it at the forefront of her display, angling the rhubarb cream pie next to it.

Silas peered over her shoulder. "Dinah, did you make all of that?"

"Well, Doc sure didn't," she half-groused.

"I thought maybe Mrs. Doc helped you."

"She's mostly confined." As soon as that slipped out, she glanced around to see if anyone had overheard, since it wasn't supposed to be common knowledge. Before she could plead with Silas not to repeat that as gossip, Esther McRae plunked her basket down across from Dinah's.

Esther made a big show of displaying her food. Jam tarts. Cheese biscuits. A fluffy meringue pie with brandied fruit compote. Sardines in a cream dill sauce. Then she startled coquettishly. "Oh! Hello, Dinah. I didn't see you standing there."

"Hello, Esther."

Then Esther's gaze shifted to Silas. "Why, Deputy McKay. I'm positive-ly *thrilled* you decided to attend one of these Founder's Day picnics."

"I'm sure you're right that my brother would much rather be here shootin' the breeze than alone in his office, playin' with his star and his gun."

Esther blinked with confusion. "Pardon?"

"I'm not the deputy. I'm Silas McKay, the deputy's brother."

Dinah saw Esther's speculative look flit between them.

Then she all but dismissed Dinah and focused on Silas. "Shame on me.

I'm Esther McRae."

He started to respond but Esther spoke first.

"I wasn't aware that the deputy had a brother, say nothing of a *twin* brother. How did your mother ever tell you two apart?"

"Lately it's easy to see tell the difference as I'm wearin' bad decisions on my face."

Esther tittered. "And you have a sense of humor as well! Did you just move here?"

"Nope. I've been a landowner for years. I just don't make it to town too often. When I do, it's usually to Labelle."

"Labelle," she sniffed. "No wonder you don't like coming to town. There's nothing to do there."

"*You're* from Labelle," Dinah pointed out.

"My daddy's lumberyard business is there," she retorted. "We *live* in town. Anyway, Mr. McKay, you have no idea what you're missing. There are so many entertainments found in Sundance. The horseracing held here at the track. The bowling lanes in the basement of Farnum's. The fine dining at Pettyjohn's. Now that baseball has started there are games during the week. On the weekends there's usually a dance. The municipal band puts on lively concerts. We have a bicycle riding club and—"

"Sounds like people in town have more free time than we ranchers do," Silas said dryly.

"What's the point of working hard if you can't have fun too?"

Dinah bet Esther had never worked a day in her life, let alone knowing anything about what hard work entailed.

"Well, one man's leisure is another man's vice." He smiled. Then he pointed to Esther's bounty of food. "It appears you went to a lot of *hard* work whippin' up them fancy vittles."

Fancy vittles? Wasn't he laying the hick rancher act on a bit thick?

"Oh, listen to you. Nothing fancy about this. Just a few things we had in the larder."

Dinah emitted a disbelieving noise that brought Esther's attention back to her.

For a moment.

But she smiled at Silas and cooed, "You're certainly welcome to sample anything I have displayed, Mr. McKay. Anything at all."

Heavens. Could she be any more forward?

"That is downright kind of you, Miss McRae. I've a mind to take you up on that if I don't overfill my belly on Dinah's spice cake, which she baked specially for me since it's my favorite."

"How sweet," Esther hissed with her forked tongue.

"Mmm-hmm, my lady is as sweet as the day is long." He offered Dinah his arm. "Been a pleasure visitin' with you. If you'll excuse us."

As soon as they were shot clear of her, Silas bent down to whisper, "That's one."

They strolled through the attendees, garnering questioning looks and whispers. Silas corrected no less than three more people who'd mistaken him for his deputy brother.

The most unsettling confrontation happened when Sheriff Eccleston demanded to know why Deputy McKay had left his post in Labelle to galivant around at a picnic. Silas assured the man Jonas was happily keeping the peace, while he, Jonas's brother, took a day off from ranching.

After the sheriff walked away—laughing that he'd forgotten Jonas had a twin—Silas mused, "Musta been the suit that threw him off."

Dinah sent him a look for that peculiar response. "Why would you say that?"

"You think *I* have a suit this nice? No ma'am. This here suit belonged to Jonas. He's a bit of a dandy when it comes to his duds. Lucky we're the same size, huh?"

"Jonas knows you're wearing his clothes?"

"As a matter of fact, he gave this to me, bein's my best shirt got ruined after the card game."

Ignoring the "best shirt" portion of his comment because he had to be joking, she gave him a once over. "Your brother just passed his entire suit on to you?"

"His words were something along the lines that I wasn't allowed to court you lookin' like a cow-punchin' saddle bum."

"I'll tell him thank you for that."

"'Tween you'n me? Him givin' me one of his slicked-up suits is an excuse for him to go get a new one made. I swear that's what he spent his extra 'outlaw' money on."

Dinah reached up and straightened his tie. "And you spend your extra money on…?"

"Darlin', I don't have any extra money. That's the problem."

He seemed embarrassed to admit that as soon as he'd said it.

"Perhaps it makes me petty, but I'm glad you aren't familiar with the entertainments that Sundance has to offer." She continued to fuss without meeting his eyes. "Although, maybe I should be worried about you seeking entertainments in Labelle at Sackett's and Ruby Red's when you do have extra jingle in your pocket."

Silas placed his rough fingers beneath her chin, forcing her to look at him. "No extra money means I usually drink my whiskey at home, not at a saloon. I prefer to play cards with Jonas, so gamblin' has a specific purpose for me. Payin' for a few hours of female companionship is an even rarer occurrence. That said, I don't fault men who do them things. But you don't gotta worry, sugar pie, that any of them vices are gonna be an issue between us or that I can't come up with a bit of extra money to court you."

In a moment of panic, she blurted out, "Why court *me*, Silas? With the way these ladies are eyeing you, you could've courted any woman at this picnic."

Anger crossed his face like a sudden storm.

When he saw her panic and that she tried to jerk back from him, he banked the fire in his eyes and snaked his arm around her waist to hold her closer. "Don't do that."

"What?"

"Pull away from me. I'd never hurt you."

"Then don't glare at me! It's scary."

"I get in a mood when I hear you sayin' silly things like questioning why I wanna be with you. I don't know how you can't see that you are light and goodness and sweetness and fire, woman. There ain't no one like you."

"Silas—"

"No, you listen. I was drawn to you from the first time I saw you last fall at Robinette's, your shiny blond curls so pretty tied up with a green ribbon that matched your dress. You had a shopping basket hooked on your arm, patiently waitin' as Jimmy picked out a sweet. A sweet that I saw you pay for along with a book, some fabric and thread, and a tin of lemon drops. You looked like an angel to me and you were kind as one to everyone you spoke with."

"You saw me? Why didn't you say anything?"

"Darlin', Robinette only lets me in the back door since I usually have cow dung from my hat to my boots. You'da took one look at me and run.

Next time I was in Labelle was the night of the blizzard."

As that sank in, she murmured, "You truly don't come to town very often, do you?"

"Not if I can help it. Besides, Jonas is in one town or the other at least five days a week. If I need something, he'll get it and bring it home." He stroked her jawbone with his thumb. "But I'd come to town twice a day if it meant I could see you. Believe that."

Warmth spread through her chest.

"Getting kinda handsy for being in public, McKay," Doc said as he wandered up. "I ain't the only one who's noticed."

Dinah briefly turned her head into Silas's hand, placing a soft kiss at the base of his thumb before she stepped back. "Perhaps they oughta be more concerned with getting this picnic underway."

"It is underway—not that the pair of you noticed. Soon as I'm done eating, I plan to head home to check on my wife." Doc tipped his head back to look at Silas. "Is your horse broke to a buggy?"

"Yessir."

"Good. I'll ride home and leave you two the buggy since I suspect you'd like to stay a while."

"That is thoughtful, Doc," Silas said. "Thanks."

Dinah handed Doc and Silas each a plate, took one for herself, and they were the last three in line.

The butcher had donated two huge pigs that'd been pit roasted. The grocer had donated potatoes, carrots and onions that had been cooked over open fires in cream canisters and then were dumped on the tables with the newspapers.

After they'd filled their plates, Doc wandered off, and the only seating left was by Sarah White and Mary O'Brien.

Pasting on a smile, Dinah sat across from Sarah.

Silas set his plate next to hers and put his mouth on her ear. "Lemonade?"

"Yes, please."

"Be right back."

She adjusted her skirt, then her plate before she met the glowers she'd felt.

Sarah scowled.

Mary held her gaze and then laughed.

Don't ask. Eat so you can leave.

Took an effort to tune out their whispers and giggles, but thankfully Silas returned quickly with two tin cups of lemonade.

Sarah smirked. "It appears you forgot to bring cups with your picnic supplies, Dinah. I hope they didn't overcharge you for those, Mr. McKay."

Shoot. He'd had to buy them?

"Two for five cents. Not bad. I could always use a couple extra cups."

Dinah looked at Silas. "Thank you."

"My pleasure, darlin'." He smiled and dug into his meal.

Mary leaned across the table and addressed Silas. "I'm surprised you're feeling up to being out and about, after your Friday night…mishap."

Silas squinted at her. "Beggin' your pardon, Miss…but do I know you?"

"No, but I know of you. I'm Mary O'Brien. I believe you're acquainted with my fiancée, Zachariah West." She practically waggled her ring-clad finger in his face.

He went still.

"I heard about my soon-to-be brother-in-law, Zeke West, getting the best of you Friday night."

"Oh, he's lucky he didn't get the worst of me." Silas's smile was all teeth. "Funny, ain't it, how much he brags about it when it ain't ever a fair fight."

Dinah sent him a sharp look. Why wasn't it "ever" a fair fight?

Mary studied him, taking in the bruises, scratches and swelling on his face. "I'm honestly shocked you're willing to show up at a public function with your face bearing the shame."

"Yes, ma'am, it *is* hard bein' here with the pocketful of Zeke's money that I won and a *shame* there's no place open to spend it all." He cocked his head, studying her in the same condescending manner. "I'm surprised your *fee-on-say* 'fessed up to bein' at Sackett's on Friday evening. Funny though, I don't remember seein' him at the card tables. I wonder where *else* he might've been."

Dinah thought it was polite of her not to point out Mary's face had turned the same color as the lettering on the *Ruby Red's Boardinghouse* sign.

"Where is your intended?" Silas asked.

"He's at work. The trains don't quit running on Sundays," she said haughtily.

"God don't give cattlemen a day off neither."

"When are you getting married?" Dinah asked.

"In July," was all Mary said.

Uncomfortable silence lingered as they returned to their food.

But the reprieve didn't last.

Mary shoved her plate until it bumped into Dinah's and said, "Oops, sorry," before stretching her arms above her head and sighing. "Lord, I've got *such* aches and pains from setting up housekeeping this week. I swear even civilized men would be happy living in a cave. But I told Zachariah that our house would be perfect *before* we lived there."

Spinster Sarah nodded as if she had a clue as to what "setting up housekeeping" meant. "It was sweet of Zachariah to surprise you and build a new house as a wedding gift."

"It *is* a blessing he has the means to support us." Mary's eyes narrowed thoughtfully on Dinah. "I'd just finished telling Sarah that I won't be teaching in Sundance in the fall. So maybe if you apply, Dinah, you'll get lucky and land a *real* teaching job."

Both Mary and Sarah laughed.

And...Dinah had had enough. She grabbed her plate and her cup and said, "Excuse me," rising to leave. Skirting the groups of people who'd already started playing games, she stormed to the buggy.

Nasty, mean cow, saying whatever nasty, mean thing that popped into her small mind.

She wanted to scream. Throw things. Challenge Mary to a fight to see how well a *real* teacher could defend herself.

She froze. *Fight* her? Why had that jumped into her head? Fists never solved anything.

It was that brawler McKay's fault.

"Dinah?"

Speak of the devil. "What?"

"What was that remark about you not bein' a real teacher?"

"I don't want to talk about it."

He spun her around and then stepped back. "Uh-oh, sugar pie, I don't like the mean glint in them pretty eyes. So I'm gonna go get my horse and hook up to the buggy. Then we'll leave."

"I have to get my picnic basket."

"Best be doin' it then."

Maybe she acquired a small sense of satisfaction seeing that Esther's *fancy vittles* sat mostly untouched while only a crust of bread remained of the food Dinah had brought.

She packed up everything and returned to the buggy, still angry about the exchange Silas had witnessed.

"Gonna make a suggestion. While I'm hitchin' up, you go refill our cups. Might as well get our money's worth."

"Silas. I don't care about that."

"Trust me on this, okay? Look. There ain't nobody over there so it ain't like you gotta make nice. Now git."

She might've flounced off at his *now git* command. And she might've stood there and poured herself a cup and drank it before she refilled their cups.

"I was hoping I'd see you!"

Dinah turned and was enveloped in a hug and a cloud of peony perfume.

Then Beatrice Talbot gawped over her shoulder at the man messing with the buggy. "*Please* tell me Deputy McKay is courting you."

"Silas McKay, the deputy's twin brother, is courting me," she said with a little pride.

"Heavens, there are *two* of them? How is that even fair?"

She laughed. "They may look exactly alike but they are different as night and day. Anyway, how are you?"

"Feeling guilty that we haven't seen each other since school let out."

"I know. But I heard you were visiting family in Billings for the summer?"

"I was there for two weeks for my sister's wedding. There's so much going on with building this new house and the bank that I can't be away for long."

"I would love to catch up with you," Dinah said. "When would be a good time for me to ride over for a visit?"

Bea tapped her chin with a gloved finger and then her face lit up. "Andrew has bank business in Casper, and he's been fretting about leaving me alone since I can't come with him. You should stay with me! That would kill two birds with one stone."

"When is Andrew leaving?"

"A week from Friday. You could ride over in the afternoon and we could do something fun that night. Andrew will be back late Saturday night."

That did sound like fun. Beatrice was the only real friend she'd made in the last year. "If Andrew's plans change, let me know. Otherwise, I will be there."

Beatrice clapped and hugged her again. "Feel free to bring a bottle of that plum wine you made last summer."

"I will." Dinah grinned and hugged her one last time. "I'm so happy we ran into each other."

"Me too. Ta-ta." Beatrice flitted off.

After she refilled the cups, she meandered back to the buggy, lost in thought.

She noticed Silas had tucked the picnic basket and his saddlebag under the seat.

"It appeared you saw at least one friendly face here," he said.

"That's Beatrice Talbot."

"How do you know her?"

"Last summer she twisted her ankle while at the hardware store in Labelle and Jimmy fetched Doc. I tagged along with him when he went to examine her. She'd just gotten married and had moved here from Casper, so neither of us knew anyone. We became fast friends."

"Who's her husband?"

"Andrew Talbot. He's a banker. His family is building the new Settler's First bank in Sundance."

"Competition's always a good thing. Not that any of them bastards would lend me money." He took the cups from her and placed them on the sideboard. Then he pulled out a flask and poured amber liquid into both cups, stirring them with the handle end of the spoon, and handed her one.

"Whiskey. On a Sunday afternoon."

"Whiskey and *lemonade* on a Sunday afternoon. Try it, you'll like it."

"You've had it before?"

Silas granted her that devil-may-care grin. "Nope."

She wasn't a fan of whiskey, but she swallowed a mouthful anyway.

The lemonade softened the sting of the booze and masked the taste. She drained the entire cup and saw Silas still grinning at her.

"That's my girl." Then he drank his down.

"It's your fault if I get drunk."

"On that little ol' snort? Nah. It'll just soothe you, that's all, and darlin', you need it." He held out his hand. "Hop up."

After he'd climbed aboard and held the reins, he said, "Where to?"

Dinah took off her hat and tipped her face to the sun. "Just drive, Silas, and get us out of here."

EIGHT

SILAS DROVE UNTIL they reached the rise that showcased the Belle
Fourche River Valley.

From this vantage point the land spread out in a carpet of green,
with towering trees, rolling hills and the snaking curve of the river.

Dinah didn't say anything for the longest time. Then she sighed. "This
is the most beautiful place I've ever seen."

"This is what made me settle here. I don't foresee a day when I'd ever
get tired of callin' this place home."

"Where's your ranch?"

He lifted her left arm up and said, "Point your finger." Then he ma-
neuvered her arm to the left. "Now look straight down your arm to the tip
of your finger. That hill? Is about ten miles as the crow flies. That's the start
of my land."

"Have you stood on that hill?"

"Yep. Too many trees to give me a view like this one. But that don't
really matter because I know the view is there…if that makes any sense."

"It does."

Gave him a warm feeling that he didn't have to explain it to her beyond that. "If we're gonna sit here a spell, I need to let my horse graze."

"I'd like to stay here, if you don't need to get back."

"Got all day to spend with you." He jumped down and winced because once again he'd forgotten about his damn ribs. He removed the harness and tied a lead rope around the horse's neck, taking him to a grassy spot. The whisper of grass alerted him and he glanced up to see Dinah moving toward him.

"What's your horse's name?"

"He don't have one."

"Is he new and you haven't settled on a name yet?"

"Nope."

She blinked at him. "How long have you had him?"

"Two years."

"Two years without a name?"

"Well, it ain't like anyone is ridin' him but me."

"Do you have other horses?"

"Yep, and they don't have names either. Neither do my oxen nor my donkey." He cocked his head. "I s'ppose your horse has a name."

"Yes, she does. Although, I didn't name her. Doc did. Her name is Folly because he thought it foolish for me to buy a horse when I could just borrow his or Mrs. Agnes's."

Silas offered her his hand. "Can't blame you for wantin' your own ride."

With her hand clasped in his, he led her to another flat, grassy spot that caught a nice updraft from the valley below. "How's this?"

"Perfect." She plopped down and stretched her legs out in front of her, giving him a glimpse of her button-up boots. Fancier than the plain ones she'd worn yesterday.

He settled beside her, close enough to touch her if she gave him a sign his attentions would be welcomed.

Time seemed to slow. Silas let himself be content, letting the guilt that he ought to be working float away on the crisp spring breeze.

Finally, she spoke. "You've been a lot of places, haven't you?"

"Yep. But that don't mean I remember 'em all."

"What do you mean?"

"Bein' on a cattle drive...it's the same thing every day. Up early, ridin' across dry, dusty land or sloppin' through a mud bog to find a place where the cattle can graze. Eat, sleep, or try to sleep if I'd been on herd watch the night before, get up and do it again. It's months of that."

"But you must've liked it since you did it for so long."

He plucked up a couple of long stems of grass. "I was good at it. And because I'd been workin' the trail for so long, the money was decent when I made it to trail boss. Not as eye-poppin' as a job with the railroad, but better than I would've earned workin' in a factory."

"The railroad dangles superior money at you until that job gets you killed, and then there's no money."

When she didn't elaborate, he bumped his shoulder into hers. "Dinah, darlin', you know you can't let them words just lie there."

"I know." She started fiddling with the grass, as if nerves were getting the best of her.

Silas placed his hand over hers. "I wanna know everything about you, sugar pie, so start at the beginning, like I did when you asked me yesterday."

"Okay." She pulled her knees to her chest and wrapped her arms around them. "I was born in Cheyenne and grew up there. My father worked for the railroad. He was a supervisor or something, which meant he was home most nights, not out in the railyard or on the tracks. My mother married him when she was sixteen. They lost a few babies before I was born. I think because of that, my dad did everything for her or hired people to do it for her. We had a day maid who did household chores as well as shopped for food. My mother did manage to cook most nights."

Silas tried to wrap his head around the fact she'd grown up with servants.

"So I attended school, took piano lessons, horse-riding lessons, had friends and social activities. We lived in a nice house, with nice things. As a child you don't know what your parents go through to keep up appearances. On the outside we seemed well off. Having hired help was an indulgence that in retrospect, we couldn't afford. I knew none of this until after my father died."

"How old were you?"

"Thirteen. There was an emergency at the trainyard. I never did hear the details, but my father was crushed by a runaway train car. My mother…went into immediate shock. She never really recovered."

"Oh, honey, I'm sorry."

"Not as sorry as I was when I learned that we didn't own the house we lived in; it was a benefit of working for the railroad."

"You didn't know that?"

"No. Neither did my mother. Although thinking back, everyone in our neighborhood worked for the railroad, so it should've been obvious it was company housing. Thankfully one of my father's friends took me in hand because he knew my mother was worthless."

He sent her a sharp look when she used that term, but she kept talking.

"I had to learn to do all those things that my mother should've known. We had to move. Mr. Jones found us a two-room apartment to rent. I sold all of our household furnishings, except a few pieces. It gave us more money to live on. Another task Mr. Jones taught me was how to run a household ledger to track our expenses, since we wouldn't have any more money coming in with my father being dead."

"Did you have to go to work?"

"Not like you, out riding the range. I continued to attend school only because...I know it sounds selfish, but it allowed me a break from my mother's grief. By age fourteen I ran our household. I cooked, cleaned, budgeted, and cared for my mother. When she got sick enough to go into the hospital for two weeks, I sold all of her jewelry—not that she owned much—to pay that bill. Out of desperation I tried to sell some of her clothing since my father had indulged her need to flit around in the latest fashions. The dressmaker paid me a pittance for the dresses I knew cost ten times that new, but even a small amount of money helped us survive another month. When the dress shop owner asked if I could sew, I admitted to knowing only the basics. She hired me on the spot. I was able to do piece work for her from home. That saved us. But there was no saving my mother. She passed on shortly before my nineteenth birthday. Does it make me sound horrible if I confess I was relieved?"

He reached for her hand. "No, darlin', it doesn't."

"Mama loved me in her own way. She just loved my father more. She once told me if it hadn't been for leaving me an orphan, she would've killed herself after he died. But the truth was, she *did* kill herself; it just took her longer to die than she'd planned."

"I'm sorry, Dinah. I truly am. After livin' in an orphanage, I saw that options were different for girl orphans than boys. When they kicked us out at age thirteen? Some girls became brides the next damn day."

"A couple of girls in my school got married at sixteen. When I mentioned my...I don't want to say *disgust* at that prospect, my mother turned mean."

"Why?"

She shrugged. "Maybe because she believed I sneered at her choice to marry that young, which wasn't true. But when I tried to explain how I felt, she said I needn't worry about marriage since no man wanted a know-it-all shrew in his bed."

Silas shook his head. "Did you remind her that if you got married she'd be on her own?"

"No. I thought of a dozen mean things I could've said back, but...how would that've helped either of us? And she was proud that I'd passed the 'normal school' teaching test on my first try. Unfortunately there weren't teaching jobs in Cheyenne. I hadn't pursued other options outside of the area while my mother was alive, but after she died, I wanted a fresh start. Rather than take Mr. Jones' offer of marriage—"

"Whoa. Hold on there. Your father's friend wanted to marry you?"

Dinah wrinkled her nose. "Yes. But I said no."

"But he could've taken care of you and you wouldn't have had to struggle at all."

Her eyes were full of fire when she looked at him. "Exactly. I did *not* want to be my mother. Ever. Perhaps it is horrible to say, but I was so angry at her, Silas, for not knowing how to do *anything*. That meant *I* didn't know how to do anything either because she couldn't teach me. I'm proud of what I learned on my own. I swore I'd learn everything I needed to take care of myself, so I'd never be stuck relying on a husband. That's why I said no to marrying him."

"Is that the only reason?"

"No. He was old."

He struggled between laughing and getting well and truly pissed off. "*And?*"

"And I hated that he didn't plan to court me. We'd be married—just like that. It felt as if he believed he was doing me a favor by marrying me."

"I'm sure he made you feel that way, while he was prolly thinkin', *Yippee! I'm gonna have this beautiful woman under me every night and twice on Sundays.*"

Dinah laughed. "Maybe he did offer for me because he was just a randy old goat."

"He would've been ruttin' on you day and night, darlin', trust me.

Anyway, keep goin'. I wanna hear the part about you not bein' a 'real' teacher."

"I'm getting there." She began to pluck at the grass again and he let her. "Schools as far away as Grand Junction, Colorado advertised for teachers in the Cheyenne paper. I was willing to go anywhere but I was aware frontier schools paid better. First part of May I saw Doc's ad for a 'new' school in Crook County. Room and board provided with him and his wife, plus transportation costs for me and a limited amount of household goods. The bottom of the ad also indicated extra income was available for teacher candidates with nursing experience." She paused. "I might've broken a finger I wrote a response so fast. I posted the letter that same day. I might've bragged a bit in that I'd been my mother's sole caretaker for years. I heard back from Doc, offering me the job, and asking if I could start right away."

"But…ain't school already out in May?"

"Yes. He was upfront that he needed my help as his nursing assistant until school started in August. I packed up and hopped on the train. Doc met me, settled me in my room in his house. Immediately I realized that his wife was in poor enough shape she couldn't do any household chores."

"Did that make you mad?"

"It made me…aware that if I didn't stand my ground from the start that Mrs. Agnes would be a repeat of what I'd gone through with my mother. I told Doc that I'd do all the cooking, cleaning and household tasks, if I didn't have to answer to—or wait on or be a caretaker to—his wife. He agreed. He never asked if I had experience growing a garden. Or milking a cow. Or putting up winter stores. Or dealing with chickens—all things that'd been neglected since Mrs. Agnes had taken ill. So I taught myself a bunch of new skills."

Silas loved her confident smile and her obvious pride. "Didja learn how to butcher too?"

"I watched Doc do it. The other thing I learned to do was keep Doc's ledgers. Many people he treated paid in goods rather than money. So I had to figure out what to do with salt pork and a bushel of apples. If we had too much of something like eggs, I'd trade them at Robinette's store for what we needed. In the fall we had a cellar full of root vegetables that I'd grown. Mrs. Agnes roused herself long enough to teach me how to make fruit preserves and wine and pickle various foods we couldn't eat right away."

"Sounds like a lot of work, Dinah."

"It was. It was also the best summer of my life. But I did have help. Jimmy chopped all the wood we needed for the winter." She paused and looked at him. "Do you know about Martha?"

He shook his head. "Who's that?"

"She's an Indian girl about the same age as Jimmy. I guess her father was a white man and after her mother died, the Crow tribe 'returned' her to Doc since he was the only white man they dealt with. He named her Martha because she refused to answer to her Indian name after the tribe kicked her out."

"Does she live with Doc?"

"She lives in the woods—that's her choice. Her mother was a medicine woman, so Martha knows a lot about plants and natural herbal cures. She helps Doc out, bringing him medicinals. She traps animals and since no one will buy from her, Jimmy trades the skins and the quills on her behalf. I bought my horse from her. Doc claims she caught it wild and broke it to saddle."

"A young girl did that all on her own," Silas said skeptically.

"I don't know why you find that surprising. Her tribe has probably been doing that for generations and that's how she learned."

"You got a point."

"Speaking of points...I got off track. Back to the school issue. Over the summer, I asked Doc if I could see the schoolhouse where I'd be teaching. He kept putting me off. Finally, I pinned him down one night and he told me the truth; there wasn't an official schoolhouse. I'd be teaching in the recovery room when he didn't have patients. Which was most of the time, since Doc preferred to make house calls. I tamped down my disappointment and asked about the students who'd be attending the school."

She paused so long that a bad feeling took root.

"Three students. That's all. Jimmy, Martha and Mr. Robinette's youngest son, Ernie."

"Good lord."

"Yes, I'd be trying to teach an orphan who bunked in a saloon if he was lucky, an Indian girl who hated being indoors, and a merchant's kid who had failed a level in Sundance for poor attendance. I didn't know whether to laugh or cry."

"Did it feel as if you'd had the wool pulled over your eyes?"

Dinah sighed. "Yes. And no. I'd been so eager to get out of Cheyenne I hadn't asked specifics about the teaching aspect of the job, so that is my fault. After I arrived here, I'd thrown myself into learning to do everything else, and working as Doc's assistant, I figured the teaching part would be the easiest." Another laugh. "That was before I learned that Jimmy had never been to school. Martha couldn't read or write. And Ernie was brilliant at math but nothing else."

"I am grateful for the factory's school and that the nuns in the orphanage made sure we could all read and write and do arithmetic," Silas said. "I can't tell you how many men I worked with on the trail that had a history like ours of bein' an orphan and they couldn't even write their own names."

"Exactly. So it did occur to me, from a teacher's perspective, to embrace the challenge. If I could teach the three of them, then I could teach anyone."

"There's a silver lining."

She sent him a sunny smile. "Thank you. I made the mistake of attending the Crook County Schools Board of Education meeting, eager to connect with other teachers. That's where I met Mary O'Brien and Sarah White. They were friendly at first, except I couldn't believe they bragged about how much they were earning teaching in Sundance and they were the highest paid teachers in the entire state of Wyoming. When they asked where I taught, guessing Beulah or Hulett, and I said Labelle…you could've heard a pin drop. Then they started tittering like drunken crows. Acting so high and mighty, snottily informing me that Doc had advertised for a teacher for over a year, but since it wasn't a 'real' school, no one had been dumb enough to take the job." She paused. "It stung at the time. I can admit now that I cried all the way back to Doc's place."

Silas leaned over and cupped her chin in his hand, forcing her to look at him. "Ties me up in knots to hear this angel face wore your tears."

"That was the only time I cried."

"Good."

She stretched her legs out and leaned into his touch. "Can I tell you a secret?"

"Sure."

"The joke is on them because Doc and Mr. Robinette are paying me twice what the teachers in Sundance make. *Twice* as much. For one fourth as many students. And on the days the kids don't show up? I still get paid."

He smiled. "Yeah, darlin', you keep makin' them dumb decisions."

Dinah lowered her gaze to his mouth.

That shy but curious glance sent his heart racing. "Can I tell you a secret?"

She nodded.

"I really wanna kiss you right now."

Her gaze flew to his. "Okay."

No hesitation. Interesting.

He let his thumb drift across her cheek. "Have you been kissed before?"

"Once. At my friend Kathryn's birthday party when I was sixteen. Kathryn's cousin Harrison kissed me on the lips. Then he tried to stick his tongue in my mouth. I didn't like it at all."

"Well, sugar pie, I'm gonna kiss you with my tongue too, but we'll work into it, all right?"

She nodded. "Do you…think it's pathetic that I'm twenty years old and I've only been kissed once?"

"It don't matter to me if you'd been kissed once or kissed a thousand boys. I just know from here on out, I'm the *only* man you'll be kissin'."

Her chin shot up. "Then I'd better be the only woman you put your lips on too, McKay."

"I promise."

"Will you also promise that if I'm bad at kissing you'll teach me how to get better?"

"I ain't grading you on your kissin' abilities, Miss Thompson."

She blushed. "But I don't want to fail at this, Silas."

"You won't." He lightly pinched that stubborn chin. "So can we get on with the kissin' part now?"

"Yes." She closed her eyes.

"Huh-uh. I want your eyes open." He kept his hand curled around the side of her face as he leaned in.

Dinah seemed to quit breathing.

He could've nuzzled his cheek against hers to start, but he'd been dreaming of those plush, petal-pink lips for months and he wanted a taste.

Silas pressed his lips to hers, holding them there against the exaggerated pucker she'd formed with her lips. Once her rigid posture relaxed, and her lips softened, he moved his mouth back and forth across hers, his heart racing in anticipation. He caught the flowery scent of her soap and his head spun when her lips finally parted on an exhale.

That's it, darlin'. Let me show you how good this will be between us.

Her eyes fluttered closed on a soft sigh when he traced the seam of her lips with his tongue, catching the fleshy inner rim.

She began to match each gentle glide of his mouth, mimicking his movements. When she placed her hand on his chest and tilted her head, he took the kiss deeper. Teasing with a soft swirl of his tongue against hers until he tasted lemonade, the hint of whiskey and the sweetness that was all Dinah.

As much as Silas wanted to devour her, to own that succulent mouth of hers, he maintained an easy exploration. Showing her that being lip-locked was only a small part of creating trust and intimacy. Gently stroking her sun-warmed face. Smoothing his hands over her soft curls that reached the middle of her back. He would've been content sharing air and swallowing her happy moans.

But Dinah wanted more. She dug her fingers into his chest like a kitten kneading its paws as she sucked on his bottom lip. Then in a move that shocked him, she pushed him back, so they were lying side-by-side in the grass.

Silas loved that her curiosity was stronger than her anxiety.

It took every bit of his willpower not to slip his leg between hers. Or align his body over hers. Or allow his hands to learn every inch of her curves. He could be patient.

Until he'd reached the end of it. He gently rolled her so he was on top, bracing himself on his arms above her, purposely only allowing their upper halves to touch.

He gifted her with soft smooches and tiny nibbles on her kiss-swollen lips as she caught her breath and the urgency between them ebbed.

"You all right?" he murmured against her cheek.

"I don't know. I didn't expect my body would get so hot and tingly and I'd feel like frogs were jumping in my belly from just kissing."

He smiled at her honesty. "Those are very good things. Means you like kissin' me."

"I like it a lot." She tilted her head back to study him. "You are such a great kisser, McKay. I want to make sure you like kissing me too. So if I need to…improve, you'll tell me, right?"

"Oh, I'll go you one better, darlin', and teach you." He nuzzled her cheek. "But to be honest, I don't have a single complaint." He smirked at her. "Except I wish we had fewer clothes on when we were kissin' like crazy."

"Sounds like a good way to get bug bites in unmentionable places," she teased back.

"You gotta be more concerned about all the places *I'm* gonna bite you before I'd let them bugs get a chance."

"Silas."

"Just statin' my intentions."

She ran her fingers through his hair.

"Mmm. I love that."

"Then I'll keep doing it."

"Let's shift a little." Silas sat up and held his hand out to help her up too. When she was upright, he placed his head in her lap. "Ah. Much better."

"I'd call you shameless, but you'd like it," she said with amusement.

"Yep."

Neither spoke for a while; she just continued petting him and he lapped it up like an attention-starved dog.

After a bit, she said, "I have an odd question."

He opened his eyes. "Shoot."

Her gaze roamed over his face. "With you and Jonas being identical twins, why are you both clean-shaven? Like today when everyone called you Deputy McKay. If one of you had a beard, that wouldn't be an issue."

"True. 'Cept we both hate beards."

"Why?"

"No choice but to have a beard on a cattle drive. Granted, we were mere hairless boys when Jeb plucked us off the orphan train. After our voices and our bollocks dropped, growin' a beard made us feel like real men. All the other cowhands had them. Then we realized there wasn't a choice. Took time, not to mention soap and water, to have a smooth face on the trail. Plus, them old hands were bastards and gave a man grief for actin' like a dandy. Or like we were getting slicked up because we were lookin' for a bachelor marriage."

"What's that?"

"Months on the trail is a long time without a woman's touch. Some of the cowhands…took to bein' with each other, as to say…sexually. Was no skin off my nose if they chose that, it just wasn't an option for me or Jonas. Soon as we were off the trail with money in our pockets, first thing me'n Jonas did was hit the bathhouse for a delousing and then barbershop for a shave."

"What about visiting a whorehouse?" She paused. "Sorry. I shouldn't have asked."

"No, darlin', it's fine. I ain't gonna lie—but I'm not braggin' neither when I tell you I spent plenty of time and money with workin' gals. It is in my past though; I can promise you that."

"I bet the workin' gals did a double take when the McKay twins sauntered through the doors. They'd probably offer their services for free."

He laughed. Hard. "Ain't nothin' ever free with the ladies. But Jonas never came with me to one of them houses."

"Never? Why not?"

"No idea. I never asked him why he passed or what he'd rather do instead."

Dinah smoothed her fingers across his cheeks. "I'm glad you don't have a beard; it'd be a shame to cover up this handsome face."

He kissed her palms, one at a time. "Thank you." Then he sat up. "What else you wanna do today?"

"Can we drive closer to Devil's Tower?"

"Of course. But it will eat up the rest of our afternoon."

Riding over to the tower meant taking the busier road. But the look on her face when she saw the size of the massive rock up close was worth dodging other buggies and ruts.

On the ride back to Labelle, Silas did most of the talking, since Dinah had questions. Lots of questions. He figured she couldn't help it, being a teacher and all. The oddest part was he didn't mind.

Back at Doc's, he stowed the buggy in the barn and said a quick hello to Doc and Mrs. Agnes before he returned outside to his horse. He might've kissed Dinah with more passion than an early evening warranted, especially since they were entwined in plain sight, but Dinah's reaction stirred a primal need in him.

"Promise me you'll always kiss me like that?" she whispered in his ear.

"Truly be my pleasure, sugar pie."

"When will I see you again?"

"I'll try to make it into town sometime this week. If that don't happen, I'll be here on Saturday afternoon for sure."

She frowned. "I hope I'm here then. Now that school's out, I sometimes go with Doc when he makes house calls."

Silas gave her one last kiss. A kiss that lingered because she sure liked kissing him. Hard to ride away from that.

But he had to.

He mounted up and she stayed to watch him. "Be seein' you soon, Dinah."

NINE

TUESDAY MORNING WHILE Dinah was out weeding the garden, she heard
hoofbeats. Hopeful, she peered around the tomato plant to see Silas
reining his horse to a stop right outside the fence line.

For a moment she let herself admire the masculine glory of him on
horseback. A rugged man in full control of the massive animal beneath
him. Even from where she stood, she noticed the powerful muscles in
Silas's thighs. His mastery in directing his horse with his knees rather than
just yanking on the reins. Not to mention how mesmerizing his backside
was as he dismounted with balance and grace.

As he tied up his horse, he called out, "Good morning, sweetheart."

"Good morning." She stepped out of the garden. "Please tell me you're
not here to see Doc because you broke, burned or sliced a body part?"

Silas laughed.

That husky, warm sound enveloped her like a summer breeze.

"No, I'm here to see my girl. Made a special trip to town and everything."

Dinah cocked her head in challenge. "Really."

"Well…no. But I had to come into Robinette's to pick up a few things
for Henrikson, since he's feelin' poorly, and I thought I'd swing by to see
your pretty face."

They were close enough to touch but separated by the chicken-wire fence.

Silas's intense gaze roamed over her, from her hat to her work boots. When his blue eyes met hers again, she felt as if he'd stripped her bare and run his hands across her skin.

Suppressing a shiver, she flipped her braid over her shoulder. "Do I pass inspection?"

"Sugar pie, as always, you look good enough to eat."

"Silas."

"Come around the fence and give me a proper kiss." He flashed her his devilish smile. "Or better yet…a very *im*proper kiss."

Dinah removed her hat and set it in the basket before she lifted the metal loop that served as the handle for the outer gate.

As soon as she was within touching distance, Silas cupped her face in his hands. His kiss was softer than she'd anticipated. A few teasing brushes of his mouth across hers. Then his happy sigh gusted across her lips as he rested his forehead to hers, his hat keeping them in shadow.

"That was very proper," she whispered.

"Mmm. You needed it sweet." He angled her head to press his lips to her temple. "I'll save improper for when Mrs. Agnes ain't gawkin' out the window at us."

When Dinah tried to turn around to see if he was pulling her leg, he held fast.

"Nope. She can have your attention later. I want you all to myself since I can't stay long." He nuzzled her hairline. "Walk with me." He took her hand.

"Where to?"

"Show me your outdoor classroom."

It pleased her immensely that he'd remembered that.

They strolled hand in hand through the long grass, still soaked with dew. It felt completely natural being with Silas, even when the anticipation of his improper kisses caused her belly to churn.

"What's going on at the McKay Ranch today?"

"I'm roundin' up cows, five or so at a time, and puttin' them in one of the two bullpens."

"How many bulls do you have?"

"Six. I've been buildin' a new pen closer to the creek, where the grass grows faster. I had two big bulls born this spring and as soon as they're weaned, they'll move into the bullpen and I'll rotate the oldest bull out."

"Rotate him out. Meaning?"

"He'll be butchered."

"Do you butcher it yourself?"

"Yeah. It ain't the best meat so I keep it for myself. It's messy work."

Dinah stopped and looked at him. "Is that hard? Killing an animal that you've cared for?"

Once again Silas curled his hands around her face. The wariness in his eyes caused her heart to skip a beat. "Will you look at me differently if I say no?"

"Not if you explain it to me so I have a better understanding of it." She placed her hand over his. "And a better understanding of you."

"Okay." Silas lowered his mouth to hers for another sweetly chaste kiss. "Come on." He led her to a fallen log and crouched down to inspect it.

"What are you doing?"

"Lookin' for ants. Them little buggers love this kinda wood. It'd be just my luck to sit down, we'd get to talkin' and then the next thing I'd see is you jumpin' up and down, ants crawlin' all over you. Then I'd have to strip off your clothes..." He stood. His dimpled grin sent her blood racing. "Maybe I oughta look for an ant-covered log, because I surely would like to see what's under that day dress."

Her cheeks warmed. "That's a little forward."

"Mmm-hmm. I want you forward and backward and every way in between."

I want that too.

Silas emitted a low rumble. "Dinah. You lookin' at me that way ain't helpin' me keep my hands to myself."

She glanced down to see he'd balled his hands into tight fists. The veins in his forearms bulged. The thought of tracing those pulsing veins with her fingers or her mouth sent a lick of heat down her spine.

"Sit." He closed his eyes and exhaled. "Please."

But after she settled herself, he silently paced in front of her.

So much for the ease of companionship between them.

"Ranchin' is a hard life. Ranchin' in Wyoming is harder yet because of the isolation and the harsh winters. It's back-breaking work. Depending on the cattle market, some years will be lean, some will be flush. I care for these animals, only to send them to slaughter. Lots of folks don't understand that, even when they're happy to have the benefits of my hard work in their butcher shop."

"I appreciate you explaining this to me."

He quit pacing for a moment and wiped the sweat from his brow. "I'm impressed that you asked the question." Then he returned to walking and talking. "This is the life I've been workin' toward since I was thirteen and on my first cattle drive. After four years here, I feel a connection to the land and a need to build something meaningful with it, something I can pass on. I can only share that life with a woman who understands that. A woman who accepts that I'm a man content raisin' cattle and ridin' the range and I don't aspire to be anything else. A woman with softness and resilience who can stand next to me and go toe to toe with me as we face life's challenges side by side. A woman who'll let me take care of her even when I know she's capable of takin' care of herself." He stopped in front of her and waited until she looked up at him. "That woman is you."

Then he removed his hat, clasping it to his heart as he dropped to one knee and reached for her hand.

Dear lord. The fierce look in his eyes made her lightheaded.

"Dinah Thompson. I intend to marry you."

She forgot how to breathe.

"I know it seems sudden to you—"

"It *is* sudden!" she practically yelled. "You officially started courting me on Saturday. It is *Tuesday*, Silas." But Jonas's warning that Silas wouldn't see the difference between courting her and marrying her rang true.

"Are you tellin' me no?"

"I'm telling you that I don't know! I like you. I like *getting* to know you."

He flashed her a cocky grin. "You like kissin' me too."

An annoyed noise burst forth—part growl, part sigh. "Why are you pushing me on this?"

"Because I've been half in love with you since the first time you yelled at me during the blizzard."

She scowled. "I didn't yell at you."

"Yes, darlin', you did." Another smile danced on his lips. "I deserved it though. Then you were sweet as you took care of me. You ate with me and read to me and fussed over me. I've never had that. Never wanted it, to be honest. But you changed that for me. I imagined havin' that kinda care from you all the time. I even imagined you lettin' me care for *you* in the same way. So this *ain't* a sudden thing for me."

How was she supposed to respond to that? When her heart was both melting and in her throat?

"Besides, I want everyone to know we're together." He kissed her knuckles. "I want everyone to know that you're *mine*."

"Then maybe you oughta just whip out your branding iron and sear your cattle brand into my backside," she retorted.

Both his eyebrows raised. "You'd let me do that?"

"Blast your ornery hide, Silas McKay, I was joking!"

He laughed. "I know, sugar pie. But I'm *not* joking when I say I'd like to call you my intended."

She opened her mouth, but he'd had enough of her protests. He brought her face to his, devouring her mouth in a kiss so delightfully improper that her entire body tingled.

Silas broke the kiss to rest his forehead above her bosom, his own chest heaving. "And then there's that."

Yes, the passion between them grew the more time they spent together.

Dinah ran her fingers through his inky black hair, loving how he trembled when she scratched her nails across his scalp and down the muscles in his neck.

He expelled a resigned sigh. "I've gotta head home."

"Can you at least stay for lunch?"

"No. It's a thirty-minute ride back." He nuzzled the rise of her breasts and she felt the heat of his breath through the thin calico fabric. If that small amount of contact sent warmth between her legs, how would she react when they were skin to skin?

Like you're burning up from the inside out.

He pushed to his feet, settled his hat on his head and reached down to help her up.

Neither spoke until they were back to the fence where he'd left his horse.

"Now that you're my intended, there's two things we need to talk about."

"Absolutely I'll let you buy me a betrothal ring," she teased.

"Sassy mouth." He kissed her. "Right now I'm responsible for runnin' two ranches. My time is limited, and we have distance separating us. I know you turned down that randy old goat's marriage offer because he didn't intend to woo you. I *am* gonna woo you, darlin'. I'm gonna woo you hard. But to be clear…it ain't gonna be a traditional courtin'."

"Well, it wasn't a traditional proposal, so I'm not surprised."

Silas smiled. "I aim to be memorable."

"That you are. What kind of wooing should I expect?"

"I'd like to come and get you on Saturday afternoon. You'd spend the night with me, and we'd be together Saturday night and all day Sunday. Now before you go getting that panicked look in your eyes, I don't expect to turn my bed into our marriage bed…until you're ready." He traced her jawline with tenderness that belied the roughness in his hands. "I want you with me, Dinah, as much as possible. With us livin' this far apart that's the only way we can spend more than Sunday afternoons together."

Maybe she should care what others in the community might think, but she didn't. She said, "Okay. I'll let Doc know I won't be around to assist him Saturday night."

Silas's answering smile was something to behold.

"What about Jonas? Will he be there?"

"Jonas spends maybe one or two nights at the ranch house. It's like he don't live there."

"Where is he sleeping when he's not on duty?"

Silas shrugged. "He ain't had to arrest anyone lately, so probably the empty jail cell. His job is his life." He ambled to the saddlebag on the right side of his horse. As he undid the buckle he said, "I brought you something. Hang on, it might take a bit to sort through this other stuff to find it."

"While you're looking for it, I'll make you a quick lunch you can eat on your way home."

Before she could turn away, Silas's hands were on her hips and his mouth was plundering hers to the very depths of her soul. Lord, the man could kiss.

The horses' snort broke them apart.

Silas planted a kiss below her ear. "I like how sweetly my intended takes care of me. Will you let me do the same for you?"

"Within reason."

He laughed and she opted not to point out she hadn't been joking. One of her favorite things about Silas was he saw her as capable, not as a fragile thing to be coddled.

Dinah still had a smile on her face when she entered the kitchen. She'd just sliced four pieces of bread when Mrs. Agnes slammed her cane on the floor, giving Dinah a fright. The woman had perched herself in the chair next to the window.

"Good morning, Mrs. Agnes. I didn't see you sitting there."

"Well I saw *you* kissing that McKay fella in broad daylight."

"That's to be expected when we're together since he *is* courting me," she said cheekily as she arranged roasted chicken pieces on the bread.

"He's dangerous. More trouble than he's worth with all the fighting and whatnot. You're a pretty girl. You should set your cap for a man without those violent tendencies. You never know if he might turn them on you."

That blanket statement about Silas's character rankled. Mrs. Agnes didn't know Silas at all. "Silas is a good man. In fact, I agreed to marry him."

"When did this come about?" she demanded.

"Just today."

"Did he give you a ring?"

"Not yet. But his promise of intent is enough for me."

"Which is all good and well, but you made a promise to my husband in writing to help him out as his nursing assistant and as a teacher for another year. You gonna run into the arms of the first man who offers to take care of you?"

Was that how she saw it? Would everyone else in the community think the same thing?

Is she wrong though?

Yes. And she'd prove it to Mrs. Agnes and any other busybodies who questioned her strength of purpose by keeping her word to Doc—and her promise to herself. If anyone would understand, it'd be Silas.

She sliced three chunks of cheese and aligned them on the bread. Then she wrapped both sandwiches in a cotton dish towel. She popped a wax stopper in the bottle of milk from this morning's milking and snagged it on her way out. "I'll be back to make you lunch."

"If you haven't given all our food to your *intended*," Mrs. Agnes grumbled.

Dinah refused to let that grumpy woman ruin her day—even when her words were something she'd chew over before she shared them with Silas.

Silas's backside rested against the fence and he held the horses' reins in his left hand. He grinned when he saw the bottle. "Milk too?"

"I fear it might churn into butter before you get it home if it's bouncing around in your saddlebag."

"Maybe. But then I'd have butter to enjoy. Thanks, darlin'. Now c'mere. Close your eyes and hold out your hands."

Feeling strangely shy, she complied. She felt a tiny flutter in her belly when Silas's soft lips touched the center of each of her palms. Then he curled her fingers around the items he'd placed there. "Okay. Now you can look."

In her right hand was a metal tin of lemon drops. In her left hand was a wide band of grosgrain ribbon the color of a robin's egg. "Silas. This is so thoughtful. Thank you."

"You're welcome. I also bought you a pie tin, but that's for our household."

Again, her heart stuttered at his casual use of *our household.* "Are you sure..."

His gaze snapped to hers. "Are you questioning whether I can afford to buy you little tokens?"

Lord, he was touchy about money. But then again, so was she, since she'd bristled at the very idea of not earning her own living. "No, I was going to say I'm sure you're hoping I'll put that pan to good use by learning to bake that sugar pie you've been telling me is your favorite."

It took a moment for his tension to leave and that devil-may-care smile to reappear. "Yes, I sure hope that pie is in my future. Now gimme a kiss that'll hold me over until I fetch you on Saturday."

Dinah wreathed her arms around Silas's neck, kissing him with every bit of joy in her heart. She whispered, "I'll miss you," and slipped away, without looking back to watch him leave.

FRIDAY NIGHT DINAH was cleaning up the exam room after Doc had reset a broken arm when she heard, "Look who's been left all alone, cleaning up after the misdeeds of men again."

She whirled around to see Zeke West leaning in the open doorway, as if posing for a tintype.

If she'd seen him out and about, she might've considered him an attractive man. He wore the finest clothes, in the latest style, on his lean frame. He kept his dark beard neatly trimmed and he'd slicked his hair back in the fashion preferred by a railroad muckety-muck, and carried himself in the same manner.

But his eyes had no light in them, the eerie brown giving the impression of endless black holes. When he bothered to show his straight white teeth, he resembled a territorial wolf baring his canines, not a man merely offering a smile.

He flat-out scared her, and that was before she'd seen the aftereffects of his violent nature.

An unwelcome chill snaked up her spine. "If you'll wait right there, Mr. West, I'll get Doc so he can find out what's ailing you."

"No need to do that. I already know what's ailing me." He pushed off the doorjamb and stalked toward her.

Dinah retreated, putting the exam table between them. "I'm not actually comfortable with you—"

He slammed his hands on the table, cutting off her response and causing her to jump. "You know what I'm not comfortable with? Know what's ailing me and makin' me sick? The rumor I heard that you're lettin' that weaselly bastard Silas McKay court you."

She didn't respond.

"Tell me it ain't true," he demanded.

She swallowed hard and said, "It is true."

"Goddammit!" he roared and swept the pan of instruments off the table, sending them flying across the room.

Please, Doc, please have heard that noise and come out here to check on things.

"I asked you last fall if I could come callin' and you said you were still settlin' in. I visited before Christmas and you—"

"Said no. Just like I said *no* the last time you asked me. In fact, every time you've asked me, Mr. West, I've been clear that I am not interested in you." Her voice shook, but at least she'd said her piece.

"You say *no* to me when I make ten times more money than that shit-kicker McKay? When I can provide you with the best of everything Sundance has to offer as I court you?"

"It's not about money. It's never been about money, which for some reason you cannot comprehend." Now she was getting mad. How dare he come in here and demand explanations from her that she'd already given him? "So let me repeat what I've said the three other times you've come sniffing around. I want nothing to do with railroad men. Ever. I will never change my mind on that stance, so you are wasting your time."

Those mean eyes of his darkened further and he bared his teeth. "McKay oughta be out of the runnin' too, because he used to work for the railroad."

She didn't let on that Silas hadn't shared that tidbit with her. "But he doesn't work for the railroad *now*, does he?"

"Because he got fired."

"For what?"

"Fightin'. And he hasn't learned his lesson because he still—"

"*You* jumped *him* last Friday night! Deputy McKay brought him here afterward, so I saw the damage you'd inflicted before you were forcibly stopped from inflicting more. That wasn't the first time I've seen Silas injured by your hands. The only lesson here is that you've built a grudge against him and I'd be a fool to let you—a man with such violent tendencies—court me."

Zeke emitted a laugh that sent the hairs on the back of her neck standing straight up. "That's all it would've taken? If I'da let McKay pound the snot outta me and then stumbled in here bloody and pathetic, you would have been sweet on *me* instead?"

"Don't be ridiculous," she snapped. "You'd still be a railroad man and I still wouldn't be interested."

"What is it about him that gets you so fired up?" He leaned across the table as if settling in to hear her confession. "Because he's a known liar and a cheat. I wouldn't be shocked at all to hear he had a couple of women on a string—the man did like his whores when the railroad crew stayed overnight in Gillette. How is it you believe him when he's actin' the part of a gentleman cowboy, sweet-talkin' you for the sole reason to get you to spread your legs for him?"

Do not give him the satisfaction of a response.

"It's pathetic he's so proud of that piece of dirt he owns. Bet he's never even taken you there since it's damn humble and he knows no woman worth her salt would ever live there."

She raised her chin. "I've been there. Beings that Silas and I are betrothed."

His body went deadly still. Zeke's gaze zeroed in on her left hand. "If he's so proud about makin' you his wife, then why ain't you wearin' his ring?"

"Because—"

"He's too broke to buy you one."

His snicker cut at her since Silas had gotten defensive over her questioning whether it'd been too much for him to buy her a pie plate, to say nothing of a ring.

"Or maybe he's convinced that buyin' another piece of dirt for himself and your 'future' together is worth more than you wearin' sparkling stone." He snickered again. "Can't run cattle on a diamond."

"Get out."

"Aww, don't be sore. But I do have a secret to share with you."

"I don't care to hear anything you have to say, Mr. West."

Faster than she saw it coming, Zeke wrapped his fingers around her wrists, pinning her hands in place on the table. He angled close enough she felt his breath on her face. Her gut clenched with fear, but she didn't move.

"I'm gonna tell you anyway. Here's what I know about your land-hungry, cash-poor betrothed…he's got ambitions. His ambitions include owning everything around him. It just so happens there's a sliver of land between McKay and his neighbor Henrikson, ain't big, maybe twenty acres. Griffen, the fella who bought that land two years back, didn't know the bottom tip of his parcel crossed the creek. If he was raising cattle, they could cross the stream. But he's raising sheep so that land is worthless to him, because he doesn't want to get between two cattle ranchers, bein's sheep and cattle can't mix. Sure, he could fence those twenty acres at a huge cost. I bet even a pretty little teacher like you can do the math on how that ain't a wise investment."

"Why are you telling me this?"

His eyes glittered with satisfaction. "Because *I* bought that land. Me'n McKay are gonna be neighbors. Won't that be fun? Maybe when he's gone, out ridin' the range, and you're home alone, I'll come over and get me some sugar from you."

"But…how did you know…"

"This particular situation came up when me'n Zachariah were at Griffen's buyin' lambs to stock his ranch."

Dinah didn't have to feign confusion. "I thought your brother worked for the railroad."

"Like McKay, Zachariah has been usin' his railroad wages to buy land. Soon as he and Mary are married, he'll be sheepherding fulltime. While we were there, Griffen was complaining about Henrikson's disinterest in buyin' it from him. I convinced him to sell it to me before he offered it to McKay."

"How?" Wasn't there some code in the West about offering land bordering yours to your neighbors first?

West shrugged. "I insinuated that McKay wouldn't have the money to buy it until the fall after he sold cattle—probably not a lie at any rate. No surprise Griffen took my immediate cash offer. He's kept the deal under his hat and the Crook County register of deeds is slow at updating their records. But McKay will know soon enough."

The calculating look in West's eyes changed and Dinah's fear caused her to blurt out, "What does any of this have to do with me?"

Keeping his gaze locked on hers, Zeke began stroking the insides of her wrists with his thumbs. "Now that you've turned me down outright, I'm offering you another deal. I'll sell you that piece of land McKay wants so badly…for one dollar and one night with you."

"No."

"You sure?" he said silkily. "What would one night of pleasure with me matter, when you'll have the rest of your life to perform your wifely duty with McKay?"

She repeated, "No," hating that her voice shook.

"Even if it's our little secret?"

Dinah shook her head.

"But think of how grateful he'd be. Isn't that your lot in life as a wife? To do whatever it takes to make your husband happy?" Zeke brushed his bearded cheek against hers and it burned like acid. "Or are you afraid if you fuck me that you'll see what a poor option Silas McKay really is?"

"Stop. Please."

"Make the deal with me, Dinah. Because I promise you that if I offered this same deal to McKay? He'd find a way to shove you into my bed even as he was convincing you that virtue is fleeting but land is forever."

"You don't know him. Silas wouldn't do that."

West laughed softly next to her ear. "That quiver in your voice belies the confidence in your words."

"I'm shaking because you're scaring me."

"A little fear makes passion so much stronger." His hands moved up her arms as he breathed heavily in her ear. "I'll prove it to you...if you give me what I want."

"Or you'll just take it?" she said through gritted teeth.

Immediately Zeke released her with a shove. "I don't have to force women into my bed."

"No, you have to pay for them first." Oh god. What had possessed her to say that?

But Zeke laughed. "All men end up payin' for pussy one way or another. Maybe you oughta make yours worth something special."

Dinah kept the distance between them despite the fury boiling over that he'd touched her, threatened her, cheapened her and had taken shots at Silas's character. "Not with you. Ever."

He sighed. "Your choice. But just remember...whatever happens next is all on you. *You* could've prevented it."

"*I* will prevent it when I tell Silas—"

His hands smacking the table cut her off again. "Don't threaten me. You won't tell Silas a damn thing."

"Watch me."

"Oh, I'll watch him lose that temper of his and come after me." A truly evil look settled on his face. "You've seen the damage I've done to him in the past. I'll gladly do it again, except maybe worse if he gets it in his fool head to challenge me over your so-called virtue...or anything else."

She stared at him and didn't bother masking her horror.

"And you won't tell him about my land purchase either, because deep down you *are* afraid he'll confront me."

Yes. Silas's first reaction was to come out swinging. He wouldn't consider Dinah's fear over losing him enough to not engage with Zeke again. He'd fight, he'd lose—because West always seemed to get the best of him—and then he'd plan for the next time he could mix it up with his nemesis.

"The truth is, you'll keep your mouth shut. Because either way...you have more to lose than I do." West turned and strode to the door. He paused in the doorway. "On second thought, go ahead and tell him everything. I'll be ready and waitin' for him."

As soon as West had gone, she sank to the floor. Her entire body shook, forcing her to bring her knees into her chest as she curled into a ball.

Breathe. He hasn't really hurt you.

A tiny voice in her head piped in with *not yet*.

Silas would lose his mind to hear that Zeke had threatened her—if he knew Zeke had put his hands on her, he'd crack. What was she supposed to do? She'd never been in this situation. Where the result of one man's reaction to another man's actions rested entirely in her hands. For being such a good man in so many respects, Silas didn't seem strong enough to withstand Zeke's goading.

Would Silas ever take into account that he could die during these skirmishes? Or what if in a fit of rage he killed Zeke and ended up wearing a noose? If his own brother, who was the law, couldn't get him to stop, what chance did she have?

Apparently Silas had missed the "turn the other cheek" lesson in Sunday school too.

Could she do it? If she were in that position?

Yes. Because she wouldn't subject the man she cared about to seeing her in pain. She wouldn't choose to stay and fight for something that didn't matter and no one remembered at the end of the week anyway, when she could walk away first.

That was the core difference between them.

The biggest question for her was if Silas would continue to let this rivalry define him? Choosing to fight every time rather than learning to talk it out? Not just with others who vexed him, but with her?

So if she said nothing about this little visit, it'd save Silas a beating.

If she shared everything with him, including her fears that grew after every run-in with Zeke, she'd hope that this time Silas would change and choose not to fight.

But it wasn't really a choice. She'd do whatever she could to save him from more pain. Even if she had to lie. Even if it made him mad.

She pushed herself to her feet and gathered up the scattered medical instruments to scrub them. The hot water had the added benefit of cleansing the memory of West's hands on her.

TEN

INAH'S SADDLEBAGS WERE packed when Silas arrived on Saturday afternoon, saving him from having to make forced small talk with Doc and Mrs. Agnes. But his intended immediately seized his saddlebags too—how much stuff did one woman need for an overnight visit?—and filled both sides with wrapped bundles.

Her preoccupation with the saddlebags ended when he kissed the daylights out of her.

With her arms twined around his neck, she caught her breath. "I like the way you kiss me, Silas."

"There's plenty more where that came from." He smooched her lips. "The way you kiss me back...you're a quick study, teach." He forced himself to disentangle from her embrace. "Let's ride."

Silas kept up a steady pace that didn't allow for conversation. After passing Henrikson's much nicer, much newer, much larger homestead, he feared Dinah would judge his small cabin as lacking.

In truth, it was.

Would she regret her decision to marry him and make this their home?

"Silas?"

He looked over at her. "Sorry, darlin'. Did you say something?"

"I asked if we needed to check cattle first or turn the horses out."

We.

Made him a sap but he loved the sound of that.

"We can turn the horses out. I spent all mornin' doin' cattle checks so they oughta be good until tomorrow."

"All right. I don't know any of this cow stuff, so I hope it doesn't bother you that I'll probably ask a lot of questions."

Cow stuff. He grinned. "I'm lookin' forward to sharin' my world with you, sugar pie."

She dismounted. "Speaking of...we need to talk about our longer betrothal before I bring it up with Doc."

What the hell? Why was this the first he'd heard of a "longer betrothal"? "I don't follow."

"There's not much to follow. I signed a two-year contract with Doc. I intend to fulfill it. Which means I'll continue to live and work there as I'd planned. Stay with you when I can. We can be married next spring."

"No."

Those piercing blue eyes narrowed on him. "What do you mean *no?* It's not your decision. I agreed that you could call me your intended, since you were all fired up to put a name to this, but we never talked about an actual wedding date."

"You want to live apart for another goddamned year? How am I supposed to—"

"If you say *take care of me*, Silas McKay, I will hop right back on this horse, right now." She stormed over. "My word is just as important to me as yours is to you. Doc can't run his practice on his own with his wife being infirmed. My students need a teacher. Not to mention the money I—"

"Hush." Silas placed his fingers over her lips. "Not a word about money. You hear me?"

Growling, she tried to nip his fingers. "Don't you *ever* hush me."

"Sorry, sweetheart. Shit. I'm so sorry." He kissed her. Or he tried to kiss her, but she kept her mouth closed. But he kept coaxing her to accept his apologies and his kisses, murmuring, "Please, forgive me. I don't know what got into me, I promise it won't happen again."

Dinah relented and kissed him back. When they broke apart, she rested her cheek against his chest. "I have a lot to learn in the next year about becoming a ranch wife anyway."

Don't ask how she plans to learn it once a week from thirty miles away, don't do it, man, just smile and nod.

He gave her a quick peck on the forehead. "That you do." Then he picked up both saddlebags. "I'll be right back so we can deal with the horses after I put these in the house."

He showed Dinah where to hang her tack in the barn and where he kept the pitchfork for shoveling hay. Once their horses joined the others in the paddock, he spread out hay while Dinah refilled the water trough.

Then the moment of truth had come. He held out his hand. "Ain't much to the house tour, but I reckon you're curious."

"I am." She slid her fingers into his. "I wasn't sure what you had on hand as far as food staples, so I brought a little of everything."

"How about this: you tell me what we need and I'll order it at Robinette's."

She gasped and held her other hand to her forehead in a mock swoon. "You'd make a special trip into town for it? You must *really* like me, McKay."

He laughed at her poking fun at him. "That I do, darlin' Dinah, that I do." *Long enough to wait a damn year to marry you.*

They passed by the immense wood pile and he pointed out the outhouse in case she'd missed it when she visited last Saturday. He paused in front of the door, which he'd left open. He gestured for Dinah to precede him inside.

The cabin stayed pretty dark, even during the brightest part of the day since there were only two small windows that faced east. The rock fireplace was centered on the far wall directly across from the door. Above it hung a huge gilded mirror that'd come with the cabin. Silas had tucked his bed in the right corner, with the footboard facing the door. He'd tacked up a heavy wool blanket behind the headboard.

Dinah's gaze moved between his bed and the smaller one in the left corner. "Which is yours?"

Ours. "The bigger one. Jonas built in a wardrobe along that wall, so his bed is smaller." His brother's wardrobe held his collection of fine suits and his firearms. Silas hung his clothes on pegs he'd hammered into the logs or he packed them in the trunk along the wall.

She skirted the two rocking chairs in front of the fireplace, stopping at the side of his bed. "I like the blanket on the wall. It makes the space cozier."

"Oh, this cabin is the very definition of cozy," he said dryly.

Dinah bypassed him, her gaze on the cookstove against the same side wall as his bed. "Hey. We had this model in Cheyenne, so I'm familiar with all the quirks." She smiled at him. "That'll make cooking easier." She peered around the side of the stove.

"You lookin' for something in particular?"

"Do you have a larder?"

"Nope. Am I supposed to?"

"It's handy for keeping food close by. Especially once I start canning and need a place for my supply of staples."

"I can build one," he offered. "Would you like it right next to the stove?"

She crossed over to the other side of the cabin. "Actually, I think this corner would be better. That stove tends to get hot. The food would stay cooler on this side."

"There will be more room over there once Jonas is out."

"With the bed gone? Definitely. But I'm claiming the wardrobe for my clothes. Plus, I'll need space for my sewing machine, desk and trunk."

"So what do I need to fix first?"

"I'd ask you to add shelves to the wall by the stove for dishes." She ran her hand along the table beneath the window. "Then build a wider table with more storage shelves underneath. We could abut this skinnier table at the end, closing off the space. The wash tub and water pitcher could go on top here. We could even store the kindling sticks for the cookstove below. Then if you build the larder in that corner, there'd still be room for the table and chairs and my credenza under the window."

He grinned. "You've been here five minutes and you're already makin' changes."

Dinah wheeled back around. "Does it bother you? Because I'm not saying we *have* to do all of it. I'm not bringing even a full wagonload of things with me, but I will need places to store my things as well as basic household items and an area to prepare our food—"

"Hey." He tugged her against his body and kissed her. "I'm not bothered. I'm happy you're seein' the potential of this place." His face heated but he kept his gaze locked to hers when he admitted, "This cabin ain't much. I wish I could build you a house like Henrikson's—"

She pressed her lips to his. "I haven't had a home since my dad died." Her mouth curved into a sheepish smile. "So I might've gotten a little carried away. Besides, we're not getting married until next summer. There's time for setting up housekeeping."

"But knowin' exactly what you want done would give me something to work on when I'm here alone and missin' you over the next year."

"If you truly want me to write things down, there's paper in my bag."

"Let's get them bags unpacked."

Silas got sidetracked watching all the items Dinah pulled out. Flour and lard in glass jars. Sugar, eggs, a crock of butter, and a bottle of milk. Fresh greens, a bunch of small carrots, dried apples, and dried beans. When she glanced up and saw him staring, she blushed. "I didn't know what staples you had on hand, so I brought the necessities."

"Keep goin'. I'm curious to see what else you deem necessary."

She hugged a mysterious wrapped bundle to her chest and walked to his bed to shove it under the pillow. She wouldn't meet his gaze when she returned.

Interesting.

"You could help, you know," she suggested.

Silas peeled the flap back to his bag and pulled out a handkerchief that'd been tied at the top. After untying it, he dumped out...ten sprouted potatoes. "Is this for supper?"

"They're for planting. If you turn over some dirt tomorrow, I'll cut these, plant them, and cover them with dirt and straw. Hopefully it's not too late in the season to grow enough to fill your root cellar with potatoes this fall."

He rubbed the back of his neck. "Ah...about that. What if I tell you I don't have a root cellar?"

"Do you have an icehouse?"

"In the winter. It's called the creek."

She flapped the bandana at him. "You'll have a shovel in your hand tomorrow so you might as well dig another hole."

Amused, he said, "Where?"

"Close by. Where the ground will be cool, but dry." She propped her hand on her hip. "Where do you store meat?"

"In barrels in the far corner of the barn. Salt beef and brined pork. I'm low on both, which is why I'm happy for the summer when the huntin's good."

"What can you catch for supper? I'd planned on making stew and dumplings."

"Probably easiest to shoot a rabbit."

She smiled widely. "Can you teach me how to skin them and clean them?"

"Whoa, you sure you're ready for that?"

"Yes. Martha trades us rabbit meat for milk and eggs. But she keeps the skins. I've wondered what it'd take to clean buckshot out of the meat and tan the hides."

Silas moved closer to touch her, just because he could. "You don't gotta learn how to do everything in one day, Dinah."

"You're right. Shame though."

"What?"

Her exaggerated sigh sent his warning bells clanging. "I'd looked forward to learning how to make you a sugar pie since it's your favorite, but since I don't gotta *learn how to do everything in one day*, I'll just make apple brown betty instead—"

Dinah shrieked when Silas picked her up, spun her around and set her in front of the cookstove.

"I was wrong, woman. Please please please make me that pie. Right now."

She laughed and slumped against him. "Gonna tie me to the stove until I do?"

I'd rather tie you to my bed and eat up every inch of you until you moan.

His body reacted to the idea of a naked Dinah, squirming beneath his hands and mouth.

"What were you thinking about just now? The truth."

Pulling her hair aside, he found a spot to taste and tease on her neck. Then he sank his teeth in, latching onto her upper arms when her knees went weak. "How I can't wait to learn all the ways to touch you that make you thrash and beg and come undone," he murmured.

"But…I thought you said we weren't…"

"Oh, it ain't gonna happen tonight." At least not the act of him rutting between her thighs. "I'll keep my word about that. But you oughta know: I can make my body behave, but my mind wanders to us rollin' around bare-ass nekkid in my bed…pretty damn often actually."

Dinah turned her head and nipped his jaw. "Mine too."

That shocked him.

And excited him.

Mostly it sent his thoughts careening back to ones where they explored this mutual desire.

She disentangled from him. "Stop distracting me. Go catch us a couple of rabbits and let me start making our supper."

Yep. She'd be as bossy with him as she was shy with others, and he wouldn't have it any other way.

SILAS RETURNED WITH two fat rabbits and a young wood duck.

And he'd picked her a handful of wildflowers.

She fussed over them as if he'd given her gold. After arranging the purple, yellow and orange blooms in a water-filled glass jar, she set it in the center of his table—which was now covered in a lace tablecloth.

Already making her mark.

Even though she'd left the door open, the scents of yeast and sugar filled the cabin.

A tray of biscuits cooled on the table beneath the window, next to a creamy yellow pie and two apple scrambles she'd baked in the tin cups he'd bought at the picnic. A towel covered a loaf pan, which he could see held a mound of rising dough. A pot of water boiled on the stove and she'd left a pile of chopped carrots, snap peas and onion next to a dish of butter.

Damn. The woman worked fast.

"Smells great in here, darlin'."

"Thank you." She slammed the cookstove door and straightened to face him. "Where are we skinning the rabbits?"

"Outside by the handpump. Less messy. I filled the tubs with cold water."

It hadn't occurred to him that Dinah wouldn't be bothered by butchering until she mentioned she'd grown accustomed to seeing blood, bones and skin working with Doc.

After cleaning up the rabbits and tacking up the skins on the sunny side of the barn to dry, he brought the pot of boiling water outside. He dunked the duck in it until the pin feathers were easier to remove. Since she'd never dealt with duck, he showed her all the ways waterfowl were different from domesticated chickens, including how to pluck them. He gutted, cleaned and quartered the duck. Then he started the first step of rendering duck fat by plopping the pieces in his biggest cast iron pan with lard and salt and covering it with a lid. It'd take two days on the coolest part of the hot stove, but he swore the end result was worth the effort.

Silas thought it was sweet she wrote down everything he told her.

She scrubbed out the stockpot and began boiling water for one of the rabbits, casually mentioning if she had another pan, she could've fried up the other rabbit like chicken for Sunday lunch.

Silas made a mental note to add that piece of cookware to his next Robinette's order. He wouldn't fret about the cost of all of this, he'd just…make up the difference somehow.

While the stew cooked, they staked out a place for the root vegetable garden. Then they'd gone inside and she'd drawn out a basic design for the cold storage/root cellar, based on the ones Doc had. She sketched the spacing for the shelves next to the stove, where to place the hooks above the stove for pans, and even tacked a birds' eye view of how her outline would utilize the most space.

If he hadn't already been in love with her, he would've surely fallen that afternoon. Working with her didn't seem like work and she filled his house—and his heart—with lightness and joy.

With the bread cooling and the stew simmering, they sat at the table. Silas poured them each a mug of beer from the growler he'd picked up at Sackett's.

Dinah was busy writing. She'd brought three different workbooks with her. One had lines like the ledger he used for ranch finances. One resembled a school primer—that's where she'd rendered her drawings. The last one had a leather cover tooled with flowers. Fancier than the others, it also had a buckle and strap across the top and bottom to keep the stack of thick papers bound inside.

Curious, he picked it up, only to have her try and snatch it back.

"Don't open that."

"What's in here?"

"None of your business."

"Recipes?"

"No." She held out her hand. "Give it back."

"Not until you tell me what it is."

"It's my journal."

"Your teacher's journal?"

"No. It's my personal journal."

"What do you write about?"

"Everything."

A wide grin split his face. "I'm in here, ain't I?"

"Yes."

"How many times?"

Dinah glared at him.

He let loose a low whistle. "*That* many times, that you don't wanna talk about it, huh? Woman, you've got it bad for me, doncha?"

"No! But those thoughts are private, Silas."

"What did you write about me, darlin'?" He held it up as if contemplating the contents. "Is it poetry? You comparing my eyes to jewels and my manly form to one of them fancy marble statues like in the Vatican in Rome?"

She snorted.

"Or did you draw nekkid pictures of me?" He tipped his chin to the sketches sitting in front of her. "Because you *are* pretty good at drawin'."

"The only thing I'm gonna draw is my fist back, aimed at your face, if you don't give me my journal right now."

He clucked his tongue. "So violent. Darlin', I worry your temper is gonna lead you into ruin. First it's just verbal threats and then next thing you know...you're pickin' a fight in church and throwin' pews over some woman's stupid comment about your hat."

"SILAS."

"All right. I'll give it back. But only after you tell me one *nice* thing you wrote about me in here."

The woman smirked at him. "I wrote that you didn't whine too much after Zeke West tried to rip your arm off."

His mouth dropped open. "Now that ain't nice at all, Dinah"—he glanced at the journal cover and noticed her full name embossed on the bottom—"*Louise* Thompson."

Her nose wrinkled. "Don't say that. I hate my middle name."

"Aw, Louise ain't bad, sugar pie. It could be something worse like…Prudence." He pointed to her mug of ale. "Or Temperance."

She cocked her head toward his bed. "Or Chastity."

Silas threw back his head and laughed. "Damn, woman, I love you." When she didn't retort with outrage or disbelief, he glanced over to see her entire body had gone stiff. "What?"

"Do you mean that?" she said softly.

He set the journal on the floor and said, "C'mere."

"Silas."

"Come. Here."

She stood and took the two steps to his chair.

Silas tugged her onto his lap, parting her legs over his so she straddled him.

Then his lips were on hers, kissing her with every bit of passion he'd tried to temper. Treating her to a drawn-out, teasing, wet, tongue-tangling, hungry clashing of mouths. His left hand clutched the nape of her neck while he used his right hand to outline her face. Stroking from her temple down her jawline and back up.

But each caress went a little further. First to her chin. Then down her throat to the slope of her shoulder. Then lower to tease the swell of her breasts.

She didn't bat his hand away; instead, she arched closer.

His cock went rigid beneath her. His heart beat so fast and loud in his ears he swore she had to've heard it. Could she feel his hardness throbbing in the cradle of her thighs where they were pressed together?

Dinah's fingers began to mimic his touch on her face. She wiggled her bottom against him and he groaned with need for more.

Finally, he broke the kiss and trailed his lips down the path his fingers had traveled. When he sank his teeth into the upper curve of her bosom, blowing a warm puff of air through the cloth, she moaned.

"Yes, I meant it," he said against her chest as he tried to catch his breath. "You got a little prissy when I suggested I call you my intended after courtin' for two days, so I figured you might act the same if I told you how bein' with you fills me with joy and hope and purpose. I've never been in love, but I reckon this is how it feels."

"Silas." She clamped her hands on his head, forcing him to meet her gaze. "Thank you."

"For?"

"Not being afraid to tell me how you feel, even if it seems fast." She outlined his lips with hers. "You listen to me. You teach me. You don't mind I'm a little bossy even when I don't always know what I'm doing. So I can admit…I've been sweet on you since you showed up at Doc's. I love being with you because I *like* you more every time we're together."

This sweet woman deserved better than a cash-poor rancher, but he couldn't wait to prove she'd made the right choice by going all in with him. "Well, that's handy, bein's we're gonna be married and all. In a goddamned year."

Dinah laughed.

They stared at each other with their goofy love faces and he'd never been happier.

"I got something for you," he said after kissing her for a good, long time. "But I'm afraid I can't give it to you until we settle a couple of things."

"What things?" she said, right back to wearing that cute look of skepticism that said he wouldn't get away with nothin' around her.

"Your journal. Now darlin', I suspect how this'll go. You'll fill that journal up. I'll buy you a new one that has *Dinah Thompson McKay* on the bottom. Over the years I'll keep buyin' you fancier journals because I'll secretly love how dedicated you are to putting our life together into words and writin' it down on paper as our history for our family to read." He pushed her hair over her shoulder. "My family's history died with my parents. I have no idea about their families or the lives they led in Ireland. I don't even know if McKay was the name they brought here or the name they gave themselves when they started anew. But you are changin' that for future McKays. They'll have a past to look to with pride." He paused dramatically. "That said, darlin', I'm gonna insist you rewrite the incident that happened between me and Zeke. See, I can't have anyone believin' that lowlife bastard got the best of me. How'll that make me look to my future kids, grandkids and great-grandkids?"

"Oh, I don't know…like you were an honest man?"

He snorted. "No. I'll come across as a lousy fighter. So when you rewrite that, you gotta say that it took Zeke *and* Zachariah West to take me down. And they broke my arm, not just sprained it."

"So I should leave in the part about Madam Ruby from the whore-house dragging you to Doc's?" she demanded hotly. "Because that'll make you look like some kind of stallion to future McKay males?"

"Jesus, Mary and Joseph, *no*. That part can stay out."

"Good. Then I will…revise it." She raised an eyebrow. "Slightly."

Silas grinned. "There's my girl."

"However, in the interest of fairness, I'll expect if something happens that leaves me in an unflattering light, then I have the all clear from you to revise it."

"Only slightly," he teased.

She whapped his shoulder. "Now, you said you had something for me?"

"Yep. Hang on." He stood with her still on his lap and hiked her butt up higher so she could tighten her legs around his waist.

"This is indecent," she huffed.

"You like it, sugar pie."

She buried her face in his neck. "You are insufferable."

"Mmm. You like that too." He half dropped, half flung her on the bed. "Now cover your eyes."

Silas walked backward to Jonas's side of the room and warned, "No peeking!" when he saw her hands move. He pulled the box out from Jonas's wardrobe and brought it over, setting it beside her. "Okay. Now you can look."

Dinah opened her eyes. "Two gifts? Really? What did I do to deserve this?"

He shrugged away his embarrassment. "I realized I like buyin' stuff for you. Open it."

She undid the paper around the first gift and said, "*The Red Badge of Courage* by Stephen Crane."

"Have you read it?"

"No. I wanted to, though." She turned the book over in her hands. "Have you read it?"

"Nope. I hoped you could read it out loud for us like you did that last one."

Her smile seemed to add an extra glow to the room. "I'd love that."

"I made sure I've got plenty of lamp oil." Then he nudged her knee with his. "Open the next one."

Dinah unboxed the Asian-themed teapot covered in cherry blossoms and red pagodas. The set included two cups and saucers, a matching sugar bowl and a cream pitcher. Her shocked gaze met his. "Silas. How did you...?"

"I asked Robinette if there was anything you kept lookin' at when you were browsing in his store. He said you were drawn to this set from the first."

She ran her finger over the domed top of the teapot and the curved bamboo handle. "My mother had one similar to this set. It got broken when we moved." Her eyes were watery when she looked up again. "Thank you, Silas. It means so much. It's a perfect addition to our household goods."

He leaned over and kissed her. "You're welcome. I also bought a tin of tea and a chunk of honeycomb."

"It appears we're having tea with our sugar pie instead of coffee." She tucked the paper back into the box. "Come on. It's time for supper."

ELEVEN

WHILE DINAH CLEANED up the supper dishes, Silas headed out to the log pile to chop wood into smaller pieces for the cookstove.

It'd been an amazing day. Exciting and yet strange to consider this would be her home. The best part had been Silas's willingness to teach her whatever she'd asked.

And his gifts. She never would've believed the man had such a sweet side.

As much as she wanted to use her new tea set, until she had a proper shelf for it, it'd be best to leave it in the box. She started coffee to go with their dessert.

Silas returned and only had eyes for the pie she'd dished up.

Dinah only had eyes for him. He'd rolled his sleeves past his elbows, revealing his strong, sinewy forearms. He'd also left his shirt unbuttoned midway down his chest after washing at the pump, revealing that thatch of midnight hair she'd found so fascinating every time she'd glimpsed his torso at Doc's. He'd slicked his hair straight back after scrubbing his face. The man was striking looking. Such handsome features deserved her admiration.

Not that he'd caught her appreciative glances.

"Darlin', I've been chompin' at the bit to sink my teeth into this pie."

"Sit. The coffee's almost done."

"We're not havin' tea?"

"I'd rather leave the tea set boxed up for safekeeping until I have a special place for it."

"Understood." He pulled the chair out and plopped down.

That's when she noticed he'd taken his boots and his socks off. There was something intimate about seeing a man's naked feet. She tried to imagine getting used to seeing all of him bared to her; heat rose up her neck and flushed her face.

After filling two coffee cups and setting them on the table, she sat across from him. "Don't be shy. Dig in."

Silas sliced through the creamy yellow filling and popped the bite in his mouth. He groaned. Swallowed. Took another bite before he spoke. "That is the best damn sugar pie I've ever had." He cocked his head. "You were pullin' my leg when you said you'd never made it before, weren't you?"

"No. I asked Mrs. Agnes if she'd ever heard of it and she had a recipe. After I looked at the ingredients, I realized this pie is similar to the custard my mother used to make. That one didn't have a crust either and the sugar on top is browned almost to the point of burned."

"Feel free to make that dessert for me anytime you want."

She smiled. "You have a taste for sweet things."

"Mmm-hmm. That's why I picked you." The rest of his pie vanished in about three bites.

Dinah hadn't eaten any of hers.

"You don't like it?" Silas said.

"I'd rather have something fruity. With a double crust. Or with meringue."

He pulled her plate in front of him. "Hate to see this go to waste."

She chuckled and sipped her coffee. "What time do you usually turn in?"

"Depends. If it's been a long day, I often don't make it much past supper. If Jonas is here, we end up talkin' or playin' cards, so I hit the hay later. Most mornings I'm up with the sun. I deal with my cattle first since Henrikson ain't an early riser. Then I head over and take care of his livestock."

"Does he ever help you?"

"Sometimes. Usually only when he's sick of his own company. Then after I've finished the cattle check, I work on building fences. Or depending on the time of year, I'm putting up hay. If I'm lucky, I'll get two cuttings out of the hay field in a growin' season. I've gotta show improvements on the land and that requires me plantin' trees, so I do that too. Which is kinda crazy because I also spend a goodly chunk of my time clearin' the deadfall outta the forested parts of the land. I load the logs in the wagon, haul them here and cut 'em so they dry out before winter hits, so I don't freeze to death." He took a swig of coffee. "Probably more than you wanted to know...but why you askin', darlin'?"

"I'm wondering where I'll fit into that. Will you need me to help you? Or maybe the better question is will you *want* my help? I understand I'll be in charge of the household, but I thought maybe you get tired of doing things all by yourself. Plus, what if you took sick? Henrikson probably won't come over and help you. I don't know any of your other neighbors. It makes sense that you teach me how to do all the cow stuff. When I'm a ranch wife I'll need—"

Silas stood so abruptly his chair tipped over. Then he just plucked her up off her chair and carried her to his sleeping area, falling back onto his bed so she was on top of him.

"Silas!"

Laughing, he rolled her over until his body covered hers. Then he kissed her with sweetness and gentle coaxing that turned warmth into fiery need. She squirmed, not to get away, but because her body wanted more...even when she wasn't sure what that more was.

Silas broke the kiss—chuckling when her lips chased his—to string openmouthed kisses down her neck. Then back up to reconnect with her mouth. Once their tongues tangled furiously, she heard him growl. She felt the vibration down to where his hardness pressed against her.

He inched his lips over to her ear and whispered, "Maybe I'll keep my wife so spent from lovin' on her all the time that she won't be able to get outta this bed in the mornin'." Then he dragged his tongue to the other side of her throat, drawing lazy circles over her damp skin. "I could just nibble on you day and night, sugar pie."

"I'd like that." She trapped his face between her palms, forcing him to look at her. "But that still doesn't answer my questions."

"It sure as hell answered mine."

She waited for him to explain.

He angled his head close enough to rub his lips back and forth across hers while keeping their eyes locked. "I liked bein' with you before I understood that you are all in with everything that it means to be a rancher's wife. Not because you feel it'll be your duty, but because you wanna share all parts of this life with me."

"I do."

"Then I'll teach you anything you wanna learn."

"How to shoot a gun?"

"How to shoot all *three* kinds of guns I own." He paused. "You really want to learn how to hunt?"

"Yes. And how to protect myself."

Those blue eyes narrowed with suspicion. "Why would you need to know how to protect yourself?"

"Because I'll be living out in the middle of nowhere and you won't always be around."

"And?"

She sighed heavily. "And Martha lives in the woods and I can't tell you how many times she warned me about bears and coyotes. She's even seen a mountain lion. Not to mention snakes." Her shudder was genuine. "What if I'm out picking berries and I come across a bear and a rattlesnake? I need to know how to shoot them for my protection."

He relaxed his posture. "Bears are unlikely. Coyotes usually run when they catch wind of humans and I haven't seen a mountain lion around here. But I'll teach you how to use my shotgun, rifle and pistol, okay? Next time I go huntin' you can come along." He studied her. "Anything else I need to put in my teacher's lessons?"

"How to rope?"

"Sure. But I don't see that you'll have much use for that."

"How to cuss like a cowboy?"

"Yep."

"How to brand and doctor calves and all the weird cow stuff?"

He snickered and kissed her nose. "You sayin' *cow stuff* busts my gut every damn time."

Dinah smirked at him. "I like that you're not laughing *at* me, McKay."

"Never." He shifted on the bed, knocking into the bundle she'd tucked under the pillow. "What's that?"

"My bedclothes." Her cheeks warmed again. "I didn't know what to do with them."

"Don't need to hide them from me, sweetheart. I'll be seein' them soon enough."

Her heart hammered. No man had ever seen her bare. And she wasn't sure if she was just supposed to get ready for bed while he watched or if it'd be better if she undressed privately.

"I see the questions in those pretty eyes. It's about us sleepin' together, ain't it?

She nodded.

"I know you haven't been with a man before. Showing me your body before sharin' it with me is a big step. I told you we wouldn't turn this into a marriage bed until you're ready…even if that means I gotta wait until we're actually hitched." Silas pressed his mouth to the side of her neck, for more of those kisses and licks that caused her to wiggle like a worm on a hook. "But that don't mean we can't touch each other and learn how to be lovers." He blew in her ear and gooseflesh erupted. "Let go of them nerves. You're beautiful and I can't wait to get my hands and mouth all over this body. But I'd never pressure you for it to happen before you're ready. Okay?"

"Okay."

"Now, since I already took my boots off and I'm in for the night, I'll crawl in bed while you head to the outhouse. I'll keep my back turned until you tell me you're ready. Sound fair?"

"Sounds more than fair, Silas. Thank you for being so patient with me."

He sank his teeth into the spot where her neck met her shoulder and she moaned. "No need to thank me. I've no doubt you're worth the wait." He pushed back onto his knees. "That said, it gets mighty warm in this cabin in the summer. I'll wear this union suit tonight, but there'll come a night where I'll come to you in just my skin."

She bit back her response of hoping that was sooner rather than later.

Silas hopped off the bed. "Grab the lantern on the table before you head outside. Leave the cabin door open and holler really loud if you need something."

"I will."

After using the hand pump in the dim lamplight, Dinah decided to ask

Silas to put a washstand inside the cabin too.

True to his word, he kept his back to her as she removed her day clothes.

Since her room at Doc's was always cold, she'd brought her flannel nightgown. Standing in the stuffy cabin, she hesitated. If she put this on, even without lying next to another warm body, she'd roast.

In a bold move, she grabbed the shift she'd worn beneath her dress. The fact that the cotton was thin enough to read a newspaper through meant she'd stay cool. Especially without pantalets.

Forcing her hands to her sides and her chin up, she said, "You can turn around now."

Silas flipped to his side so fast she feared he might've given himself whiplash.

His gaze moved from her bare toes, curling into the wood planked floor, up to the tops of her knees where the shift ended, over her legs—his gaze lingered on the vee of her thighs and the dark patch of hair visible through the flimsy white material. His perusal felt as intimate as a caress as it followed the curves of her hips and passed over the plane of her belly, coming to a dead stop at her full bosom. The cloth was tighter on top to control her breasts since she refused to wear a corset. With the way he studied her, with such hunger, her nipples tightened. After rubbing his hand over his mouth, his scrutiny shifted up to the square neckline that showed nearly all of her upper chest and neck, to her face.

Then he swallowed hard. "Goddamn, woman. That's gotta be my favorite piece of clothing you've ever worn."

"But Silas. There's nothing to it."

"That's exactly why it's my favorite." That devil-may-care grin fit him so well and she loved that he flashed it at her without shame.

He patted the spot beside him. "Crawl in. After you grab the book I bought you."

"I already brought a book to read. We'll start the one you gifted me after we finish this one."

"What's the name of it?"

"You'll see." She held the lamp. "Put a side table on your list of household items. I need light if we're reading every night."

"Here." He took the lamp and placed it on the thickest spot of the headboard. "As long as we're not slammin' into the headboard like animals, it oughta stay in place."

Slamming into the headboard like animals. Dinah knew what that meant. Growing up she'd frequently heard that banging sound coming from her parents' room. Even now she heard it occasionally from Doc and Mrs. Agnes's bedroom. And to think someday soon she and Silas would be doing the same thing.

But good Lord, how hard would he have to rut into her to make the headboard wobble? Would it hurt?

Silas must've read her look as panic because he said, "I'll build a side table this week for you."

"Thanks."

Clutching the book, she slid under the covers next to him.

Immediately Silas rested his head on her chest. He sighed. "Just as soft and sweetly scented as I'd imagined. However..." He scooted down so the side of his face was on her belly. "This'll be more comfortable for you. And you can run your hands through my hair when you're readin' because I surely loved when you did it before."

Thankfully she'd done something right in the way she touched him. "I might have to rest the book on your shoulder."

"Fine by me."

"We need to make sure we don't fall asleep with the lamp burning."

"We won't."

"What if my voice puts you to sleep?"

He lifted his head up and looked at her. "You're in my bed for one night out of seven if I'm lucky. I ain't gonna waste any more time sleepin' than I have to." He returned to his previous position. "Now tell me, sugar pie. What are we readin'?"

"*Pride and Prejudice* by Jane Austen. It's one of my favorite books."

"Then I'm lucky you're sharin' it with me. What's it about?"

"Love and family and expectations in English society at the start of the century."

"Any dueling pistol matches at dawn in it?"

"No."

"Any shipwrecks with pirates, a secret treasure and a pet monkey?"

"Not that either."

A sigh.

"You don't get to be disappointed before I even start the book, Silas."

"All right. I'll stop askin' questions and listen."

Dinah picked up the book and turned to the first chapter. "*It is a truth universally acknowledged, that a single man in possession of a good fortune, must be in want of a wife.*"

Silas snorted.

"What's wrong now?"

"Nothin'. The language is strange, but the words are true. In my head I just changed the word *fortune* to *ranch*."

She snickered. "Can I keep going?"

"By all means."

When Silas didn't interject another noise or comment after the first chapter, Dinah kept reading. However, she stopped when she began to yawn.

Immediately he wiggled into an upright position, turned off the lamp and slid back down next to her.

He gathered her in his arms and his mouth zeroed in on hers, kissing her with surety. Legs twined together, his hands soothing her until she melted against him. He whispered, "Night, my angel," and settled her head against his chest as if it was the most natural thing in the world. Like they'd done it for years instead of it being the first time.

SHE WOKE ALONE in the bed the next morning, but Silas had to be close because she smelled coffee.

Then she heard whistling from outside the open cabin door.

Might've been the happiest sound she'd ever heard.

Dinah stretched and sat up.

She had no idea what time it was.

Silas ambled back in. He bestowed a glorious grin on her. "Now there's the prettiest sight I've ever seen. My beloved in my bed."

She might've sighed loud enough for him to hear.

"I've got the horses saddled. Soon as you're dressed, we'll get to work." He pointed to the row of pegs across the wall. "Feel free to hang your nightgown up there for next time you're here."

"Is that your way of bragging to Jonas that I'll be in your bed regularly?"

"Yep."

"Well, too bad. I'll need to wear this under my dress today." She dropped her feet to the floor. "But I'll bring this one back and leave it here next time I stay, all right?"

"Next time?" He frowned. "I thought you could be here with me every Saturday night."

"As much as I wish I could, I *am* beholden to Doc, for at least some Saturday evenings, remember? You'll be fine with me here only half the Saturdays and Sundays between now and next May. Plus, think of how much more cow stuff you can buy when I'm saving up my earnings to contribute to the McKay Ranch fund."

He didn't act happy about that like she'd expected.

"What's wrong?"

"You think I can't provide for us?"

"I never said that." Her traitorous thoughts returned to what Zeke West had said about Silas always being broke.

"You didn't need to. But the look on your face says someone else put that idea in your head." He paused. "Who? Doc? But that wouldn't be right because I always pay my bills with him and you'd know that."

"Silas—"

"Who?" That dangerous glint entered his eyes. "Tell me you ain't been talkin' to West."

This just drove home the point that she couldn't brink up Zeke's visit Friday night because Silas would go after him. She hated she had to lie in order to keep him from fighting, especially when his *pride* had created this particular rift, not his past with West.

"Dinah."

"You are the one who told me you don't have extra money. You even admitted that you play cards as a way to earn more. So why are you so angry at me?" How did she get him to see this anger scared her?

"I ain't takin' the money you earned, Dinah. No way, no how. You spend that on yourself."

"What?"

"You heard me."

"I'd hoped I heard you wrong."

"You didn't."

She leaped out of bed and stamped over to where he'd taken a belligerent posture—feet braced apart, arms crossed, jaw set. "Then you don't get to spend your ranch earnings on me, McKay. Not. One. Red. Cent."

"Bullshit. I can take care of my wife."

"I am not your wife yet. I don't need you to take care *of* me, Silas. I just need you to care *for* me."

"Same difference."

"Nope." She poked him in the chest. "You listen. If you insist on me spending the money I earn on *myself*, I will hire someone to put in the shelving and larder and to dig holes for the root cellar. I won't allow you to spend *your* money on enacting the changes I've suggested."

"That don't make a lick of sense."

"It makes about as much sense as you telling me to throw away what I earn on fripperies."

"I don't even know what the hell that is."

"Exactly my point. The money I earn can stay in the bank for all I care, until we do need it. But I want the right to invest in our life."

"Fine. But I want the right to give you…fripperies or whatever the hell I want without havin' you look at me like I wasted my money or I'm gonna go hungry because the purchase left me short on funds that month. I know you can buy your own books and sweets, but I want to spoil you a little because it makes me happy, okay?"

"Fine. I know you can buy your own cow stuff but I want to contribute to it because that would make me happy, okay?"

Silas loomed over her. "You are one stubborn woman."

"So what's it going to be?"

That's when his focus dropped to her chest and he bit his lip.

For the first time since the argument started, she remembered she was barely dressed. If the lustful expression on his face was any indication, his brain lost functionality when her breasts were within touching distance. She wondered if she stripped out of her nightgown…would the man agree to anything?

It's bad behavior to take advantage of his distraction and need, her conscience warned.

Oh hang it, she could do whatever the heck she wanted.

"Silas."

"Huh."

She stepped back, pulled the shift over her head and let it drop to the floor.

Silas's jaw nearly landed on top of it.

Took a long time for his eyes to meet hers.

The raw hunger she saw in those blue depths gave her a rush of power unlike anything she'd ever felt.

"You're nekkid."

"I needed to get your attention."

He shook his head as if to clear it. "That ain't helpin' at all. Christ, woman. I already had to jerk one out first thing this mornin' with your ass all up on me when we were sleepin' last night. Now seein' you so..." He gestured to her body but seemed at a loss for words. Nor had his gaze traveled back up to her eyes.

Perfect.

"So the question upon you, Mr. McKay, is if you prefer me to waste my money on layers and layers of fabric frippery and finery, I'd be flitting about in it all the time so you could admire me in it." Pausing, she boldly ran her hand down the center of her body. "Why, I'd so rarely be *nekkid* because I'd definitely need to get my money's worth from my fancy clothing. Don't you agree that'd be a shame?"

"A damn cryin' shame," he said to her bosom.

She might've laughed.

That's when his blazing blue eyes reconnected with hers.

Silas took one step forward. "Oh, you are the very devil, Miss Thompson."

"Me?"

"Yes, you."

Another step.

"I never would've believed my betrothed would stoop to teasin' me with her beautiful body to get her way..." He laughed. "But I'm goddamned impressed, sugar pie."

"You are?"

"Uh-huh." His last step meant no space existed between them. "So I'll agree to lettin' you contribute to our home, in whatever way you see fit— with the exception of hirin' some other man to come in here and build the things that *this* man wants to do for his woman to make her happy in our home."

"Okay. Umm. Thank you."

"That said, darlin', you played dirty."

His lips floated across the shell of her ear as he spoke in the deep tone that stirred her blood.

"Very dirty," he whispered. "Deliciously dirty. And I'm afraid dirty is as dirty does and you've brought out my competitive side first thing this mornin'."

Her entire body trembled when he blew in her ear.

"I can play dirty too." His teeth tugged on her earlobe. "Very dirty." Another soft breath. "Deliciously dirty."

Her throat had gone so dry she couldn't make a sound.

"I've always said you look good enough to eat. Now I'm gonna prove it." He palmed her breasts and squeezed the flesh while kissing a path down the side of her neck, over her collarbones and the heaving rise of her bosom. After a pause to angle his head, he latched onto her right nipple with his lips.

Dinah gasped at the first wet lash of his tongue. Oh heavens. She'd never felt anything like *that*. Velvety warmth and then cool wetness when the air hit her skin. His wicked, wandering tongue followed the slope to her other nipple, where he did the same thing.

Except harder.

Then softer.

Then harder again.

Blindly, she reached out to find her balance and ended up gripping his hair in her fists as he fed on her. She arched forward for more—rather than trying to pull away—when he used his teeth.

When Silas lightly swirled his tongue around the hard tips, her knees stopped supporting her entirely.

Chuckling, Silas dropped his hands beneath her bottom and lifted her, continuing to bite and suck on her neck as he carried her backward to the bed.

But he didn't return to kissing and stroking and sucking on her nipples. He placed his hands on the insides of her knees and pushed her legs open and dropped to the floor. Then he lowered his mouth to that secret part of her and began kissing her there.

Dinah was shocked...then the feel of his silky, flickering tongue all over the throbbing part of her caused the last of her modesty, any protest and all sanity to flee.

Silas emitted growls that caused her belly to flutter in anticipation as he gently licked and fiercely sucked on her. The very masculine, very pleased noises gave off the sense that having his mouth on her was as much of a treat for him as it was for her. He snaked his hand up her belly to pinch and caress her nipples, never missing a beat in proving how thoroughly he intended to eat her up.

She let him. With absolute abandon.

It wasn't long before all the nerve endings in her body fired at one time, in one place, and sent shock after shock of tingling, pulsing sensations to the spot he sucked.

Gasping and writhing without shame, she couldn't believe her body was able to give her this much pleasure. Over the years she'd touched herself, but it'd never been like this.

As she floated down from the fuzzy headspace he'd sent her into, she understood that Silas gave her the pleasure. Not her body alone. He'd turned the tables once again, proving this was another way he intended to care for her.

She had not a single complaint about that.

Sighing, she flopped back, her legs splayed wide, her body damp with a sheen of sweat and feeling…everything.

Silas's smug laugh pulled her out of the haze of pleasure. "Thought you might wanna learn another way to kiss and make up."

Dinah managed to lift her head. "You are a scoundrel, Mr. McKay."

He laughed. "I liked you readin' that book to me last night. Scoundrel is a good word for me. Lucky is another." Then he kissed the insides of her thighs, each hipbone, her bellybutton and the valley between her breasts. Finally, he planted his hands by her head. "Better buy some new bedding with all that money you're earnin', 'cause darlin', we're gonna wear them sheets out."

She touched his face. "You liked doing that?"

"I *loved* doin' it. You tasted just as sweet and hot as I imagined." He pressed his lips to hers and flicked his tongue across the seam to slip his tongue inside her mouth.

So odd….and oddly satisfying to taste the intimate part of herself from his mouth and catch her scent on his face. Whatever embarrassment she thought she'd feel was strangely absent.

He rested his forehead to hers. "Get dressed, sugar pie, cattle need tendin' even if it's gonna be hell to ride with my cock this hard."

Shyly, she asked, "You'll teach me all the different ways to...ease you?"

Silas groaned. "Yes, but I ain't gonna think about your hand on my cock or my cockstand will never go down." He tapped her ass. "Be outside in five minutes."

AFTER THEY CHECKED the McKay cattle, Silas sent her back to the cabin and he dealt with Henrikson's cattle on his own.

Dinah fried the other rabbit for lunch. While waiting for Silas to return, she turned over the soil for the root vegetable garden, planted the pieces of potatoes and covered the patch of dirt with straw.

Then she packed up for her ride to Doc's.

Silas ate heartily and praised her food. She liked taking care of him and was glad he'd have some of her cooking to get him through the week.

She left the drawings and the list of staples on the table, next to the flowers.

The more time she spent here the harder it would be to leave.

The ride to Doc's went too fast. She and Silas barely spoke at all. He greeted Doc and Mrs. Agnes while she unsaddled her horse and hung up her tack.

Silas kissed her and hugged her for a long time before letting her go.

"Is there a chance you can come here for supper this week?" she asked. "Maybe Wednesday?"

"I don't know, darlin'."

"It might be our only chance to see each other. I'm staying at Bea's Friday night and Doc probably expects me to be around on Saturday night and Sunday during the day."

"No promises, but I'll try." He ran his knuckles down the side of her neck. "Gonna miss you."

"I'll miss you too."

TWELVE

FRIDAY NIGHT ROLLED around and Silas was bored.

Dinah was at her friend's place; Jonas was working.

Sadly, Silas didn't even have a dog to keep him company.

Sackett's in Labelle was his usual hangout on the rare nights he had free. But after his run in with Zeke West the last time—and Jonas being on duty—he'd be better off heading to Sundance.

On the ride into town, he decided he needed to buy Dinah an impressive betrothal ring, even if it set him back a bit. Maybe he'd have a good run playing poker tonight.

After leaving his horse at the livery, he walked to the farthest section of Main Street.

Sundance had several saloons; one boasted dancing girls as entertainment. But when a man wanted to drink, smoke a cigar and gamble without the distraction of a saloon girl flirting to earn tips, Pettyjohn's was the place to go.

The Pettyjohn family owned the Sandstone Building. The street side was the main entrance to Pettyjohn's Restaurant. The back door at the rear of the building led upstairs to the gambling hall.

Silas took a moment to ready himself. Brushed the dust off his clothes. Counted his money. Readied his poker face. He'd had enough success gambling that the little rituals mattered.

With the uncharacteristic warmth of the night, the door to the upstairs had been propped open. Trying not to appear too eager, he climbed the stairs.

Gordon Pettyjohn, the biggest of the owner's sons, blocked the entrance. He alone chose who passed inspection to gain admittance.

He scowled at Silas. "No chance I'm lettin' you in tonight, Deputy McKay."

Silas groaned. "Every damn time I show up you think I'm my brother, Gordon."

His expression didn't soften one iota. "Prove you ain't the deputy."

"Last time I was here, oh, round about November, I reckon, after the hall closed, you and I played four rounds of poker and we tied two games to two games. Rather than have a tiebreaker, we each drank four shots of whiskey and I am lucky that my horse knew the way home."

That's when Gordon grinned. "Glad to have you back, Silas, even though it's been too long."

"Been a rough winter."

"I hear ya." He angled his head toward the jar sitting next to him. "Buy in is a buck."

Another Pettyjohn's distinction: pay to play. "Sure." Silas handed over the coins.

"Got a faro table and a twenty-one table runnin' for those who ain't interested in the high stakes table."

"What's the high stakes table?"

"A tournament. Overall winners of the individual poker tables compete. Regular cash game until it's down to the last two players and they decide on the stakes."

Silas managed a bland expression despite his interest. "That's new."

"Been holdin' it monthly after my father saw how it was done in Deadwood over Christmas. Last time, the high stakes winner ended up with a pair of Colts. Month before that, winner ended up with a bull. Before that, winner got four hours at Ruby Red's." Gordon shrugged. "Keeps things interesting and the players around, drinkin' and makin' side bets even after they're outta the tournament, so it's worth it for us since we don't gotta provide the final payout."

"Smart."

"Get on in and get you a seat at the table. There's only three open chairs left." His eyes narrowed. "Fair warnin', you gotta have something other than money to offer if you're one of the last two players."

"I hear ya." Silas grinned. "I know exactly what I'll offer up."

Gordon nodded but his focus was on whoever was coming up the stairs.

Silas stopped at the bar for a drink, asking for beer rather than whiskey. He wondered what'd possessed him to tell Gordon a bald-faced lie: he had no idea what his final barter would be. His worldly possessions were few. His firearms weren't fancy enough to wager. His livestock options were limited unless he offered up cow/calf pairs. Since he was already Henrikson's hand, he couldn't hire himself out for a week's worth of cowboying.

He was half-tempted to forego the high stakes poker game and play a few hands of twenty-one. He'd come here with the intention of winning cash, not some unknown stake that might not be tradeable for the cash he needed.

That's when a deranged laugh echoed back to him.

"Look who cleaned up and headed to town, hopin' to clean up here too."

Zeke West.

Of course that dirtbag would be here on a Friday night. Probably just got paid.

Too bad they weren't playing for cash, because he'd love to take that mouthy fucker's money again.

"Are you playin', McKay? Or are you afraid that without your brother here you won't get away with cheatin'?"

Silas didn't respond even when every eye in the place turned his direction.

But the dealer at Zeke's table warned, "Another allegation of us allowing cheaters to play here, and Gordon will toss your ass out. Understood?"

Zeke nodded.

West sat at the far rear table with his bootlicker railroad buddies. Then Zeke spoke to them and they both got up, each relocating to different tables, which left the two open spots at Zeke's table.

A blatant challenge for Silas to play next to him.

Maintaining eye contact with Zeke, Silas took the last seat at the table directly in front of him—not the one by West.

Game on, asshole.

The men who'd come in behind Silas promptly filled the empty spots at Zeke's table.

The manager explained the rules: five card, one draw, ante increased by one every round, play continued until only one player remained at each table.

One table had a winner within ten hands.

The other four tables lasted longer.

There seemed to be more good-natured ribbing among this crowd than Silas was used to. He couldn't figure out if the men at his table were all just crappy card players, or were here for fun, or if he'd just gotten lucky with his cards.

You're always lucky at cards, Jonas's complaint echoed in his head.

When Silas outlasted the barber in the final hand, his tablemates' congratulations were genuine. They even promised to root for him as the representative of table two.

Silas studied the table one winner closely, outright dismissing him as real competition when he knocked back his second whiskey in five minutes.

Both of Zeke's buddies won their respective tables.

Zeke and another older gent were the last two players vying for the final slot.

Dealer shuffled and dealt.

West must've gotten a good card on the draw because he went all in.

He won…barely. Three of a kind—tens—over two pairs—kings and nines—but the blustering way he acted made him look like a fool.

The dealers dismissed everyone to the bar while they set up for the final game.

Silas allowed himself one more beer as he took stock of the situation.

Zeke and his buddies were talking among themselves. Without doubt Zeke was demanding his cohorts throw the game so the final players would be him and Silas.

The only concern on Silas's mind was what stake he'd offer. West would sneer at the offer of Silas's horse or any of his livestock. Since he'd already let Zeke beat the crap out of him in public without fighting back, he couldn't even suggest they mix it up for the entertainment of others as a potential stake.

Or you could purposely lose before becoming a final player, walk away and be out nothing.

He told Jonas's pesky voice of reason in his head to shut the hell up.

You know it won't end at the table regardless if you win or lose. Beating him is essentially you daring him to come after you. Don't give him the satisfaction. Please.

Great. Now Dinah's voice joined with his brother's.

Then maybe you oughta listen.

But Silas had a good feeling about his odds and he'd never backed down from a challenge to his skill as a card player. It amused him to decide on wagering the black suit Jonas had just given him. It'd smack Zeke's pride that Silas suggested a dirty, poor rancher dressed better than a highly paid railroad worker. It also relayed the message that he'd never give Zeke an option to take anything of worth or anything that mattered to him.

Gordon moved in next to him where he rested against the back wall. "I hear you and West have a history."

"Yep."

"This ain't Labelle, Silas."

"Meanin' I rely on my brother to ride to my rescue?" he said sharply.

"No, I'm sayin' we don't put up with brawling in here."

He snorted. Like he was the only cowboy in Wyoming who got into fights on the regular. "West prefers to hide in the dark and jump me when there ain't no one else around."

Gordon sighed. "Figured as much."

Silas scanned the crowd. "How's your relationship with Sheriff Eccleston?"

"Good. Why?"

"You might wanna alert him now that he'll have to settle a dispute between me and West tonight after I win. Because I guarantee that blowhard will accuse me of cheatin'."

"Fuckin' sore loser."

"Always." Silas drained his beer. "Fair warnin' to you. I won't throw the first punch, but I promise I *will* throw the last one."

Big talk. If it becomes physical, you'll take the first and the last punch.

Silas sauntered over to the table positioned in the middle of the room and took his seat.

Zeke immediately plopped into the chair opposite him.

His buddies flanked him; the youngest ended up on Silas's right.

Drunk player number one stumbled into the chair on Silas's left.

The rest of the previously eliminated players formed a circle around them.

Silas saw money exchanging hands as those players made bets on who'd win.

The dealer restated the rules. Five card, one draw.

Throughout the first six hands, Silas kept a close eye on Zeke, although anyone watching him would believe he ignored West completely.

And Silas did let Zeke win—mostly to keep Zeke's confidence level high.

Drunk player number one, with the fewest coins, went all in on hand eleven. With two pairs—jacks and queens.

Which Zeke joyfully trounced with three eights.

The drunk player swore he thought he'd had a full house.

That caused laughter to fill the room and cut the tension.

Two hands later Zeke's buddy with the lowest pile of coins bet it all on a flush.

Stupid move. Unless the flush had face cards, it was almost always a losing play.

The third player lasted three hands until he, too, bet it all. He actually had a decent hand—a full house with sevens and fours.

But it wasn't enough to beat Silas's cards—a full house with kings and tens.

No surprise it'd come down to the two of them.

Silas stacked his coins neatly and waited for Zeke to start mouthing off because he loved being the center of attention.

"So McKay, let me tell you about the exciting purchase I recently made."

He glanced up and feigned surprise. "How recent? I thought I won all your wages the last time we played."

"You did. But I make that much *every* week, so it wasn't the big loss for me it might've been for a rancher with no regular income."

Don't take the bait.

West played with his coins as he spoke. "Still, it stung, you bein' so *lucky* that night." He uttered *lucky* as if it were a curse word. "I thought that maybe if we spent more time together we wouldn't have this mutual loathing between us."

"Yeah, I don't see that happenin' anytime soon, so cut to the chase."

"I doubt our fellow players are aware of your obsession with buyin' land. I mean, the purchases are there on the county registers, but I don't think they know just how fast you snap it up, since you keep to yourself out in the middle of nowhere. Maybe you have an inside track when parcels come up for sale since your brother is a county employee."

"Jonas's job is to keep the peace, not to scout for land deals," Silas said coolly.

"Pity then that you didn't know about it, because an exciting opportunity was recently offered to me."

The bad feeling that started in his gut and was rarely wrong took root.

"I, too, would like a place to call home. An investment in my future and build ties to the land. So I can proudly say that creekside section, round about twenty acres once owned by Griffen and between you and Henrikson? Well, I bought it. You're lookin' at your new neighbor."

No. He wouldn't. West wasn't that goddamned vindictive to go behind his back and make an offer on land that was all but worthless to anyone but him or Henrikson.

But he was. The look on Zeke's face was smug to the point of evil.

Silas's guts squeezed but he affected a carefree grin. "Aww. I'm beginning to think you're a little sweet on me, Zeke darlin', given your obsession with me. In fact, I think you know more about me than even my sweetheart does."

The laughter that rang out turned Zeke's face dark red.

But Zeke regained control quickly. "Such a joker you are, McKay. But I'm glad you brought up the lovely Dinah. Because she is part of this game."

The hell she is. But Silas managed a droll, "You ever gonna quit flappin' your gums and state your stake instead of blatherin' on and stalling to save face?"

"Yes, by all means, let's get down to brass tacks. I'm offering up the land I recently bought that would make us neighbors. And since you don't own a single thing of value or interest to me, I'll let you put your sweetheart up as your stake."

Silas stood abruptly, anger filling every molecule of his being. "You shut your mouth. Don't you even suggest something like that, you dirty-minded motherfucker."

And Silas had played right into Zeke's hands while Zeke played it cool. "Simmer down. Since our fellow players like a wager that's interesting, I was only about to suggest that if I win, I'll expect your promise to break off your engagement with Miss Thompson. I heard you haven't even given her a ring yet anyway, so I'm being generous with *allowing* that as your stake."

Expressions of disbelief and laughter taunted him.

While everyone around them talked and laughed at the audacity of the wager, Silas leaned in so only Zeke could hear him. "Why are you doin' this?"

"Because you stole my life."

That made no sense even when that wasn't the first time this crazy asshole had said that to him. "What's that have to do with Dinah?"

"You used your injuries to trick her into believing I'm a violent monster and now you're with her instead of me. So I want her to know who the real monster is when she hears her intended is willing to gamble her future away for just another piece of dirt."

This guy was plumb crazy.

"And if I get up and walk away from this poker game?"

"You won't. You'd rather lose her than take a chance on havin' me for a neighbor for the rest of your miserable goddamned life."

That wasn't true...was it?

If it isn't, then forfeit right now.

But...this was all drama, all for show, all to make himself look like the most powerful man in the room. To get people talking about how audacious Zeke West was.

But won't they be talking about Dinah too?

Yes, but if West could showboat, then Silas could too. If he lost the bet—which wasn't likely—he could humble himself in the most public manner to get back into her good graces. It might take some time to win her back, but heck, they weren't even getting married until next year anyway.

Silas couldn't pass up his chance to get that land. Dinah would understand. Besides, by the time she heard about this wager, he could...slightly modify the details in the retelling. Tall tales got started this way by a bunch of drunken men. He'd downplay what happened and convince her to see the humor in it.

He hoped.

"So what's it gonna be, McKay?"

Adjusting his hat, Silas said, "Fine. I accept those stakes."

The din around them increased tenfold. Money exchanged hands between the spectators.

After several long minutes, the dealer shushed the audience.

Somehow Zeke had procured a piece of paper. He shoved it at Silas. "I want it in writing that should you lose, you will end your relationship with Miss Thompson as your ante in this game."

Silas scrawled those words across the page and signed it. Then he ripped the paper in half and shoved it back at Zeke. "I want it in writing that should you lose, you will turn over the deed to the aforementioned land immediately as your ante in this game."

Smirking, Zeke complied.

The dealer set aside the papers. "Bets are made. One hand, gentlemen. One hand, two draws, no wild cards, need an ace shown to me for a draw of four." Then he broke open a new deck of cards with a Chinese dragon image on the back so there'd be no chance of card switching.

That annoyed Zeke.

Silas eyed the long sleeves of West's suit coat, guessing he'd probably hidden a couple of cards up there. Contrary to Zeke's claims, Silas hadn't been kicked out of a saloon for cheating, but Zeke had.

The dealer shuffled half a dozen times. He cut the deck in half and set a half in front of each player. "Highest card determines who gets first card and first draw."

They flipped over their cards simultaneously.

Zeke flipped a nine of hearts.

Silas flipped a six of diamonds.

Another smirk from Zeke but Silas was relieved his opponent would have to draw first.

The dealer shuffled again and dealt Zeke, then Silas until they each had five cards.

Silas's heart thundered as he lifted the edges of his cards. Ace of diamonds, queen of clubs, queen of hearts, two of spades and jack of spades. Not the worst hand, but nothing but a pair of queens, and pairs didn't win hands.

Zeke threw down four cards and showed the dealer his hand.

So his opponent also had an ace. It was likely Zeke hadn't been dealt any face cards or he wouldn't have tossed four.

Silas slid his jack of spades and two of spades forward as his discards, signaling for two new cards. He peeked at his new cards, seeing the queen of spades and the jack of diamonds.

For the last draw, Zeke took two. He couldn't mask his grin.

Silas discarded just the jack of diamonds, wondering if he should've kept the jack of spades. Then he saw that his final draw was the last queen in the deck, the queen of hearts.

Somehow that seemed appropriate given what he was betting with.

Still, he frowned. His bastard opponent could gloat all he wanted, but odds were in Silas's favor that Zeke didn't have four kings because that was the only hand that would beat his.

"You don't look so confident, McKay," West taunted him.

Silas didn't respond because that's exactly what he wanted West to think. Then he shuffled his cards in his hand as if trying to reconfigure them.

West said, "Let's make a side bet." He pulled out a twenty-dollar bill and tossed it on the table. "An extra twenty to the winner."

"Pass. We've already made our bet. So let's get this over with."

Zeke tucked the money back into his outer front jacket pocket. "All right, *neighbor*, read 'em and weep." He milked the drama, turning over one card at a time.

Ace of clubs.

Ace of spades.

Ace of hearts.

He paused to let the crowd revel in their excitement.

Then he flipped over a ten of hearts and a ten of diamonds.

A full house, aces high.

Silas just stared at the hand.

"Go ahead and cry if you want."

Laughter.

Silas signaled to the bartender. "Two shots of whiskey."

"Doublin' up already, McKay?"

"Yep."

"You're gonna be the bigger man and offer me a toast?"

"Something like that."

The booze arrived and Silas held up the first shot glass. "Zeke West, the cockiest card player I've ever met." He threw back the whiskey, welcoming the burn. "Who once again proved that his cockiness ain't nothin' but a bunch of hot air." Silas flipped his entire hand over at once. "Read 'em and weep, West." Then he knocked back the second shot and raised the empty glass to Zeke. "Go ahead and cry if you want."

The room exploded with shouts and laughter and general melee.

Zeke stared at the winning hand in utter disbelief. Then he stood up and roared. "This was fucking rigged!"

Before West could throw aside the table and come after him, Sheriff Eccleston slapped his hands between them. "I heard there might be trouble, so I've been watchin' since the game started. And you listen to me, West. There will be *no* accusations of cheatin' or of Pettyjohn's rigging the game. McKay won fair and square. I saw it as did everyone else in this room."

"Of course you'd take his side," Zeke sneered. "His damn brother is one of your deputies."

"Don't matter. You lost. Don't make it worse on yourself by bein' a sore loser. You chose the stakes. You gotta live with them. So along those lines, I'd better hear of you visitin' the county courthouse in the next week and puttin' McKay's name on that land deed." He got right in Zeke's face. "We clear on that?"

"Yeah." Zeke retreated. After sending Silas a blazing look, he and his friends slipped through the crowd.

Then the sheriff came over and clapped Silas on the shoulder. "Heck of a card game, McKay."

"Thanks. I appreciate you comin' by. If I'da known West was here I'd've skipped this place tonight."

"I've heard you've tangled with him before."

"Last time I beat him at cards, he jumped me about an hour afterward and whipped up on me bad enough to send me to Doc's." No need to share why he'd let that beating happen.

The sheriff's eyes turned hard. "He the cause of them bruises I saw the day I mistook you for your brother?"

"Yes, sir."

"I ain't puttin' up with that kinda shit in my town. I'd likely toss you both in the jail since you both need to learn to act like adult men."

Silas nodded even when he knew it was a bunch of horseshit.

"You headed home?"

"I reckon. Had enough excitement for one night."

"The ride will give you time to think about how you're gonna tell your girl about the role she played in your winnin' hand."

"Ah, I'm hopin' to avoid that confession entirely."

The sheriff laughed. "Son, word of advice. She's gonna hear it from somebody. It'd be best if that somebody was *you*."

That was true. Plus, he'd won the land, but he hadn't won the cash needed to buy Dinah that ring, which was why he'd come to town in the first place. He sure as shootin' wasn't going home empty handed now.

"On second thought, maybe I will stick around for a bit and see if my luck holds."

That's when a folded note was hand delivered to him.

THIRTEEN

"**B**EA. I DON'T think this is a good idea."

"Darling, you look wonderful. Wearing a little lipstick and rouge won't turn you into a harlot." She snickered. "Well, *more* of a harlot than you've turned out to be, you cheeky thing, getting engaged three days after your first outing with the very persuasive Mr. McKay."

Dinah smiled...and smeared lipstick on her teeth. This waxy stuff was more trouble than it was worth.

"Although, I am disappointed you're not wearing his ring yet."

Why did everyone point that out? It wasn't as if a ring would make them more betrothed.

Wednesday night, Silas had surprised her and shown up for supper. Mrs. Agnes had felt well enough to dine with them and had slyly asked when he planned to make the engagement official and give Dinah a ring. Silas had quipped that it'd taken him this long to find the perfect girl; it'd take him longer than a week to find the perfect ring. Then he'd happily dug into the mahogany cake with raisins Dinah had made and changed the subject.

"Dinah? Are you all right?" Bea asked.

"Fine. Just woolgathering."

Bea moved in behind her, pressing her cheek to Dinah's as they faced the mirror. "Try darkening your eyelashes with this." She passed her a gold tube. "I'll be right back."

Dinah set the tube aside; with her luck she'd jab herself in the eye.

She'd visited Bea several times the past year, but this was her first foray into her friend's elegant bedroom. Half of the space belonged solely to Bea. Her hand-carved black walnut armoire had been aligned along the far wall (her husband's matching armoire echoed in placement across the room) with the dressing table positioned next to it and a velvet-tufted chair tucked beneath. This allowed Bea to sit in front of the gilded mirror with a view of the four-poster canopied bed behind her. She stored her "unmentionables" in a *chiffonier*, which Dinah decided was a fancy word for a tall, narrow chest of drawers.

She'd never put much thought into the type of luxurious life Bea was accustomed to as a banker's wife. Even the Talbots' temporary residence while their new house was under construction was much nicer than anyplace Dinah had lived. She might've been intimidated by Bea's wealth, if not for the fact Bea was genuinely sweet, fun to be around and the schemer of outrageous ideas that had not come to fruition, thank goodness.

Dinah still hoped to talk her friend out of the plan she'd concocted of dressing up for a ladies' night dinner at a restaurant in Sundance. During her years in Cheyenne, Dinah had dined out with her parents, but she hadn't enjoyed it. She remembered the food being weird and a meal taking forever. So she hadn't sought out dining experiences in Sundance.

"All right," Bea said, reentering her room, her arms piled high with garments. "Andrew bought these for me this spring when he had business in Chicago. Apparently these are all the rage among women in cities."

Bea tossed a bronze-colored bundle of fabric on the bed. She held up a black, bell-shaped skirt at her waistline. The billowing layers with a satin sheen changed the fabric from black to silvery gray. "What do you think?"

The skirt stopped mid-shin. "Are you adding a fabric underlay? Because as is, it's much too short."

She laughed. "Oh, that's not the most shocking feature. Watch." She ran her hand down the center of the skirt and midway it separated into two pieces, like men's trousers.

"Bea! Why are you showing me your bedclothes?"

"I'm not. These were designed for women's bicycle riding. See? When you're walking down the street they look like a normal skirt. But when you want to ride…voila! You can sit on the bicycle seat without having to yank up your skirt. Isn't it the cleverest thing?"

"It is," she admitted. Then she studied Bea. "I didn't know you had a bicycle."

"I don't. But these are perfect for horses too." She reached over and plucked up the bronze material, holding one skirt in each hand. "Which one do you want to wear tonight?" Bea gave her a once over. "The bronze for you, I think, since you're wearing brown boots."

"Beatrice Talbot. I am *not* wearing something like that out in public!"

"Yes you are. We *both* are. And we will be the absolute talk of the town."

That's what Dinah was afraid of.

"But…"

Bea dropped the clothes and snatched Dinah's hands. "Please? As a favor to me?"

"Tell me why this is so important to you."

"Because after the bank is built and our house is done…I'll be expected to act in the manner that's appropriate for a banker's wife. Not to mention how staid and upstanding I'll have to appear when children start arriving." Bea squeezed her fingers. "Now that you're betrothed, you needn't worry about a single night of mischief harming your chances of finding a suitable husband. We can have this one evening of fun and thumb our noses at anyone's disapproval. Plus, won't it be a hoot to show up in such fashionable clothes that no other woman is bold enough to wear? Can you imagine the looks on the faces of the ladies who've been condescending to both of us?"

Her friend did have a point.

"And the best part? If our men feel the need to chastise us for our behavior, we'll blame it on too much whiskey. Because isn't that what *they're* allowed to do?"

Dinah laughed. "You are taking that 'what's good for the goose is good for the gander' argument to the extreme. But you're right." She paused, her pulse racing at what she was about to suggest. "I have one request, however, if we are going for the shock factor."

"Name it. Anything."

"I want to attend the burlesque show at Timson's."

Bea let out a peal of laughter. "The prim schoolteacher has a wicked side. I knew it!"

For once, Dinah did feel wickedly carefree. She picked up the bronze skirt. "I do think this one is more suited to my coloring. Do you have a corset and a jacket I can borrow?"

THEY FINISHED THE entire bottle of plum wine as they finished dressing.

It was so much easier to ride a horse in a bicycle skirt. It sent Dinah's thoughts into how she could convert one of her own skirts into something similar.

After leaving their horses at the livery, Dinah and Bea strolled arm in arm through town. By the time they'd reached the baseball field, they'd caused quite a stir. Not only were people gaping at the split in their skirts, their short jackets were unbuttoned to show a glimpse of their beribboned corsets.

They delighted in drinking a mug of ale and predicting who'd approach them first.

Bea was so sugary sweet to Esther McCrae and her friend Antonia Gladswell, whose father owned the established bank in town, that Dinah wondered if honeybees were buzzing around them.

Since the baseball game held little interest for them, they left early and strolled down the shops on Sundance's main street. A few people even stepped out of the stores after they passed by—Dinah felt their stares, mostly focused on the fact they could see the tops of her boots since her skirt stopped below the knee.

Pettyjohn's restaurant had reserved a table for them in the back. The menu offered more recognizable dishes than the restaurants her parents' had frequented in Cheyenne. Dinah chose a lamb chop with mint jelly and roasted potatoes and an orange egg cream to drink.

With Bea's lively conversation, Dinah didn't mind that the meal stretched out. They'd just finished their dessert course, cups of warm chocolate and a caramel torte, when Bea noticed a commotion among the employees, and she wasn't shy about asking what had them all a-titter.

The young female server was eager to gossip. "You know there's gamblin' upstairs?"

Bea nodded as if she was aware but that was news to Dinah.

"There's some kind of poker tournament. Right now, the two men playin' against each other ain't doin' it for a money prize."

"Whatever are they playing for?" Bea asked.

"A fancy fella wagered a land deed. The other cowboy fella offered his betrothed."

A gasp from Bea. "What! You're sure he wagered a person?"

"Oh, oops sorry, no. The cowboy offered to break up with his girl-friend and never see her again. Ain't that just something? Everyone is talkin' about it. I mean *everyone*. I'd hate to be the lady whose intended wagered his life with her against a piece of land." She flitted off, shaking her head.

Dinah had gone still, her cup stopped halfway to her mouth as she stared at the server's back.

"Dinah? Darling, whatever is the matter?"

She slammed her teacup into the saucer. "She's talking about me, Bea."

"Oh pooh." Bea flapped her napkin. "The monthly tournament with the unusual wagers is old news at Pettyjohn's Saloon. Andrew and I have laughed about some of them."

"You're not hearing me." She paused and leaned in. "I told you about the bad blood between Zeke West and Silas. What I haven't told you—or anyone—is that Zeke came to see me last week."

Her eyebrows rose. "Alone?"

Dinah nodded.

"What did he want?"

"For me to spend one night with him in exchange for the land deed that he knew Silas wanted."

She gasped.

"I refused. I knew if I told Silas about West's offer—not just the bed-ding me part but the land purchase part—he'd go after Zeke and they'd end up brawling. I'd hoped by not telling Silas anything that Zeke would drop it and that'd be the end of it, but apparently it was just the beginning."

"Dinah. What are you going to do?"

"Wait until the game is over. Then I'll know which one of those bas-tards I'll deal with first."

When the server returned, Bea explained the situation and why they needed to know the outcome of the wager. Upon hearing this, the server brought them each a double shot of whiskey in a teacup—her version of tea and sympathy, apparently.

A raucous roar sounded above them, indicating the game upstairs had ended.

Normally Dinah would've shrank with embarrassment at being the topic of such gossip among the kitchen staff, the other restaurant patrons and the gentlemen upstairs watching the card game. But tonight, she burned with fury. She would not suffer this humiliation in silence.

The server's tentative approach to the table sent Dinah's heart pounding. "Ah…it appears the cowboy fella won the game." She grinned. "So he got the land *and* you."

"I guess we'll see about that, won't we?"

Bea snickered.

Dinah offered the server a smile. "Would it be possible for someone to deliver a note to the *cowboy fella* upstairs?"

"Yes ma'am. I'll bring you paper and a pencil."

After the server left, Bea said, "Are you sure this is a good idea?"

"No. But it wasn't a good idea for him to offer me up like livestock either."

Sighing, Bea signaled for more "tea."

Dinah scrawled her message, folded the paper in half and handed it to the cook who'd appeared.

"Do you want to head back to my house after this and forego the show at Timson's?"

"Absolutely not. We *are* going to that show." She lifted her cup to Bea's. "Besides, you wanted to be the talk of the town, and this will really get those tongues wagging."

AFTER SENDING THE note, Dinah paced in front of Pettyjohn's windows.

Hard strikes of bootheels alerted her to Silas's presence on the boardwalk and she wheeled around to face him.

She kept her stance wide and her hands on her hips, squaring off against him like a gunfighter.

Silas hadn't dressed up for his trip into town. He wore his work clothes with the exception of donning his dress hat. It annoyed her, that surge of pride she felt, seeing that he looked ten times better in his plain duds than the dandies who wore fancy suits.

Not helping, Dinah.

Silas's gaze started at her knees, where he saw the full shaft of her boots as well as the split in her skirt. Then that gaze traveled up, following the brass buttons on her russet and cream jacquard-patterned short jacket to where they ended at her cleavage. His eyebrows drew together. "What the devil kind of getup is that?"

"It's the latest fashion."

Closing the distance between them with four steps, he held up the piece of paper. "What bullshit is this? You're breakin' our betrothal in a fucking note?"

"You were willing to break it off with me for a chance at a piece of fucking land," she shot back.

His eyes widened at her cursing.

"Whatever the bullshit is between you and Zeke West…I'm done with it."

He deflated. "Dinah, darlin', it ain't what you think."

"No?" She stepped forward. "I think I was having a nice dinner in Pettyjohn's only to hear whispers from the employees about some asinine bet between two men upstairs, involving land and a woman's hand. Land, Silas! God. I hate that I immediately knew who would do that."

"You don't understand."

"You're right, I don't. But I *do* understand that the man I thought I'd pledged my life to was perfectly happy to gamble it—and me—away. So *you* should understand, Mr. McKay, that we are done."

That shocked him. Then his jaw ticked with anger. "No, we are *not* done. Not by a long goddamned shot." He latched onto her upper arms, but his focus was momentarily sidetracked by the up-close view of the tops of her breasts. A growling noise rumbled in his chest and then his hands moved as he attempted to button up her jacket.

"Stop it," she hissed, batting his fingers away. "You lost the right to touch me."

"But every other person in town gets to see them private parts of you?"

he demanded.

"Yes."

"Like hell they do."

Just to be ornery, Dinah stepped back and hastily undid the remaining buttons. Then she took off the jacket, dropping it on top of Silas's boots. Her chest heaved as she stood in front of him—and anyone in town who was gawking at the spectacle—in a peach satin and lace corset that barely contained her bosom.

"Christ almighty, woman, would you cover yourself back up!" He leaned down to retrieve her jacket.

"Don't you want to see what you won the rights to?" She flattened her hands on his chest, shoving him back a step. "Except in using me as part of your wager in this stupid feud with Zeke West, you lost me." Snatching the jacket out of his hands, she angrily put it back on. "Now if you excuse me, I have someplace else to be." She spun around and sashayed away.

"Dinah. Wait."

"No. Go to hell."

Silas spoiled her dramatic exit by sneaking in behind her, picking her up and throwing her over his shoulder. "I already told you woman, we ain't done."

"Put me down, you bastard!" She thrashed against him. "I mean it, McKay! I will kick your tiny bollocks—"

"Now that's just plain mean, sugar pie. You have no idea what size my bollocks are."

"I hate you!"

"No you don't."

"Yes I do! Put me down."

"Nope."

"I'll scream!"

"Go ahead."

More bootsteps thudded and Silas stopped.

"Everything all right, McKay?"

Fuming, Dinah tried to turn so she could see who he was talking to as if she wasn't hanging upside down like a side of beef.

"Yes, Sheriff. But as you can see, me'n my lady are havin' a bit of a row."

A male laugh. "I take it Miss Thompson heard about the wager?"

"Yes I did, Sheriff Eccleston, and I want this man arrested!" she yelled.

The sheriff crouched down so he could look her in the eyes. "I don't blame you for bein' upset. So how about a compromise? You hear him out. If you still want me to arrest him afterward..." He paused and frowned. "What exactly would I be arrestin' him for?"

"Stupidity," she snapped.

Sheriff Eccleston laughed. "Sorry to say it, but that ain't a crime. If it was, damn near everyone in the county would be in jail." He stood and clapped Silas on the shoulder. "Good luck. And keep the town's decency laws in mind when you kiss and make up or you *will* find yourself behind bars."

"Understood, Sheriff."

They'd reached the end of the walkway and Silas set her down.

Before she could bolt, he'd towed her around the edge of the building and pushed her up against it with his body. He put his mouth on her ear. "Settle down."

"Leave me alone, Silas."

"Not a goddamned chance in hell of that happening *ever*."

She closed her eyes and refused to look at him. It took every bit of her resolve not to cry.

"Will you listen to me?"

"Do I have a choice?"

"Yes, darlin', you do." Those rough-skinned hands framed her face. "Will you please open them pretty blue eyes and look at me?"

Dinah opened her eyes and glared at him.

"There's my girl."

"Say your piece."

"The wager wasn't my idea."

"Whose was it?"

"West's. And I didn't wager you. I wagered my happiness." His eyes searched hers. "The bet was if he won, I had to break it off with you."

"How is that not betting me?"

"Because it was *not* my choice. I didn't say, hey, *the only thing of value I have in my life is this beautiful, smart, perfect woman who's agreed to be my wife and losin' her would destroy me.* I'd planned on anteing up the suit Jonas gave me."

She was not letting the sweet words from that sly tongue distract her this time. "So you're thrilled that you finally got that creekside piece of land between yours and Henrikson's? Does it feel better to have won it than if you'd paid for it, especially since Henrikson passed on buying it when Griffen offered it to him first? What makes you *happier*, Silas? That you won't have to worry about Griffen ever running his sheep there? Or that you and Zeke won't be neighbors and he'll never be able to stop over and borrow a cup of sugar from me?"

Confusion darkened his eyes. "How did you know exactly where that land in the deed was and who owned it before Zeke bought it?"

This was why she didn't keep secrets. How was she supposed to believe that Zeke wouldn't have bragged that to Silas that he'd paid her a visit? Now she looked guilty.

"When?" he demanded with that quiet anger that scared her far worse than his blustering.

"A week ago."

He took a moment to breathe. "Why didn't you tell me?"

"Because West both warned me against telling you *and* encouraged me to tell you that he'd visited me when he saw I was alone at Doc's. He knew you'd be furious and go after him."

"That motherfucking cocksucking son-of-a-bitch. I'm gonna fuckin' kill him."

Dinah latched onto Silas's vest when he reared back, as if to leave. "That is *why* I didn't tell you."

"That's not your choice, Dinah."

"To keep you from starting yet another pointless fight with West and getting yourself hurt again? Yes, it is the choice *I* made to protect you, even from yourself, you idiot. You have no idea how out of control your anger is, do you?"

"Did. He. Touch. You?"

She shook her head.

Silas leaned in until they were nose to nose. "You're lyin'. Something else happened."

"Yes, something else did happen. Zeke told me you used to work for the railroad." Surprise flashed in his eyes. "Why didn't you tell me?"

"Because you made it clear how you felt about railroad men. I didn't wanna be lumped in with them. Especially not after he and I…" He snapped his mouth shut. "It don't matter."

"Yes, it does. Tell me the truth about why you and West hate each other."

He retreated. Took a moment to calm himself. "I couldn't afford to ranch fulltime so I applied for a part-time railroad job. About a month in, I got a new boss. Ezekiel West. He hated me from the start. I couldn't do nothin' right. Thing about railroad men is they expect your after-work hours belong to them too when you're out of town on a run. The nights we stayed in Gillette, we all went out on the town."

"I remember my mother used to complain about my father and his buddies living in each other's back pockets even when they weren't at the rail station."

"It's still that way. West liked to gamble. But he was terrible at it. I'd been playin' cards around the campfire since age thirteen so I'm damn good at readin' players. Anyway, first night out at the saloon with my new boss, I made the mistake of beatin' him at cards. He accused me of cheatin', and he and I had words. Then I was reassigned and I knew it was because I'd shown him up. So from that point on, anytime we ended up playin' cards, I let him win."

"Silas."

"Not only did I let him win, I never stood up for myself when he gave me what for on the job. Bastard had me cowed. I'll admit, my temper got the better of me one night. We started fightin' and I beat him so badly he ended up in the hospital. I lost my job—which I lied about to my brother, tellin' him I quit. Zeke has been gunning for me ever since.

"I haven't handled it well and he won't let it go. Now he's brought you into the middle of it. I hate how damn weak I am. I decided that even if I lost tonight, even if what I agreed to wager felt like humiliation to you, I could fix it. I could somehow win you back."

"You never even considered walking away from that wager he offered, did you?"

"I did when I heard both yours and Jonas's voices in my head. But I didn't listen. Now, I have to admit West hit it dead on; I lost you anyway."

Dear lord. Were his eyes filling with tears?

Silas curled into her—more childlike than she'd ever imagined a man who was a foot taller than her could pull off. "I'm sorry. Goddamn, Dinah, I'm such a sorry, selfish son of a bitch. You deserve better. I wish I would've walked away. I wish I had that damn time machine we read about and I could start this night over." His rapid exhalations gusted across her bosom. "I'd do anything to make this right."

"Anything?"

"Anything."

Dinah placed her hand on the back of his neck. His skin was clammy with nervous sweat. She tugged on his hair to get his attention. "Okay. There's a couple of things we need to settle between us to fix this."

He finally looked at her again, but wisely didn't speak.

"My condition for not breaking this engagement is this: no more fighting with Zeke West, for any reason, ever again. Ever," she repeated.

"You'd forgive me?" he asked hopefully.

"If I have that promise from you, then it would fulfill the first condition."

"I promise." Silas took her hand and kissed her knuckles over and over and over again, saying, "Never again," between each press of his lips. "What's the other condition?"

"Bea and I are attending the burlesque show at Timson's. While I'd like to seem daring, I don't know if two women showing up there unescorted is brave or stupid. So you'll be accompanying us—but you'll remain in the gambling area until the show is over, and then you will escort us back to Bea's house."

"Lemme get this straight; you're ordering me to…gamble?"

Her eyes gleamed. "Oh, gambling isn't the real reason you'll be flashing that cocky grin at the card tables. As you're playing, you will use that charm of yours to weave a new narrative about what really went down at Pettyjohn's. Yes, you won land; no, you didn't bet your future with your betrothed to get it. Figure out another 'prize' they'll believe. Showing your face—and mine—together will quiet any rumors. The sooner you do that, the better and the faster it'll all go away."

"Done." He grinned. "You are brilliant." He kissed her hard. "Brilliant and I'm luckiest man in the world for this second chance."

"Yes, you are. And the last condition is about my journal. I'm detailing our life together, so it's necessary to include the 'Silas won a piece of land in a poker game' as a family legend. But I'm exercising my right to *slightly modify* the event, so our future children, grandchildren and great grandchildren won't know that you wagered…your happiness with me."

"I'm good with that too."

She tilted her head back. "Since we're in public, a proper kiss will do. But next time we're alone? I expect the other improper 'kiss and make up' type of kiss that you showed me."

Smiling, he nuzzled her cleavage. "Liked that, did you?"

"Mmm-hmm." She puckered her lips. "Kiss me quickly."

"Nope. I'm gonna kiss you right."

And kiss her he did. By the time he finished, she was grateful for the brick wall behind her holding her up.

Silas straightened her clothes. "By the way, sugar pie, I love them britches you've got on. Feel free to wear them any time you want."

FOURTEEN

SATURDAY NIGHT DINAH hastily donned her apron outside the door to Doc's examining room as she juggled the hot teakettle.

An exasperated female voice said, "You're being ridiculous. I'm fine."

"You're bleedin', madam. Mrs. Mavis said she'd box my ears if I didn't bring you here and I'm way more skeerd of her than I am you," Jimmy blurted out.

So the midnight patient was Madam Ruby.

Dinah stepped beside Doc and poured the warm water into the ceramic bowl he'd placed on the table.

It'd been a long day for him and he looked a fright with his hair sticking up all over and his robe thrown on over his long johns. He dried his hands on a towel. "Dinah, dear, bring that lantern closer so I can see the damage to Miss Ruby's cheek."

Doc had rigged up a lantern in a long, milky-white glass tube that was much brighter than a regular lantern. He'd attached it to a base with a rope and pulley system so he could move it and adjust it to various heights. He turned the flame to high and light blazed across the space.

Miss Ruby's eyes were wide, her gaze moving between Dinah and Doc. She held a frilly lace handkerchief cloth to her face—it might've been ivory but now it was bright red.

"Turn your head, please."

Ruby dropped her hand and stared at the ceiling. Blood ran in a thin red stream from the apex of her cheekbone and dripped onto the table. The skin around the wound had already become swollen, making it difficult to see the size of the cut.

"Ruby, dear. Tell me how you got this gash."

Her gaze zipped to Jimmy then back to Doc.

Without missing a beat, Doc said, "Jimmy, wash your hands and go to the icebox. Break off a big piece of ice, wrap it in a clean rag and bring it to me."

"Yes, sir."

As soon as Jimmy was gone, Ruby said, "Thank you. Although I don't know why I feel the need to protect him."

"Because he's a good boy with a soft heart," Doc said as he began cleaning the wound. "Continue."

"We had a new customer. Traveling salesman of some type. He acted like a big spender and I sent him to Millie, who is my best girl. After he finished with her—they were in the room for about five minutes—he complained I was cheating him with a new whore. He claimed that a seasoned whore would've spent the entire fifteen minutes arousing him. Then the snooty bastard demanded his money back or he wanted his remaining ten minutes with an experienced whore. Namely…me. I refused, told him to leave and never return. He backhanded me with the finesse of a man used to striking a woman. Of course he wore a big, tacky ring to inflict more damage."

Dinah was absolutely riveted and repulsed.

"Dangerous business you're in," was all Doc said.

"It's been a long time since I've personally had to deal with this. Millie was so outraged by his insult to her skills and that he'd dared to hit me, that she kicked him in the bollocks."

Doc winced. "And then?"

"I grabbed my Winchester and poked him in the ass with it until we reached the door to Sackett's. Blubbering fool was bent over, clutching his cock when I left him with Dickie. Then Mrs. Mavis called for Jimmy and forced him to bring me here."

"It's likely no surprise that you'll need stitches. Six, maybe seven."

Dinah's stomach turned over. Ruby was a stunningly beautiful woman with flawless skin. No pockmarks, or scars at all. She didn't even have wrinkles, so it was impossible to gauge her age. She had to be devastated by the fact her perfection would be ruined.

But Ruby merely sighed. "Get on with it then."

Doc's hand trembled when he reached for another cloth.

While Doc was able to stitch a gut-shot man back together and save his life, that didn't mean his stitches were anything besides serviceable. With the late hour and the fact Doc had already had a full day of delivering a baby, and resetting a broken bone, he shook with exhaustion. He'd sew Ruby up, not without care, but to the best of his ability.

And Dinah's sewing ability far exceeded his.

That's when Dinah noticed a single tear rolling from the corner of Ruby's eye before it disappeared into her hairline.

So the madam wasn't as unaffected as she pretended.

Dinah set her hand on Doc's arm. "Doc? If it's only a few stitches, let me do it."

Both Doc and Ruby stared at her.

She locked her gaze to Ruby's. "I'm a seamstress and I specialize in fine embroidery. No offense to Doc, but I will make much finer, smaller stiches than he does, so the chances of scarring will be less. Provided you follow post-surgical infection prevention."

"Have you ever stitched on skin?"

Dinah nodded. "One of my students sliced her hand open and Doc was gone so I stitched her up. I've helped Doc a few other times."

"Dinah, dear…you're sure?" Doc asked.

"Yes. You're exhausted. You've already cleaned it. I just need to numb the area and dose her with a relaxant, right?"

"Right." He fixed his gaze on Ruby. "Dinah is being square with you, madam. She'll do a better job than I would in this case. She's competent and compassionate…but the choice is yours."

Ruby looked between them. "I'd rather not look like Frankenstein's monster, so it appears I'm entrusting you, Miss Thompson."

Dinah smiled. "While I adored Mary Shelley's story, I promise I won't try to replicate Victor Frankenstein's work on your face."

Jimmy returned with the chunk of ice, wrapped in cloth.

Doc placed it on Ruby's cheek. "Ten minutes ought to numb it. What relaxant do you prefer?"

"Rum."

"Dinah. Two full shots."

"Yes, Doc."

Doc and Ruby murmured in low tones while Dinah prepped the surgical supplies. Doc used both a sewing hook and a needle, but both of them were too large for such delicate work. So she excused herself and returned to her room for a better needle.

By the time she'd scrubbed her hands and sterilized the needle, Doc declared the area of skin numb enough.

He patted Jimmy on the shoulder. "Come along. There's pie leftover from supper. Then you can stretch out on the couch until it's time to escort Madam back to town."

Dinah inhaled a deep breath before she settled on the stool next to Ruby's head. "Fair warning; the first stitch is the worst. Hold very still."

"I will."

It's just a thick piece of fine leather, Dinah told herself as she poked the needle inside the bottom edge of the wound.

Ruby hissed out a breath and said, "Goddamn that man's little prick straight to hell."

Thankfully the only thing that moved were her lips.

Dinah blotted the blood that welled out of the center. "That's more to the point than Silas's outburst the last time he was in here."

"If I hadn't seen Silas's injury firsthand the night of the blizzard, I might've believed he'd injured himself so he could spend more time with you," Ruby offered.

"Oh, he did that once too." She paused. "Thank you for taking the risk and bringing him here in that snowstorm."

"Better here than in one of my rooms where I would've had to care for him," Ruby retorted. "And you're welcome."

"He was an impatient patient. But I didn't mind." She inserted the needle again, pressing the skin and pulling the thread simultaneously.

"Holy mother of god, that hurt just as much as the first stitch," Ruby said through clenched teeth.

"Yeah, I kinda lied about that. They're all gonna hurt." Dinah tugged on the thread, better aligning the skin for the next stitch. "Is this the first time you've had stitches?"

"Yes," she hissed out. "But not the first time I've been on the receiving end of a man's fists."

"I can't imagine. Did you report him to the deputy?"

Ruby released a husky, bitter laugh. "Miss Thompson. Whorehouses are illegal. There's plenty of folks that'll say I only reaped what I sowed."

"Not Deputy McKay. He's a good man."

"He *is* a good man, but that doesn't change the fact I am a lawbreaker. Ow, motherfuck that hurts."

She paused for moment.

"Besides, I can't run to a man to save us every time another man raises his hands to me or one of my girls. I'm the one *they* run to. And to be honest, I'm glad that idiot struck me and not Millie."

The wound had started oozing again. Dinah reached for the ice. "Hold this here. Cold slows the bleeding." She figured Ruby could use the break. Doc's estimate of the number of stiches was about half as many as it'd actually take. "Would you like another shot of rum?"

"Yes, please."

Dinah handed her the glass and Ruby lifted her head only enough to drink and swallow.

Silence stretched between them.

Finally Ruby sighed. "I'd rather we keep talking."

"About?"

"Anything to keep my mind off of this."

"Your dress is gorgeous." The burgundy velvet was off the shoulders with cut away cap sleeves. A black silk horizontally pleated bodice showcased the tops of her breasts and the deep valley between them. The low and formfitting waistline of black lace had been sewn atop the velvet, giving that section of the dress the appearance of an entirely different color. The skirt wasn't voluminous, in keeping with the latest slimmer style.

"Thank you. I reworked the top and cut enough fabric from the skirt I could almost make another dress out of it."

"You sew?"

Ruby turned her head and looked at Dinah. "Out of necessity, yes. No dressmakers in Labelle and the ladies' shop in Sundance refused my patronage. Their loss. I have four women to dress who adore pretty things, so I've learned to adapt."

"Is it offensive if I ask how you became a madam?"

"Seeing how you're fixing my face and I've had enough rum not to care what you think of me, I'll grant you the true sordid saga of Ruby Redmond."

That barbed comment got Dinah's back up. "Should I thank you for lumping me in with the other judgmental idiots who live here? Because you're not the only one who's been subjected to ugliness and rumors, Miss Redmond."

Ruby's eyes turned sharp even beneath the glassy effects of the rum and pain. "I like to hear you snap back, Miss Thompson. Most women are too flustered in my presence to say much of anything. Or they're frothing pure venom out of their mean mouths. There's usually no in between."

"I'm not bragging when I say I'm not like most small-minded women in this town." She paused. "And please. Call me Dinah."

"Okay, Dinah. Where are you from originally?"

"Cheyenne."

"What brought you out here?"

"Money. Frontier teachers make more. I've been on my own for the most part since I was thirteen."

"Me too."

Dinah's focus dropped to the ice pack and she narrowed her eyes. "If you can't keep that where it's supposed to be, we'll have to stop talking."

Ruby smirked and adjusted the ice. "Better?"

"Yes. Now my life history is boring. Tell me the sordid saga."

"My parents joined the throng of people migrating to Deadwood, intending to get rich striking gold, except they got there too late. I was ten, my brother Eddie was fifteen."

"Where did your family move from?"

"Minnesota. For two years we lived in a miner's camp and when the fever went through, it took both my parents. Eddie and I survived the fever and the mining camp for another year. My brother had bigger aspirations than scrabbling in the dirt for gold or felling timber. And caring for his sister wasn't in his plans. So he sold me to Madam Marie of the infamous Deadwood Gold Nugget brothel."

Dinah's mouth dropped open.

"At the time I was thirteen, but Eddie told Marie I was sixteen. I'd developed a womanly shape early so that was believable. Marie had a harder time believing I'd retained my virginity living in a miner's camp.

Until I told her I dressed in baggy men's clothes, forewent baths and didn't venture from our campsite. Our parents had been savvy enough to pick a spot against a hill with a small cave. The only reason we survived the winters was because that dirt cave kept us dry and out of the wind and snow. The front section under the canvas offered a windbreak for a campfire."

"You're probably numb enough." Dinah removed the ice pack. "Keep talking."

Ruby faced the ceiling but kept her eyes closed. "Eddie worked odd jobs that year it was just the two of us. He hunted and fished. I cooked what he caught. I hauled water and if no one was around I hunted for berries and other edibles in the forest."

She froze when the needle pierced her skin and Dinah followed it with a quick tug of thread. "And?"

"And we were barely surviving. So maybe I should've been more upset when Eddie dumped me and took off. But at the Golden Nugget I had regular baths with warm water. I had two meals a day. I could choose from dozens of fancy gowns to wear. Other women fussed over me, braiding my hair, calling me little sister. Telling me I was pretty. Heady stuff for a thirteen-year-old girl who'd endured two years masquerading as a boy. Madam Marie gave me a frank discussion of what physical acts would be expected of me as a whore. For a month, I watched sex through one of the hidden peepholes, in a carnal education of every possible sex permutation. The ladies taught me how to flirt and play coy. How to be bold. How to fake an orgasm."

Dinah flinched at that phrase, jerking the needle harder than she'd planned. "Sorry. I just…"

"Wasn't expecting the dirty details? Honey. That's part of my story. How I learned to do all of the dirty things men love better than the rest of my house sisters is the reason I ended up a madam and not just another two-bit whore. That said, the only choice Marie allowed me was *which* man got to buy my virginity. I impressed her when I informed her that I should choose three men, not just one, since I had three places on my body that had never taken a man."

When Dinah went still, Ruby smiled. "No shame in being a virgin, darling, and not knowing those three places are cunt, mouth and ass."

"Men…I mean, I knew about them using the mouth, not the

ah…other one."

"Ass fucking is a particular favorite of married men because most wives refuse to allow it. That's why that service costs them more money."

Dinah must've blushed to the roots of her toenails. Somehow she made the next stitch with a steady hand.

"I was a working girl for Madam Marie until five years ago when she gave me her blessing to strike out on my own. Beulah already had a whorehouse—not up to Madam Marie's standards, but I had no interest in competing with Gigi and her sole proprietorship. I found it unusual a town the size of Sundance didn't have a bawdy house. Then I realized the Sundance City Council would've run any woman out of town before building construction started. Luckily Darby Sackett and his brother had a falling out and Darby wanted to open his own place in Labelle. He bought the existing saloon and agreed to let me add a boardinghouse onto it and create an entrance into my place with a door on the second floor. No one tried to run me out of town. In fact, the community—or at least the men in it—embraced the idea of a whorehouse because construction only took one month, and we were open for business."

"Do you ever worry about having a falling out with Darby?"

"We're both making too much money. But it could happen eventually, I suppose."

"Just three more stitches to go."

Ruby frowned. "How many have you already done?"

"Nine. They're small."

A few quiet moments passed as Dinah pressed a cloth to the wound to quell the bleeding before she finished stitching.

"I take it you've forgiven Silas for his poker game bet?"

She studied Ruby's placid face. "That happened in Sundance. Just last night. How did you hear about it?"

"People talk."

"Who talks?" she demanded. "And where? If you mean that Silas has been in your—"

"No, no, darling, it wasn't Silas telling bordello tales. I actually over-heard Jonas talking about it. It was clever for you to send Silas right back into the thick of possible rumors."

An immediate burst of anger swamped her that Silas's brother was gossiping about the incident. Then she realized that Ruby had called

Deputy McKay by his first name, as if they were on familiar terms. So after Silas had confessed to his brother...maybe Jonas hadn't been gossiping to anyone but Ruby. "To answer your question, yes, I've forgiven Silas. It might've been different had the wager come from Silas first, but Zeke West created the situation. And I demanded Silas end their feud as a condition of forgiveness." She pinched the skin together and quickly made the final stitch. After tying off the thread and wiping away fluid, she bent closer to peer at her handiwork. Evenly spaced stitches, not too tight. "Done."

"Thank the heavens."

"You can sit up. But keep the ice on it for ten minutes at a time or until it melts. It'll help with the swelling." Then Dinah busied herself tidying up. She'd return in the morning and scrub the surfaces and douse them with boiling water, but she was too tired to deal with it tonight. When she turned around, Ruby was studying her.

"You're free to go. Keep the wound clean and Doc will want to remove the stitches in ten days."

"Thank you. Truly."

"You're welcome."

"If there's anything I can do for you..."

There is. I have questions. Specific questions.

No. She couldn't.

Yes. Just ask her. She offered. And when will you ever get another chance to get firsthand carnal knowledge from an expert willing to share?

Still...Dinah, hesitated, keeping her focus on the same spot she'd been scrubbing for a very long minute.

Then Ruby's throaty laugh echoed through the small space. "Go ahead and ask me, Dinah."

"Ask you what?"

"You know. 'The' question. Don't be shy."

Dinah folded her arms over her chest and met Ruby's curious gaze. "All right. I'm a virgin. Silas and I have kissed and touched and...stuff. Doc has some detailed human anatomy books as well as a few explicit novels I've read. I have a grasp of the mechanics of what goes on between a man and a woman, but how do I keep Silas happy enough in our bed beyond the first year or so that we're married that he won't want to visit a whorehouse?"

Ruby laughed. "That's a much better question than the one I usually get."

"Which is what?"

"*If my husband shows up at your whorehouse will you please refuse to take his money?*" She made a face. "It's not my job to monitor someone's husband. And some men desperately love their wives, but they also want sexual acts their wives won't do." She shrugged. "I don't judge. I definitely don't turn away customers. I run a business. Selling pleasure is no different than selling anything else. So my first question for you is…do you like how you feel when you and Silas have kissed and touched?"

"Yes. Very much."

"You're what…nineteen? Twenty?"

"Twenty."

"Since you're on your own here, I'm guessing it's not the worry of parental disapproval holding you back from dispensing with your maidenhead. Maybe you're religious, I don't know. What I *do* know is it's solely your decision whether you decide to fuck Silas before marriage or after your vows. But once you're in that intimate partnership with him, *talk* to him. If he does something you don't like, don't immediately freeze up and say *no*. Suggest trying something different that you *do* like. Becoming sexually compatible is work, but sex is not a chore. It is a lovely intimacy like no other. It's supposed to be fun and raunchy and passionate and sweet…but it doesn't have to be all of that at the same time."

Dinah expelled a nervous burst of laughter. "Thank you. Since Silas and I started this…*lovely intimacy*…I don't have anyone to talk about this."

Ruby gave her a soft smile. "I'm glad you asked for advice. Nothing that happens in private between a man and a woman is dirty if they both want to do it."

"So noted."

"The last thing I'll tell you is to know your own body. Because if you aren't familiar with what gives you pleasure, how can you tell Silas what you need?"

She nodded because that did make perfect sense.

"It's late. I appreciate you stitching me up with such care."

"You're welcome. And don't worry that I'll blab far and wide about this incident. I'm the epitome of discreet."

"Says the woman who had a screaming match with Silas McKay on Main Street in Sundance, on a Friday night," Ruby said dryly.

Dinah rolled her eyes. "A different situation that called for zero discretion on my part since the man had already turned me into a public spectacle."

"Don't let him smother that fire inside you, Dinah."

"He won't. I think he appreciates that his charm doesn't always work on me." She paused in the doorway. "I'll send Jimmy out to escort you. Take care, Miss Ruby."

FIFTEEN

L ATE SUNDAY MORNING Jonas stormed into Sackett's Saloon.

The place wouldn't get busy until later, so no one stopped him from hoofing it up the stairs to the second floor. No one manned the door between the saloon and the whorehouse, so he just waltzed right into Ruby Red's social parlor.

Mrs. Mavis glanced up from the book she was reading as she lounged on a red and gold chaise. "Is there a reason you're bustin' in here when we ain't open for business yet, Deputy?"

"I need to speak with Miss Ruby immediately."

She opened her mouth to protest and he cut her off.

"I know she's here. I just saw her in Robinette's." *And she fucking ran from me.*

"She left word she wasn't to be disturbed."

"Tough." He pointed at the bell pull that was a direct line to Ruby's rooms. "You can ring her. I'm headin' down." Without waiting for a response, he hustled through the hallway that housed the working rooms, stopping to open the door that led to the stairs. A narrow ladder rose up to the wide attic trapdoor to the third-floor loft where the girls lived. A cramped staircase opened into a small kitchen behind the boarding house's street side entrance. Jonas cut to the left and saw the door to Ruby's private rooms was still closed.

He knocked politely. But he warned, "Don't think to leave me hangin' out here, or I *will* beat this damn door down."

The lock clicked on the other side, but she didn't open the door.

So Jonas did.

Once he was inside, he turned the key behind him. Then he noticed Ruby had her back to him.

She'd clenched her hands into fists at her sides. "I do not appreciate your high-handed behavior, Deputy."

"That's what you think this is?" He moved in behind her and curled his hands over her small fists, hating that she flinched when he touched her.

"That's what it *was* in Robinette's."

Jonas hated that the only time Robinette allowed Ruby to shop was on Sundays when "decent folk" were at church. That was the first place he'd gone after getting off the train this morning. His heart had skipped a beat upon seeing her through the windows. He'd ambled in, nodded at Robinette as he started his own shopping. Putting a loaf of bread, a wheel of cheese, a pint of cider, and a cake of soap on the counter. Then he'd wandered down the aisle where Ruby had been browsing.

She'd worn a drab brown coat and a matronly bonnet that covered her glorious hair and kept her face in shadow. She'd placed a bottle of ointment and a tin of tooth powder in her basket, as well as a thick stack of white fabric and a spool of thread.

"Mornin', Miss Ruby," he said after sidling up to her.

"Good morning, Deputy." She didn't offer anything else, just kept running her fingers over the bolts of colorful fabric.

He put his hand over hers and murmured, "I missed you."

Ruby eased her hand away from his. "It's been less than a day."

"Did you miss me?"

"I missed specific parts of you." She ducked her head to hide her smirk.

Sassy little woman. "Can I guess what parts?" he whispered closer to her ear.

"Tend to your own shopping, Mr. McKay."

"I am. I wanted to ask if you've hidden licorice whips in the bottom of your basket?" If she hadn't treated herself to her favorite candy, he'd add some to his order.

"Why? Have you been bad and need a whipping?"

"Suggesting that will get your ass paddled for sure, Ruby girl."

The bell on the door rang and she'd automatically turned to see who'd entered.

That's when Jonas saw the black stitches and swollen skin marring her cheek. Without thinking, he took her chin in his hand. "What the hell happened to you?"

Ruby jerked away from him. "Nothing."

"Goddammit, Ruby—"

"Stop," she hissed. "You're causing a scene."

"Oh, you ain't seen nothin' yet. What happened?"

She whirled around and strode up to the counter, setting down her basket. "Mr. Robinette, put this on my account and please have Jimmy deliver these to the boardinghouse later today."

Then she all but ran out of the store.

He'd forced himself not to run after her.

So here they were.

Jonas pressed a kiss to the top of her head. "I'm sorry. Will you please tell me what happened?"

Ruby sighed. "A customer didn't like what I told him. He lashed out with his fists. I'm fine."

No, sweetheart, you ain't even close to fine. "Will you turn around and look at me?"

"It was a long night and I'm still tired. It'd be best if you just left."

"Darlin'—"

"I'm not in the mood for private entertainment, Jonas."

Stung, he let his hands fall away. "I didn't come here to fuck you."

"Then there's no reason for you to be here at all, is there?" she said coolly.

A laugh rumbled out. "Gonna hafta do better than that to chase me off." He gently turned her around.

She didn't fight him. Nor did she fuss at him when he tipped her chin up to get a better look at the gash on her cheek, but she did close her eyes.

Jonas hissed in a breath. "Still hurts?"

"It throbs and I swear I can feel the skin growing back together."

"Who stitched you up?"

Her eyes opened. "Why do you ask?"

"Because they did a damn good job." He let his thumb sweep across her cheek below the stitches. "Bet in a year or two you won't have much of a scar."

"Your soon-to-be sister Dinah sewed me up. She shooed Doc out and claimed as a seamstress she'd do a better job." Ruby's eyes searched his. "You've seen men patched up before. How does this compare?"

"It doesn't. Like I said, it looks great. It's hardly swollen either."

"I kept ice on it last night."

"Did your customer get shots in anywhere else?"

"Not besides at my establishment. He was unhappy with Millie's service and when I refused to refund his money, he backhanded me. Darby and Dickie escorted him out. He's not a local so I doubt I'll see him again."

"Good." Jonas's gaze roamed over every inch of her face. "Now that that's out of the way...can I kiss you hello?"

Ruby moved into him and said, "I need this first." She pressed her unmarked cheek against his chest and wrapped her arms around him.

He rested his chin on the top of her head and breathed her in as he gathered her close.

They stayed like that for a long time.

When she tilted her head back, he covered her mouth with his. Giving her tenderness. Sweetness. And she lapped up every bit of his gentle care, clinging to him, not immediately trying to turn up the heat between them like she usually did.

Before Jonas lost his head completely and they ended up in her bed, he slowed the kiss to soft smooches and a fleeting glide of his lips across hers. He whispered, "I missed this."

She murmured, "So we've both said."

That was the closest she'd ever gotten to admitting that she'd missed him too.

"Spend the day with me."

Ruby leaned back and squinted at him. "Why do I get the feeling you don't mean here in my rooms?"

"Because you're smart." He kissed her nose. "Let's go for a ride together."

"Jonas—"

He silenced her with a kiss. "No one will see us, if that's what worries you. I've got a spot in mind on Silas's land where nobody can find us."

"What would we do?"

"You could bring a blanket and we could have us a picnic. I'll even bring the food."

Again, those amazingly blue eyes of hers studied him. "This is important to you."

"Yes, darlin', it is."

"Why?"

"It's a beautiful day and I wanna share it with you. Just us."

"Okay."

He grinned at her quick agreement. "Great. I'll meet you on the backside of Doc's place between the woods and the creek in one hour."

"All I'm supposed to bring is a blanket?"

"And your naughty, lovely self." He kissed her nose. "You won't regret this. I promise."

JONAS WAS HALF afraid Ruby wouldn't show up.

But she came into view on a horse he recognized from Blackbird's Livery. For the first time it occurred to him that she probably wouldn't have the need for her own horse. She rarely left the boardinghouse—not that there was much going on in Labelle anyway—and she wasn't welcomed in Sundance. That increased his determination to make today extra special for her.

As soon as her horse was next to his, she said, "Deputy, can we not race these animals wherever you're planning to take me? I'm not a very experienced horsewoman. Micah said this was his easiest mount."

"We'll take it slow and enjoy the scenery, all right?"

She nodded.

They meandered along and he was grateful for this rare glimpse of her and her sense of wonder.

It amused him when she slowed to ooh and aah over wildflowers. She laughed when a fish jumped in a placid section of the stream. "It's like they're taunting us for not having fishing poles."

"Do you fish?" he asked.

"My brother did when we lived at the Deadwood camp. He didn't have much success because there were a lot of miners trying to catch their food. He did better with hunting and trapping. How about you? Do you fish?"

"Only when there are no other options. I had enough seafood when we lived in Boston to last me a lifetime."

She smirked.

"What?"

"Looking at you all cowboyed up atop your fancy horse, wearing a hat, vest, gun and badge, I forget that you were raised a city boy."

He snorted. "That seems a lifetime ago."

"No desire to ever return to the big city?"

"Not a single one." He cut around a rock outcropping and turned to watch to make sure her horse followed his.

"Sometimes I think my life would be easier if I lived in a big city," she mused.

"Probably. Bein's you don't consider yourself much of a horsewoman," he teased.

"I haven't had much opportunity to become one," she retorted. "In the hours I'm not running a business, I can't saddle up and indulge in a long ride. Not only because I'd get hopelessly lost, but riding by myself isn't a good idea for me even more so than other single women." She snapped the reins when her horse seemed more interested in stopping to eat than moving along.

Jonas would take her riding every day if she'd let him. He didn't offer, knowing that would get her back up.

"So thank you for today, Jonas. This truly is a peaceful place."

He looked around. "It is, ain't it? Silas has a vision for the McKay Ranch. As much as I hate to admit it, he's gone about his land purchases the right way." Another snort. "With the exception of the card game with Zeke West. But to be honest, Zeke got what he deserved in bein' dishonest and double dealin' with our neighbor. That just ain't right."

"I noticed you said 'our' neighbor. Does that mean Silas has convinced you to spend more time ranching?"

"Nope. He's got the name McKay on the deeds he owns, which ain't uncommon when families stake claims, officially puttin' just their surname down. Anyone over the age of twenty-one can claim one hundred and sixty acres, and naturally, any family that settles wants their land adjoining. Silas did the same for us a little over four years ago when we turned twenty-one."

Ruby reined her horse to stop. "So how much of what I can see is McKay land?"

"All of it. Well, at least what we've been ridin' on since we followed the creek."

Her eyes widened. "Jonas. How much land does Silas have?"

He clucked his tongue at her. "Greenhorn move, woman. You don't ask a man the size of his spread or how many head of cattle he runs."

"Is that against some 'code' of the West?"

"Nope. It just ain't considered polite. It's like askin' a lady her age."

"Ah. Understood. Thank you for the ranching etiquette lesson."

He wheeled his horse around, taking in a three-hundred-and-sixty-degree view. "Just so you know...in this part of the country, a cattleman needs roughly thirty acres per cow."

"Thirty acres for *each* cow?"

"Yep. Cattle need to eat a lot to get fat for market and ranchers want them grazing when there's grass available. Winter months are easier on the ranchers in some respects because the livestock needs hay to survive, so they'll herd together in closer quarters rather than bein' spread out lookin' for a food source. But if you can't grow enough hay to get your herd through the winter, then you've gotta buy it, and there goes part of the profit."

"Listen to your cattleman speak," she teased.

"It's the life I lived for many years. I still got one boot in the world most days." He pointed to a line of scrub oaks bordering the creek. "That's where we're goin'." He spurred his horse and headed for the biggest tree.

Ruby followed at a more sedate pace.

Jonas helped her dismount. Then he removed the saddlebag. "If you wanna set up in the shade under that tree, I'll deal with the horses."

"Deal with them...how?"

"Gotta take the bits outta their mouths so they can eat and drink."

"Do you tie them up?"

He shook his head. "My horse ain't gonna bolt. If yours does for some reason, well, darlin', I *did* wrangle livestock for a livin', so I can catch a fat, slow mare pretty easily."

She might've murmured, "I'd sure like to see that," before she turned away.

When he returned, he saw she'd spread out a quilt. She'd taken the food out of his saddlebag and set it on a flat rock.

She had her hands on her hips as he approached. "You are sure that no one will be riding along and catching us out here?"

"Ain't no one gonna bother us, Ruby."

"Good. Then I'm taking off these blasted hot clothes."

Jonas watched slack-jawed as Ruby undressed.

She unhooked her skirt, stepped out of it and laid it in the grass. Then she unbuttoned her shirt and tossed it aside. On her upper half she wore a plain white shift that left her arms and shoulders bare and exposed her skin down to the tops of her breasts. On the bottom half she wore pantalets that ended above her knee. She plopped down and removed her lace-up boots and stockings. She fell back onto the quilt, her limbs akimbo, toes wiggling as she sighed gustily. "This is more like it."

He let a warm, giddy rush of possessiveness flow through him. No one else got to see her like this, relaxed and carefree. Shadows and sunlight dappling her exposed flesh, a breeze tousling her hair and a secret smile curling her lips.

"Are you just gonna stand there staring at me, Deputy? Or are you planning on joining me?"

"Can't blame a man for bein' addle-brained with a beautiful half-nekkid woman spread out before him in a private feast."

She laughed. "God. I love that sweet-talkin' almost as much as your dirty talk." She propped herself up on her elbows. "Did you bring a knife?"

"It's in the bottom of the left saddlebag."

He undid his gun belt and set it on the ground. His vest followed. Then he removed his hat, boots and socks and lowered next to her.

She'd sliced wedges of cheese, nestling the chunks into the pieces of bread she'd torn off. She handed him a piece and a dark brown bottle with a flip top.

"What's this?"

"Wine." She opened up a red bandana between them. "I brought plums and honey corncakes too."

"Thanks." Even though he wasn't a huge fan of wine, he took a swig from the bottle. His eyes widened and he took another sip. "Dang, darlin'. That is good."

"Mrs. Mavis makes it special for us from the fruit she has leftover in the fall. We girls hoard it. That is my last bottle."

"Then I am grateful you're sharin' it with me."

Tiny, sweet plums, sour bread and tangy cheese, golden, crumbly honey-cakes, all washed down with spiced fruity wine and shared in the sunshine with the woman he loved—it was the best meal he'd ever had.

After they'd stuffed themselves, they stretched out on the quilt. Jonas reveled in how easily Ruby snuggled into him, her head on his chest, her legs entwined with his.

She made a soft humming noise. "I love this."

And I love you.

He stayed quiet and kept caressing her back.

The food, the wine, the warm woman at his side and a cool breeze drifting over them from the creek lulled him into a peaceful place.

Content, he dozed off. Ruby had too, he noticed, when a hawk's cry awakened him. He turned his head and saw both horses still grazing in the meadow between the hills.

Ruby stirred. "I guess I was tired."

"Yep. The snoring gave it away."

She poked him in the side, and he laughed.

"I nodded off myself."

"How was your trip to Gillette with Silas?"

"Good. He was skittish about bein' on the train, thinkin' he might run into Zeke West since he's now forbidden from ever fightin' with him again. I thought once we were at the stores he'd relax, but he was wound tight."

"From what?"

"Nerves. It ain't every day a man buys his intended a ring."

She lifted her head off his chest and gaped at him. "*That's* the reason for the emergency trip you two took into Gillette yesterday afternoon?"

"Yeah. It bugged Silas that people kept askin' Dinah why she wasn't wearin' his ring." He groaned. "Took him two damn hours to pick one. Then we went to a tailor. He's havin' a courtin' suit made. I told him it looked like a funeral suit since it was all black, but he argued he liked plain, so I let him be. He bought a bunch of material, lace and other frilly stuff for Dinah to make a bicycling dress out of. I refused to help him pick out household goods and went to the saloon for a drink."

"Poor Jonas. Not interested in setting up housekeeping," she teased.

I'd set up a household in a hot minute with you.

"When are they getting married?"

"Next summer."

She frowned. "Why are they waiting?"

"Dinah promised she'd teach and help out Doc for another year. Silas says he'll use the time to improve the cabin, build chicken coops, add on a stall for a milk cow, till up a garden area, plant fruit trees. Hell, I think he might even be planning to sew curtains for the windows."

Ruby laughed. "It's sweet that he wants to make it a home for them." She paused. "Where does that leave you?"

"Bunkin' at the jail some weekends since Dinah plans to spend every other Saturday night and most Sundays with Silas. I thought about askin' Sheriff Eccleston if I could start workin' in the Sundance office. At least there's a hotel there." He nudged her hip with his. "Too bad Ruby Red's ain't a real boardinghouse, 'cause I sure could use a room to rent."

She stiffened beside him, as if he planned to ask if he could stay with her more often than he already did.

"Anyway, when I was havin' a drink at the Last Chance Saloon in Gillette, I saw an outlaw huntin' buddy of mine. He was headed to Butte, Montana. Guess there's been some issues between the miners and the mining company, and he's been hired to help keep the peace." He paused. "Said if I was tired of breakin' up barfights in backwoods Wyoming he'd hire me. The money they were payin' him would turn any man north to Montana."

"Are you seriously considering it?"

"If I'm bein' honest…I came here because of my brother. If he's got a wife and his own family, I don't know that he needs me around. Especially since he finally understands that I ain't interested in ranchin' with him." He snorted. "But no way in hell would I move to Butte for any amount of money. Dirty, stinky-ass town."

"You've been there?"

"I've spent a lot of time all over Montana. First workin' the cattle drives. We drove the herds to Miles City more times than I can count. Then workin' the outlaw trail, a lot of them wanted guys headed to Butte or Great Falls. I didn't mind it there. Seemed to be more big-city-like though, with the dams powering electricity."

She trailed her fingers up and down his belly. "Right after I set up

Ruby Red's I had a customer come through from Montana. He kept telling me about all the money I could make if I set up a house in Helena."

Jonas laughed. "Yeah, Helena does have more than its share of dance halls, saloons, and bawdy houses. It *is* a mining town, after all. That said, because it's the capitol, and it's set at the base of these truly spectacular mountains, it's a lot classier city. But it still feels...untamed."

"That appeals to you."

"That whole area from Helena to Missoula to Kalispell appeals to me. Beautiful country. Lots of opportunities."

"Sounds like you're lamenting lost opportunities." Ruby sat up and shifted over to sit on her knees, straddling his hips. "Speaking of lost opportunities..." She fell forward, bracing her hands by his head. Then she kissed him. Consumed him. Seduced him fully with the rolling press of her curves against his chest and the tease and retreat of her tongue. She nipped along his jaw, stopping to blow in his ear.

He groaned and tilted his head for more of that.

"I did miss you, Deputy," she murmured into his neck. "And since I've been the first for you for so many things, it's only fair that you get to be the first for me for something too."

Jonas gently trapped her face in his hands, mindful of her stitches, to stop her wicked mouth from rendering him stupid. "A first for what?"

"I've never fucked outside."

"Never?"

She shook her head. "Always inside. I mean, I'm grateful I never had to be a camp whore, but still, this will be fun. We can be as loud as we want."

He stroked the hollows of her cheeks as his eyes searched hers. "You know it's a first for me too, darlin', since you're the only woman I've ever been with." He didn't bother masking the longing in his face that silently told her she was the only woman he ever *wanted* to be with.

Her eyes darkened. "Jonas. I—"

Placing his thumbs on her lips, he said gruffly, "It'll keep." Gently, he pushed her back so he could sit up. "Now get nekkid, woman, so we can teach the birds and the bees a thing or two."

Ruby happily complied, even if she did seem skittish and immediately sat back down on the quilt, looking around as if swarms of bugs would attack her bared skin.

After Jonas ditched his clothes, he removed the box from his pants pocket and palmed it before he scooted in behind her. He allowed himself to be momentarily distracted by the beautiful visual of her black hair floating against the creaminess of her skin; the ends nearly brushed the indentions above her buttocks. When he kissed the slope of her shoulder, she rested more fully against him, igniting his blood with her scent.

He said, "I have something for you."

"Mmm. I can *feel* what you have for me poking me in the back."

He chuckled. "Oh, I plan on givin' you that too, but this is something else. Close your eyes." His heart thundered as he opened the box and held it in front of her. "Okay. Now you can look."

She gasped. "What is this?"

"A little something I picked up when I was in the jewelry store in Gillette."

"Jonas. It's beautiful." She reached out and traced the golden heart. "Is that…?"

"A ruby? Yep. That's when I knew I had to buy it for you."

She gently tugged the necklace from the box and held it up by the chain, letting it swing like a pendulum. The gold charm glinted in the sunlight. Then she turned her head and grinned at him. "Can I wear it now?"

Relief swept through him that she hadn't refused his gift. "Of course. Lean forward and I'll fasten it."

Once the chain circled her neck, she pressed her fingers over the gold charm where it rested in the hollow of her throat. "Thank you. I will always treasure this."

Jonas kissed the side of her neck. "I know you don't wanna hear this, but I'm gonna say it anyway." He covered her fingers with his own. "Ruby at the center of my heart. That's you. That'll *always* be you."

She twisted in his embrace and pushed him onto his back. She kissed him with devotion. His chin. His lips. The dimples in his cheeks. The corners of his eyes. His temples. His forehead. The shell of each ear. The spot below his ear. More long kisses that were sweeter than the plums and went to his head faster than the wine. When she started kissing a path down his throat and his chest, he had the fortitude to stop her.

Then she found herself pinned beneath him. "You've taught me that ladies come first."

"I'm not a lady."

"You're better than that." He nuzzled the delicate skin at the base of her jaw. "You're a temptress." He breathed across the damp skin just to feel her tremble. "A goddess." He scraped his teeth down her throat. "A siren." He kept inching down her body with open-mouthed kisses. "And I'm gonna make you scream like a banshee."

"Why?"

"Because you're the one who mentioned that we don't gotta be quiet out here." He teased her a bit more. "Ever come so hard that you screamed?"

She snorted. "That is a myth."

He smiled against that glorious curve of her hip. "Is that a challenge?"

"It's a fact."

"Really."

"I'm a whore and a madam of a whorehouse and any screams I hear are pure theatrics."

Jonas chuckled. "Gonna prove you wrong, Ruby girl."

She arched up at the first contact of his tongue wiggling into the secret spot just below the rise of her mound.

He dove in, growling at the musky-sweet taste of her. Spreading her thighs wide enough to accommodate his shoulders because he planned on staying there a while.

Her first orgasm happened quickly; he barely started sucking on her clit and he felt the throbbing contraction of her intimate tissues against his face.

Ruby gasped and clutched his hair as she arched closer, but no scream.

His second attempt involved his fingers and just the tip of his flickering tongue on her clit. Her legs quaked, and she babbled—begged, really—but when she fell over the edge into bliss after a longer climb, she said his name over and over like a mantra but the scream he craved remained elusive.

"Jonas," she panted, "enough," trying to scoot away from him.

He held fast to her thighs when he looked up at her across the soft cushion of her belly.

Their eyes met. Hers were sated and yet somehow, still hungry.

His cocky expression likely annoyed her but he'd earned it. "What, my love?"

"Get up here and fuck me."

"I will." He burrowed his tongue into her channel, lapping at the sweet proof of her arousal. "But first I wanna hear you really let go, darlin'." He sucked her pussy lips past his teeth and rubbed her pouting pearl with his top lip.

"You're teasing me! Stop."

"Never." He tormented her with the erotic movement of his mouth until she swore at him. He chuckled and the vibration against her tender flesh had her cussing him even as she moaned louder. He eased back long enough to say, "That's it. Scream for me, darlin'. Scare the birds from the trees with the sound of your joy."

"I can't."

"You can." He nibbled on the insides of her smooth thighs. "You do this for me and I'll fuck you so hard you'll feel it for days."

"I wanna feel it *now*."

Her petulance made him smile. He teased and petted her pussy, making her think he was taking his time until she could take direct contact on her swollen bud.

Jonas had other plans. Dirty plans. Plans she'd love. Which was why he didn't tell her those plans, he just enacted them.

He flipped her over on her belly and hiked her ass in the air. Tilting her hips to where he got an eyeful of both those tempting openings. He flattened his tongue and licked her slit. Slowly. Savoring the tasty mix of the sweet cream flowing from her and the salt of her sweat. When he reached that sweet little pucker, he painted it with his tongue.

"Oh God. Jonas. Please."

He slapped her left butt cheek and then her right.

She went still.

His next two smacks were harder yet.

Then Ruby gave him the sign he'd sought; she slid her knees out wider.

The sound of his hand connecting with her flesh echoed back to him, spurring him not to hold back like when they were in her bedroom. He spanked her until every inch of her milk-pale cheeks was cherry red.

And hot. He trailed his fingers over her reddened skin, and she flinched from the contact of his stubbled cheeks scraping the sensitive spots.

There had been a time when he might've worried that he'd gone too far. But the insides of her thighs were wet from her arousal. She loved this.

She'd taught him how to toe that line between pleasure and pain. And he'd been a damn attentive student.

When Jonas snugged his groin against her heated backside, grinding the hair surrounding his cock against her abraded flesh as he stretched his body over hers, she let out the sexiest sound he'd ever heard. "Your ass looks so pretty marked up by my hands," he panted in her ear.

"Please."

"Obedient *and* needy is a good look on you, darlin'." He breathed in the warm floral scent of her hair and exhaled against the damp curve of her shoulder. "Ready for your reward?"

Ruby made another wordless noise and tightened her leg muscles to try and keep them from shaking because she anticipated what came next.

He dug his fingers into her burning ass cheeks and spread her wide, lowering his head and spearing that rosette with his tongue. Lapping and licking and toying with that tight ring, jamming his tongue inside, then sliding down to treat her pussy to the same slavish devotion.

Jesus. He fucking loved this. Loved that she gave herself over to him with such trust. Loved she'd taught him all the wicked little raunchy sex tricks that turned *her* mindless with need.

When she started rocking her hips, he sensed she was close to detonating. He gave that dark, dirty, delicious part of her one last lick and layered his body across hers.

Except this time he grabbed a handful of her hair, forcing her head up.

"Scream for me," he growled as he slammed into her to the hilt.

Ruby screamed.

He rode her with ferocity until she started to come.

Her cunt clamped down on his cock with such force he had to slow his thrusts. He'd never felt her spasms this deeply before. He rode the waves out with her, his pelvis keeping time with those pulses. When her interior muscles relaxed, he kicked up the pace. His greedy eyes taking everything in, the long lines of her body, the tangled mass of her hair, the rapid rise and fall of her shoulders.

His ass cheeks clenched with each wet slide out of her body. His hips thudded into her reddened backside with each hard thrust in. His breathing labored. Sweat coating his skin. Naked in body and soul.

Jonas had never felt more alive.

A tingling started in his tailbone and quickly rolled through him when his cock released his seed. The intense pleasure had his toes curling and his jaw tightening against roaring out like a beast.

When the blood stopped pounding in his ears and his focus returned, he pulled out and laid down beside her, wrapping her in his arms.

After they'd caught their breath, Ruby laughed softly.

"What?"

"You actually made me scream, Deputy. Another first."

He kissed the back of her head. "I aim to please."

"Mmm." She squirmed away and rolled over to face him. "What now? We round up the horses and head back?"

"No."

"But—"

"I fed you and fucked you and you think we're done?" he said tightly. "Wrong. I wanna spend the day with you, Ruby. The *whole* day." He swept her hair over her shoulder. "As much as I love makin' you scream, there's more we can do together than fuck."

"Like?"

"Talkin', dancin', nappin'."

She blinked at him. "Naked dancing."

"Sure. Or we could put our clothes back on and dance barefoot in the grass."

"You are a romantic, Jonas McKay."

He put his mouth by her ear. "Shh. Don't tell no one."

"Your secret is safe with me."

"Or we could also go swimming," he offered.

"Where?"

"There's a bend in the stream up a ways. It's ain't a lake, but it's deep enough to sit in and cool off." He cocked his head. "Ever been nekkid in a stream?"

"By myself? Yes. I lived in a mining camp in South Dakota, remember? How else was I supposed to get clean?"

Jonas leaned over and rubbed his lips across the dew gathered on her chest. "I could lick you clean."

"Tempting as that is…I am sticky. I wouldn't mind cooling off the sting in my ass."

"Complaining about that, darlin'?"

"Never. It was…" Her eyes glazed over. "You give me what I need

Jonas, without me having to ask."

"I know. And you do the same for me. Let's go." He popped to his feet and held out his hand. "You wanna walk? Or you want me to carry you?"

She raised an eyebrow. "Is this where you call me a tenderfoot?"

He laughed. "*I'm* a damn tenderfoot. I figured I'd slip my boots on for the walk to the creek and kick them off once we got there."

"In that case, I want you to carry me." She sent him a mischievous look. "Piggyback."

He crouched down, waggling his ass in her face. "Mount up, sweetheart."

Ruby bit him on the butt hard enough that he'd be wearing her teeth marks for a few days before she launched herself onto his back with a whoop of joy.

It felt good to laugh with her. And splash around with her like they were a couple of kids.

It really felt good to sit on a flat, sun-warmed rock and just hold her as the breeze dried their river-cooled skin.

They returned to their picnic spot and shared the bottle of cider, which left them both drowsy. Once again, they curled up together and drifted off.

Upon awakening, Jonas made love to her slowly. Face to face. Eye to eye. Heart to heart.

Her deeply contented sigh and whispered, "I love it like this with you," meant as much to him as her scream borne of passion.

After dressing, they ambled hand in hand through the meadow, taking the long way to retrieve the horses.

The sun had dropped behind the hills when they reached their parting point.

Neither one of them wanted to be the first to go.

Keeping her eyes on his, Ruby lifted the heart charm to her lips and kissed it. Then she spurred her horse away, leaving Jonas staring after her like a lovesick fool.

But he had no regrets. It'd been the best day of his life.

SIXTEEN

S ILAS DID NOT want to attend the Sundance Fourth of July rodeo, let alone compete in it.

He would've preferred to spend the day at the ranch with Dinah. For the past several weeks she'd been staying with him one night each weekend and riding out one day a week to learn his routine. Seeing her three days out of seven—if he was lucky—had him questioning why he'd agreed to a longer engagement.

"Hurry up."

He sent Jonas a dark look as he changed into *something better than that dirty rag you call a shirt.* Jesus, Joseph and Mary, his brother fussed over his appearance more than Dinah did.

"Stop glarin' at me," Jonas said. "Everyone in the county will be there today, which means you ain't gonna embarrass your betrothed by showing up lookin' like you just spent months on a dusty cattle drive."

"Don't make sense, Jonas, to get fancied up when we're competing in bronc bustin', team ropin' and rope'n ride. I'll be covered in dirt and shit anyway, except now I'll be covered in dirt and shit wearin' my best damn shirt."

"Maybe the next time you're in Robinette's you oughta buy a couple of new shirts for yourself instead of another gift for Dinah." Jonas's gaze moved to the shelving alongside the cookstove that held the tea set, and the three new pans that dangled on hooks above the cookstove.

Good thing his snoopy brother didn't know that Silas had also given Dinah a bottle of lilac perfume and the cameo choker that Henrikson paid him with last week instead of cash. "Says the man who spends all of his money to look dandy for the ladies that I ain't never seen him with."

"Bugger off. I don't dress nice for the ladies. I dress nice because I'm a public figure."

Silas snorted.

"Speaking of gifts, why in the devil haven't you given Dinah that ring we had to make the special trip to Gillette for? You know that folks will be talkin' about why she still ain't wearin' one."

"I intend to make it special when I put it on her finger. Been so busy I haven't come up with anything—"

"Romantic," Jonas said and made kissing noises.

"At least I *got* a romantic side."

Jonas's eyebrow winged up. "Brother, the last person I'd show my romantic side to is you." He walked over and tossed one of his new shirts on Silas's bed. "Wear this."

"Why?"

"Because it's completely different from the one I'm wearin'." The shirt Jonas had already buttoned up was navy blue, striped with light gray and red. "Don't want anyone mistaking me for you and vice versa."

"They wouldn't anyway since you'll be wearin' your badge," Silas shot back. But he did put on the shirt. It was nice. Simple. The pale blue color reminded him of Dinah's eyes. The button-up, cotton fabric wasn't too heavy for July or too flimsy that it'd bust out at the seams when he moved. "Thanks for the shirt."

"You're welcome. You can keep it."

"Aww...see? There's your romantic side."

Jonas slipped on the leather vest Silas had given him for Christmas. The vest that matched the one Silas intended to wear, with the McKay cattle brand seared in the back.

His brother had made it clear he'd be willing to help out on the ranch whenever needed, but he wouldn't hand in his badge to do so fulltime, so it touched Silas that Jonas was willing to wear the family brand in public.

"Hurry up, slowpoke." Jonas pinned his badge onto the vest and headed for the door.

"Whoa. Didn't you forget something?" Silas pointed to Jonas's gun belt.

"No need for that today since I'm cowboyed up for the ranch rodeo."

As if Silas needed the reminder.

SILAS HAD NEVER seen so many people in Sundance. Made him want to turn around and spur his horse for home.

But Jonas had an agenda, which didn't even allow for them to stop so Silas could have a word with Dinah. They headed directly to the racetrack north of town where the horse races and ranch contests were being held. Horses and buggies lined the area with still more people.

"Christ. I didn't know there were this many people livin' in the entire state of Wyomin'," Silas groused.

"This is a big event. People are here from Beulah, Hulett and Labelle. Guess the Spearfish baseball team is playing against Sundance this afternoon."

"Are you goin' to that?"

Jonas shrugged. "We'll see. There's other activities happening in town that might be more interesting."

"*Anything* is more interestin' than baseball," Silas shot back. He'd given in to Henrikson's request to do something "civilized" earlier in the week and accompanied the man to the Zane Hotel for lunch, and they'd attended a baseball game afterward. The kinda men who had time to take off from work during the day to play games obviously weren't ranchers. While he understood Henrikson's loneliness, Silas would've preferred spending time with Dinah rather than folks who had too much time to waste.

"Agreed." Jonas pointed. "That's where we're supposed to be. The first round of horse racin' has finished."

Someone had created makeshift pens on one end of the dirt track. One pen held horses, most of which were bucking their displeasure, one held calves, and one farther away from the livestock pens held...sheep.

Jonas and Silas rode side by side until they reached two poles jammed in the ground with wire strung between them. A man Silas didn't know waved at them enthusiastically.

"The McKay boys! We're excited you're participating in the ranchers competition this year."

"We appreciate you thinkin' of us," Jonas said smoothly. "Allen, I don't believe you've met my brother Silas. Silas, Allen here runs the Sawtooth Mine. But today, he's head of the community games."

Silas leaned over and offered his hand. "Pleasure to meet you, Allen."

"Same here. We think the world of your brother."

Doesn't everyone.

"We've got you both signed up for the bronc bustin' event, the team ropin' event, the ride'n rope event, the horse skills event and the ropin' challenge. Since contests like these ain't nothin' new to boys such as yourselves, ain't no need to explain the rules, right?"

Jonas said "No" the same time Silas said, "What're the sheep for?"

"Sheep ranchers have a separate competition. Course, there ain't as many participants in that class. Shame, really, since the prize money is the same amount as for the other ranch contests."

That caught his interest. "You don't say. Can any man enter the sheep competitions?"

"Well, sure, I guess. The events don't run concurrently. But most men stick to one or the other competition, not both."

Silas grinned at him. "Well I ain't most men, Allen, so sign me up."

"No foolin'?"

"It's all about givin' the people a good show, ain't it? I can't think of nothin' funnier than a cattle rancher tryin' to wrangle sheep."

Allen laughed. "You've got a point." Then he looked at Jonas. "Sign you up too, Deputy?"

Before Jonas could say *hell no*, Silas answered, "Oh, we *McKay boys* do everything together. Of course the deputy *that everyone thinks the world of* is eager to participate for the good of the community he serves."

Jonas said, "Jesus Christ," under his breath.

"That is simply great. I'll let 'em know. Now the first cattleman's event is the horse handlin' skills." He pointed. "Other fellas are already down in the cattleman's class since we're about to get underway."

Silas tipped his hat and reined his horse that direction.

Jonas trotted alongside him. "What in the hell is wrong with you? We don't got any business fuckin' around with the sheep ranchers."

"Yes we do. Did you see who's over there all cowboyed up? In the cattleman's section." He paused. "The West brothers."

"Goddammit, Silas, then we really don't need to tangle with them in the sheep class too."

"Wrong. We're gonna show them up in *both* classes."

"What is *wrong* is this vendetta you and Zeke have goin'."

"It's in the past. I promised Dinah no more fightin' with Zeke. Ever." He smirked. "But she didn't say a damn thing that I couldn't compete with him on my turf."

"Turf." Jonas snorted. "Happy as I am that Dinah forced you into walkin' away from that fucked-up feud you and West had goin', what was it even about? I'd put my money on you giving up because you'd get tired of him kickin' your ass."

Silas had held this in for far too long. He'd told Dinah a portion of the issue between him and Zeke, but not all of it. Getting this off his chest would truly close this ugly chapter in his life. Fuming, Silas pulled his horse to a stop. "I'll tell you what it's about. Zeke ended up bein' my boss at the railroad. He humiliated me every chance he could get. I took every bit of nastiness because I needed the railroad money to stabilize my ranch. During forced social time with him, I had to let him win when we played cards or else he'd punish me when we were at work. I put up with it for a damn year. Until one night we were at a saloon outside of Rockypoint. He'd been drinkin' and made a comment to me about how I'd stolen his life—made no sense then, or now. He said now that he knew where I intended on puttin' down roots, he'd do everything in his power to dig up those roots one at a time and kick the dirt in my face. He threatened to burn down my cabin. Rip apart my fences. Poison my cattle. Those things? I could laugh off to some degree." His jaw tightened. "But when he said it'd be a shame if my law-abiding twin ended up on the wrong end of an ambush or a gunfight, I lost my head. I beat him near to death, Jonas."

All the blood drained from Jonas's face. "Christ, Silas. Why didn't you tell me this before?"

"Because I was protecting you. West wound up in the hospital. I went to see him and he said if I ever laid a hand on him again or fought back when he tried to settle our blood debt…he'd kill you, not me." Silas looked over to where the West brothers stood apart from the cattle ranchers. "So I never fought back. Not once. Even that hasn't held him in check. He paid Dinah a visit when she was alone. He bought that section of land by mine with every intention of buildin' a house there. No matter what I do—or don't do—he's gonna keep fuckin' with me. I promised Dinah no more fightin' with him. I intend to keep that promise. But this competition will drive home the point that I ain't afraid of him."

Jonas didn't say anything. Then he sighed. "I hate that you felt you had to go it alone, Silas. We're brothers." He paused. "I will always have your back. How could you forget that?"

Today was a good time for that reminder to resurface.

Another long-suffering sigh gusted from Jonas and Silas braced himself. "We'll do this. On one condition."

"What?"

Jonas grinned. "You owe me a bottle of whiskey after I kick your ass in the horsemanship competition."

Silas laughed. "Deal."

"Let's go have us some fun, brother."

IT TURNED OUT that the West brothers were not competing in the cattleman's class. They'd just wanted a better view of the events.

More spectators gathered around, and Silas tried to focus on the competitions rather than all the folks staring at him while he participated.

Jonas won the horse handling skills contest. The only one who came close to handling his horse with such finesse was…Silas. He took second place.

The bronc bustin' contest was for fools and show-offs. Still, Silas hopped on a wild horse, if for no other reason than to show up his brother and to remind himself why he didn't buy unbroke horses. Only one other fella managed to stay on longer than him, and that meant another second-place finish.

Afterward, as he caught his breath, he noticed Dinah standing with a group of ladies—Bea Talbot, Esther McCrae, Mary O'Brien and Sarah White were the only ones he recognized. With her jaw set in a hard line and her full lips flat, he sensed she wasn't happy to be in their company.

"McKay! You're the last one up," echoed to him and he reluctantly turned around.

Ride'n rope was a challenge where a rider chased down a calf on horseback, roping it, dismounting the horse and tying the calf's four legs together—all as quickly as possible. Maybe he should've been working his rope between events, but since he did this every day, he figured he didn't need the practice.

Turned out he was right. He'd beat his next closest competitor— Jonas—by nearly fifteen seconds. Valuing speed more than accuracy didn't really reflect a rancher's daily skills, but a win was a win.

Silas and Jonas were partnered for the team roping. They were picked to go first. They didn't even have to discuss who was doing what beforehand. As soon as the calf raced into view, they were after it, Jonas reining his horse to the left side to rope the calf's head and Silas reining his horse to the right side to rope the calf's back legs. Didn't take them any time at all. They were pleased they'd broke the previous years' record by ten seconds. No other team came close to beating them.

The McKays winning streak didn't win them any friends among the other cattlemen. Beloved Deputy Jonas could soothe their ruffled feathers and bow out of the last event just as long as he didn't expect Silas to follow suit. Because that event was where Silas excelled: roping.

He'd never participated in this style of competition. First he'd have to rope a moving object while he remained in one spot on the ground. Then on horseback he'd have to rope and drag a stationary object.

The first object was a pan hanging on the right side of a saddle horn. Easy peasy. The second challenge was easier yet: roping a log and dragging it twenty feet through the dirt.

Again, Silas won.

Few congratulated him for winning three first places and two second places.

He would've preferred cash to store credits in Sundance, but at least the credits were at the hardware store. Every little bit helped.

During the break between the cow and sheep classes, he looked for Dinah but couldn't find her. Maybe she'd headed back to town because she believed he'd be done competing. But it wasn't like her not to wait for him. Especially since he'd been the big winner. He'd sorta hoped for a victory kiss from his girl.

The crowd milled around as the event coordinators set up.

Allen yelled out for all sheep competitors to approach.

Jonas and Silas didn't look at each other as they stepped forward.

But it sure seemed as if everyone else was looking at them.

Allen clapped his hands for attention. "First up is the sheep dip contest. This is where boys eight and under ride a sheep to the finish line. Fastest time to the finish line wins. Follow Miss O'Brien over to the fence."

"What about girls?" some woman yelled from the back.

"Boys only." He scanned the papers in front of him. "Second competition is penning. Team competition. Two men on horseback sort and pen the specific number on the sheep." He held up a piece of a paper with a number written on it. "Each sheep in the fenced area will have a number clipped to it. Your job will be to sort *only* the sheep wearing this number into the pen as quickly as possible."

Silas leaned closer to Jonas. "Like separatin' the mama's and babies for brandin'."

"Yep."

"Third competition is dally ribbon ropin'. Team competition. One man on horseback ropes the ram's horn. One man on the ground as the runner has to remove the ribbon from around the ram's neck after it's been roped and he then runs to the finish line."

"That's new," Silas said.

Allen said, "And the last event: sheep shearing. You'll shear your own sheep. This is an individual competition, not a team. And if you didn't bring sheep, you can't participate."

Some smart-mouth said, "That means you, McKays."

Jonas rolled his eyes. "It's odd that they only have three events."

Silas snickered. "Because it'd be indecent if they had them publicly compete at what sheep-fuckers are best at."

"Jesus, Silas."

"What? You were thinkin' the same damn thing, Deputy."

Jonas's lips twitched. "Yeah, but thinkin' it and sayin' it..."

While the parents prepped their boys for the sheep dip, Zeke West stormed over.

"What in the hell do you two think you're doin'?" Zeke demanded. "You ain't runnin' sheep. Which means you ain't allowed to compete."

"You ain't runnin' sheep either, West. You work for the railroad, remember?" Silas pointed to Zachariah. "You don't even live on his place anymore."

Zeke glared at him.

"Besides, we cleared it with Allen. He said we were welcome to compete. You don't like it, take it up with him." Silas stepped closer. "And I hope you do. I'd like to see that temper of yours flare up and get you kicked outta this competition entirely."

"We won all the events last year," Zeke bragged. "They ain't about to deny the reigning champs a chance to repeat."

Silas watched Zachariah amble closer. "You saw the cattleman's competition. So you're aware that a few of the bronc bustin' guys weren't ranchers. No different for us not bein' sheepf"—he paused, as if to stop himself from finishing that thought—"farmers."

Jonas choked back a laugh. Then he offered his hand to Zachariah. "Good luck."

Zachariah grunted his response, but he did shake Jonas's hand.

Neither Silas nor Zeke pretended they could put their differences aside even for a simple handshake.

The whistle blew as the signal to start the sheep dip race.

Silas and Jonas both busted a gut watching kids being tossed around as they attempted to ride fluffy sheep. The winner had gotten thrown off four times but had climbed back on and had ridden to victory.

But there was a collective booing in the crowd when the winner was revealed to be Edna Mae and not Ed. The second-place finisher was awarded first place, which Silas thought was a bunch of sheep shit.

It was time for him and Jonas to mount up again. As they walked back to their horses, they heard someone shout "McKay!" and they both turned around.

Dinah waved to him. Silas hadn't seen her because she'd been under the shade of a lacy parasol, standing next to…Madam Ruby…who was holding the parasol.

Jonas went utterly still beside him. "What the devil are the two of them doin' together?"

"Dinah's likely checkin' to see how Miss Ruby fared. 'Bout two weeks back, Miss Ruby showed up at Doc's needin' stitches and Dinah ended up stitching her up."

"I know that," Jonas snapped.

Silas stopped. "How do you know? You weren't on duty, since it hap-pened the night we were in Gillette." Then he paused. "Guess I never thought about the sheriff's office getting involved, but it makes sense since someone got hurt. Anyway, don't worry about it. Dinah can hold her own. Come on."

Since only five teams were competing for the penning prize, they drew straws to see who went first.

"West brothers, you're up first. Followed by Andrews and Hall. Then the McKays."

With a team buffered between them, Silas and Jonas could watch the Wests compete.

And Silas almost felt sorry for the West brothers.

Almost.

If Zeke would've listened to his brother, they probably would've done fine. But Zeke's horse kept fighting him. Finally Zachariah yelled, "Just get number eight outta here."

As soon as Zeke was out of Zachariah's way, he had the six sheep penned.

Silas started to shout, "Better luck next time!" as the West brothers rode off, but Jonas snapped, "Leave it."

They mounted up and took their horses away from the crowd, giving them room to move.

Jonas seemed agitated. Luckily for him, Silas wasn't the type to let him brood like an old mare. "What's got a burr under your saddle?"

"Nothin'."

Like hell.

"McKay brothers, you're up," the event leader shouted.

"Well, whatever's got you so sore, leave it until after we win this damn thing, okay?"

"Yeah. Come on." Jonas spurred his horse, leaving Silas to follow.

Once they were in the paddock, Jonas deferred to him.

Fifteen sheep were released. The leader shouted, "Number two."

There could be as many as nine number-two-marked sheep, or as few as three number-two-marked sheep.

Jonas went left; Silas went right.

Silas yelled out his count first. "I see seven."

"Yep. Seven."

Rather than attempting to sort in close quarters, Silas scattered the entire flock of sheep. Jonas's horse had more dexterity, so he cut and penned the number twos one at a time after Silas moved the other numbers back.

It took them four minutes from start to finish.

The cattlemen who'd stayed to watch this competition clapped enthusiastically when the McKay brothers' time—a new record—was announced.

Zeke West glared and didn't notice when Zachariah gave them a quick hat tip.

They hung around until the last team finished and the McKays were announced the event winners. The prize was another store certificate to Farnum's in Sundance.

Silas thanked the event coordinators and the sponsors. Then he left the competition area and scanned the crowd until he spied who he was looking for. He dismounted before approaching her.

She didn't return his smile. She studied him with her arms crossed over her chest. He didn't blame her.

"Hey there. I gotta say, you were the best sheep wrangler in the sheep dip competition, and you won fair and square, Edna Mae. So if it's okay with your folks, I'd like to give you our winner's certificate to make things right."

Edna Mae's eyes widened. "But you had the best time. The best time ever! Don't you wanna buy something special?"

Silas shrugged. "We already got a certificate in the cattlemen's competition. I'll probably spend it on something boring. But *you* deserve to get yourself something special for bein' the best. So what do you say?"

Her mother said, "Are you sure, Mr. McKay?"

"Yep. Just as long as you let Edna Mae spend this however she wants." He winked at the girl. "Even if she uses it all to buy candy and fireworks."

"That's generous of you." She prompted her daughter. "What do you say?"

Edna Mae grinned at him. "Thank you, Mr. McKay."

"You are welcome."

Silas walked his horse back over to the pens behind the competition area, leaving it in the hands of the stable boy since he wouldn't need it for the last competition. He turned around and Jonas was right there.

"Now before you get mad—"

"Why would I get mad? I'd planned on doin' the same damn thing."

"Oh. Well. Okay." He adjusted his hat. "We ain't so different after all."

Something in the distance had caught Jonas's attention as he sat on top of his horse. Without looking away, Jonas said, "How I wish that were true, brother."

SEVENTEEN

R UBY HAD PLANNED to spend the Fourth of July in her room cutting out fabric pieces to create a new jacket. She'd given her girls the entire day and evening off; customers were always scarce on a family day devoted to picnics and frolicking. She'd expected her girls to hang around the boardinghouse since they likely wouldn't be interested in attending the celebration in Sundance.

But they'd surprised her. Millie had organized an outing for all the girls, plus Mavis and Dickie, to the Belle Fourche River, where they could swim. Then afterward, they'd head to Hulett for that township's celebration. They'd invited her to join them, but she knew they'd have a more relaxed day if she declined.

Even Sackett's had closed.

Her rooms were stifling. Given her recent outdoors excursion with Jonas, she was having a harder time than usual staying inside.

As brave as she considered herself to be, the idea of rolling into Sundance by herself filled her with dread. But the thought of hiding away in her rooms on such a glorious day gave her pause too.

Damn them all. As a citizen and as an American she had every right to be there. Every right to celebrate.

She exited her rooms and headed up to the second floor. The snoring coming from behind the closed door to the smallest room indicated she wouldn't have to go far to find who she sought. She knocked once.

A mad scramble ensued inside, and a sleepy Jimmy flung open the door. "Miss Ruby. I'm sorry. Mrs. Mavis said it was all right that I slept here last night, and I didn't mean to stay this long. Please don't—"

"It's fine, Jimmy."

"Okay." He yawned. "I'll be out in a jiff."

"Actually I was looking for you."

"What do you need?"

"What are your plans for today?"

"Nothin'. Might go fishin'. Why?"

"How would you like to go to the Independence Day celebration in Sundance?"

His eyes lit up. "No foolin'?"

The more she thought about it, the more she realized it was the perfect solution. "There'd be a few things I'd need you to do, but they're basic and I'd pay you. You'd also have time to take part in the celebration."

"Heck yeah, Miss Ruby, that'd be swell!" He furrowed his brow. "But wait. Can Martha come? I'd told her we could spend today doin' stuff since I didn't hafta be at Sackett's."

"Jimmy darling. I know she's your friend," she said gently, "but I don't think an Indian girl would be any more welcome in Sundance than I would be."

He grinned. "She's good at hidin' herself. She dresses like a boy and no one pays no attention to her."

"If you promise to be responsible for her, then yes, she can come. I'll need you to go over to Blackbird's and get us a horse. And a buggy big enough for three."

"Martha will want to ride her own horse. She don't like to be beholden to nobody."

"No, she'll have to ride with us, Jimmy. A lone rider riding bareback will cause a stir among the crowd in Sundance, and honey, that's not blending in."

"Fine. I'll tell her."

"I'll be ready in an hour."

"Me too." He turned away but she caught him before he got far.

"Ah-ah-ah. Not so fast, mister. You *will* wash. With soap. I'll be sitting next to you in that buggy, so I will know if you skip it. You hear me?"

"Yes, ma'am."

Ruby chose her outfit carefully. With this heat the less fabric the better, but folks expected to see her wearing outrageous clothes meant for the boudoir. Yet donning a prim and proper high-necked blouse with full sleeves to her fingertips guaranteed she'd sweat. She opted for a shirtwaist the color of ripe strawberries with three-quarters-length mutton leg sleeves and a sweetheart neckline with white satin piping. She paired that with a plain gray lightweight cotton skirt. Her hat was a gorgeous monstrosity, small-brimmed with silk rosettes the same hue as her blouse, with loops of ivory silk ribbon, sprays of pearls and glass stones fashioned to look like clusters of raspberries, and finished with tufts of silvery gray netting and downy white feathers. She snagged her fanciest parasol with the white tulle and lace and slipped on her comfiest pair of boots.

Just in case none of the food vendors would sell to Jimmy, Ruby packed a lunch for three, comprised of cheese sandwiches, black walnut sugar cookies and fresh figs. Just in case her nerves got the better of her, she packed a big flask of cherried brandy.

Jimmy and Martha pulled up in front of the boardinghouse exactly on time. At least she believed the small person driving the buggy was Martha. Jimmy had been right about one thing: Martha easily passed as a boy.

"Miss Ruby, this here is my best friend, Martha. Call her Marty when we get to town." Jimmy hopped down and stowed the basket of food and the parasol before he helped Ruby into the buggy, crowding in beside her on the small bench seat.

"It's nice to meet you…Marty."

She flashed teeth that shone white against her beautiful skin tone. "Same, Miss Ruby." Her gaze encompassed Ruby's hat. "If you ever need quills or rabbits' fur for your fancy hats or clothes, tell Jimmy and I'll bring you stuff. Nice skins. For less than you'll pay at the general store."

"That's thoughtful. Thank you."

Jimmy chattered like a chipmunk all the way into Sundance. Marty mostly grunted in response and he left Ruby no time to respond at all.

"Where to?" Marty asked Ruby.

"Last night in Sackett's I heard a man say horse racin' and livestock events were at the racetrack north of town," Jimmy said.

"Let's go there."

Spectators had lined their buggies around the perimeter. Marty found a spot and parked. But they were so far away from the events they might as well have stayed in Labelle.

Ruby jumped down without Jimmy's assistance.

"Looks like the horse racin' just finished."

Marty scoffed. "I'da beat them all. That's why they never let Indians compete."

Jimmy nodded. "Marty's horse would whip up on anyone's." Then he pointed. "Livestock competition is over there."

"I'd like to set up there to start." She left the food but pocketed the flask, and grabbed the picnic blanket she and Jonas had used and her parasol.

A couple of families gave them a wide berth as they crossed the dirt track to get a better view. But Ruby didn't pay them any mind. Especially not after Jimmy said, "Hey! I see Deputy McKay."

Jonas and Silas were both on horseback. Even if the deputy hadn't pinned his star to the front of the vest identical to the one his twin wore, she could've told the brothers apart. She knew exactly how Jonas McKay moved, regardless if he was atop a horse or atop her: with an innate awareness of his body as he gently—but firmly—controlled the animal beneath him.

God. The man was magnificent.

She kept walking until she reached the best viewing area. It was no skin off her nose if other families didn't want to sit close to her.

It wasn't until after she'd popped open her parasol that she noticed Jimmy and Marty whispering back and forth. "What?"

"People ain't any nicer to you, Miss Ruby, than they are to us. You want us to stay here by you for a spell?"

Such a sweet boy, trying to protect her feelings. "If you have any interest in watching the competition, I'd say yes. But I'm guessing you two would rather go over to where the tents have been set up for the carnival."

"I see enough ranchin' stuff every day. This is the first time I've been to a town celebration so me'n Marty wanna have a look-see."

"I don't blame you. Keep aware of who's around you, all right?" From the small miser's purse, she pulled out a dollar's worth of coins. "Don't waste this on games of chance. Don't spend it all in one place."

"Aww, thanks, Miss Ruby."

Marty and Jimmy exchanged a quick grin and scampered off.

A breeze eddied about, kicking up swirls of dirt. Even through the dust she could see Silas searching the crowd for his betrothed. Whereas beside him, Jonas messed with his rope.

How she wished Jonas knew she was out here rooting for him.

Although Silas hadn't spotted Dinah, Ruby had her within her direct line of sight.

Dinah stood with a group of overdressed ladies. The pleasant smile affixed to her face slipped when one particular woman spoke. Ruby suspected most of the ladies' conversation was lost on Dinah because she was concentrating on Silas. Little doubt she was entertaining licentious thoughts watching him in his element, the same way Ruby lusted after Jonas.

Ruby gave into her smug sense of satisfaction that none of those snooty-looking women had a male like one of the McKays in their beds. If they had, they wouldn't give two pins about gossip; they'd be too enthralled watching their virile man publicly prove his prowess.

When two newcomers joined the clique, Dinah discreetly turned her back and conferred her full attention to the competition.

Jonas was the first contestant in the horse skills contest.

Ruby's mouth went positively dry even as her pantalets went damp at seeing Jonas and his expertly trained horse barreling through the requirements, as if demonstrating perfection.

No other contestants begrudged his first-place finish, especially not his brother, who'd finished second.

During the switchover to the next event, she lost track of Jonas and Silas in the milling crowd of men and sea of hats.

The announcer called out the start of the bronc busting.

Ruby assumed Jonas would cheer on his brother during the contest, but wouldn't enter it himself.

Wrong.

Jonas was announced fourth in the line-up and Silas sixth.

She held her breath from the moment Jonas climbed on the back of the beast until the moment the animal tossed him in the dirt.

He laughed, dusted himself off, and went to help his brother get ready for his attempt.

Silas fared better than all but one of the buckaroos and he ended up in second. Pity he couldn't see Dinah cheering for him and his consecutive second place finish.

The announcement for team roping caused a large portion of the crowd to leave, which didn't make sense to Ruby. This was the real-life skill set ranchers used on a daily basis. This was what she'd been eager to see...or maybe she just wanted to witness how well Jonas and Silas worked together.

And she wasn't disappointed in the show they put on...because it wasn't a show. These men had a nonverbal communication that transcended their bond as twins. They were in tune with their individual responsibilities yet created a seamless team transition that made roping a frightened animal look easy. Ruby knew if she questioned either of the McKays about it, they'd be humble, chalking it up to luck and well-trained ranch horses, and not their skills.

The brothers vanished in a cluster of men on horseback to ready themselves for the next event.

Two couples with assorted children approached Ruby until the younger man—who'd been a longtime regular customer—realized who she was. He sent her a panicked look as if she'd announce to his wife, three children and in-laws that his kink was having a glass dildo shoved up his ass while getting his cock sucked. She really wished these men would give her more credit; if she blabbed their secrets far and wide, how would she ever stay in business? Still, she turned the other cheek and scanned the people standing around the tents to try and catch a glimpse of either Jimmy or Marty.

No luck.

When she faced forward again, she jumped because Dinah had appeared in front of her.

Directly in front of her.

Wearing a friendly smile.

"Ruby. How are you?"

She offered a tentative smile in return. "I'm good."

"How long have you been here?"

"Since the start of the cattlemen's events." She paused. "The McKays have had a great showing, haven't they?"

"Outstanding. Although I'd be happy never to see Silas climb on the back of a bucking bronc again."

Ruby didn't say anything.

Then the event coordinator announced the last event.

Dinah turned and stepped to the side. "Do you mind if I watch from here?"

"Won't your friends..." *Stare and demand answers on how you know Madam Ruby?*

"Only one of those women is my friend. The others are sycophants since Bea's husband is building the new bank in Sundance."

"I see."

"Before you say something insulting like I should care about my reputation by acting as if we don't know each other, I'll point out we have more in common than you might imagine."

Ruby managed not to snort with disbelief and offered a cool, "How so?"

"We've both fallen for a McKay."

That left Ruby speechless.

"I've not said anything to Silas—or to anyone else, for that matter—about you and Jonas being together."

"How did you arrive at the conclusion we're together?"

"When I stitched you up, you called him Jonas. Especially telling since most people refer to him by his title. Silas says Jonas only stays at the cabin maybe two nights out of the week. He believes his brother is sleeping at the jail. Maybe he is some nights. With no boardinghouse in Labelle...there is one place he could stay regularly and no one would question his comings and goings."

Ruby continued to stare straight ahead, neither confirming nor denying.

"I believe you brought Silas to Doc's in a blizzard because you were taking care of him when Jonas couldn't, and it was your way of helping your man's family."

Dammit.

"The only way you could've known about what was said between Silas and me after the incident in Sundance was if Jonas had told you—after Silas had told *him*—because no one else heard our conversation. And I'm pretty sure that Silas and Jonas tell each other everything."

"Not everything," she said dryly.

"You have a point. I'm not saying any of this because I want to hold something over you."

"Then why?"

Dinah paused. "Because like me, you're actually here to watch them compete."

"They're nearly done, right?"

"This is the last cattleman's event." She stood on her tiptoes. "Looks to me as if the deputy isn't competing."

"Shame," Ruby said off-handedly, grateful if he'd foregone climbing on the back of some wild, bucking animal.

"I see Silas tossing his rope, so I'm betting it's a roping contest." Dinah attempted to discreetly wipe the sweat from her brow. "I don't know how I forgot to wear a hat today."

"Because it would've messed up your lovely hairstyle. Come. This parasol is ridiculously big. There's plenty of shade to share."

Dinah blinked those big blue eyes at her. "You're sure?"

"Absolutely."

"Thank you." She scooted closer. "Did you come here with someone?"

"Two someones actually. Jimmy and Martha, although she is dressed like a boy and is insistent on being called Marty today."

"That sounds like her. You're only missing Ernie Robinette and you'd have my entire school with you."

Ruby glanced at her. "Only three students in your school? That's it?"

"Yes. Once I got over the shock and disappointment, not to mention the jokes at my expense of not being a 'real' teacher with a 'real' schoolhouse…I embraced the challenge. Traditional schooling didn't work for any of those kids. Ernie is brilliant at math and science and doesn't see the point of wasting his time on other academic avenues. Martha could teach a master horticulturist a thing or two; she's an excellent hunter and horse trainer, so traditional jobs relegated to females hold no appeal for her. Jimmy absorbs whatever is placed in front of him when he's not falling asleep from exhaustion at being a twelve-year-old boy who works any job asked of him in order to survive."

Ruby hadn't expected to hear such admiration from Dinah for kids who most people—teachers included—would discount.

"Oh, it's starting."

Once again, Silas McKay had no competition and took first place.

When Dinah saw him looking around, likely for her, she waved the parasol and shouted, "McKay!"

Everyone turned and looked at them.

Everyone.

The attention didn't bother Dinah a bit. She didn't notice; she was too busy getting moony-eyed over her man.

That's when Ruby believed she and Dinah were kindred spirits.

Especially when Dinah leaned over and whispered, "It's actually funny how hard the deputy is trying *not* to look over here at you every thirty seconds."

Ruby laughed. "He's failing miserably, don't you think?"

"Yes. Does it bother you?"

"What? That I can't yell his name and blow kisses at him in public?" That sounded a little salty. "Sometimes, yes. But it'd be worse for him to be publicly dragged down for doing something as silly as falling in with a prostitute."

"I'm sorry. I truly am. One can only hope with the suffrage movement some of those biased and unfair judgments toward women will change."

"Amen, sister, but I'm not holding my breath."

"You might want to." Dinah wrinkled her nose. "The sheep events are about to start."

"Oh. Do sheep stink?"

Dinah cocked her head. "They smell like oil and dirt and manure to me."

"Not like sunbaked, rain-cooled wool from the misty moors?" Ruby asked slyly.

"No. In that furry form you won't catch the crispy roasted meat with mint jelly aroma either. Which is a pity because that's my favorite." She frowned. "Why are the McKay brothers mixing with the sheep ranchers? Are they not aware that Zeke and Zachariah West are right there?"

Since Ruby was taller than Dinah, she could see that Dinah hadn't been mistaken. Jonas and Silas were with the other sheep event competitors. "Surely they aren't..."

"Damn Silas's ornery hide, I'll bet that's exactly what he's done: entered to put Zeke West in his place." She sighed heavily. "You deal with men all day long. What is *wrong* with them when they just can't let something go? Why do they have to keep poking the bear? Even after they've promised to stop poking the bear because the bear pokes back?"

Ruby twirled the parasol. "Dinah, if I'd figured out what makes men do what they do, I'd have more money than the Hearst family, the Vanderbilts, and the Rockefellers combined."

Dinah snickered.

"Men will always have pissing contests to see who has the bigger pecker."

Silence.

Ruby leaned closer. "Pecker is another word for cock, darling."

"I sort of gathered that."

Their conversation lost momentum while they watched the bizarre contest of putting small children on the backs of sheep.

But they voiced their outrage when a girl placed first and she wasn't allowed to claim the prize.

Ruby casually said, "In the interests of female rights, I feel we should have a little celebratory toast to Edna Mae's accomplishment."

"Agreed."

"Hold this." She handed Dinah the parasol handle when she bent down to get the flask out of her stocking. "How about a nip of cherried brandy?"

"Sounds delicious." Dinah swapped the handle for the flask. She took a big swig then passed it back. "Oh, that's good. Like summer in a bottle. Thank you for sharing with me."

"You're welcome. Have more."

They passed the flask back and forth until they'd emptied it.

They might've gotten a bit enthusiastic when Jonas and Silas set a new record for sheep penning. And when Silas gifted Edna Mae with their winning certificate.

Dinah revealed her tipsiness when she confided, "That's the father of my future children. I'm thinking some intense baby-makin' practice is in our immediate future whenever I see that man mount up. Or when I watch him ride."

"Or even when you just watch him walk. With purpose, but also as if he has all the time in the world to get to you. And when he finally reaches you? Wild horses couldn't drag you away from him, but he wouldn't let you go anyway even if they tried."

"God. You get it, Ruby. You really, really get it."

Ruby bumped her with her hip. "I get it far more often than you do, *virgin*."

"I believe it. I took your advice, *madam*."

"Which advice?"

Before Ruby could respond, Jimmy and Marty tore up. Their pow-dered-sugar-coated faces and grins were something to behold.

"I take it you kids had fun."

"The most fun ever. But we…" Jimmy and Marty both eyed their teacher and whatever they were bursting to tell Ruby wasn't for Dinah's ears. So she let Jimmy lead her away and the three of them huddled with their heads close together.

Ruby lowered her voice. "What did you do?"

"I know you warned us not to play games—"

She started to tell them not to feel guilty about losing the money, but Jimmy blurted out, "But we played, and we *won*."

"What did you win?"

"Two dollars," Marty bragged.

"Two *whole* dollars," Jimmy emphasized.

"What game?"

"The shell game. A guy put a silver dollar under one of three shells and then kept movin' them around. When he stopped, we had to guess which shell the money was under. Marty guessed right both times and we got to keep the dollar!"

"Did you make them mad when you won?"

"Just the last time because we took the money and wouldn't play double or nothin'."

"So what are you doing back here? Are you hungry?"

Jimmy and Marty exchanged another look.

"Oh for heaven's sake, just tell me."

"Well, we wanna know if we're s'ppose to pay you back the dollar you gave us. Now that we got our own money."

These kids. Two bucks was everything to them. "My dollar was a gift. Fun money. You don't have to pay it back."

"Truly?"

"Truly."

"All right! So we're gonna go back. But we promise we ain't playin' no more games."

"Have fun. But keep checking in so I know you're all right."

When Ruby turned around, Dinah was gone. Apparently Silas was done competing if she'd taken off that fast.

Maybe she was slightly peeved that Dinah had just tossed the white parasol onto the ground. As well as the flask. That seemed rude.

And completely unlike the polite schoolteacher.

Frowning, Ruby bent down to pick up the flask and spotted a couple of large pieces of white fluff that weren't from her parasol.

How hadn't she noticed these? With the ground being so dusty, they would've stuck out.

Because the pieces of wool hadn't been there before she stepped away to talk to Jimmy and Marty.

A bad feeling flowed through her.

Scanning the crowd didn't get a glimpse of Dinah's pale blue dress. She spun around and didn't see her in any direction. Then she called out to Jimmy.

He immediately returned. "It's okay if you've changed your mind, we'll give it back."

"It's not that. Before we started talking, did you see where Miss Dinah went?"

"Nope. But I saw that West feller that Silas don't like sneakin' up behind her. I tried to warn her with my eyes, like Dickie's been tryin' to teach me, but it didn't work, and she turned away to talk to him. Then we were talkin' and when we were done, she wasn't there."

"Jimmy, before you return to the carnival, I need you to find either Silas or Deputy McKay. Tell them to look for me because I'm trying to find Dinah. I'll have this white parasol."

"Should I tell 'em about that West guy? 'Cause Silas gets so mad—"

"Yes, tell him."

"What can I do?" Marty asked.

"Look for her—them—where the buggies and horses are kept. If you see them, do not approach. Zeke is a dangerous man and he won't care if he has to hurt you to get rid of you. Promise me, Marty, you won't do anything but look for them."

"I promise."

Ruby took a deep breath and marched toward the center of the crowd.

She was so anxious to find Dinah that the whispers and comments rolled right over her.

Her panic increased with every moment that passed and she didn't catch sight of her friend.

Too many kids and people and dogs and noise; how was she supposed to concentrate?

Ruby stopped walking to focus on the movements of others. Without knowing West's agenda, she couldn't be sure if he'd try to hustle Dinah away to the outskirts of the crowd or if he'd remain in the thick of it.

Then she saw them. Her relief didn't last long. With the hold West had on Dinah's arm, she wasn't going with him willingly. But she wasn't actively fighting him either, which meant...

Sweet baby Jesus, he was forcing her cooperation in some way.

She had to stop this now. So she did the unthinkable; she drew attention to herself. Putting her fingers in her mouth, she let loose an ear-piercing whistle.

Twice.

The sound caused West to stutter a step and look around for the source.

Which was long enough to capture Dinah's attention. Embracing her Madam Ruby persona, she yelled, "Dinah! Where do you think you're going? Get back here right now."

West kept ahold of Dinah's arm as he marched her through the crowd toward Ruby. "If it isn't the town whore. Business slow today that you're out recruiting schoolteachers to work on their backs?"

Her hand tightened on the parasol handle. She could whack him with it if it came down to that and she'd enjoy every hard blow. "I don't believe Miss Thompson appreciates your vulgar sense of humor any more than I do."

When Zeke reached her, he said, "How much will she cost me?"

"Let go of her," Ruby said sharply.

"Give me a price range. Let's say I want her mouth, cunt and ass. I'd also want to fuck these sweet titties. How much?"

"She's not a working girl, Zeke, which you're fully aware of. Stop being a pain." Ruby thought maybe she could get the upper hand and get Dinah away from him if she acted annoyed rather than petrified.

"Not a working girl? Then why did I see you two laughing and talking together? And don't try and convince me you're *friends*." He sneered at a silent Dinah. "Ruby don't have any friends. Most people would like to see her strung up."

"What are you getting out of causing a scene?" she demanded, stalling for time in the hope Jonas would soon arrive and put a stop to this.

Dinah opened her mouth to answer and then a look of pain crossed her face.

"No talkin' out of turn, Miss Thompson," Zeke chastised her. Then to Ruby he said, "Me'n my friend Dinah were about to have a private celebration."

"I'd think you'd want to hide your face in shame, not celebrate. Losing the sheep competition to a couple of cattlemen."

"You shut up."

"Let the girl go and I will."

"What do you say?" Zeke mock whispered loudly to Dinah, ensuring that Ruby heard every word. "Shall we share the details on the private celebration I had planned? You. Me. Alone in the woods. All the time in the world to explore our urges. No one to bother us. No one except me to hear you scream with pleasure…or pain. No one will ever find—"

"You just threatened to kidnap, rape and kill her," Ruby snapped. "Now it's her word *and* mine against yours—"

"What's the word of a whore worth?" He shrugged. "Not as much as one of your holes, that's for damn sure."

His malicious gaze flicked to something behind her. Immediately his expression turned self-satisfied and Dinah's face drained of all color. "Now it's about to get interestin'," Zeke said. "Look who I found keepin' company with a whore. You should thank me for tryin' to save her reputation, McKay."

"Get your fuckin' hands off her," Silas snarled.

"Certainly." He shoved Dinah away from himself with such brutality that she skidded across her hands and knees in the dirt several feet away.

Silas flew at Zeke, knocking him to the ground.

They exchanged words and a few punches until Dinah gasped. "No, Silas, don't! He has a knife!" as Ruby helped her upright.

That did get Silas's attention.

He pushed to his feet and stormed over to her. "Did he hurt you?"

Dinah shook her head.

Silas looked as if he didn't believe her. "You're sure?"

She nodded.

He pulled Dinah into his arms, trying to control her trembling before he focused on Zeke. "If you *ever* come near her again, I'll kill you. Do you hear me, West? I *will* motherfucking kill you."

"Oh, I heard you." He gestured to the crowd gathered around them. "So did everyone else."

That bastard. That's what this drama had been about.

And Silas had played right into his hands.

Silas continued to glare at Zeke.

Dinah had her face buried in Silas's chest, refusing to look at anyone.

Zeke West sat on the ground in his fine clothes, the embodiment of pure evil.

That's the scene Deputy McKay arrived at.

Ruby ached at the reality that she couldn't go to him. She had to watch him weigh his fear for his brother with his anger that Silas hadn't learned anything from his previous altercations with Zeke and balance that with his responsibility as the law.

Jonas had to listen to Zeke whine and spew lies about feeling threatened by Silas when he'd been trying to do the man a favor. She hated that it wouldn't make any difference in the way Deputy McKay had to handle this, if she told him that Zeke had intended to kidnap, rape and kill Dinah.

The deputy stopped Zeke mid-rant to shoo people away. "Okay, show's over folks. Move along."

Zeke stood and brushed the dirt from his clothes. "Since you're not takin' this seriously, I demand to speak to Sheriff Eccleston about your brother's continued threats when I was merely havin' a conversation with his *friend*, Dinah, in order to help her."

"She's more than my goddamned friend, and you know it," Silas spat.

"And yet...I still don't see her wearing your ring."

Deputy McKay held up his hand to quell any further outbursts. "If you can find him in this crowd, West, you're more than welcome to speak with him," Jonas said evenly. Then he pointed to an object on the ground behind him. "Just make sure you tell him why that knife was necessary when you had a 'conversation' with Miss Thompson."

Zeke glanced over his shoulder at the knife. "I have no idea what you're talkin' about, Deputy. That's not my knife."

"My mistake." Jonas crouched down and picked it up. He didn't bother examining it; he just pushed the switchblade closed and dropped it into his pocket. "Shame that someone lost such a nice piece. I'll keep it in the deputy's office in case the owner comes lookin' for it."

God, she loved this man.

"I believe the sheriff is officiating the three-legged race. Best be getting over there if you wanna have a word with him before it starts." Then he turned his back on Zeke, making sure he understood that Deputy McKay wasn't afraid of him.

Zeke slunk off. Alone. It appeared even his brother had abandoned him.

Silas started to speak but Jonas held up his hand. "You've said enough, doncha think? Head on home. I'm right behind you."

"We have to make a stop first."

"Fine. But I'm gonna make sure that 'stop' is in the opposite direction from the one Zeke West went."

Silas took Dinah's hand and they walked away toward the horse paddock.

Then Jonas stepped in front of Ruby. "You okay?"

"Not really. I'm scared for her. Something isn't right with him. This is beyond card games, and land rivalries and missed courting opportunities."

"I know. But the hell of it is...I don't know what to do about it." He scrubbed his hands over his face. "Tell me what West said."

Ruby made a show of examining her parasol. "As West pointed out, the word of a whore isn't worth anything, so I'll save my breath."

"That ain't fair."

"No, it's not." She looked at him. "I can't do this anymore, Deputy."

Those eyes darkened with an emotion she'd never seen before. "Do what?"

Watch you hurting. Pretend I don't care about you deeply. Hide from you that I love you like I never imagined I could love another living soul.

But she couldn't tell him that. Not here. Maybe not ever.

Brusquely, she said, "You know *exactly* what."

"Christ, Ruby. What am I supposed to say?"

"Nothing. We're both very good at doing that." She popped open her parasol and turned to walk away.

And Jonas let her.

RUBY'S TEARS HAD dried by the time she'd cleared the end of the race-track. It startled her to see Gigi from the Beulah Brothel approaching her. She offered Gigi a genuine smile. "It appears they'll even let old whores like us celebrate with the decent folk today."

But Gigi wasn't smiling. She seemed out of breath, as if she'd been running. "I didn't come here to celebrate. I came here to find you."

"What's wrong?"

"Madam Marie. She's been sick but she took a serious turn for the worse yesterday. I got a telegram today because they sent one to you yesterday, but no one would deliver it you."

Not the first time that'd happened.

Gigi took a breath. "Marie's girls are catfighting and the whole house is in chaos. Dorothy fears that if things aren't sorted quickly, the Lawrence County Sheriff will seize the chance to close Madam Marie's down after she's dead, since it's the last workin' whorehouse in Deadwood."

"What am I supposed to do about that from here?"

"That's the thing; Marie has requested we both come to Deadwood to restore order to the house, pick her successor and stay for her funeral."

Dammit. Going to Deadwood and handling this would take more than just a day or two.

"She's going to die, Ruby. This is the last thing she's askin' of us. We owe her."

Ruby knew Gigi was right. "It'll be at least tomorrow before I can get transportation—"

"You don't understand." Gigi grasped Ruby's hands. "Marie sent her carriage for us. It's waitin' on the opposite side of the tracks."

"Right now? God. This really is dire." She looked around. "But I can't just leave from here. My girls—"

"Will be fine. Send word to Mrs. Mavis that Dickie should expect a telegram at Sackett's from you as soon as you're in South Dakota. If we went to Labelle to get your things, we'd be wastin' time that could already have us halfway to Deadwood. Marie has everything you need—except extra time. We have to leave now."

Ruby had no choice. "All right. I'll write Mavis a note and make sure Jimmy gets it to her. Then we can go."

EIGHTEEN

THE COMMUNITY CELEBRATION had lost its appeal after their run-in with Zeke.

Silas insisted they return to the ranch and forget everything that had happened after the rancher's competition. It'd surprised Dinah that Jonas had agreed and was waiting for them when they'd arrived from Sundance.

Now the brothers were outside arguing while she'd opted to stay in and cut up the chicken Silas had bought from Farnum's.

He'd also bought her a gun.

Which was why the brothers were arguing.

Silas had been so overwrought that he was chopping wood like a mad man. Shirt off, muscles in his arms bulging, sinew in his back straining as he swung the axe over and over. Sweat dripping from his brow. Sweat running down his torso. The man was a sight to behold even in his anger.

Maybe especially in his anger.

Dinah had been so distracted by Silas working half-naked, all those perfectly sculpted muscles flexing right outside the window, that she'd nearly sliced off her finger. So she forced herself to listen to their conversation through the open door instead.

"I know I threatened him. I know everyone around us heard me threaten him. What you're not hearin' is me apologizing for doin' it because I'm not sorry. Not even a little bit."

"So you've said ten fuckin' times. That's not the point I'm tryin' to make," Jonas snapped.

Thwack. Crack. Then a hollow thud as he pitched the chopped piece into the pile.

"Then get to the fuckin' point, Jonas."

"What did West say to her?"

Dinah's stomach tightened. She'd been relieved that Silas hadn't pressed her for details because she couldn't remember beyond someone tapping her on the shoulder. She'd turned to find Zeke West shoving a knife against her belly and he'd warned her not to make a scene.

She'd gone with him willingly. But fear had overtaken her. Her thoughts were on Silas and how he'd react if he saw West with a knife, not to mention the bruising grip Zeke had maintained as he'd marched her through the crowd. She'd chanted *please don't hurt me* so loudly in her head that Zeke's voice in her ear had been a blur of sound, as if he'd been speaking to her through water.

Her shock had left her addle-brained even after Ruby had bravely tracked them down. Dinah remembered standing across from the fierce-eyed madam, watching her lips moving and yet not hearing anything she'd been saying—thankfully nothing Zeke had said registered either. But she had felt the tip of Zeke's knife twisting into her spine as a warning while he'd conversed with Ruby.

What had shaken her out of her mental stupor was Silas bursting onto the scene. Her fear hadn't abated; it'd increased at witnessing the fury on Silas's face at seeing Zeke with his hand on her. The burning sensation of the knife puncturing her flesh forced her out of her physical stasis seconds before Zeke had hurled her to the ground.

After warning Silas about the knife, Dinah had attempted to hide her injury, knowing if Silas saw red, nothing could've stopped him from killing Zeke, right there in public.

Nothing. Not even his promise that he'd never fight with Zeke again.

Then Deputy McKay had shown up.

At that point Dinah had come back to herself. Jonas had more to deal with than just Silas's outburst, so she had to buck up. The best way to handle Silas was to act as if this incident had just been another unfortunate run-in with Zeke. She wouldn't berate Silas for breaking his promise not to fight with West. She wouldn't confess her fear she'd never see Silas again. She especially wouldn't share her gut feeling that Zeke had tried to separate her from the crowd because he'd intended to rape her and kill her.

After they left Jonas with Ruby, they mounted up.

Silas had insisted on stopping at Farnum's to use his newly won store credit. She'd stayed with the horses and wasn't aware he'd bought more than two fryer chickens and a big bottle of whiskey until he'd set the purchases, including the gun, on the table in the cabin.

The moment Jonas had seen the gun, he'd lit into Silas and wouldn't let up.

That's also when she'd become theatrical about their fighting and kicked both men out of the house. That allowed her privacy to change out of—and to try to clean up—her blood-stained dress.

Examining the stab wound had proven difficult given it was in a spot she couldn't see—not even with the help from her hand mirror. She could only feel the length of it, but if she touched it, it bled. Treatment of the wound beyond cleaning it would have to wait until she returned to Doc's.

The bruises on her arm would be harder to hide.

Zeke had wrenched her arm so violently she understood why Silas believed his arm had been broken the time he got into it with Zeke. It'd been agony holding the reins on the ride home. Lifting her arms to get undressed. Using force to cut through chicken bones. She still had pie crust to roll out and if Silas saw her struggling, he'd demand to know why and she could not—*would* not—tell him.

Keeping her injuries from him was a matter of life or death this time.

She'd used her mother's best trick, adopting a chipper "can-do" attitude to mask her emotions, even when part of her was bothered that Silas believed everything was fine and dandy as soon as they'd reached home and hearth.

"Listen to me," Jonas said sharply, outside the window, snagging Dinah's attention again. "Gimme the gun."

"Nope." *Thwack. Crack.* "You have your own collection of guns. A big collection."

"They're not all mine. They're ones I've confiscated after they've been used in a crime."

"This one ain't ever been fired, so back off on your need to confiscate it."

"Maybe, you stubborn bastard, I'm tryin' to head off a crime before it happens."

"Is that a new law enforcement tactic? Or just one you're usin' on your younger, hotheaded brother?"

Dinah shook her head. Silas could be so ornery sometimes, especially with Jonas. Jonas was the older twin only by twenty minutes. But to hear Silas tell it, Jonas acted years older. Sometimes she saw it—like now, when Silas overreacted like a petulant child.

Whatever Jonas said in response, Dinah didn't hear.

But Silas's derisive snort was loud and clear.

Then the thwacks became louder. Faster. Not in a natural way. She listened as she dredged the chicken pieces in flour. That done, she stepped outside to wash her hands and saw Silas and Jonas each with an axe, chopping wood as fast as they could.

"What in the world is going on out here?"

"No time to talk, darlin', me'n Jonas is havin' a contest. The winner gets—"

"Silas McKay, didn't you learn your lesson the last time you took a bet?" she demanded.

He grunted.

Jonas laughed and Silas told him to piss up a rope, which only made Jonas laugh harder.

Even laughing, Jonas didn't miss a swing in his quest to finish his log pile first.

Dinah rounded the corner of the cabin to the new cold storage box Silas had built. She pulled out two eggs and a jar of cream. She purposely ignored their huffing and puffing as she walked past them into the house.

She scooped a dollop of duck fat into the biggest cast iron pot. As she waited for it to heat, she mixed up milk batter, adding a touch of vinegar, and dunked the chicken into it. After tossing all the pieces into the pan, she slid the lid on and moved on to her next task.

"Dinah, come quick!"

She raced out of the house muttering, "I *knew* one of you would get injured."

Silas and Jonas were both bent over, air soughing in and out of their lungs.

"What's wrong?"

"Nothin'," Silas wheezed. "Whose is bigger?"

"Excuse me?"

He gestured to the piles. "Who has more wood."

This was what the "Dinah, come quick!" had been about?

They were both looking at her as if they had every right to interrupt her work to play mama and declare a winner in their petty games.

Nope.

Propping her hands on her hips, she said, "Well, stand up and drop your drawers."

"What?"

"That's what this is about, isn't it? To prove which one of you has a bigger c—"

"DINAH!" Silas yelled. "That ain't what we were doin' at all!"

"Oh. Right. If you're identical in all ways then you're probably endowed the same, so you have no need for me to be out here judging the size of your…wood…when I need to be inside making sure my damn chicken doesn't burn."

She flounced back inside.

Jonas huffed out a laugh. "I like her. I mostly like that she's already got a hold of your bollocks nice and tight."

After hearing that, she slammed the door.

SHE'D JUST FINISHED frying the chicken when the door opened and Silas yelled in, "Is it safe to come in or are you still sore?"

"Come in. It's your house."

Silas moved in behind her and kissed the nape of her neck. "It's *our* house, darlin'."

"Did you work off your extra energy?"

"Some of it." He pressed another kiss to her temple. "I'm savin' the rest for you."

She whirled around, biting back the wince of pain, and noticed he still hadn't put on a shirt. Peering around his arm to make sure his brother wasn't watching, she lapped at the sweat that had pooled in the hollow of his throat. "Mmm. You still taste angry though."

He hissed in a breath. "Don't start something we can't finish."

"Then put some clothes on. If your brother is half-naked tell him the same."

He held fast to her arm and the agony from it nearly knocked her to her knees. "Sugar pie, have you been drinkin'?"

Whiskey dulled the pain, so she'd been sneaking a nip as needed. "Yes. It's a day for celebration. And after the morning I had, I have every right to get rip roaring drunk."

Unsurprisingly, he didn't have a response for that.

Dinah dished up the chicken, potatoes and gravy, green beans and cream biscuits. She'd mixed sugar with the leftover sour cherries to create a sweet drink. But it wasn't sweet enough. "Silas, do we have rum? Or just whiskey?"

"Just whiskey. If you want rum—"

"Put it on the list" they finished together and laughed.

That's when Jonas sauntered in. He sent them an amused smile and pulled out his chair. "Dinah. This looks outstanding. Thanks for cookin' for us."

"My pleasure."

There wasn't much small talk during the meal. Dinah wondered if it was a habit with them or if they were avoiding a specific conversation about the morning's events. "What are your plans for the rest of the day?" she asked Jonas.

"Heading back into town. Gotta make sure none of the kids burn the buildings down with their fireworks."

Maybe he and Ruby had made plans to meet up later.

"Sundance?" Silas asked. "Or Labelle?"

"Labelle. There's a community dance in Sundance after the city fireworks. I expect it'll be quiet in Labelle since most businesses are closed, unlike Sundance where everything is open later than usual." He wiped his fingers. "Are you stayin' here tonight, Dinah?"

"I'd planned on it. But now I wonder if I should be at Doc's in case there are fireworks injuries."

"Nope. You're stayin' here. He can do without you for one damn night." Silas picked up her hand and kissed her knuckles. "I can't."

"Aww. Listen to you sweet-talk me, McKay." She winked at Jonas.

"You think his need for me to stay has something to do with the fact I haven't finished baking that cherry pie yet?"

Jonas laughed. "Maybe."

After they finished their late lunch, the brothers rode off for "a bit" without saying where they were headed. Dinah washed the dishes, put the pie in the oven and wandered out to check on the potatoes and other root vegetables she'd planted. But even that brought her pain. Since she was alone, she allowed herself to give in to tears.

Silas returned alone. In a somber mood.

After he dealt with his horse, he returned inside and immediately came back out with the box containing the gun he'd gotten at Farnum's.

"Darlin', come here. I wanna show you how to load this."

"Why?"

"Because it's different than the Winchester 30-30 rifle and the Colt revolver we practiced with last week."

"I'm not in the mood." God. She ached. There was no way she could hold up a gun for more than a second or two.

His fingers circled her wrist, keeping her from flouncing off. "Then get in the mood, because we're target shootin' with this."

"It's...little," she said when he held it up.

"Got enough stopping power to make you rethink that little comment." He held it out for her to inspect. "It's a Remington Model 95 derringer. Over/under double barrel. Ammo is .41rimfire and I got you a box of that too."

"Silas. I don't—"

"Just hold it." Then he dropped it in the palm of her hand.

"It's heavier than I expected."

"And yet, it'll fit in your apron pocket."

Her gaze flew to his. "I can't carry a gun around all the time."

"I don't expect you to. You can put it under your pillow when you're sleepin'."

"That's not funny."

"Wasn't meant to be." He opened a box of bullets. "Let's get it loaded so you can practice doin' it yourself and then we'll target shoot."

There was no arguing with him. Nor had he given her a chance to sneak inside for a sip to dull the pain that would accompany all this movement.

After she'd shot and reloaded five or six times, she understood why Silas had picked this model for her. It fit her hand. Dropping it in her pocket didn't weight it down any more than a large apple would. Because she had a better grip on the smaller gun, her accuracy was higher than with the Colt. Within an hour she could blow a pinecone off the top of the fencepost nearly every time.

Silas had seemed pleased.

And she'd understood his seriousness about her learning how to use it when he'd foregone pie in order to teach her.

Later that night, after they'd read from *The Red Badge of Courage*, and they lay cuddled together in the darkness, Silas spoke. "I didn't break my promise to you today. I didn't go off half-cocked until after Zeke threatened you."

"What?"

"After I knocked him down, he promised he'd take you away from me. He wanted to prove how easy it'd be and how much he looked forward to seein' me fall apart."

She shivered and he tightened his hold on her. "Did you tell Jonas what he said?"

"Yeah. But it don't matter. No one heard that exchange but me'n Zeke. Zeke made sure no one heard it."

"Is Jonas going to tell the sheriff?"

"Says he plans to, but he warned me it won't change anything. It's my word against West's. And if he got to the sheriff first…"

She tipped her head back to try and read his eyes, but the darkness was absolute. "Where did you and Jonas go today?"

"I showed him where I'm hidin' my money. In case something happens to me."

"Hiding your money," she repeated. "You don't keep your money in the bank?"

Silas snorted. "I don't trust banks."

"But you 'trust' your money is safer…buried?"

"Yep."

How hadn't she known this about him? "Handy that you have your own bank. What do you call it? The Stinky Old Boot Savings and Loan?"

"Not funny. Bankers are crooks. Plus, banks get robbed all the damn time. The money is safer with me. I just needed Jonas to see where I'd stashed it."

"Why didn't you show *me* where you keep it?"

"Because we agreed not to talk about money. At least not until we're married. Remember?"

Was he really throwing that in her face now?

"Jonas needs to know where stuff is because he'll take care of everything for me."

"Am I one of those things, Silas?"

"Now, don't go getting all het up about this. My brother has a better understanding of what needs done. And I did it because I don't want you to worry."

"About some 'man' stuff I can't understand? Piss off, McKay." Dinah tossed back the covers and limped out of the cabin into the cool night air.

Silas barreled out, right behind her, not giving a fig that the only thing he wore on his bared flesh was moonlight. And she was so mad she forced herself not to look at his manhood, since he'd chosen now as the first time he'd displayed it to her.

"Hey now. That ain't fair."

"You're right. It's not." She propped her left hand on her left hip. "What else did you and Jonas talk about?" Then, as if the wind whispered it to her, she knew. "You asked him to take care of me if Zeke does the unthinkable to you. No, you asked him to *marry* me."

"Dinah—"

"Tell me I'm wrong."

He sighed. "You're not."

"Goddammit McKay, you can't demand that of your brother! He has a life and his own love story to live. Not to mention I am not some...prized heifer to be passed on to the next big bull that comes along. I can take care of myself."

"Jesus, woman. Settle down."

She shrugged off his touch and stepped away.

He followed and tried to put his hands on her shoulders.

"Don't touch me."

"Sugar pie, you don't mean that," he said softly and attempted to circle his arms around her waist.

Dinah spun around and her new little derringer was in her hand, pointed at his chest. "I said back off, McKay."

His hands went up. "Okay. Let's just take a moment here. And please lower that loaded pistol, darlin'." He paused. "Please."

"Fine." She let it dangle by her side.

"Hell fire, woman. I didn't even see you snatch it off the table."

"Maybe I had it under my pillow like you suggested," she cooed.

"Christ. You're in a mood."

"Yep, a bad mood. If you were smart, you'd say *yes darlin'* when I told you I wanted to mount my horse and head back to Doc's."

Then he loomed over her. "Like hell that's happening. You wouldn't even get there until midnight."

"I can tell time," she snapped. "And I know you'd follow me regardless if I told you not to, which means you wouldn't get back here until one a.m. and I know you have to get up and check cattle early. So I'll stay. But I'm mad at you. Go to bed and leave me alone. I'll come in when I've worked off my mad, but I'll be sleeping in Jonas's bed, not yours."

Silas growled at her.

She pointed at the open door with the gun. "Now get in there before you get bug bites on your pecker."

His eyes narrowed. "Where'd you hear that term?"

"From a friend."

"I'm leavin' the door open," he groused, giving her a great view of his tightly muscled rear end before he disappeared into darkness.

Dinah watched the stars, trying to empty her mind.

But it didn't work. She hated that Zeke had done what he'd promised: made it so not a day went past that they didn't think about him.

When she couldn't quit yawning, she padded back inside and quietly closed the door. After setting her gun on the table, she cut to the left and climbed into Jonas's bed. She didn't really want to sleep there, but she had to stick to her guns.

That phrase made her smother her laughter in Jonas's pillow.

But her hysteria gave way to tears.

Almost immediately, she found herself airborne and then tucked into a warm male body.

"I'm sorry, darlin'. I tried. But you belong in my bed, next to me, not across the damn room." He nuzzled her ear. "I especially can't listen to you cry and not have you in my arms."

"Silas."

"Am I the cause of them tears?"

"No."

"Thank god for that."

After she'd found a position that hurt neither her arm nor the knife wound, she nestled her cheek against the downy hair on his chest. His scent, his strength, the way he tended to her needs was everything she'd ever wanted. He cared for her enough to give her the independence she needed, but in doing that he compromised his protective nature and that in turn was hard for him. That gave her the courage to tell him the decision she'd come to when she'd considered what they were truly up against.

"What's churning in that brain of yours?" he said softly.

"That I'm scared."

"Me too, darlin'."

It was a big step that he'd admitted that to her. "Our fear—our future—is worth more than money."

"I don't follow."

"Fulfilling my work promise to Doc isn't more important than the promise I've made to you. The money I'd earn in the next year teaching and working for him would help us, but not as much as us being together will give us peace of mind that money can't buy. You can't protect me from thirty miles away. I know that it's eating at you, Silas, that Zeke can get to me when I'm in Labelle. So the logical solution is to get married as soon as possible—we'll be together and able to protect each other all the time."

Silas shifted to stare into her eyes. "You mean it?"

"I do. We're stronger together than we are apart."

"Yes, that we are." He kissed her with such love and tenderness her eyes welled up again. "Christ, woman, I do love you."

"I love you too."

"Tomorrow after cattle check, we'll hitch up the wagon and get your things from Doc's. We'll swing by the Crook County Courthouse and see about getting a marriage license. Doubt we can get it tomorrow, bein's Mondays are their busiest day, but you'll be Mrs. McKay this week for sure."

Of all the decisions she'd made today, this one had been the easiest. "I can't wait."

"Me neither." He blew in her ear and expelled a cocky chuckle when she shivered and moaned. "Now get some sleep, because as soon as you're my wife, we ain't gonna get much sleep when we're in this bed."

NINETEEN

THE DAY HAD gone to hell from the start.

Silas had awoken before Dinah—not unusual. He'd done his morning business, washed up, and made a pot of coffee. He'd poured Dinah a cup and carried it to where she still slept, curled into the bedcoverings as if still hugging him.

Her shift had risen up her thighs and his admiring gaze moved over her half-nekkid form.

That's when he noticed the blood.

At first, he'd believed she'd just gotten her monthly flow, but none of the red was between her legs. It seeped through her nightgown on the lower right side of her back. When he leaned closer to get a better look, he also noticed the bruising on her right arm. Hand shaped bruises in two spots, the impressions deep enough to make out the individual demarcations of each finger.

Zeke had hurt her yesterday. In three different spots that he could see—who knew if there were other places she'd hidden from him?—and she'd fucking lied about it.

Lied.

To his face.

What the hell had happened to her promise that she wouldn't keep things from him?

It's not as if you're not keeping things from her too.

Yeah, but those things were for her own good.

Maybe she believed this was for your own good. How would you have reacted yesterday if you'd known she was bleeding and bruised at the hands of Zeke West?

Silas would've killed him. Right then and there.

And he'd be in jail.

Even if she would've shown him the injuries last night, he likely would've gotten up, ridden to the snake pit that West crawled out of and killed him.

So he'd be in jail.

Either way—the end result was the same.

He forewent his impulse to ease back into bed and snuggle up to her, coddling and cuddling her—which given her stubborn nature would be a worse method of getting answers about her lies than merely shaking her awake.

Instead of poking the bear, he parked his ass on a chair and drank his coffee as if he had all the time in the world to do so.

He'd finished his second cup when Dinah began to stir. He loved watching her come to wakefulness. Blinking away the haze of sleep that looked damn close to her drowsy look of pleasure. The way she stretched her whole body, swaying her clasped arms above her head, rolling her back into an arch from her hips to her shoulders, rocking her neck side to side, pointing and flexing her toes and then expelling a soft sigh.

But that's not how his beloved awoke this morning. She moved her arm gingerly and emitted a soft wail. If that tiny movement caused her to cry out, how in the hell had she cooked, cleaned and target shot yesterday without yelling in agony?

Because like you, she is damn good at pretending everything is fine.

And Dinah did yelp when she caught him sitting at her bedside, staring at her.

"Silas? Is everything all right?"

"Nope." He drained his coffee. "How'd you sleep?"

"Umm…okay. Why—"

"You must've been restless since it caused the wound—I'm guessin' a goddamned *stab* wound—to reopen in the night, since you've got blood on your nightgown."

She started to retort but he shook his head.

"Don't bother to pretend it's your woman's time because even I know that you don't bleed from your lower back. Or maybe"—he stood and shuffled closer—"we oughta discuss all them bruises on your arm. Bet it hurt like hell to have that arm wrapped around me last night."

"Fine. I'm in a lot of pain. Is that what you want to hear?"

"No. I never wanna hear that you're hurtin'. But what's worse is you didn't trust me enough to tell me the truth when I asked you about it yesterday."

Dinah closed her eyes. "You know why I didn't."

"Yep, I do. So darlin', I hate to do this, because I know you're sore, and this ain't about me punishing you for not comin' clean about him hurtin' you, but I can't risk leavin' you here when I check cattle." He wished he could just kiss her on the forehead and tuck the covers around her so she could rest. "Since I took most of yesterday off, I gotta do a full check, so you'll have to get up and come along. I promise we'll get you to Doc's as soon as possible so he can take a look at you."

She threw back the covers with her left hand. "If I can walk, I can ride. If I can ride, I can check cattle." She stood. "Ain't that right, cowboy?"

At any other time, he would've laughed. But not today. Today he just felt sad and kind of sick that his damn cows had to come before her. "You need help getting dressed?"

"No."

"Now...how'd I know you were gonna say that?" Silas pressed the other coffee cup into her hand and kissed her forehead. "I'll saddle up your horse and be waitin' for ya outside."

THEY DIDN'T SPEAK beyond Silas instructing her and her obeying, mostly because they were both in a rush to get this done.

With their late start, they didn't finish until one in the afternoon and then he still had to deal with Henrikson's cattle.

Henrikson was a real prick about it too.

Normally Silas had no problem staying civil and nodding when Henrikson complained and berated him. But he'd had enough of everyone's shit that he wasn't about to swallow another mouthful.

"You know what, Garold, if I'm doin' such a piss-poor job takin' care of your cattle then it's time we parted ways. You can deal with your own livestock or hire someone else to do it, but I'm done." He tipped his hat. "Good luck to you." Then he turned and tore off toward home.

By the time Dinah caught up to him, he'd had his horse turned out and the oxen hooked up to the wagon.

"Good lord. Those things are huge."

"They'll get the job done."

"Are they mean?"

"Nope. They were castrated early so they're calmer. That's why they're best for pulling and plowing."

"I don't imagine they have names."

Silas snorted and adjusted the modified horse collars he used instead of a yoke.

"Since as of tonight I'll be in permanent residence at the McKay Ranch, from here on out, I will be naming our livestock." She dismounted and approached the ox on the left side. "This one is Beast. The one on the right will be known as Beauty."

"Whatever you want, darlin'. We gotta get a move on if we're gonna get loaded and get back here and unloaded before dark."

"That doesn't leave us any time to go to the courthouse today, does it?"

"Nope. The best day of my life is gonna have to be tomorrow." He pulled the cinch. He turned and Dinah was right there.

"I get so mad at you, McKay, and then you go and say such heartfelt things that I just melt."

Grinning, he stole a kiss. "It's my job as your husband to make you melt at least once a day and twice on Sundays. Then I'm gonna take my own sweet time licking you up."

"I'll be right back." Dinah kissed him. "I've gotta grab something out of the house."

It took twice as long to get to Doc's by wagon as it did on horseback.

Dinah had gone inside to speak with Mrs. Agnes, since Doc was out on a call. She seemed to've been gone a long time. Maybe the crotchety old woman was informing her that Doc wasn't releasing her from their agreement as easily as she'd believed.

Silas caged up the two chickens and rooster that his intended had purchased in the last month. He wandered through the barn, wondering how much Doc would ask for the milk cow, since it'd go un-milked if Dinah wasn't here to do it.

A clanking noise outside the barn caught his attention.

Thinking it was Dinah, he peered around the corner to see Zeke West leaning against the corral, gun clutched in his hand.

After yesterday, Silas should've been scared, but today he was just tired of this. Yes, he'd played a part in things getting to this point, but how much more would he and Dinah have to put up with?

"Come on out, McKay. I know you can see me."

"Why are you here, West? Can't you just let it go?"

"I'm getting really tired of everyone tellin' me that."

"If everyone is tellin' you that, then maybe you oughta listen."

Bootsteps shuffled in the dirt, making Silas wonder if West was drunk.

"Get out here," Zeke said. "I'd hate to have to shoot your—"

Silas hustled out with his hands above his head. "I'm here. I'm un-armed. Now what do you want?"

"A fair fight. Not a fist fight or a game of chance. Let's settle this Old West style." He snickered. "Get it? I'm the same old West?"

Jesus. This man had rocked off the rails completely.

"As to your question, I want one thing I've been denied." Zeke spun the Colt on his index finger, forward and backward, stopping it with his palm. "A real gunfight."

"I told you, I'm not armed."

"Well, that's just plain dumb, McKay. I told you I'd be gunnin' for you. I would've thought after yesterday, when I proved I can get to Dinah any time I want, that you would be all puffed up with anger and armed to the teeth."

"I'm a rancher. That's it. I never aspired to be a railroad tycoon, or a card sharp, or a gunfighter. All I wanna do is live my dream of raising cattle with my woman by my side. I'm no threat to you, Zeke. I never have been."

"That's all I ever wanted too. To live my dream. But you stole that dream from me. You McKays took it and you didn't even know it." Zeke lifted his gun and aimed it at Silas's forehead. "So I lied. I don't want a fair fight. I just want you dead so I can put you outta my misery." He smirked at his play on words. "You threatened me yesterday so there ain't a judge that'll hang me for defending myself." Keeping his pistol in his right hand, Zeke reached into his vest pocket for another gun. A derringer, just like the one Silas had bought Dinah yesterday.

For a brief, horrible moment, Silas thought Zeke had gotten to Dinah and it was Dinah's gun in his hand. But hers didn't have those fancier pearl grips.

"Now, I can't shoot an unarmed man," Zeke taunted, "so you'll have to think fast."

Silas stepped to the side to dodge the derringer that Zeke intended to throw at him.

Two shots were fired so quickly that Silas wasn't sure where they'd come from until he and Zeke hit the dirt at the same time.

Except Zeke didn't get up.

And blood began to spread out from beneath his body.

Silas looked over and saw a white-faced Dinah standing by the back of the wagon, arm straight out, her derringer still clutched in her hand.

Her shooting arm began to wobble, and she said, "Is he dead? Oh god, did I really kill him?" She raised teary eyes to his. "Silas?"

Silas jumped to his feet.

Her horrified gaze dropped to the blood on Silas's frontside. "Did I shoot you too?"

"It ain't my blood."

The gun dropped from her hand and thudded into the dirt.

Then she swayed and fell to her knees before she listed to the side and passed out.

He raced to her.

The next three things happened simultaneously.

Silas picked up the derringer and nearly plowed into Mrs. Agnes as she exited the house.

She yelled, "I told you kids to stop foolin' with fireworks, the holiday is over…" She saw the gun in Silas's hand and her wide-eyed gaze moved to Zeke, prone on the ground.

The jingle of a harness sounded behind him. Still holding the derringer, he spun around and saw Doc's buggy pulling up.

"What the devil is going on here?" Doc bailed out of the buggy and dropped beside Zeke.

Silas stood there in shock, watching Doc struggle to find a pulse in

Zeke's neck.

This wasn't happening. Any second he'd wake up in a cold sweat and he'd be goddamned grateful it'd just been a fucking nightmare.

Mrs. Agnes shrieked, "Silas McKay killed Zeke West. I saw him do it. He's still got the gun."

Doc's shrewd gaze moved from the gun in Silas's hand to the two bloody holes, one on either side of Zeke's spine. "You shot him in the back?"

"No! I…"

But his focus had moved beyond the dead man. "Dear lord, what happened to Dinah?"

"After Zeke…she…"

Mrs. Agnes hadn't even noticed Dinah on the ground behind her. She gasped. "Is she dead too?"

Doc hustled over and did a quick exam. "She's in shock. At least I can treat her." He stood slowly and held out his hands. "Silas. Son. Put the gun down. Nice and slow."

"I didn't hurt her, Doc. I'd never hurt her."

"I believe you. And you can help me help her. Let's get her moved into her room. She'll be more comfortable there." He looked over at his wife. "Agnes. Please get the door."

Silas set the derringer on the back of the wagon. Then he bent down and gently scooped Dinah into his arms.

After he lay her on the bed, he sat on the chair beside her, pulling her feet into his lap so he could unlace her boots.

"Silas."

He glanced up at Doc.

"As you know, my wife is not strong. She needs to tell the deputy what she saw before she relapses. So I'll have to lock you in here with Dinah while I fetch him."

"I get that, Doc. And don't worry. I'll stay put. I won't cause any trouble."

Doc rubbed his eyes. "Yes, you've caused plenty of trouble for one day. For one damn lifetime, McKay."

The lock clicked behind him.

Silas pressed his face into Dinah's belly. Breathing her in. Wondering if this was the last time he'd ever be this close to her. There'd be no marriage this week—or ever. No making room for her things in his house. No good-natured ribbing from his brother about finding a new place to hang his hat.

He'd swing for this, for sure.

The bad blood between him and West likely meant there wouldn't be a trial. A circuit judge would hear Mrs. Agnes's claim that she'd seen him shoot Zeke, and that'd be that.

Even if it wasn't true.

But he'd go to hell himself before he told anyone the truth about who'd fired the gun.

Maybe it made him the most unfeeling bastard in the world, but he wasn't sorry Zeke West was dead. If the man would've been less inclined to blow hot air, Silas's body would be cooling outside right now. Maybe Dinah's too. Or worse, he might've taken her and done unspeakable things to her.

"I'm sorry, darlin'. I screwed this up nine ways to Sunday. Maybe Zeke was off his nut, but I could've been the bigger man. The better man. Now it's too late. I should've listened to my brother when he said my actions will be the death of me. But I will do everything I can to make sure my actions won't be the death of you too."

Silas had no idea how long he remained in that position. He just knew he was reluctant to move even when his damn neck hurt, and his leg had fallen asleep.

The lock clicked and the door creaked open.

"Is she okay?" Jonas asked behind him.

"Still in shock."

He harrumphed. Then his hand landed on Silas's shoulder. "I've gotta take you in."

"I know." He cleared his throat. "I need to have a word with Doc."

"I'm right here, boy."

After gifting Dinah with a kiss on the forehead, then the mouth, and a whispered, "I love you," he straightened and faced Doc. "Zeke stabbed her yesterday so she's got a puncture wound on the lower right side of her back. He also wrenched her arm—just like he'd done to mine—and she's been in a lot of pain from that. Plus he left other bruises on her arm. I'm askin' you to keep her comfortable for however long it takes for her not to be in pain as she heals."

"Of course I'll see to her."

"Thank you." He brought Dinah's hand to his mouth and kissed the finger that should've been bearing his ring. "And if I am to hang, I don't want her there. I don't care if you gotta lock her in this room, that ain't something she needs to watch, no matter what she says."

"Again, McKay, I think of her as a daughter, so I'll make sure she's protected."

"I appreciate it."

Behind him, he heard Jonas say, "The oxen are in the paddock. I'll be by tomorrow sometime to return them to the ranch."

"I'd appreciate it."

After one last look at his beloved, he turned and walked out.

TWENTY

TWILIGHT HAD PASSED to full-on dark when Jonas escorted his brother down the dusty road from Doc's place to the deputy's office.

He hadn't bothered to restrain him; Silas was resigned to his fate.

Word hadn't spread yet about the shooting, so the raucous noise drifting out from Sackett's was the mix of piano music, laughter and rattling glassware, same as any other Monday night. No rubbernecking townsfolk stood on the boardwalk, watching the McKay boys take their last stroll together.

Their last one until Jonas accompanied Silas to the hangin' tree.

Neither of them would pretend that wasn't in Silas's future, even when it wasn't fair.

Jonas knew that Silas wasn't the one who'd pulled the trigger—regardless of what Mrs. Agnes claimed. He'd seen enough deaths, examined enough bodies shot up every way that a man could meet a bullet, to know there was a pattern to blood when it was violently forced out of a body. The blood on Silas indicated he'd been standing off to the side of Zeke when the bullets had been fired.

But that wouldn't matter.

Silas had threatened Zeke yesterday in front of dozens of people and today Zeke was dead.

Mrs. Agnes seeing Silas holding the gun near to where the gun had been fired was the first—and last—nail in the coffin of his condemnation.

The Wyoming District One court judge wouldn't waste time with a trial. He'd be here on Wednesday morning and Silas would be convicted that same day. *When* they fit him for the hangman's noose was up to the sheriff's department.

Jesus. It made him sick to think about it.

Jonas had helped Doc move Zeke's body into the "coroner" hole in the shadows behind his barn. It'd been over a year since it'd been opened up and it stunk to high heaven because it'd only ever had one purpose: body storage. With life more settled in the Labelle township due to cattle and railroad traffic spread out across the state and not concentrated in one area, there'd been little need for an official coroner of late.

"Is Big Jim waitin' in there to take over your shift?" Silas asked.

"Big Jim and his family are in Belle Fourche at some church revival. He'll be back late tomorrow night."

Jonas should've sent a messenger to Sundance so Sheriff Eccleston could take stock of the situation, but between dealing with the body and sending word to Zachariah West about his brother's death, contacting the sheriff had slipped his mind. Now it was late, and he wasn't about to task a lackey from the saloon with heading over to Sundance to rouse his boss.

Besides, this might be the last night he ever had with his brother.

Everything else in the world could wait until morning.

They stopped in the small grove of birch trees at the edge of the building. "If you need to take a piss, do it now or else you're pissin' in a bucket."

Silas took a few steps forward and relieved himself.

After Jonas had unlocked the door and ushered Silas inside, he turned the lamp on his deck to a low flame.

"Here's how this works. You strip to long johns; I pat you down and put you in the cell. You get water. That's it. Someone will take over as your jailer tomorrow mornin'. But for tonight, it's me."

"Just like old times when we finally hit a decent-sized town on the trail. You tellin' me to wash my cock before and after visiting a bawdy house or warnin' me not to gamble all my wages at the card table."

"It's a lot different, Silas. We've never had iron bars between us before."

His brother didn't say anything after that.

He felt damn ridiculous watching Silas like a hawk as he removed his clothes and boots inside the tiny cell. After Silas tossed his clothes out, Jonas locked the metal-barred door.

"How many nights a week do you sleep in here?" Silas asked.

Fewer than you might imagine. "Enough to know you ain't gonna be comfortable."

"Where will you be sleepin'?"

"At my desk. But I don't know that there'll be much sleepin' as I've got paperwork to fill out on account that my brother killed someone." He paused. "But in truth, he didn't kill someone and that don't make a lick of difference, 'cause I still gotta do the goddamned paperwork."

"I killed Zeke, Jonas."

"Like hell you did."

"I might not've pulled the trigger, but I'm the one who bought her the damn gun. I made her carry it in her pocket. Way I see it...I'm fully responsible for his death."

Jonas took off his hat and tossed it on his desk. "You ain't gonna tell the truth of what happened? You ain't gonna even try to defend yourself?"

Silas snorted. "Even if Dinah were to try and take the blame—which I'd never allow—it's too risky. Yeah, West had acted untoward several times, previously payin' her a visit when she was alone and scaring her, but she had no witnesses to the fact, then or now. West took her away at knifepoint yesterday. Stabbed her in the back. Manhandled her enough to bruise her, yet she didn't voice a single complaint to you when you were right there. Why not?" He paused. "Because West could've explained his actions away just like he did about that knife not bein' his. Then he would've tacked on that Dinah had 'misunderstood' his intentions and I overreacted like I always do. So yeah, I gotta swallow the truth that she didn't report what he done to her to keep *me* from killin' him." He looked at his brother. "See how this is gonna go?"

"Silas—"

"I ain't done. I suspect Zeke told Ruby exactly what sick fuckin' things he planned to do to Dinah before she'd stopped him from takin' her, but it woulda been her word against Zeke's. A man she's kicked out of her brothel multiple times, if Jimmy's been tellin' the truth. The word of a whore ain't worth much, sadly."

Jonas flinched at the word but his brother didn't catch it.

"Then there's the threat against Dinah that Zeke leveled at me—after I tried to beat his face into the dirt, a threat that no one except me heard. Whatcha think my word is worth? Given the fact Zeke West and I have been doin' the *who'll be first to the hangman*'s dance for over a fuckin' year. Oh, and let's not forget that I threatened to kill him yesterday. Anyone who was there knew I meant it. Add in me holdin' the gun that killed him, Zeke never getting a shot off from either of the guns he had in his hands, and it looks as if I done the cowardly thing and shot him in the fuckin' back. Even in his goddamned death he's pointing the finger at me."

"Then tell the judge Dinah did it."

Silas shook his head. "I'll hang for a crime I didn't commit long before I'd *ever* let her hang for one she did." He closed his eyes and his grip tightened around the iron bars. "She's gonna hate this. It'll ruin her. Savin' me from Zeke plugging me full of holes only for me to die anyway." He laughed harshly. "The one goddamned time Mrs. Agnes decides to leave the house, the one goddamned time I've *ever* seen her outside, it had to be today, of all days. Christ. That's just my luck, ain't it?"

"Is what you told Doc true?"

"About how badly Zeke hurt Dinah? Yeah." Silas's eyes were haunted when they met Jonas's. "She cowboyed up all day yesterday. You saw her. She was in agony and she hid it from me because she was tryin' to keep me from doin' something stupid. And I ended up doin' something stupid anyway."

Jonas waited for Silas to continue, his heart in his throat.

"We had a fight last night. Not about her bein' hurt and lyin' about it, but about the talk me'n you had yesterday."

"You told her about that?"

Silas shook his head. "She guessed the part where I asked you to marry her and take care of her if something happened to me. Christ, Jonas, she was pissed. She pulled a goddamned gun on me. She said I had no right to demand that of you. That you had your own life, your own love story to live."

Last night, Jonas's biggest fear in going to see Ruby had been that she'd intended to give him the boot, but he'd found out she'd returned to Deadwood—probably for good—to run her mentor's brothel.

His biggest fear today was watching his brother die because of some perverted sense of honor he'd recently ascribed to.

Jesus. This was about the most fucked-up situation he'd ever been a party to.

"We were supposed to get married tomorrow," Silas said softly.

"What?"

"Even before I knew how much Zeke had hurt her, she understood that I'd be frantic about his threats toward her. She said no amount of money she could earn was worth me not havin' peace of mind that I could protect her. The promises she'd made to Doc weren't as important as the promise she'd made to me when she agreed to become my wife."

"That's why you had the wagon at Doc's," Jonas said.

"Yeah. We were movin' everything of hers to the cabin." Silas paused. "For what it's worth...I was gonna ask you to stand up for me tomorrow. But I guess that don't matter now."

He let a minute pass...and he was done.

"Fuck that." Jonas pushed to his feet. "I'll stand up for you now."

Silas squinted at him. "What?"

"This is all bullshit. You hangin' to save Dinah when she saved you, and me just sittin' by and watchin' it happen because I'm such an upstanding deputy who follows the fuckin' rules. What kind of man would I be if I let my own brother die when I have the means to prevent it?"

"You been hittin' the bottle when I ain't been lookin', bro?"

"Nope. I feel like I'm seein' clearly for the first time in ages." He stormed over to the cell and curled his fingers around the bars, nearly coming nose to nose with his twin. "Here's the truth. I don't like this job. I never have. Big Jim is a dipshit—and a mean one at that. I've stuck around because you're my brother and because..." *Just say it.* "Because I'm in love with Ruby Redmond."

Silas's eyes widened. "You and Madam Ruby? I'll be damned." Then he sent his brother a sad smile. "That'd explain why you're mopey half the time. That's a hard row to hoe."

"Yeah. I don't begrudge you bein' with Dinah. She's good for you. But it's just driven home the truth that this...ain't no kinda life for me, Silas. Solitary lawman. Pinin' for the woman I can't have. I'd be relieved to move on from Wyoming." He swallowed hard. "But you wouldn't. You love it here, you've got a woman who loves you even when you're a hotheaded fool. There's no doubt in my mind Zeke West would've succeeded in killin' one of you. What Dinah did was defend her family against a threat. I know it, you know it, she knows it...does anyone else really matter?"

Silas stared at him for a long time. "I guess not when you put it that way. That don't change nothin'."

"It changes everything."

"How?"

"Remember when we were kids and we used to switch places and see how long it took our folks to notice?"

Silas snorted. "They *never* caught on to that game, if I recall correctly."

"Exactly. So let's me and you switch places. Not for a day or a week, but permanently."

Wariness entered his brother's eyes. "What?"

"Silas McKay makes a jail break. He beats the shit out of his too-trusting brother, locks him up in jail and takes off for unknown parts, never to be seen again." When his confusion didn't clear, Jonas said, "Meaning I leave as you; you stay here as me. The land deeds are in the name McKay, so you'd still be doin' what you've been doin'. No one would fault Jonas for resigning as deputy after he let his murdering brother escape. The fact you'd stick around here after that throws off any suspicion we'd cooked something like this up."

"What about Dinah?"

Jonas shrugged. "You can still court her and marry her. I doubt she'll have an issue with the name change when her other option is that you're dead."

"True. What about you and Ruby?"

That was a harder pill to swallow. "She and I aren't meant to be. I could move on from her." He never would, but saying that sounded pathetic.

"There's just one wrinkle in this plan, Jonas. You and me? We could never see each other again. *Ever.* For the rest of our lives. Silas McKay will always be a fugitive. The McKay boys, the McKay twins, the McKay brothers would be no more."

"I know. But if I don't do this, we'll never see each other again anyway because they'll hang you."

They stared at each other for the longest time. Then Silas said, "You think anyone will believe that I'm you?"

"My damn *boss* thought you were me just a few weeks back. Plus you've been a hermit besides your few forays into town to play cards, so no one really knows you. You can be me...but a better me. Because you'll be happy. I can live with that, brother, pretty damn easily."

"I feel like you're getting the short shrift, Jonas. I get to keep my ranch and my woman and get the respect I haven't earned, and what do you get?"

"A chance to figure out who I am when I'm not trying to live your dream. I'll have the freedom to find my own."

"You mean that."

"More than I've ever meant anything."

Silas didn't try and hide that his eyes had filled with tears. "I'm gonna miss you every day for the rest of my life. *Every* day."

Jonas rested his forehead to his brother's through the bars. "I know, brother, me too."

After a bit, he stepped back and wiped his own tears. Then he unlocked the cell. "I really hafta do the paperwork first. While I'm doin' that, open the gun cabinet drawer and lift up."

Silas crouched down and jerked the drawer. The false bottom gave way and loose bills of every denomination spilled everywhere. "Christ. So this is where you've been keepin' your money."

"Well, someone else in the family already claimed the good spot under the fencepost by the creek."

He laughed. "Dinah called it 'The Stinky Old Boot Savings and Loan' last night."

"She's got a smart mouth—I like that about her."

Silas went still. "Thank you for this...chance."

"Don't thank me. It's my chance too."

Silas didn't speak again until he'd stacked all the bills and secured them in his leather fold-over wallet he'd taken from his jacket pocket. "Now what?"

Jonas exhaled. "At some point we'll have to fight. So the jail break is believable."

"Do we need to do that right now?"

He shook his head. "There's a few things you'll need to know about the office in order to maintain credibility, just for one day."

"Okay."

Afterward, they allowed some time to reminisce. To laugh and bullshit and remember.

Jonas peered out the window. "Sackett's is closed."

The time had come.

Silas sat on the floor of the jail cell, dejected.

"I don't know that I can actually hit you," Jonas admitted.

"You have to. It's the only way this will work." Silas raised his head and managed a small smile. "Make it hurt, so the outside matches the way I feel inside."

They were both bleeding by the time they were done.

Crying too, not just from the cuts and scrapes and bruises.

Jonas locked his brother in the cell. "Toast us on our birthday every year, yeah?"

"Yeah." Silas waited until Jonas reached the door until he said, "Be happy, brother. That's the only way I can stomach doin' this is if I know you'll have a better life."

"I will."

WHEN THE SUN came up three hours later, "Silas" McKay was an outlaw.

He kept his horse headed south and didn't look back.

TWENTY-ONE

SILAS HAD SPENT all day building fence. He was hot, sweaty, hungry and more than a little heartsick not knowing if he'd—they'd—done the right thing.

It wasn't something he could talk to Dinah about. Mostly because he and Dinah weren't talking. They'd agreed to remain apart for a while. The evolution of a relationship between them would be more believable to the community if they stuck to a traditional courtship.

All social situations Silas had avoided.

But he wasn't Silas anymore. He was Jonas. And Jonas had been a sociable guy. Hence, Silas masquerading as Jonas meant he'd have to become that. Embodying his twin just drove home the pain that he missed his brother something fierce.

Even when it'd only been two weeks since they'd said goodbye, he knew this hole in his life wouldn't heal. He feared it'd only expand as the years went on.

Years Silas would spend living as Jonas McKay.

Years wondering how his brother's life had played out.

If he'd discovered a new occupation.

If he'd settled into one place and had become part of a community.

If he'd found a different woman to love.

If he'd raised children.

If he'd missed his brother like Silas missed him.

While he understood brooding solved nothing, he couldn't help it.

This switch had worked out easier than he'd thought possible.

Even Henrikson had bought into the ruse, sharing a couple of disparaging remarks about Silas when "Jonas" stopped over to inquire whether he still needed a ranch hand.

Robbie O'Neil had ridden out to the McKay Ranch to share gossip about how the townsfolk felt about Zeke's violent end and Silas's disappearing act. How no one had been surprised, but everyone felt sorry for Jonas and Zachariah West for the damage their brothers had done to both families. Robbie had been tight with Jonas and hadn't guessed he wasn't Jonas, so that had been another test passed.

Robinette offered "Jonas" a line of credit at the general store as he acclimated to his new life on the ranch.

McCrae Lumber offered "Jonas" a longer-term payment plan on a bulk order of fence posts.

The only people not happy to see the ass-end of Silas McKay were Dickie and Darby at Sackett's Saloon.

Sobering stuff to acknowledge that Jonas had made a bigger mark in the two years he'd lived in the area than Silas had made in twice that long. No one ever stopped by the ranch to see if Silas needed anything.

But already Sheriff Eccleston had popped over to ask if Jonas would consider changing his mind about working for law enforcement in some capacity after everything leveled out. Silas figured it was some kind of test, so he'd been firm about being done with that.

As far as he'd known, no one had put out a reward for Silas McKay's capture. If Zachariah had money, he might've done it, but he didn't have the kind of cash that would warrant interest. Although Zeke had worked for the railroad, since the murder hadn't affected the railroad's operation, they wouldn't put up a reward either.

Every night Silas prayed his brother used his knowledge of the outlaw system to stay one step ahead of—or a thousand miles in front of—the law.

His bad day got worse when he noticed a lone rider approaching. Before the man dismounted, Silas ambled over with his hands in the air. "I ain't armed, Zachariah. Like I told you twice before, I don't know where my brother is."

"Like I said twice before, Deputy, I ain't about to shoot an unarmed man."

"I'm no longer a deputy." A pause. "What are you doin' here?"

Zachariah's jaw tightened. "I have no fucking idea."

Silas waited.

Finally Zachariah sighed. "He was all I had. He's dead and buried and I'm pissed off and I don't know what the hell to do with it, okay? It's screwed up, but the only person who came to mind to talk to about it was you." He paused. "I see know how stupid that was. I'll just go."

"No. Stay." Silas moseyed closer. "As long as you're here and not lookin' for revenge, we may as well drown our sorrows in whiskey."

"Why would *you* need to drown *your* sorrows, McKay?"

He locked his gaze to West's. "Because you ain't the only one who lost brother. Mine ain't dead, but he may as well be, because I know in my gut I'll never see him again."

Zachariah seemed to take that in. Then he nodded and dismounted.

"I'll grab the bottle."

When Silas returned, West had turned his mount out into the corral. He seemed to be studying—and judging—the house, barn and paddock. For once, that didn't bother him. He'd been so happy to be home after getting dismissed from the jail that he'd fallen to the floor in gratitude.

"You got a flask?" Silas asked.

"Yeah." West pulled it out of his inner vest pocket.

The lack of weight indicated it was nearly empty. Silas poured the amber-colored booze into the flask and passed it over, keeping the half-empty bottle for himself.

After West took the first pull, he grunted. "As least you got good taste in whiskey, McKay."

"Silas left it."

West grunted again.

When it didn't appear Zachariah intended to start the conversation, Silas did. "You and Mary O'Brien still getting hitched?"

"Yep. Was supposed to happen last week but I just…" He knocked back another glug of booze. "Couldn't. I needed more than a damn week to deal with losin' one person in my life before I gained another." He propped his boot on the lowest rung of the fence. "I'm still marryin' her. Just not until the end of the summer."

"At least she ain't in Dinah Thompson's situation. My brother broke every promise he'd made to her and left her high and dry." Silas tipped up the bottle and drank. "But she's probably relieved he's gone."

"You haven't spoken to her?" Zachariah asked.

"Not really. I'd planned on checkin' in with her next week. There's some stuff here Silas bought for her. Don't know whether she wants it, but I oughta ask."

"I think folks are surprised she's stayin' around here. Mary indicated she's the type to turn tail and run."

Silas tamped down his anger and offered a shrug. "No one would blame her after what Zeke did to her."

In a small voice, he said, "I never knew that side of him. I certainly never saw it when he was with women or I would've stopped it, believe me. It sickened me."

"I don't believe your intended is familiar with Dinah at all if she thinks that woman would run at the first sign of adversity. She's much tougher than she appears."

"You know her well?" West asked in a casual manner that wasn't casual at all.

This was another one of those situations where he had to tread lightly, reacting as Jonas. "Only from what Silas told me about her and the times I'd seen her assisting Doc. She knows her own mind, that's for sure." He took another swig. "Some recent nights...I've wondered if this'd all be different if I'd've asked to court her like I'd wanted to."

West choked on his whiskey. "You and the schoolteacher?"

"Ain't that far-fetched. I'd actually met her in Labelle before Silas had. But after she'd patched him up the first time, she was all he could talk about. I..." Silas felt his cheeks warm. "I let go of any ideas I might've had when she preferred my wilder-edged brother."

"I hear ya. Mary couldn't stand Zeke when he was alive but now that he's dead, she's elevated his status." He shook his head. "Taken to wearin' black and explaining how we couldn't possibly have such a joyful occasion as a wedding in the midst of my grieving. Theatrics and attention for her. In some ways...I think she and Zeke would've been a better match than her'n me."

Silas sensed that Zachariah wasn't keen on marrying Mary, but he intended to buck up and follow through with it. After meeting her, Silas wouldn't wish that shrew on his worst enemy—which he was starting to believe wasn't this surviving member of the West family.

Their conversation lulled and Silas expected Zachariah would take his leave.

But he didn't.

"Six people attended Zeke's service. Those six included me, Mary and the priest." He swiped his hand across his mouth. "No one liked him. Hell, more than half the time *I* didn't like him neither."

That had to've been painful to admit. The hell of it was Silas understood. "Don't know if it'll make a difference, but if it'd been Silas wearin' a bullet, no one would've come to pay their respects to him neither. Since he's been gone, I've been getting a clearer impression of how solitary his life was."

"Maybe that's why he left. No one to vouch for his character meant he'd swing for sure."

Silas braced himself for a barrage of nasty observations about Silas's character—or lack thereof—from West, but that seemed to be it. After a few moments, he sighed. "How'd we end up in the middle of our brothers' feud anyway?"

Zachariah sent him a sharp look. "You don't know?"

"Know what?"

"Why Zeke hated you."

He shook his head. "Why would Zeke have hated *me*? I never arrested him. I barely spoke to him even when I'd caught him beatin' the tar outta Silas."

"You are Jonas," West muttered. "Good to know. I'd wondered."

Silas managed to keep his look confused, refusing to let it morph into panic. "You ain't makin' a lick of sense, West."

"You really don't know, do you? About why Zeke hated the McKays?"

"All's I know is that when Silas took a job workin' for the railroad, Zeke ended up his boss. Zeke made Silas's workin' hours hell. What I didn't know until the last time Zeke whupped up on Silas was that my brother hadn't quit his railroad job; he'd gotten fired."

"Did he tell you why he'd gotten fired?"

"Yeah." He swallowed another mouthful of whiskey. "I wasn't aware of it until right before the competition started. Then Silas said he visited Zeke in the hospital—"

"After he'd *put* him there," Zachariah interjected.

"Zeke warned Silas if he ever touched him again, even to defend himself, that Zeke would find a way to kill *me*."

That caused Zachariah's head to whip toward him. "What?"

"You heard right. Apparently Zeke said ambushes or incidents could befall a deputy in Wyoming." He tapped his hand on the fencepost. "I gotta say…it'd never made any sense to me why Silas kept losin' fights to Zeke. For years I'd seen my brother fight for fun or if he was pissed off and I'd seen him lose maybe twice. He told me he'd never fought back again after Zeke threatened to kill me."

"Fucking moron," Zachariah muttered. "My brother, not yours."

"So you tell me: why did Zeke hate Silas so much? They never even met until Silas started workin' for the railroad. I doubt Zeke felt his position was threatened by Silas because Silas never hid the fact his railroad job was temporary, and ranching was his first priority."

Zachariah remained quiet for a long time. Then he said, "You really don't remember, do you?"

"Remember what?"

"The orphan train station."

"What about it?" His thoughts scrolled back to the constant noise and the stench and sound of kids crying, but specifics beyond that were a blur. "Were we on the train from Boston together?"

He shook his head. "Me'n Zeke were on a train from Pittsburgh. Our father fought in the war between the states on the Union side. Our mother nursed him back to health and they got married. Because of his war injuries he'd been told he'd likely never father children. Our mother bragged it'd been a shock and a blessing when they discovered she was with child. Only…she'd been pregnant with twins."

Silas's jaw dropped. "You and Zeke were twins too?"

"Yep. But obviously not identical like you and Silas. Anyway, our father died when we were three and our mother raised us alone. Factory work took its toll on her and she died when we were twelve. Factory management secured our placement on one of them trains they sent orphans on out to a farm community in Nebraska, but Zeke convinced me to jump trains in St Louis and we ended up on a train headed west to Denver."

Silas started to have a bad feeling.

"The entire train ride, all Zeke could talk about was workin' as horse wranglers on cattle drives. He had this idea that we'd immediately get chosen since we were twins, two workers for the price of one. We'd learn horse handlin' skills and survival skills. Then when we were old enough, we'd follow the miners wherever the next vein of gold, silver or copper was discovered in the West and strike it rich.

"'Cept when we got to Denver, we had to lie about losin' our placement papers, which meant we were placed with open call orphans. Those kids only got seen after the placement kids were picked. Zeke..." He shook his head, but a fond smile curled his lips. "He'd always found a way to get information. He learned what the drovers comin' to find horse wranglers looked for in workers. He set his sights on one company in particular that preferred brothers. They finished their cattle drive in Montana in the thick of mining country and they'd be at the open call the end of the week. So he traded all our food rations to the kids who'd been there the longest, so we were pushed to the front of the line."

"How long were you in Denver before bein' seen at the open call?"

"Two weeks. I was starved and pissed off at Zeke for him thinkin' he had the right to make decisions for both of us. Especially when I was the older of the two of us, and bigger."

"I guess your size difference is why it never crossed my mind that the two of you were twins."

He nodded. "Zeke was a sickly babe. Almost died several times, according to our mother. That's why even as an adult he was so much smaller than me. When we were boys, the difference wasn't as obvious, but it was there. So I didn't understand why Zeke thought we'd be a good investment for a cattle company when folks warned us that life on the range was the hardest of all options."

"As long as we're bein' honest, those years on the cattle drives were brutal. Every bone in my body hurt, every damn night. For years. But Silas loved it. He never complained."

"Did you?"

"Occasionally. I did the work, learned a lot. But as soon as the chance to take a different path opened to me, I took it without hesitation." He adjusted his hat and remembered the conversation he and Jonas had about Jonas striking out with the outlaw hunters. "But when we were boys on that train, I'd been just as eager as Silas to ride the trail."

"That's probably what made Jeb choose you and Silas over me and Zeke."

Silas felt as if he'd taken a hoof to the gut. "What?"

"Me'n Zeke were there that day. You and Silas were pushed past us and everyone stared because you looked exactly alike. Caused quite a stir. Kids whispered. Even the people in line to view open call kids were watchin' you. That's when Zeke got so mad. He just kept sayin' over and over because you two looked alike, people would think you were special, but you weren't special *because* you looked exactly alike, but you'd still get chosen first. And you were. Jeb never even talked to us. Zeke blamed you both for takin' the life he'd wanted."

Finally, Zeke's accusation of *you stole my life* made sense. Silas gulped down more whiskey before speaking. "Okay, but we didn't have any control over that."

"I know," Zachariah admitted. "But Zeke heard your last name and never forgot it."

"He has—*had*—a very long memory if he recognized Silas when he went to work for the railroad since it'd been a decade since he'd seen him. You're tellin' me he'd carried a grudge that long, specifically for my brother?"

Zachariah shook his head. "The grudge was for both of you. Silas just was unlucky enough to be the McKay that crossed paths with him first. Zeke took it to mean that Silas considered workin' part-time for the railroad as bein' a step down from cattle ranching. It didn't help matters in Zeke's mind that me'n him went to work for a sheep ranching family from the Currans area after Jeb didn't choose us." He grunted. "Zeke hated workin' sheep. Hated it. Not an hour of any day went by when he didn't complain about it."

"How about you?"

"Well, I'm still in the sheep business so that oughta be obvious I didn't hate it. The family we ended up with were good folks. But Zeke never saw what they were, just what they weren't. Soon as he turned eighteen, he signed on with the railroad. That suited him. But even when he moved up into management and earned four times more money than I did, he harped on the life he'd—we'd—lost out on."

"That's just plum stupid, blamin' Silas."

"Ain't gonna get an argument from me on that. But maybe you ain't aware of Silas's issues with sheep ranchers, and that also was a check against Silas as far as Zeke was concerned. Still…I didn't condone Zeke buyin' that land from Griffen. If he wanted to invest in land so badly, he should've helped me." He glanced across the paddock. "Times have been lean. Even twenty acres could've made a difference in my yearly yields. He chose revenge over family."

Hearing West phrase it like that…Silas needed to temper his response. "Silas did the same thing at the rodeo. Entering the sheep competition because he wanted to prove his superior ranching skills."

"Well, I gotta say, Silas did have those."

Don't preen.

"It appears that, like Zeke, you didn't follow the path our families were set on that day in Denver."

This wasn't the first time this question had been asked, nor would it be the last. "I worked the cattle drive for six years, so it ain't like I'm a greenhorn. When I signed on as a bounty hunter, I wanted the experience and skills. At age nineteen it'd been easy to overlook more years of sleepin' on the ground, racin' hell for leather to the next town on a moment's notice because the thrill of the chase was worth it." He paused. "Until it wasn't. I did that for four years. I was ready to have a more settled life and stayin' in one place appealed to me. I came here because my brother had put down 'McKay' on land for me, but none of it ever felt like mine because he had his own vision for it. He never listened to a damn thing I said or suggested."

Zachariah grunted his understanding.

"That's why I took the deputy job. But as much as Crook County needed a law presence in Labelle, I didn't have any real power there. Only so much breakin' up bar fights and settlin' neighbor's disputes. Until Labelle incorporates, it would've continued like the situation with Silas and the land: a part of it, yet not. I'd talked to Sheriff Eccleston about workin' in Sundance as a deputy, and I might've done that had my brother not made me look like ten kinds of fool." He swigged from the bottle. "How was I ever supposed to hold my head up in law enforcement around these parts? I'd always be the deputy who let his murdering brother get away—no matter how that ain't even close to the truth."

"You two fought? At the jail?"

"Like two wet cats in a burlap sack."

"Why didn't you send someone to the sheriff's office in Sundance right after the shooting happened?"

"Who? I thought you oughta be told first. The one guy I relied on to get word to you fucked that up." Jonas had sent Robbie to the trainyard to get word to Zachariah. Those idiots had put Robbie on a train to Gillette to tell West in person. Robbie had gotten lost so nearly twenty-four hours passed before Zachariah returned to Labelle. "I didn't have anyone else to send to Sundance. And Silas was my brother. I never imagined he'd act so cornered."

"I didn't take the news well that he'd gotten away."

"I never blamed you for that. I'm plenty pissed off at Silas for the chickenshit way he run off. For what he did to Dinah. To me. He even took my fuckin' horse. Maybe your brother had a point about Silas not bein' who he said he was." He shifted his stance and sighed. "As family, we couldn't see the flaws cause we're too close to 'em and that'd force us to look deeper into our own."

"Christ. Amen to that. Even Mary keeps yapping on about a blood feud. Especially after I got the letter with the money yesterday."

Silas's head snapped around. "What letter? What money?"

From inside his pocket, Zachariah pulled out an envelope and handed it over. The postmark on it read Cheyenne. Inside was a folded piece of parchment paper with the word SORRY printed in big black letters across the center. Silas passed his thumb over the bills. "How much is here?"

"One hundred dollars."

"No shit."

"I'm assuming it's from Silas," West said.

It wasn't. Silas doubted Jonas had sent it either. Outlaws didn't do things like that, lest they wouldn't be outlaws for long.

Then his belly did a flip and he felt the whiskey rise up his throat.

Dinah.

She'd sent this to Zachariah. Out of guilt.

"You didn't know about this."

A statement. "No. I ain't been in Cheyenne since I got snowed in back in February at a lawman's conference." He looked up as he passed the envelope back to Zachariah. "Are you gonna talk to the sheriff about it? I mean…it is a clue as to where Silas has been."

He sighed. "I'd intended to. Then Mary pointed out the sheriff might keep the money as evidence. She said if it's 'blood money' then it belongs to me and I oughta do something good with it. I'm leaning that direction. Course, I'll have to get Mary's promise not to talk about it outside our family."

"You do what you gotta. I'm forgetting I ever saw it."

Zachariah tucked it back in his pocket. "Blood money. Name feels right even when everything about keepin' it feels wrong."

Neither spoke for a while.

"You're stayin' around these parts?"

"Yep. Several land improvement requirements will be met next year, and I'll own the land. Me. Not Silas. I can run things my way, instead of his hard scrabble approach. Makin' the ranch bigger—and better—would be satisfying. As would becoming involved in local and state cattle issues—another thing Silas never cottoned to doin'."

When West didn't respond, Silas thought maybe he'd laid it on too thick.

Then Zachariah lowered his foot and stepped back from the fence. "I hear ya. I'll admit, this wasn't the conversation I expected to have, but I'm feelin' better for havin' it."

"Me too."

"That said, if I ever see your brother around here again, Jonas, I *will* kill him. After his escape and break ain't no one would fault me."

"I know that."

"So maybe we have us a gentleman's agreement." West secured his gaze. "I'll stay outta the cattle business and you stay outta the sheep business. We needn't ever cross paths again." Then West offered his hand.

Silas shook it. "Agreed."

There wasn't anything to say after that.

West mounted up and rode off.

Silas remained out by the corral, long after Zachariah had gone.

He finished the bottle of whiskey. In his drunken state he realized he'd meant every word he'd said to West. Silas was as good as dead. He was Jonas now.

In order to thrive, he'd have to do everything differently.

He just hoped Dinah would be on board with it.

TWENTY-TWO

R UBY HAD LOST all sense of decorum as she paced in Doc's exam room.
Heaven help her, she'd actually snapped at the infirm Mrs. Moorcroft in her desperation to speak with Dinah.

Of course Dinah and Doc were out making rounds.

Of course Mrs. Moorcroft didn't know when her husband and his
assistant would return.

Of course the local whorehouse madam wasn't allowed to wait inside
the Moorcrofts' home. Mrs. Moorcroft hadn't even offered to let Ruby wait
on the property, suggesting that she return later in the evening. After dark.

To hell with that.

Ruby had let herself into the examination room. Doc could deal with
his sputtering and indignant wife about the "liberties" she was taking. She
planned to remain right there until she could talk to Dinah about what the
devil had gone on in the past three weeks that she'd been in Deadwood.

Jimmy had seen the open door to the exam area. If he'd been shocked
to see Madam Ruby muttering to herself and pacing, he hadn't shown it.
He'd agreed to do a favor for her and return the horse and buggy to
Blackbird's Livery, and he'd left her to her pacing.

Two full hours passed while she waited. She forced herself not to run
out when she heard a buggy come to a stop.

Mrs. Moorcroft came out of the house—no doubt to head off her husband and complain about his patient who'd refused to leave the premises.

As soon as Dinah had seen Ruby in the exam room doorway, she sent Doc and his wife into the house and returned alone, closing and locking the door behind her.

"Where is Jonas?" Ruby demanded. "And don't give me some cocka-mamie story about that being *him* on the ranch. I rode out there as soon as I heard what happened with Silas and Zeke West. The man who greeted me like we were goddamned...*strangers* is not *my* Jonas McKay. Where is he? God. Is he okay? Please tell me he's not dead."

Dinah studied her.

Ruby knew she looked a fright. Her chest heaving. Her sweaty face the same crimson color as her gown. Her hair hanging down after she'd pulled the pins out while pacing.

As much of a mess as she was on the outside, inside was worse. Her heart raced. Her stomach churned. The tears she'd been holding back threatened to overflow like a spring dam.

"Sit." Dinah pointed to a chair.

"You cannot—"

"If you want to hear this, you'd better sit down before you fall down, Ruby. Because what I'm about to tell you will send you into shock."

That got her butt to connect with the chair.

Dinah dragged another chair across from her, sat and took Ruby's gloved hands in her own. "Your Jonas is alive as far as I know."

"As far as you *know*? Where is he?"

"That, I do not know. What I'm about to tell you...just hear me out until the end, all right?"

"Then you'd better start explaining every single detail right now."

As Dinah relayed the story, Ruby's dismay increased. While she genu-inely understood Dinah's panic and fear at the hands of Zeke West, she forced herself not to snap at Dinah to get to the part of the story where Jonas disappeared.

"So I shot Zeke."

Ruby's mouth fell open. "*You* did?"

"Yes. That part is as clear as day. It's the aftermath that is a complete blur for me."

"Why?"

"Because Doc dosed me with laudanum. He believed me to be traumatized because I'd watched Silas kill Zeke. Then he'd seen the body trauma Zeke had inflicted on me and kept me sedated to heal. I didn't witness Jonas hauling Silas off to jail. While I was under sedation, Silas broke out of jail and left town to avoid hanging for Zeke's murder. When I finally could function again, a week had passed. Zeke was in the ground, Silas was a fugitive, and Jonas had resigned as deputy."

"Except that's not really what happened?"

She shook her head. "Mrs. Agnes saw Silas pick up the gun after I'd shot Zeke. She didn't see what'd happened, but she told everyone she *did*. Doc wasn't certain how it'd gone down but he couldn't call his wife a liar—"

"Even when a man's life and freedom were at stake?" Ruby demanded.

"Even then. Maybe especially then. Because everyone heard Silas threaten Zeke at the racetrack that day. If I would've called Mrs. Agnes a liar and confessed to pulling the trigger, no one would've believed me anyway. No one, Ruby. They would've accused me of protecting Silas. When the truth was...he took the blame to protect me." She swallowed hard and looked down at her hands. "I think Doc might've known what Silas and Jonas intended to do and if I was unconscious, I couldn't be a party to it."

Ruby wanted to yell at her for allowing Doc and his wife their manipulations. "Go on."

"As soon as I could, I rode out to the ranch to talk to Jonas, because I honestly believed Silas had skipped town. As soon as I saw Silas...I knew what they'd done."

"Switched places," Ruby said.

"Yes."

"So it wasn't Silas taking the blame to protect you, but Jonas. Jonas, who had to leave town, and remain on the run as an outlaw so his twin brother could pretend to be *him* for the rest of his life? Christ almighty. How is that fair to Jonas?"

Dinah raised her tear-filled gaze to Ruby's. "It's not. I never wanted this. Silas never wanted this. Jonas never wanted this. The only person who wanted to annihilate the McKay family was Zeke West...and he succeeded." She started to cry in earnest. "I should feel horrible for killing Zeke, but I don't. Not at all. But I do feel guilty for Silas and Jonas having to say goodbye forever. For Silas having to pretend to be someone else as long as he lives. For Jonas to be all alone and having to start his life over as someone new. I will blame myself for that for the rest of my life, so don't you dare think this is easy for me."

Ruby patted Dinah's shoulder as she cried. Her sympathy was half-hearted at best...but only because the wheels in her mind were churning as fast as a locomotive.

Her Jonas was getting a fresh start. Her thoughts scrolled back to all the times Jonas had spoken of an outlaw's mistakes. How personal connections were impossible to sever for most people and almost always created a followable trail which would get a man caught.

As far as anyone in Crook County knew, Jonas didn't have any personal connections besides his brother.

No one besides Dinah knew that she and Jonas had a connection.

For the first time ever, she believed she'd made the right choice to tell Jonas no whenever he'd asked to court her. She'd known nothing would ever change who they were in the eyes of the community: the whore and the lawman.

During their picnic he'd told her about his restlessness. How he'd considered making a change and taking his outlaw-chasing buddy's offer. Granted, this situation might've been forced on him, but she suspected that he'd volunteered to uproot his life since he hadn't really set down roots here. Not like Silas had.

Jonas knew how to think like an outlaw and a lawman. He'd utilize both skills until he found which skin fit him best. In a place where no one knew he had a brother who looked exactly like him. Where no one knew he'd given his heart to a whore.

He'd drift for a while, just to make sure he hadn't left a trail. Maybe he'd even become a city-boy to cover his tracks. But Ruby knew he wouldn't stay in a city forever. He'd eventually end up in the area he called the most beautiful place on earth.

No one besides Ruby knew where that was.

"Ruby?"

Her gaze met Dinah's. "I'm sorry. I'm just in shock. I wasn't listening to you at all. What did you say?"

"I asked how...Jonas responded when you went out to see him today."

"Confused as to why Madam Ruby was making a social call, to say the least."

Dinah laughed and dabbed her eyes.

"I knew immediately, of course, that he wasn't *my* Jonas." Her eyes narrowed on Dinah. "You didn't tell your McKay about me being his brother's dirty little secret?"

"First of all, didn't *you* inform me nothing that happened between a consenting man and woman was dirty?"

Ruby rolled her eyes. "You know what I mean, virgin."

"And you know what I mean, *madam*. What you and I talked about? Is between us. No one else. Not my McKay. Not yours. If your Jonas told Silas about you, Silas is keeping mum to me about it because he hasn't mentioned it to me, so fair is fair. But given what happened while you were gone, I have to know why you weren't here the one time you should've been."

Ruby explained about Madam Marie's funeral and settling her estate. What she didn't share was receiving the shock of her life when Marie had left all of her earnings to Ruby—more money than Ruby could've imagined. But that caused a different issue: how to transport those earnings, mostly in gold. She'd never trusted the stagecoach line nor any livery-for-hire services. The railroad didn't connect to any larger towns. She wasn't competent enough with a horse to make the return trip to Labelle on her own. All's it would've taken was a whisper about her inheritance—not a far-fetched fear in a town Deadwood's size—and she'd be set upon by bandits.

She'd discreetly hired a bodyguard rumored to be a Pinkerton and they'd taken a convoluted route to Gillette in a carriage he'd purchased in Spearfish. He'd posed as her husband "Mr. Ruby" which allowed her to convert the gold into cash. Then as Mrs. Ruby, she was able to open an account with a progressive bank that allowed her to deposit—and withdraw—money without the presence of a man. "If I would've known things were dire here, I would've returned sooner."

"Why couldn't your girls send you a telegram about the situation in Labelle?"

"Because like I told you, no one knew Jonas and I were involved. So they wouldn't see his resignation as anything other than a nuisance as we wait to see who'll take Deputy McKay's place." Ruby bit her lip. "But we do have cause to worry."

"Why?"

"Big Jim barely tolerates our presence. If the sheriff allows him to choose a new deputy with the same mindset, we will be closed down sooner rather than later."

"Is that such a bad thing?"

"Excuse me?"

Dinah lifted her chin and challenged, "Do you see yourself doing this for the rest of your life? Did your madam friend intend to die in her bawdy house?"

No. That'd been Marie's last request. That Ruby didn't end up like her.

Now she had enough money to give each of her girls a chance to do something different with their lives. They were young enough to move on.

So are you.

Some days she forgot to subtract the three years her brother had added to her age, making her thirty-one, not thirty-four.

Over the past year, Mavis had suggested turning Ruby Red's into a "real" boardinghouse with a restaurant since there wasn't one in Labelle. While that had never been in Ruby's wheelhouse, Mavis and the other girls should have the opportunity to choose before the choice was taken from them by the law.

"Ruby?"

She glanced at Dinah. "I'm sorry. What did you say?"

"Nothing yet, but I was about to ask if you're going after your McKay."

"He's not my McKay."

"Yes, he is, and you know it. You also know that he would've taken you with him if you'd been here."

"I would've refused to go and saddle him with more worries!"

"Bull. Your mouth is telling me one thing but your eyes say something completely contrary." Dinah stood abruptly. "You're good at giving me advice, so I'll return the favor. Don't be scared or stupid or both. Your McKay loves you. I recognized it because I saw it every time that mine looked at me the same way."

Cheeky little thing.

"Don't let doubt get a foothold because once that happens...it'll trample you until you feel you can't get back up."

Ruby stood and latched onto Dinah's arm. "What makes you say that? Nothing has changed for you."

Dinah whirled around; her chin wobbled before she firmed it. "Let's set aside the obvious fact that I took a life and don't have to answer to the law for it as an action that has changed me profoundly."

Damn. It'd been callous for Ruby to disregard that ugly truth.

"*Everything* has changed for me. Silas gave up his brother. I worry that he already regrets it. He'll have to spend the rest of his life acting like someone he's not and he resents me for that too. And if that's not bad enough, everyone in the community is eyeing me with pity. Which they'll continue to do when 'Jonas' decides to start courting his brother's former fiancée—not that many believe we were a love match anyway because everyone reminds me that Silas couldn't be bothered to give me an engagement ring."

Ruby's heart hurt for this couple.

"I miss Silas, the man I fell in love with, not the shell he's become. We can't go back to how we were before. I can't spend a Saturday night with him at the cabin. There won't be any surprise visits during the week with him bearing gifts and kisses. We have to keep our distance. I worry that the relationship we'd started to build isn't strong enough to withstand this immense…damage. Not to mention we'd just started to explore the passion between us. I'm still a virgin. Now I'll remain one until my wedding night. Because with my luck, if I threw caution to the wind, I'd wind up pregnant, forcing my McKay into a hurry-up wedding that would make me look even more like a charity case."

Dinah burst into tears.

It was useless for Ruby to try and hold back her tears. So she hugged Dinah tight and wept right along with her, for what they'd both lost.

But she had to believe there was something good to be gained out of this.

When they were down to ragged sniffles, Ruby stepped back and handed Dinah her extra handkerchief and then dabbed her own eyes.

Dinah shuffled over to the cabinet and pulled out a flask. She took a generous swig and then waggled the silver flask at Ruby. "Rum?"

"Just a taste." She palmed it and tipped it back. The sickly sweet, boozy taste kicked in her gag reflex, but she forced herself to swallow it. "Thank you."

"You're welcome." Dinah knocked back another slug. "I'm finding rum helps me make it through the day."

"Don't rely on it," Ruby warned. "It'll become a habit faster than you can blink. Take it from someone who has watched that 'helper' do serious damage to many, many friends. What you need is a plan to get your McKay back."

"Excuse me?"

"Remember when I said you needed to talk to your man about what you wanted from him in the boudoir? You still need to do that, Dinah. Maybe now more than ever because he is finding his way in what amounts to a new life. You need to assure him that what's between you two might look different to the outside world, but in your private time, in your private space, you're still those two people who fell in love. You need to reestablish your place in his life, Dinah, so he can reclaim his place in yours."

"What do you suggest I do?"

Ruby shrugged. "Start with a French perversion…or as we called it in Deadwood, a French cocksucker. That'll get his attention."

Dinah opened her mouth. Shut it. Blushed bright red and gulped another mouthful of rum before she blurted out, "I need specific instructions on how to do that."

Upon finishing the demonstration with detailed directions, Ruby said, "After that, you get to the most important part: talking."

"I'm pretty sure after I do this, he'll consider *that* the most important part," Dinah said dryly.

Ruby laughed. "Perhaps. But it truly is just a door that reopens intimacy."

"Thank you." She exhaled. "I've been floundering. Wallowing. Replaying the past instead of forging a new future. Now I feel ready to fight for what I want with him, based on what we had."

"Exactly."

"Now let's talk about whatever plan you've concocted to get *your* McKay back."

Ruby fussed with her heart necklace. "My plans will take more time to implement than just riding my horse over to his place and getting on my knees."

"But you *are* going after him."

"Yes." She squared her shoulders. "He—we—deserve the life we were denied here."

"Amen, sister."

They stared at each other. Then they both started to speak at the same time.

Dinah laughed. "Sorry. You go ahead."

"No. You first," Ruby said.

"I would've liked to have you for my sister," Dinah said shyly.

"Same goes." She reached for her hand and squeezed. "But in our hearts, we'll always be connected by the men we love. Even if they have different names. Even if they're unaware that through them we've created this bond."

"Agreed." She gave Ruby another hard hug. "When will you go?"

"Soon. Change is in the air and I had a good run here. But I'm ready to move on."

"Please try and get word to me. It doesn't matter if it's next year or in ten years, but I need to know that you're all right."

Ruby frowned. "I'll try. But won't it be obvious—"

"No. Like you said, he won't have the same name and I doubt you will either." She smirked. "Jimmy told me about your secret codes. Ours will be you mentioning being my friend from Cheyenne, and I'll know it's you."

"You're sure?"

"Yes, because I haven't kept in contact with anyone from Cheyenne." She laughed. "Done."

"Take care, sister."

"You too."

Ruby felt lighter on the walk back to the boardinghouse. She kept her head held high as she bypassed the deputy's office. Neither Big Jim nor the weaselly looking man leaning in the doorjamb, wearing a shiny new tin star, acknowledged her.

No matter.

Madam Ruby was about to disappear for good.

TWENTY-THREE

May 1898
Sundance, Wyoming

"A S REGISTRAR IN the city of Sundance, in Crook County, in the great state of Wyoming, this union is officially recognized as legal and binding. Jonas McKay, kiss your bride."

Jonas curled his rough-skinned hands around Dinah's face, the metal from his wedding band cool on her cheek. He whispered, "Finally," before his lips connected with hers in a kiss that lingered just enough to be improper.

Some things never changed with her man.

Dinah turned and accepted a hug from Bea Talbot, although hugging her these days was difficult, given the size of Bea's pregnant belly. Then she hugged Doc and Martha.

Next to her, her husband accepted congratulations from Andrew Talbot and Ulysses Gilbert of the Wyoming Brand board, who'd become Jonas's closest friends after Jonas joined the Wyoming Cattleman's Association.

After former deputy Jonas McKay learned that his outlaw brother had left him as one of the largest landowners in Crook County, he'd become involved in the community. He also sat on several state licensing boards to ensure that landowners' and cattlemen's rights were being served. Dinah was proud that not only had Jonas embraced that "new" part of his persona, he'd actually enjoyed it.

"So what now?" Bea teased.

"Now, I take my wife home," Jonas said, slipping his arm around Dinah's waist. "We'll see you all tomorrow night."

Bea and Andrew had moved into their new house just last month and Bea had begged to host their wedding reception. Jonas had agreed—provided the reception wasn't the same day as their wedding. Because tonight was just for them. They'd finally forge that final intimacy as husband and wife.

Dinah switched her bouquet of wildflowers to her free hand as they exited City Hall.

Jimmy waited with the horse and buggy, grinning like a loon because he'd tied tin cans to the back of it below the sign JUST HITCHED. Points for her former student that he'd spelled everything right.

"Congratulations, Mr. and Mrs. McKay! Everything you asked is done," he told Jonas. "Buttercup was milked, chickens were fed, I put Daisy out with Beauty and Beast. You don't gotta worry about nothin'—livestock wise—until late tomorrow mornin'."

Jonas said, "Thanks, Jimmy," and passed him a few folded bills. Then he offered Dinah a hand up. "Let's go home, Mrs. McKay."

While they rode along the familiar path, Dinah's thoughts veered to all the changes the last year had wrought.

After Dinah's conversation with Ruby, she'd immediately gone to sort things out with her McKay. It'd been a difficult discussion for both of them, to be candid about whether they could go forward after the complete implosion of the life path they thought they'd be on.

But that honesty had saved them.

It'd taken a few months to believe that their love was strong enough to survive.

In those months, Jonas had publicly wooed her in the manner that Silas never would have. They attended dances, community events, church socials. Their fears that people would be suspicious at how easily Dinah Thompson had switched her affections from one McKay to the other were largely unfounded. Perhaps because they'd both shown their eagerness to grow their roots in Crook County, individually and as a couple. When

Jonas proposed during the annual Christmas ball, presenting her with a beautiful aquamarine and diamond engagement ring, women had swooned and men had congratulated him for not wasting time in stating his intent.

And yet, they preferred the time they spent alone together. When they could cuddle up and read just like they used to do before. Share meals together. Check livestock. Laugh and argue and kiss and make up. Continue with their plans of creating a home that would be a place of joy and solace. A private oasis where they could explore intimacy in any way they chose.

Tonight they'd take that final step of being fully joined in body. Over the past month as they'd combined their individual lives into one, Dinah had joked she'd come to their marriage bed a virgin, but not innocent.

Not even *close* to innocent.

She was proud that some of the more…unconventional sexual avenues they'd chosen to express their mutual desire would probably even shock Madam Ruby.

Her man had such deliciously dirty ways to use that silver tongue of his.

"Sugar pie, are you all right?"

Dinah turned and looked at him. He only called her *sugar pie* these days when they were alone. "I'm enjoying the happiest day of my life."

"You're awful quiet while you're enjoyin' it."

"Mmm. Just fantasizing about how it'll feel to have your cock shoved inside me over and over."

He grinned and kissed her. "I love how only *I* know how filthy this sweet mouth of yours can be." He reined the horse to a stop. "I'm just as anxious to shove my cock inside you over and over, but I have a surprise for you first." From the inside of his suit jacket, he pulled out a long piece of black silk. "Since I don't trust you not to peek, I'm gonna hafta blindfold you."

She raised an eyebrow. "I'll agree to the blindfold, but no ropes."

"No ropes…*this time*. Come on now, turn to the side."

"You'll mess up my hair."

Then Jonas's lips were on her ear. "Like you give a shit about that. Now turn."

Everything went dark.

"Can you see?"

"Not a damn thing."

"Good. Hold on."

It was strange how she had no sense of where they were or how long she'd been blindfolded when the buggy finally stopped.

Jonas gave her a firm, "No peeking" warning before he bailed out to unhitch the horse.

She tilted her face to the sun, glorying in the heat and the pine-scented breeze.

"Okay, darlin', gimme your hand." He lifted her out of the buggy and cradled her to his chest, with one hand under her rear, keeping her ivory skirt out of the dirt as he strode along.

"Carrying me over the threshold, Mr. McKay?"

"Yep. We're doin' this once and I'm doin' it right."

A door creaked, which was odd; he'd oiled the door hinges just last month.

Dinah didn't have time to dwell on that.

Jonas removed the blindfold and said, "Welcome home, Mrs. McKay."

She blinked. Once. Twice. Her eyes had to be playing tricks on her because they were not in the cabin.

He set her down.

She knew where they were, but she was shocked to see *their* chairs in front of the massive stone fireplace. She turned and *their* table was in the room off the kitchen. Her things—their things—were all over the place.

He moved in behind her and held her tightly. "Surprise."

"This is Henrikson's house."

"Nope." He kissed the edge of her jaw. "This is *our* house. Our home now."

"What?" She tried to take that in. "But…when? How?"

"Henrikson had been talkin' about leavin' here for months. I never took him seriously. But after the one-year mark passed that he'd lost his wife and his child, he was ready to move on. He wanted to sell to me, but I didn't have that kinda money." He paused. "So I talked to Andrew Talbot at Settlers' First Bank."

Dinah whirled around. "You actually went to a banker?"

"Yep. And he actually lent me the money." He smiled and shook his head as if he couldn't believe it either. "I guess showin' him that we wanna be part of the community for the long haul was all he needed to get the loan approved. That said, I had to buy Henrikson's cattle and I've agreed to turn over one hundred percent of the money earned when we sell at market this fall. But I've done the math, darlin', and we *can* afford this. Even without your money from teachin' and Doc. I can even afford to hire a ranch hand until we make little ranch hands of our own."

She sidestepped him and walked to the "parlor," which didn't have a stick of furniture in it. Oh, but it had so much potential.

"I also got a little extra money for you to buy furnishings or whatever you want. Since Doc is movin', he said to tell you he'd *give* you anything from his house that caught your eye. Says he's too old to cart a bunch of crap with him or to try and sell it."

She laughed. That sounded like Doc. And she knew, too, that his offer partially came from grief. Mrs. Agnes had passed on in February. He'd decided that after Dinah and Jonas got married, he'd quit practicing medicine and move south, where the winters weren't so brutal. Since Martha and Jimmy were more like his kids than his servants, they'd chosen to leave with him the end of the month.

"This is why you kept me away from the cabin the past two weeks."

He chuckled. "Yeah. Jimmy helped me move everything over. Today he relocated all the chickens and…well, you heard. Been hard keepin' this from you, but I wanted to give you something special today of all days."

Dinah faced him. "You're special *every* day and everything I could've hoped for in a husband. This…is almost too much."

"Hey now, no cryin'." He fastened his mouth to hers, teasing her lips open with the tenderest of kisses. Caressing her arms with his big hands, slowly gliding the palms up and down as if to warm her.

She was definitely getting all kinds of heated up.

Jonas rested his forehead to hers. "Let's go to bed."

"Yes."

"I'm gonna be in you as soon as you're nekkid."

"Yes, please."

He scooped her up and ran with her to the back of the house.

In a bedroom the size of their entire cabin was their bed, covered in their bedding, the book they were currently reading, *The Prisoner of Zenda* by Anthony Hope, on the side table next to their reading lamp.

Jonas started to touch her. "You looked beautiful today. I love that you designed this dress just *slightly* scandalous." He drew his finger across the square neckline in ruched ivory satin that rested midway across her chest, and up the capped sleeves covered in silk roses.

"You look pretty handsome yourself, Mr. McKay." While plain workday clothes were still his preference, he'd gotten used to donning the suits and nicer pieces of clothing his brother had left behind.

"Please tell me you brought a button-hook for all these blasted buttons."

She froze. "There's one at the cabin. In my sewing supplies."

"That's the one thing I didn't move because I figured you wouldn't have a lotta time for *sewin'* these next couple of days."

"Oh."

Against the upper swell of her breasts, he groaned a frustrated noise of a man being denied something he really, really wanted.

"Jonas," she whispered in his ear, "the dress is slightly scandalous, but what's underneath is *completely* scandalous."

"What's that, sugar pie?"

"Nothing but my pantalets." She nipped his earlobe. Hard. "No shift. No slips. You take the pantalets off and you can take me."

"Christ, Dinah." He rubbed his lips across her cleavage. "This ain't the way I wanted this to happen."

She flitted away from him. Watching his hungry gaze, she lifted up her skirt, untied the waistband of her undergarment and shimmied the cotton down her legs. She let him look his fill of the fluffy tulle and satin dress pulled up to her waist, her legs bare, save the stockings peeping out of the tops of her white boots. "Do you really think we're the first newly married couple who don't get all of their clothes off before they're rutting against each other?"

He stood back, legs braced apart, one hand on his hip beneath his jacket and his other hand moving back and forth across his chin.

Sighing dramatically, Dinah threw herself onto the bed, her wedding dress pooled behind her in a white cloud, fully exposing her lower half to him with her boot heels hooked into the wood slats of the mattress box and her sex brazenly on full display. "I'll just wait...until you decide to take what's yours."

He released the sexiest roar she'd ever heard and his pants were only to his knees before he was on her.

In her.

They both groaned after that first deep, hard thrust.

God. This feeling of fullness was...everything.

His chest was heaving just as hard as hers.

Their eyes met.

She angled up to kiss him. "Keep going."

"You're okay? No pain?"

"A little." She rocked her hips. "But I don't want you to stop."

Jonas pulled out and eased back in. "You feel good. I don't ever remember it bein' like this."

"Me neither."

"Smarty." He chuckled and his mouth came down on hers. Kissing her with that single-minded passion that curled her toes in her boots.

But he'd stopped moving his bottom half.

Dinah reached around and clamped her hands onto his butt cheeks. Kneading that firm flesh. Then pulling him against her as a hint to get pumping.

He peppered kisses down to her chin, then dragged an openmouthed kiss up her jaw to her ear. "Dinah, I love you. I love you so much." He traced her hairline with his nose, his lips following with little sugar bites that sent tingles across her scalp.

"I know. I love you too." The way he kept nuzzling her, without meeting her eyes, caused a tiny bubble of worry to pop up. "Am I doing something wrong?"

"No, sweetheart, this is amazin'." His lips returned to hers, teasing and tormenting for several long, luxurious moments as his body remained motionless atop hers.

Those long, deep, slow kisses had the opposite effect of soothing her; they inflamed her. She wiggled and moaned but he didn't budge. "Please."

"I need something from you," he said softly.

"Anything."

That's when he fastened his dreamy blue-eyed gaze to hers, showing a vulnerability she hadn't seen in ages. "Just this first time tonight, will you call me Silas?"

Her heart cracked wide open for this man who'd given up so much for them to be here in this moment together. "Yes, I will." She nipped his chin, then sucked on his bottom lip before she released it and whispered, "Fuck me, Silas."

He groaned and withdrew from her body, then thrust back in.

She arched hard. That time she felt a bit more pain from her body stretching to admit his girth at the base, but more pleasure too.

Strong, callused, seeking hands glided up the insides of her thighs as he pushed them farther apart.

That one adjustment changed everything as he began to ride her.

"Next time," he panted, "I want you nekkid so I can see your tits bounce when I do this." He slammed into her.

"Yes, Silas, more like that. Please."

The sensations were dizzying as the intensity began to build. Over the past few months, they'd become intimately acquainted with each other's physical needs and fulfilled each other's desires. She'd had orgasms. She'd given orgasms. She'd believed she understood every way her body could react to this man's.

But this was different.

This fullness, this hardness, this shift and arch and slide and thrust was life and rebirth and everything.

Every. Thing.

"Please, tell me you're close, sugar pie, because it feels so fuckin' good I'm about to blow."

"I think I am," she panted. "But I might need more…"

"Of this?" He twisted his hips against her hot, wet flesh, drawing a circle.

"Yes. Right there. Do it again. Grind harder." Her belly clenched and that fizzy feeling of anticipation sucked her closer to the pinnacle. She breathed against the strong column of his neck, loving that he shuddered above her. "God, Silas, you are so good at this."

"And it'll only get better." He growled, "Come on, little wife of mine, give me what I want from you."

One more kiss on her throat and a few rapid snaps of his pelvis and Dinah was done for.

Done for.

She came so hard she might've ripped the bedding. She said his name over and over, his real name, kissing his cheeks and his jaw, holding on as he emptied himself into her and they sailed off the edge of the world together.

In the panting, sweating, throbbing-in-new-places aftermath of love…with his weight above her and her virginity finally behind her, she giggled.

Jonas paused, gifting the bared skin of her bosom sweet kisses, and regarded her. "What's so funny?"

"Of all the things you've guided me through in learning to be a ranch wife, this is by far my favorite duty. It's not a duty at all. I could do this kinda duty every day—"

"And twice on Sundays," he finished with a grin.

She ran her fingers through his hair. "Thank you, Silas, for loving me like you do."

"It's my life's joy, darlin'."

Then she slapped him on the butt. "So…Silas got first crack at me. Let's see what skills 'Jonas' is bringing to the table."

Her husband lifted his head. "You wanna do it on the table next? I'm game for anything."

TWENTY-FOUR

Three years later...
July 1901
Livingston, Montana

"YOU ARE CONSIDERING it... Right, Mack?" Richie, the baby-faced junior agent, asked.

Agent Mack Jonas scratched his dark beard and his gaze flicked to the map of Montana tacked on the wall. "I don't know, kid. The fact that Park County is hirin' more enforcement agents means that Livingston is getting too damn crowded."

"So that's why, if you took the other job, you could probably be appointed Sweet Water County Land Commissioner in five or six years."

"But I'd have to live in Big Timber."

The kid rolled his eyes. "I know there's a couple of nice hotels, since you'd rather rent a room than own an entire house."

"I work all over the county. Makes no sense to buy a place that I'll rarely be in. Plus, there's something about ordering a meal anytime I want one that makes the Grand Hotel perfect for now." Dumb name for the place since it was a glorified boardinghouse. But it was located down the block from the coalition office, and it'd served as his home base the two weeks a month he worked in Livingston.

Two knocks sounded on the door. His secretary, Mrs. Burgess, popped her head in. "There's someone to see you, Mack. Dierdre from the hotel sent her over."

"Who is it?"

"Mrs...." She tapped her chin. "Shoot, sir, I already forgot her name. Do you want me to send her in?"

"Nah." He stood and stretched, then picked a couple of pieces of white fuzz off his navy-striped suit pants. "I'll talk to her in reception. It's getting to be that time I'm meeting Hultenschmidt at Dixie's for lunch." He rounded the desk and headed down the hallway to the reception area, his mind already on half a dozen other things he and the commissioner needed to discuss.

His visitor had her back to him. He pasted on a smile. "Good mornin', ma'am. I hear Dierdre from the Grand Hotel sent you here to talk to me?"

"I hope it's not an imposition." Then she turned around.

Midnight black hair framed her exquisite face. Turquoise eyes blinked at him. Then her lush red lips curved into a smile.

"Ruby?" he whispered, half afraid his mind was playing tricks on him.

She emitted the husky, dirty-sexy laugh that he hadn't heard in three long years. "We're calling each other by our last names now, Mr. *Jonas*?"

"This is Mrs. Adeline Ruby," Mrs. Burgess said.

"I know who she is," Mack said, shifting closer to take Ruby's—Adeline's—gloved hand.

"Yes, my late husband and Mr. Jonas were associates. Thick as thieves if you'll pardon the expression." Her eyes kept searching his face. "I quite honestly couldn't believe my luck when Dierdre at the front desk referred to a Mr. Jonas, who is a permanent resident at the hotel. At first, I thought to myself, 'Addie, Jonas is a common last name, it's unlikely that this is the same Mr. Jonas you're acquainted with'...but here you are in the flesh. In Livingston, Montana."

Mack couldn't tear his gaze away from her extraordinary face. "You look amazing, Mrs. Ruby. A sight for sore eyes." *And a wounded heart.*

"*Mack*," she mock chided. "We've known each other too long for such formalities. Call me Addie."

"Very well, *Addie*. What brings you to Livingston?"

She cocked her head coquettishly. "Wanderlust. I've been directionless since my man passed."

"I was sorry to hear he'd gone so suddenly. That had to've been hard."

"It was. I didn't get to say goodbye or anything."

Mack knew that if Ruby had been in Labelle the night he'd stolen away, he would've taken the chance to say goodbye.

"You must miss him very much," he said softly.

"Yes. But I decided it's time to move on. So here I am. This part of Montana is every bit as beautiful as I'd heard."

They stared at one another, each just drinking the other in.

When he noticed she still wore the heart necklace he'd given her, he feared he might fall to his knees and begin to blubber.

"Anyway, I'm staying at the Grand Hotel, and I heard this odd noise last night. When I inquired about it at the front desk this morning, they had no knowledge of it. But Dierdre suggested that since you're in residence most nights, in the room right next to mine, maybe you can tell me what it might be?"

"Not without hearin' it first. Maybe I could come by right after lunch—"

"Sorry to interrupt, Agent Jonas," Mrs. Burgess said, "but you do have a full afternoon scheduled following your lunch with commissioner Hultenschmidt."

Addie glanced over at Mrs. Burgess, sitting at her desk, who'd been openly listening to their conversation. "I apologize for interrupting Agent Jonas's day. My little issue can wait." Then she smiled at Mack. "Thank you for taking time to meet with me."

"Happy to help. Would you like to have dinner with me this evening, Addie?" That name didn't even sound weird tumbling from his mouth. It fit her: classy, forthright, yet dragging out each syllable, *Ad-e-line*...as he dragged out her pleasure, held a certain dirty appeal too.

"I'd love that. What time would you like to meet in the hotel dining room?"

"Not sure when I'll be done here, so I'll come to your room sometime after five." Mack's coworkers couldn't see when he brought her gloved hand to his mouth to place a lingering kiss on the bare skin on the inside of her wrist, gliding his lips across that soft, sweet-smelling flesh. He allowed a cocky grin when she attempted to suppress a shiver. "I do need to see if I can figure out that noise anyway."

"Yes." She granted him a mischievous smile. "I'll see if I can't narrow down where odd noises might be coming from."

Sassy thing.

Addie retreated. "I will see you later." She waved goodbye to Mrs. Burgess and sailed through the outer door.

Richie whistled. "I can't believe you know a woman like her."

Mack whirled on him. "What's that supposed to mean?"

"She's beautiful and cultured. And…did I mention beautiful?"

He relaxed his fighting stance.

"And she's fashionable," Mrs. Burgess added. "Lord. That lavender dress was divine."

She could've been wearing sackcloth and ashes and Mack wouldn't have noticed—not solely because he was remembering the bounty beneath her attire.

"She seems like a lovely person. Pity about her being a widow."

That's when Mack grinned at Mrs. Burgess and then at Richie. "Mark my words, she won't be known as a widow for long, because I'm gonna marry that woman."

Richie's jaw dropped. "But you just met her."

"No sir. My history with her is complicated, but I'll tell you that this time I won't be too late in stating my intentions toward her. Call it fate or fortune or whatever you want, but she ended up in Montana for a reason. Because we are meant to be together."

"Maybe you oughta be tellin' her this, instead of us," Richie offered with a snicker.

"Oh, the way they were looking at each other?" Mrs. Burgess said dreamily. "That woman knows exactly how this man feels." She cleared her throat. "Now get a move-on to Dixie's. You don't want to keep the commissioner waiting."

AT ONE MINUTE past five, Mack knocked on Addie's door.

It'd been the longest goddamned afternoon of his life.

At four o'clock Mrs. Burgess had kicked him out of the office, suggesting he shouldn't show up to "state his intentions" with empty hands. Which was how he ended up juggling a bouquet of flowers, a box of mint chocolates and a bottle of huckleberry cider.

Now he felt foolish. His heart raced and his throat tightened the longer he waited for her to open the door.

And then she did.

The pleasure that lit her face at seeing he'd arrived bearing gifts was definitely worth it.

"Jonas—shoot, I mean, Mack—all this for me?"

"Yep. I couldn't decide on one thing, so I got all three. Hope that's all right?"

She ushered him inside. "It's wonderful. Thank you. I'll put these in some water." She plucked the flowers from his hand and gestured to the sitting area. "Put the rest down anywhere."

When she turned around after plunking the posies in the water pitcher, Mack was right there. He cradled her head his shaking hands, his thumbs pressed into the edges of her jaw, his fingers curled around the back of her neck as his eyes took in every nuance of her face.

"I dreamed of what I'd say if I ever saw you again. Now that it's here, and I have my hands on you and your scent is in my lungs and I know I ain't dreamin'...pretty words—hell, any words at all are escaping me." He inhaled. And exhaled.

She waited for him to get himself settled.

"I love you. I never stopped loving you. I hoped you understood when I left the way I did, that I'd no more saddle you to the life of bein' on the run with an outlaw, than you would subject me to the ugliness of people's opinions of a lawman takin' up with a whore."

Those stunning eyes remained steady on his as she nodded.

"That is behind us. And sweet darlin', I don't give two hoots whether you call yourself Ruby or Addie because I am gonna finally get to call you what I've always wanted."

"What's that?"

"My wife." That's when he kissed her.

And dear god, it was like coming home.

He murmured sweet words and promises as he kept kissing her. Wiping away her tears. Letting his own fall freely and without shame.

Then he carried her to bed and reveled in the heat and passion of their connection. Of coming home to this too.

Afterward, when they were naked and entwined in the sheets and each other, they talked.

Mack told her of the months he'd spent capturing outlaws across the southwestern states after he'd left Wyoming. Then in the spring of that year, he joined up with other horsemen and cowboys to train as part of Lieutenant Colonel Roosevelt's Rough Riders cavalry, with the goal to stop Spanish aggression in Cuba. Although they'd spent more time training than fighting, the war in Cuba had changed him.

He lit out for Montana upon fulfilling his military duty, opting not to become a rancher, but to work with the settlers and timber companies as a land enforcement agent. For the past year and a half, that'd been a good fit for him. But it probably wasn't permanent either.

"I have to know how you ended up with the name Mack Jonas," she asked.

"Outlaw rule number one: stick close to the truth. Someone asked my name and I replied Jonas, without thinkin'. The guy gave me an out when he asked first or last name. I said last and used a variation of McKay for my first name."

She snickered. "At least if I screw up and call you Jonas, it won't seem random."

"Same goes if I slip up and call you Ruby girl." Mack kissed the top of her head. "How did you become Adeline Ruby?"

Addie tilted her face up and smirked at him. "Actually, Adeline Ruby is my full given birth name. Madam Marie changed it to Ruby Redmond. None of the girls used their real names, which worked in my favor. After I obtained the inheritance from Madam Marie and sold my stake in the boardinghouse in Labelle to Dickie and Mrs. Mavis, it was easiest to call myself Mrs. Ruby. Besides, after you left, I did feel as if I'd been widowed."

"I'm sorry."

"Me too. Anyway, whether I was traveling or in the shops, people believed my claim that my late husband had left me a sizeable inheritance."

"You only had to deal with them small-minded suspicions because you're a well-off woman who is both young and beautiful," Mack pointed out.

"Not to mention becoming even more suspect when she has…" Her mouth snapped shut and she nestled back into him.

"When she has what, darlin'?"

"Strong opinions, among other things."

He laughed. "That you do."

Addie's stomach rumbled. "Good lord. We forgot to eat."

"I distinctly remember eatin' something." He rolled her to her back and began kissing his way down her body. "Maybe I need me another taste."

"Mack."

He raised his head from where he'd been licking her bellybutton. "I love hearin' you speak my name like that, Adeline."

"Same." She petted his beard. "I know I said I didn't like facial hair...but this suits you. It makes you look like a distinguished gentleman."

Growing a beard was his one concession to changing his appearance after leaving Wyoming. With only half his face visible, chances were less likely that he'd be mistaken for his twin. Keeping his gaze on hers, he teased his bearded chin across the sensitive skin between her hipbones. "Does that tickle?"

"Yes. So stop it."

"Not a chance. This distinguished gentleman is about to remind you how dirty and depraved he really is."

She groaned. "I can't keep quiet when you do that to me. That'll get the entire hotel staff up here to investigate the noises."

"Good. We can ask them to bring us some food, so we won't have to leave this bed for the rest of the night."

MUCH LATER, MACK was nearly asleep when Addie said, "Can you take tomorrow afternoon off?"

"Sure. What for?"

"It's a surprise."

"What kinda surprise?"

"The good kind."

"Adeline, darlin', the *good kind* ain't a hint of what kinda surprise it is."

"It's called a surprise so you don't know *what* it is, silly man."

"Well, how am I supposed to sleep now?"

She smiled against his chest. "Need a little...something to help you relax?"

"The last thing I am, when you put your mouth on my cock, is relaxed."

Addie poked him in the belly. "I was going to offer to rub your back."

"Oh."

Her wicked laugh tickled his ear. "My back rubs are nearly as good as my special French perversion, remember?"

"Like I could ever forget that."

TWENTY-FIVE

ADDIE HADN'T GIVEN Mack the directions to their meeting place until right before he left her hotel room to go to work.

Then she'd packed up the few items in her room and checked out of the hotel. The livery brought her buggy around and she'd forced herself not to race to the house on the outskirts of Livingston where she'd been living the past week.

Her nerves jumped like bullfrogs in her belly, prompting her to drink two shots of rum to calm down.

She paced on the front porch, aware Mack would arrive as his schedule would allow.

Hoofbeats and a whirl of dust indicated Mack was more than casually curious about this surprise; he was an hour earlier than they'd agreed upon.

Here's hoping your curiosity is stronger than your anger.

Mack reined to a stop, looking every bit the expert horseman she remembered him to be.

He dismounted and led his horse to the hitching post before he spoke. "I'm early."

"I suspected you would be."

Tugging her against his chest, he kissed her soundly. "I'm so damn glad I can do that," he murmured into her hair. "Half the reason I'm here early is because I worried last night had been some fever-filled dream and I'd ride out here to find nothing."

Oh, he was about to get way more than he'd ever imagined.

Addie took his hand and led him into the entryway. "Let's go through here."

"Are we thinkin' about buyin' this house?" he asked, trying to take in the space as she hotfooted it through the parlor. "'Cause if we are, I'd like a chance to look around."

"You'll get a chance to see it all later because this isn't your surprise."

Mack planted his boots, jerking her to a stop. "Adeline. What the devil is goin' on?"

She stood on her toes and wreathed her arms around his neck. "Please. Just trust me. Okay?"

"I do."

"Then come on. Your surprise awaits."

They exited the house onto the rear porch. A field of green spread down to the cottonwood trees lining the creek.

Before she lost her nerve, she yelled, "You can come out now."

Two little faces peeked out from behind the big tree trunks.

Two little heads with dark hair.

Two little boys raced toward her, each trying to be the first to touch her.

Addie had moved forward and behind her...Mack had gone completely silent.

The first one to reach her nearly plowed her over. "Mama, mama, I won!"

"No fair," boy two complained, trying to knock his brother away so he could climb his mother like a tree.

Addie caught the attention of the young woman who approached slower than the twins. "It's all right, Molly. Go on inside. I'll let you know when I need you."

Molly nodded and ducked around the side of the house.

Which gave Addie the impression the expression on Mack's face was scary enough that Molly didn't even want to walk past him.

Taking a deep breath, Addie turned around. The boys also turned. But upon seeing Mack, their shyness overcame them. They leaned against her legs, one on each side, and peered at him from behind the safety of their mother's skirt.

Finally, her eyes connected with Mack's. "These are my sons. Teddy"—she ruffled the black hair of the boy on her right—"and Seth." She brushed a leaf from the shoulder of the dark-haired boy on her left.

"Your sons," he repeated.

Holding his gaze, she said, "Yes. They're your sons too."

Mack fell to his knees.

The boys pressed closer against her.

"Twins," he said, dazed.

"Not identical, but close enough."

"Mine," he said hoarsely. Then he swallowed. "I mean ours."

"Yes. They turned two last March."

"Mama, who's that?" Teddy asked.

"Yeah," Seth piped up. "Who's that?"

Addie waited for Mack to respond.

The time between the question being asked and waiting for an answer seemed to last an eternity. But finally, Mack said, "I'm your father."

Teddy leaned forward and looked at Seth.

Some secret twin communication happened between them and then they both looked at Mack. Teddy shrugged and said, "Okay."

Seth said, "Okay," before adding, "Can we have a cookie now?"

Addie laughed. "Yes."

Mack continued to stare at them.

"I'll take them inside for their snack and come back out so we can talk, okay?"

"Take your time, I, ah...need a moment."

Addie herded the boys through the back door into the kitchen.

Molly already had milk and cookies set out on the dining room table. She smiled at Addie. "They look like him."

"Yes, they do."

"But they look like you too."

She was also aware of the issues that might cause.

Molly swung Teddy into the first chair and Seth right next to him.

"Did it go okay? Telling him?" Molly asked.

"We'll see." Addie smoothed down Seth's cowlick. "Will you keep the boys inside and entertained while Mack and I talk? I don't know how long it'll take."

"Of course."

On a whim, Addie opened the bottle of cider he'd given her and brought it outside.

Mack hadn't moved. Except he'd balled his hands into fists by his sides and his shoulders shook.

Goodness. Was he so angry that he was shaking from it?

Leaving the bottle on the porch, she approached him warily. "Jonas?" slipped out of her mouth before her head enacted the name change.

He leaped to his feet and enveloped her in his arms before she could take another breath.

The first thing that registered: he wasn't vibrating with anger. He was crying. Sobbing. He just kept whispering, "Oh god, oh god, oh god," over and over—a man in serious pain.

"Oh, honey," she whispered, wiping his wet cheeks. "It's okay," she assured him between kisses. "I love you. So much." She nuzzled his jaw where his beard started. "We'll work this out. I promise." More soft smooches on the corners of his eyes. "Please don't be mad at me. Please."

That caught his attention. He angled back to blink those blue, blue eyes at her. Eyes the same color their sons had inherited. "What? Why would I be mad at you?"

"You're not?"

He expelled a long breath. "No. But I'd like to know how it happened."

"Oh, the usual way," she teased him. "When two people love each other—"

His impromptu swat on the butt was surprisingly firm.

And utterly delightful.

She danced out of his reach. "Sit. I'm grabbing the cider to celebrate you finding out that you're a father."

"Christ. That's just…" He shook his head.

Addie returned to find him sitting in the grass.

He swept her right onto his lap and took the first swig from the bottle. "Tell me all of it. Don't leave nothin' out."

"I didn't realize I was pregnant until after I'd returned from Deadwood to deal with Madam Marie's final requests. Three long weeks with what I figured out was morning sickness as I crisscrossed the area with my Pinkerton bodyguard to deposit my earnings and my inheritance in various bank accounts. I returned to Labelle, fully intent on telling you the news, when I learned about Zeke and Silas. I had no idea what you'd done until I went out to speak to 'Jonas' and it wasn't you."

"Did my brother think it was odd that you'd come callin'?"

"Yes, but my poker face is even better than his." She waited for Mack to tell her whether he'd said anything to his brother about Jonas's relationship with Ruby before he'd left, but he didn't, so she kept talking. "I knew Big Jim would crack down on my business after you were gone, so I sold my half of the stake in the boardinghouse and moved to Denver. A pregnant widow was merely sad in a bigger town, not suspicious. I had a difficult pregnancy. The doctor suspected twins once I shared that the baby's father was a twin, not to mention my mother was a twin."

"No kiddin'. I didn't know that."

"I'd forgotten that until I detailed my family history for the medical record. The boys were born at the Babies Summer Hospital—"

"Whoa, wait. Summer hospital? You said they were born in March."

"They were. The Babies Summer Hospital was started by a female physician who took an interest in babies with health problems. Seth was smaller and sicklier than Teddy. I had to hire a fulltime nanny and the first year of their lives is a bit of a blur."

"I hate that you did this all by yourself, darlin'."

"I know. I also understood that the boys had to be well enough—and old enough—to travel when we set out to find you."

"You wouldn't have found me at all that first year, bein's I was chasin' outlaws and then trainin' for war," he said tersely.

Addie kissed the hard line of his jaw. "I presumed you'd be out earning bounties for a couple of years until you settled in Montana. I didn't know you'd choose to go to war. But I'm not surprised because you needed to build a new reputation. Or start a different occupation."

"How'd you track me down?"

"Pinkertons. Don't worry, I didn't give them your previous name. The version of the story I told them was we had a falling out over my pregnancy and you left. A few years had passed, and I wanted you to meet your sons. I suggested they search for law enforcement agents in western Montana."

His eyebrow winged up. "Not a rancher?"

"If you were trying to distance yourself from being Silas, then you wouldn't get into the cattle business. I also figured if anyone had been hunting for you, that's the direction they'd look since Silas's skills were as a cattleman and a card player. You had more options than he ever did. And how…contradictory would it be if the so-called fugitive was an upstanding law enforcement officer? The irony of that would appeal to you."

He chuckled. "That it did. Lord, woman, you really do know me. So how long before you received the Pinkerton's information?"

"Two weeks. I waited another two weeks before I left Colorado. For the past month we've been on trains, slowly making our way here." She paused. "The Pinkertons report didn't indicate whether you were married or courting someone, so I decided it'd be best to approach you without the boys first."

Mack turned her face toward his. "Did you really think I wouldn't want you? Or them?"

"I didn't know. Yes, I know you said you loved me then, and I believed you. But as the only woman you'd been in a relationship with, I worried maybe you'd get away from the temptations of a whore and regret those two years we'd spent together. A casual encounter between us on neutral territory gave you an out if you'd become involved with a new woman, and it would've allowed me and the boys to move on."

He kissed her with the hunger and passion that'd marked him as hers since the first time their lips had touched. "There's never been room in my heart for another woman since it's filled to bursting with lovin' you. I've not been with anyone else. Ever. Only you. I'd made my peace livin' my life with memories of you and decided it'd be enough."

She blinked away her tears that this wonderful, beautiful man wouldn't have to make do with memories. "I also had a small fear, given my previous occupation, that you might not believe the boys were yours."

"Hey. That wouldn't have mattered to me because they'd still be *your* sons, and I'd still love them because I still love you."

"Stop making me cry."

Smiling, he kissed her. "You got pregnant on our picnic, didn't you?"

"Yes." She fiddled with the button on his collar. "I never doubted you when you swore you didn't care if I had to 'do my job' but the truth is, that last year we were together in Labelle, I was only with you. No one else. Last night ended three very long years of celibacy for me too."

He shrugged. "Good to know. But even if you still had been a workin' girl, that wouldn't have changed nothin' for me. However…" Mack flipped her onto her back and pinned her body beneath his for a steamy kiss. "I'm mighty pleased to hear that I ruined my first and only woman for any man's touch 'cept mine."

She laughed. "That you did."

The door slammed. Footsteps thudded across the porch.

It was adorable how quickly Mack sat up and tried to act like they hadn't been in the midst of anything untoward in front of their sons.

The boys barreled right past them, racing and tumbling like puppies.

"Sweet baby Jesus, they're amazing," he murmured in her hair.

"That they are."

"Tell me about them. Who is the shiest one? Which one will eat sweets until he pukes?"

"Huh-uh, buddy. You'll have to figure that out on your own."

"I can't wait." He opened his mouth. Closed it.

"What?"

"I want everyone to know they're ours. But I especially want Teddy and Seth to know I'm their father. We're finally in a place we can start over and be the family I never thought I'd have. So it's especially important we do it the right way for all of us from the start."

She tilted her head to the side to look at him. "I'm open to suggestions on how to accomplish that."

"There's a job in Big Timber I've been considering. Same thing I'm doin' now. Less money, but it's a much smaller community. We show up there married, with our boys."

"And?" she prompted.

"And nothin'. That'll be that."

"Was that a proposal, Mr. Jonas?"

"A shitty one...but yeah."

She grinned at how cute he was when he blushed. "I accept."

Addie and Mack shared the bottle of cider and laughed at the antics of their sons. The boys were unsure of Mack, but curious. It wouldn't be long before he'd be such an integral part of their lives, they wouldn't remember a time when their father wasn't there. That filled her with indescribable joy.

Still, she sensed his melancholy. "Are you all right?"

"The best I've ever been. You. Our sons. Our life ahead of us." He paused. "But not a day goes by that I don't miss my brother, Ruby girl. Seein' them together...makes me remember all the times we were called 'them McKay boys'."

"I fear Teddy and Seth will be hellraisers of the first order and we'll hear plenty of complaints about them Jonas brothers."

"The Jonas brothers," he repeated. "I like the sound of that."

EPILOGUE

Three years later...
Late July 1904

JONAS RETURNED FROM town waving a letter. "You got mail. It's the damndest thing though, it don't have a return address on it. Postmaster Pete was fit to be tied."

"That is odd. Can I see it?"

"Sure." He kissed her cheek. "How you feelin'? Get a nap in?"

"Yes. But napping while you're working makes me feel lazy."

"We've got a ranch hand so you can stay on bed rest, sugar pie. That's the most important thing. I brought you a new book and one of them chocolate bars you love so much."

Dinah touched his face. "I love *you* so much."

"I know." He nodded at the letter. "I'm gonna pop outside for a few."

Meaning...sneaking out for a cigarette. She wished he hadn't taken up the habit, but at least he didn't smoke in the house, which was something.

She studied the beautiful floral stationary and the loopy handwriting and knew who'd sent it. She muttered, "About damn time," and carefully broke the seal.

Dearest Dinah,

I must apologize for the lengthy span of time between this and our last correspondence. Leaving Cheyenne and finding a place to permanently settle with Mack and our twin boys took longer than I expected.

But the good news is...we are finally in our new house! It required some convincing, but my husband agreed to indulge in my girly side, and we live in a Victorian painted-lady style home. I'm madly in love with it, even if the colors are exceedingly bright for the prairie. My biggest challenge is keeping our five-year-old sons, Teddy and Seth, from dragging critters into my parlor and having slingshot contests in the dining room.

Mack is still working for the county. He loves every aspect of his job, especially that he doesn't have to travel nearly as much. Some days I see his wistfulness and know he's thinking back on the time he spent working cattle with his family and he misses it. Every year he's invited to reunite with his buddies from the war he fought in, in Cuba, but he declines, telling me and our sons there's no glory in reliving war.

As for me, the duties of running a household and chasing after our sons keeps me busy. I did manage to open a small dress shop in town— you know how I've always loved fashion!

I hope all is well with you and you found your heart's desire. I treasure the time we spent in Cheyenne and yet sometimes it's good to leave everything behind and start fresh. Mack and I are certainly proof that patience and determination are the foundations upon which love can thrive.

All my best - Adeline J

Dinah pushed to her feet and walked to the window above the kitchen sink.

Had it really been six years since she'd extracted a promise from Ruby to contact her if she'd been successful in tracking down her McKay?

In some ways those six years had flown by. In others...each month had dragged on with excruciating slowness.

So by mentioning their sons' ages, Dinah knew that Ruby had been pregnant when she'd left Labelle.

Dinah's hand dropped to the swell of her abdomen. She and Jonas hadn't been so lucky to start their family in the five years since they'd become husband and wife. She'd had numerous miscarriages. The last two pregnancies...neither of her baby boys had lived longer than a few hours.

So on the days the grief was particularly bad, she questioned whether God was punishing her for taking a life, by not allowing her to create one. On the days the grief was tolerable, she lamented she'd inherited her mother's female troubles that made it difficult to carry a child to term. On the frustrating days, she wondered if this house was cursed, since neither she nor Margaret Henrikson had heard a baby's cry while living under this roof.

Through it all, Jonas was wonderful. He held her, loved her, and cared for her with humor, sweetness and passion. He'd never spoken of disappointment the McKay family name might be just a memory in Sundance, Wyoming. He continued to improve the land as if he would have something to pass on.

But this pregnancy seemed different from the moment she'd felt this babe quicken. Even Jonas had commented that the wiggly bump seemed like a feisty little thing like her mother. It was a blessing he didn't care if they had a daughter or a son. It was sweet how he talked to her belly like the babe was already a person. It made her laugh how he pored over the books in their parlor, then read out the most outrageous options for baby names.

But no way was she naming a child Flossie Eula. Or Festus Eugene.

She let him coddle her without complaint. The truth was, she needed it. More than ever.

The door opened and her man immediately sought her out.

He tucked his groin against her behind and placed a kiss below her ear. "You okay?"

"I'm fine."

"That letter didn't upset you?"

"No. Why would you ask that?"

"Just seemed kinda random. Who was it from?"

"My old friend Adeline from Cheyenne."

"Huh. I don't know that I've ever heard you mention her."

"Which just proves you don't listen to me," she teased.

"Do you think this is the start of regular letter writin' between you two?"

Dinah shook her head. "It was her way of letting me know she'd found what she'd been looking for. Besides, she didn't give me a return address so I couldn't get in touch with her even if I wanted to."

"I still think it's weird."

He didn't know the half of it.

And as long as she was alive…he never would.

Some family secrets were meant to go to the grave.

Author's Note for

SILVER TONGUED DEVIL

Naturally my first historical western romance would feature the McKays ☺ I've had the notes and plotline done on this origin love story for years—before Sierra did her McKay family report in *Gone Country*, or before Carolyn and Kimi West gossiped about the McKay family history in *Cowboy Take Me Away*. So if you're a longtime reader of the series, there is one discrepancy:

> Sierra McKay claims that Jonas McKay and Dinah Thompson got married in 1901.

Correction: Silas (posing as Jonas) and Dinah got married in 1898. Jonas (now Mack) and Ruby (now Addie) got married in 1901. It was a little confusing in my notes when at that time I didn't have both storylines fleshed out. So, let's chalk up that error to a sixteen-year-old girl making a mistake on a school report from unclear family historical notes provided by...me.

Moorcroft, Wyoming (known as the unincorporated Labelle township) was incorporated on October 2, 1906. The exact meaning of Moorcroft is unknown but over the years several suggested origins for the name have been an homage to Alexander Moorcroft, an early settler who built a cabin in the Black Hills of Wyoming. Or it was chosen by the community's first postman Stocks Millar after his hometown named Moorcroft in Scotland.

Most of the businesses I've mentioned in Sundance 1897 are fictional. Sackett's Saloon existed in Sundance, so creating a second Sackett's in Labelle was taking artistic license.

This book was a JOY to write! I loved doing the more extensive research, not only on the city and township, but of everything from that time in rural America—which was still very much the Old West. That said, any errors are mine alone.

Thank you for reading this McKay origin story!

Author's Acknowledgments

This book wouldn't exist without my LJ Team. Thanks to:

Lindsey Faber—my fabulous editor, who has been with me through EVERY Rough Riders book since *All Jacked Up*. She knows the fictional McKay world, but more importantly, she knows ME. She's a cheerleader, a whip cracker, a strategist, a life coach, and the best editor I've ever worked with. Over the years she's helped hone my craft and I'm a better writer because of her. Thank you, doesn't seem like enough, Lindsey, for how much you mean to me on every level.

Kim O'Connor—my PA, my BFF, my go-to for umm…everything. She does the hard stuff so I can write. She does the harder stuff when I can't write. I have to stop there, or I'll start blubbering and she will too. Love you, Bama, for all you are.

Meredith Blair—my graphic artist, who created this gorgeous cover, and who deals with my yes—no—maybe—yeah let's revisit that later—million ideas with firm humor. See, M? I GOT THIS DONE like I said I would for once—hahaha—love you too.

Melissa Frain—copy editor extraordinaire, who went above and beyond in rapid turnaround to this book that ended up…ah, longer than I said it would (no surprise, I write LONG) Melissa has also copy edited numerous Rough Riders books and I'm thrilled she had time in her schedule to do this one—thanks a ton, Melissa.

My husband, Mr. James—who has been urging me to write this story for YEARS. He's been my pandemic rock, keeping the larder full and taking care of me through the crazy six weeks I invested in writing this book. Love you—almost 35 years of living our own love story, baby ☺

Also by
LORELEI JAMES

BLACKTOP COWBOYS® SERIES
Corralled
Saddled and Spurred
Wrangled and Tangled
One Night Rodeo
Turn and Burn
Hillbilly Rockstar
Wrapped and Strapped
Hang Tough
Racked and Stacked
Spun Out

BLACKTOP COWBOYS® NOVELLAS
1001 DARK NIGHTS
Roped In
Stripped Down
Strung Up
Tripped Out
Wound Tight

WILD WEST BOYS NOVELLAS
Mistress Christmas
Miss Firecracker

THE WANT YOU SERIES
I Want You Back
Want You to Want Me

THE NEED YOU SERIES
What You Need
Just What I Needed
All You Need
When I Need You

MASTERED SERIES
Bound
Unwound
Schooled (digital only novella)
Unraveled
Caged

STANDALONE NOVELS
Unbreak My Heart
Dirty Deeds
Running With The Devil

STANDALONE NOVELLAS
Lost In You
Wicked Garden
Ballroom Blitz

Made in United States
Troutdale, OR
06/27/2024

20863796R00181